DEAD WEIGHT

Magic, Mayhem, and the Law in Precinct #153

Book 1

G.P. ROBBINS

Dead Weight
Magic, Mayhem, and the Law in Precinct #153
Book One
by G.P. Robbins

Newly promoted Detective Jace Smithson has his hands full with solving the murders of ten men and the kidnapping of a unicorn capable of producing diamonds. On the surface, the crime appears to be a classic tale of greed and violence, but digging deeper reveals something sinister has come to Cauldron City.

Securing the safety and security of those he swore to protect is only the beginning of Jace's problems. Add in his relationship with the dragons of Cauldron City along with a few personal secrets, and he's the ideal target for the killer. Surviving to tell the tale will test his wit and skills in ways he never thought possible.

But if he wants to obtain justice for the wronged, he will have to face his challenged beliefs and come to terms with the darker realities of the city he calls home.

Cover Design by Rebecca Frank of Bewitching Book Covers.

ONE

"That's a good one. Been sitting on it long?"

THURSDAY, APRIL 5, 2057
WAREHOUSE ROW, PRECINCT 153
CAULDRON CITY, NEBRASKA.

THE NEXT TIME Captain Farthan asked if I wanted to accompany him on a call, I would concoct at least a hundred and two reasons why I needed to bust my ass at my desk. Had I been thinking, I would have remembered the captain liked to test his officers a minimum of once a year. With quarterly reviews around the corner, he'd taken to the streets to better monitor Precinct 153 and its eclectic collection of residents, transients, and others.

The call, which had come from a rather notorious warehouse with a tendency of attracting trouble, should have warranted two pairs, but no.

Captain Farthan viewed himself as a one-man army. And if the man part of the equation didn't work out, he became a one-dragon army, and only an idiot pissed off a grouchy bachelor of a dragon looking in all the wrong places for his one and only.

The rust-pocked building came into view, and I began my weapon check, hoping I wouldn't need it but expecting to have a close encounter with the strange, the stranger, and the dangerous.

I couldn't remember the last time a call to the damned warehouse had gone well.

"Nervous?" Captain Farthan asked.

Raising a brow at his question, I replied, "Not at all. I have a gun and a dragon. I'm probably the best armed sentient in the entire precinct right now."

The captain snickered. "That's a good one. Been sitting on it long?"

"For about as long as the last time you sat on someone's car after they tried to race with an interceptor." When a multi-ton dragon treated a car like a skateboard, the vehicle tended to grind to a halt. As the captain preferred when his prey emerged alive, he'd turned skating using cars into an art. At least his efforts tended to keep additional property damage to a minimum. "If you do decide you're an interceptor today, sir, I do ask you come to a complete halt before leaving the vehicle, transforming, and pursuing your target."

"If you're looking for a promotion, that's the right way to go about it." The captain parked in front of the warehouse, and to my relief, two other patrol vehicles joined us, their lights on while their sirens remained silent.

That told me one thing: whomever had been using the building had already cleared out, and we didn't want to disrupt the neighborhood more than we already would showing up to do yet another cleanup.

How marvelously delightful.

I stowed my firearm, unbuckled my seatbelt, and got out of the cruiser. "Your orders, sir?"

"Let's see how much you've learned in the three and a half years you've been with us, Officer Smithson. While you were gathering your kit, I informed the other officers that this is your rodeo."

The last thing I wanted was to be part of a rodeo while at work, figuratively or literally. As my momma had raised me stubborn and my pappa had demanded I behave like a proper police officer, I saluted my captain, straightened my shoulders, and pretended I knew what the hell I was doing while heading for the main entrance of the warehouse, which someone had left cracked open.

How very helpful.

My fellow cops, two pairs of our precinct's higher level detectives, joined me.

"Welcome to the jungle, Jace," Paul said, and he held out his elbow for a bump. I'd learned early on to go with Paul's elbow bumps. Cop by day, touchy-feely elephant by night, the elbow bump was one of the ways he got his daily dose of affection from his co-workers, thus sparing us from him trumpeting his loneliness for the entire precinct to hear. He'd revealed his second nature early on in his career, as lonely elephants became grouchy elephants.

Much like our dragon of a boss, a crabby elephant could do serious amounts of property damage in a short period of time.

So far, I held the top prize of being the most normal cop in the precinct. Everyone had some form of secret everyone knew about—except me.

I had my secrets, but I held them close to my chest.

"Am I getting the nice jungle or the mosquito-filled hell

Brandon keeps telling us about that time his parents took him to Mexico?"

Paul grinned at me. "I'm going with the mosquito-filled hell. Orders are orders, so we're supposed to do what you tell us and only what you tell us, as he wants to see how badly you pooch our investigation. He took Yvon out yesterday. It was special. Yvon is going back to preschool next week until he understands he is not allowed to lick the evidence."

In Precinct 153, preschool was another word for the academy, and the captain liked sending cops back for remedial lessons if he wanted to promote them but they had more to learn than he liked. A few weeks bringing cadets up to speed and getting lectured by experienced cops tended to work wonders for the slow learners.

I'd yet to earn a trip back to preschool, and I hoped to avoid it.

"All right. I'm going to start with wear your damned gloves, put your booties on, and don't contaminate any of my damned evidence. Do we have scrubs to put over our uniforms?"

The detective grinned at me. "As a matter of fact, yes."

"Enough for even the hothead who made me come out here?"

"Cute, Smithson," the captain muttered, strolling up to join us.

"We were instructed to bring extras, as you had no idea you'd be playing detective today," Paul informed me.

"Get everyone dressed. Pretend I'm the captain and you're dodging preschool when you show me what I need to wear and how I need to wear it, allowing for us to access our firearms because we don't know what's in that building," I ordered, glaring at the open door.

"Damn, Captain. He's already ahead of the curve. Hardy, we've got ourselves a smart one."

Detective Hardy Grimstone, the grandson of a rather notorious black dragon who'd made his nest in New York City, chuckled and went to the trunk of his cruiser to start implementing my orders. "He probably doesn't want to get sent to New York. He caught my grandpappy's eye last go around, and you know how that old goat gets."

"I saw him first," our captain growled.

As the last thing we needed was two dragons duking it out when we were supposed to be solving a crime, I cleared my throat and said, "Focus. If you two want to argue about who has property rights, do so at the station where everyone can participate, make bets, and enjoy the show. What type of case do we have here?"

At the very least, I would be highly amused should they duke it out at the station, where the men and women alike would get in on the argument. Only one winner existed in such a scenario: me. Nobody would bother me while I got my work done, and I'd have a great day laughing at my fellow cops.

Captain Farthan regarded me with a raised brow before glancing in the direction of the warehouse. "We have a serious case of dead weight and a cranky unicorn we need to get down from her current position. We only know she's a her because the caller got a good look up her skirt, as the dead weight is keeping her a solid twenty feet off the ground. We think it's a standard unicorn heist."

And just like that, my day went from bad to worse. Unicorns came in two varieties: shapeshifters and natural-born. Natural-born unicorns *were* shapeshifters, and shapeshifter unicorns could produce natural-born ones. They shared most of their abilities, and both counted as endangered.

Natural-born unicorns tended to play human more often than not, leaving the shapeshifters to take the brunt of society's determination to tame, catch, or benefit from the species.

Depending on breed of unicorn, they were wanted for a myriad of different things. They came in every color of the rainbow with a few extras mixed in, and each one had a different trick. The blacks were prized for their healing abilities and were responsible for the majority of legends surrounding unicorns. Fortunately for the entire unicorn race, the instant the unicorn died, their magic died with them, so everyone wanted living, breathing unicorns.

The blues and indigos purified water along with sporting some healing arts, although they couldn't hold a candle to the blacks. The greens restored vegetation and improved crop viability. The oranges, yellows, and reds liked confusing everyone with their various abilities, although their powers boiled down to life-giving flame, prosperity, and fertility. The violets could do a little of everything, which made them among the most desired of the species.

White unicorns had the potential to do a little of everything with a twist.

Whites produced gemstones in their droppings along with the dreaded crafting herpes, glitter. In addition to that, the whites could purify just about anything, heal well enough the blacks liked keeping them around in case of emergency, and were the true masters of short-distance teleportation, an art known as blinking.

Precinct 153 had a ridiculous number of unicorns, and there was one universal truth: unicorns were trouble.

Unicorns showing up during my shift were double the trouble and would haunt me for weeks to come.

"What sort of dead weight are we talking about?" I asked, afraid of the answer.

The opal dragon huffed, and he wrinkled his nose. "The corpse kind. Someone got the bright idea to use corpses to keep the unicorn lifted up off the ground."

I sighed. Sometimes, a criminal did something clever. Hauling a unicorn up into the air counted as clever. A unicorn who couldn't touch a hoof to the ground couldn't do interesting things like blink short distances away or bring their most potent weapons into play. Shifting also became questionable; some could shift without touching hoof to ground, but most were stuck until rescued. "All right. Let's get kitted up, see if we can get anything useful off the door, and prepare to deal with someone even crabbier than a dragon fresh up from a nap with no gold to play with."

"Hey," both the captain and Hardy protested.

I raised a brow and engaged both in a stare down. "Where's the lie, gentlemen?"

"I told you this was going to blow up in our faces, Captain," Hardy muttered. "You've gone and done it now. You've put Jace in charge, and do you know what Jace's problem is?"

"What *is* my problem?" I asked, tilting my head to the side and crossing my arms over my chest, waiting for my co-worker to illuminate me. "Beyond having to pretend I'm qualified to do this job, which I'm not."

"You're too damned pretty to be that damned bossy when you're in charge of something!"

Damned dragons. Man, woman—it didn't matter to a dragon. When they encountered someone they felt was pretty, that was that. They lamented over what they couldn't have. I needed to have a long talk with my parents about their contribution to my various assets. "Just shut up and get the kits, Hardy."

"Will you marry me if I do?"

"Neither of us swing that way, and even if we did, the captain has rules. His rules say the precinct's dragons do not kidnap or marry co-workers on grounds of appearance or competence." I would not remind Hardy about the exceptions, as determined dragons usually got what they wanted. "The gear, Hardy. You can go cry to your grand-pappy later, after we investigate the unicorn, check out the dead weight, and get everything and everyone down. And no messing up my evidence. If one of you gets me sent down to preschool being reckless, I'll find some way to make you pay."

"I should be reprimanding you over the use of coercion and threats, but you're doing it with such skill," my captain complained. "How can I reprimand that?"

I uncrossed my arms, rolled my shoulders, and finally shrugged. "Personally, I have no idea, sir. Let's get this job done as though we're actually skilled law enforcement officers rather than members of the circus who were given cuffs and guns and told to play cops with the local riffraff."

"Wait, we're not members of the circus?" the elephant asked.

"We forgot the lion, and we left the ringmaster at the precinct," I retorted. The last thing any of us needed was Deputy Inspector Hagfield, another opal dragon with an attitude and a love of all things pretty, coming out to play with us. As for the lion, he'd stayed behind waiting for the drug calls, where he did his best work.

The bloodhounds would help in extreme circumstances, but they claimed dealing with the base-level drugs counted as cruel and unusual punishment, where the lion could handle sniffing out the narcotics without going half-mad from the stench.

"It seems Officer Smithson is on a roll. Let's see if that roll translates to decent investigative work," our boss said, helping Hardy pull out the scrubs and various other equipment we would need to gather evidence. "Listen up, Smithson. I only want to have to explain this once. Under no circumstances do we harm the unicorn. Beyond that, show us what you've got, ask questions, and assuming you're not an idiot, you'll dodge preschool. This time."

"Wait. This time?"

My captain chuckled, ignored my question, and proceeded to guide me through the detective's basic arsenal of equipment required to gather evidence and bring criminals to justice.

Thursday, April 5, 2057
Warehouse Row, Precinct 153
Cauldron City, Nebraska.

TWENTY MINUTES after getting kitted up and enduring a thorough lecture on why the exterior of the warehouse door would be shit for admissible evidence, we entered the building.

The dead weight, in the form of ten bodies, held up a rather sparkly white unicorn. A sizable pile of droppings exposed the motive of the crime. When my father heard about the situation, we wouldn't need to investigate anything.

He would take care of the problem himself, and he'd leave bits of the culprits spread across the entirety of Cauldron City, the capitol of the strange and stranger in the United States.

Once I got her down and home, I had a few questions for my mother, who spotted me and turned her head so she wouldn't have to look me in the eyes.

All right. As my mother had weighed in at 1,342 pounds as of a week ago while a unicorn, we had 1,342 pounds of deadweight in the form of ten bodies to contend with. The system holding her up, which involved two heavy-duty pulleys and a single length of thick steel cable, would raise or lower with the addition of any weight to a single side. Even a pound would do, albeit it would be the world's slowest descent.

Considering the rate of putrefaction in humans, I gave it no more than twelve hours before the corpses released enough fluids to ease my mother to the ground without any harm done to her. The culprit would come back to retrieve the droppings, which would be loaded with glitter and gemstones. She'd escape with little difficulty once her hooves touched the ground.

She was one of the unicorns who had no hope in hell of blinking or shifting without a hoof touching solid ground.

After that long of hanging around, she'd do what any sensible sentient would in her situation: she'd bolt for home *without* stopping to collect the wealth she'd left behind.

Well, maybe. She was my mother, and I'd learned most of my tricks from her, with a few lessons tossed in from my father.

Great. Just great. What had my mother been eating, when had she eaten it, and had her kidnapper monitored her for her diet? If fed the right balance of food prior to having to use the facilities, we could produce even diamonds. What we ate determined what sort of gems we left behind. A steak-rich diet tended to result in garnets. Lettuce created peridots. Vodka created magic and mayhem but little in the way of gemstones.

Chicken and cheese were the harbingers of great wealth, and the greater the volume of cheese, the higher the probability we'd leave diamonds in our wake.

Well, as I couldn't start catcalling my mother and informing everyone I knew every damned unicorn in our precinct, I went to work collecting the accessible evidence. Someone had caught her on the hoof, and she must have been taking my father somewhere, as her favorite bridle and saddle were abandoned off to the side. I pointed at it and said, "That probably belongs to the unicorn, so you'll want to wipe it for prints if possible. You won't get the unicorn's prints, but you *might* lift the culprit's prints. She'll want it back later. Expect it to disappear from evidence if it isn't returned to her in a timely fashion."

Every white with a single grain of sense wiped their prints off their gear just in case somebody got overly interested in acquiring easy gemstones. Most of the time, unicorns didn't require hands to work with their tack, willing it into place as needed. Some species couldn't, but my family?

We'd mastered the art of manifesting bridles, saddles,

halters, shoes, and anything else we needed. If a saddle no longer fit well, we dumped it off somewhere and manifested a new one. If we were feeling fancy, we'd go buy one properly, hiring someone to create a work of art for us.

I'd rewarded myself with such a saddle and bridle the day I'd gone to work as a cop in Precinct 153.

My mother snorted and turned her ears back.

"I see you've been studying species abilities," my captain stated, and he headed over to photograph my mother's tack. "What would you have done if this were a dragon's hoard?"

"I would have called you and stayed away. Only an idiot touches a dragon's hoard."

That got the rest of my co-workers laughing, especially Hardy, who had a reputation of getting extra crabby if someone messed with his hoard.

He kept a pile of gold in his drawer, and once a week, I made a point of shuffling the coins around before erasing my fingerprints with my special brand of magic—the same brand of magic that would make certain my mother departed without leaving any evidence of who she was when human.

"Good answer," Paul praised. "And the dead weight?"

"Let's gather the evidence on the ground before we worry about that, but getting the mare down will be easy."

"It will? How?" my captain demanded, his tone sharpening.

I pointed at the pulley system. "Give me a rope and five minutes, and I'll have her down without any issues. We'll want to photograph the bodies and get as much evidence off them as we can before we set her free, unless you happen to have, say, fifteen hundred pounds of material we can use to hold them up."

"Hardy, once we're ready to bring the unicorn down, I expect you to shift."

"Are you calling me fat, sir?" Hardy complained.

"Yes."

I snickered, as Hardy barely topped the weight I'd set as the requirement to hold the bodies up. For a dragon, he had a great deal of growing to do before he matched our captain, who had at least a few hundred years on him.

My mother might kill me when I came over to visit and ask how she'd gotten herself in trouble, but I'd go out with a bang.

I took my time walking around the site, discovering someone had done a rather admirable job of cleaning the area. "Well, the motive is easy on this one."

"It is?" my co-workers blurted.

I retrieved my phone and held it up, giving it a wave. "Search the internet for unicorns, their abilities, and look for white in the color listing."

Rather than investigate my mother's saddle and bridle for evidence, everyone dug out their phones and checked the public databases on unicorns. A few moments later, everyone stared at the rather large pile of droppings my mother had left on the floor.

"That's right, gentleman. It could be glitter, it could be gemstones. Are you brave enough to find out?" I chuckled. "It's evidence, anyway, and technically, it's her property, so even if you did want to check it out and find out for yourself, you'd have to get her permission. At most, you can investigate the evidence to establish the value of glitter or gemstones as part of the charges pressed against her kidnappers. Then you would have to return the glitter and gemstones."

I'd lost count of how many times one of my parents had vanished off for a few days to return home grumpy, hungry, and out a few gemstones after having gone through the effort of eating the perfect diet for a few weeks to maximize the odds of getting something worth decent change.

"I think he's been reading up on the law, sir," Paul said.

Paul's partner, a magicker with a wicked sense of humor and a drive to pursue justice, came up and stared at the pile. "Toxicity rating?"

I snorted. While dragons had some fairly toxic excrements when in their scaled form, unicorns came dead last in the dangerous department. "It's shit, Lovell. Don't lick it and wear gloves. You'll be fine."

That won me a chorus of snickers, and Lovell laughed the hardest. "I'll keep that in mind. Can we just bag it?"

"If the bag breaks, you'll regret it. That is glitter-trapped shit, and there is a lot of it."

As a general rule, glitter made up the vast majority of the droppings, with a light but rather hard casing protecting the treasure within. We used either hoof or horn to break open the payloads in search of gemstones to fund our various lifestyles.

I behaved more like a dragon than a self-respecting unicorn, opting to keep most of my gems unless I wanted something I couldn't realistically afford with my job. Thus far, I'd only released three of my gemstones into the world, all so I could purchase new gaming computers and go on book buying binges. My parents played at being middle-of-the-road Americans, working because they wanted to and living the high life in some other city when they weren't in Cauldron City keeping an eye on me.

They spent most of the year making sure I didn't cause

them trouble. According to my father, he would continue to do so until I was safely married. According to my mother, it was a crime a man as handsome as me had zero luck convincing a woman of any species to give me the time of day.

I hadn't had the heart to tell my mother I had no problems convincing women to give me the time of day, but finding a woman who wanted me for more than my looks took a lot of work. From the day I'd turned twelve, I'd decided I would aim for what my parents had, which involved a relationship founded mostly on love with an uncomfortable amount of lust tossed in for good measure.

Whenever the lust issue came up, I made a point of leaving their house and staying gone until certain they'd finished their various acts of debauchery.

I'd been overjoyed when I had turned eighteen and had made my way into the world. My parents had flung a year's worth of rent at me to make sure I'd stayed gone, too. I'd put the money to good use, sending in applications for prestigious colleges and universities. Once they realized I'd meant to expand my education rather than work right out of the gate, they'd both sold gemstones to pay for my efforts.

I'd earned a degree at Yale only to enroll in the police academy and take the opportunity to pursue my dream job.

Their expressions upon realizing what I had done remained a favorite memory.

I regarded my mother, wondered how my dream job had mystically transformed into a nightmare, and sighed.

My captain regarded his phone, echoed my sigh, and joined me in staring up at my mother. "The motive seems easy, then. They wanted the unicorn's shit, so they put her in a sling and hauled her up there. But why use bodies instead of sandbags?"

"Putrefaction," I replied.

"Pardon?"

"Putrefaction. The process in which a body decays. They would have matched the bodies' weight to the unicorn's weight so they balanced out, allowing them to haul her up while they set up the corpses. If they got the weight right, that's what you get—a perfect balance, where their unicorn can't escape and the corpses hold her up. During the process of putrefaction, they'd start to drip. As they'd start to drip and otherwise shed weight through the process of decaying, she would gradually lower to the floor, allowing her to make her escape. At that point, she'd be fairly spooked and run for it. The perps would then come back to a bunch of bodies on the floor and a pile of potentially valuable unicorn droppings." I waved my phone at the captain to reinforce the whole idea I'd been doing my research on the various denizens of Precinct 153.

All four detectives and my captain stared at me as though I were the unicorn rather than my mother.

Boy, did I have news for them.

"You're serious," Captain Farthan spluttered.

"Give me a rope and a grapple, and I'll show you, but I'll need a dragon who can keep the corpses from splattering on the floor once she makes a break for it. I can almost guarantee that the instant her hooves touch the floor, she will be *gone*. She'll show up at the station to collect her droppings later, I'm sure. And her saddle and bridle. I'm sure those are expensive, and she'll want them back. She'll bring a note with descriptions of the saddle and bridle, but just expect to read between the lines on the glitter and gemstones."

The directions were more for my mother's benefit than to convince my captain I had an idea of what I was doing, but with a little luck, she'd show up, get her property, and go home. Once home, I'd be there ready to scold her for adding another tally to her disappearance count.

My parents needed to stop romping around as unicorns, inviting themselves to questionable situations.

Hardy regarded my mother, heaved a sigh, and bowed his head. "I'll go get shifted. I doubt I can fly up there, but at least I can keep the bodies from hitting the floor."

"Try not to give the entire neighborhood a show," Captain Farthan ordered.

Anyone on the street would get a show, as Hardy wasn't an old enough dragon to shift without having to strip first. As he got older, he'd learn the trick of it. Most shapeshifters learned how to deal with clothes in some fashion or another as they aged.

I'd mastered the art of shedding my clothes *after* adding my thick coat over my human skin but before popping to my unicorn form in the blink of an eye. My mother and father transformed and sent their clothes home to the dirty laundry bin, and when they shifted back, they summoned something from their supply of clean clothes. I gave it a few years before I reached their level.

I could shift without tearing my clothes to shreds, and I'd learned how to fold them with magic.

Unlike my parents, I rarely went out and about as a unicorn. The idea of being left hanging lacked appeal. One day, I hoped it lacked appeal for them, too.

Within ten minutes, a grumpy Hardy, who took after his

grandfather with black scales tinged with red, sauntered into the warehouse, barely squeezing through the door. Like most in his line, he breathed fire when annoyed, although he had other breath weapons at his disposal. To keep from adding yet another incident to his permanent record, he contained himself to a few trails of smoke from his nostrils.

Lovell handled acquiring the rope and grapple for my plan, and I rigged the hooked metal to the rope, giving it a practice spin while eyeing the chain above my mother.

"If you get that first try, lunch is on me," Captain Farthan stated, staring at the sling and chain holding my mother up. "And I'll give you a pass from going to preschool for two weeks. That's going to be quite the shot. Whatever you do, don't hurt that unicorn."

"I'm sure she'll be fine."

"Those are famous last words. Mess this up, and you'll be going to preschool for at least a month."

TWO

"Have you been sneaking to preschool without telling anyone?"

THURSDAY, APRIL 5, 2057
WAREHOUSE ROW, PRECINCT 153
CAULDRON CITY, NEBRASKA.

AS I LOVED my mother and didn't want to hurt her, I showed off one of my tricks, coiling the rope and grappling hook around the steel cable a solid fifteen feet over her back, jerking to secure it into place. At worst, the hook would tangle in the assembly rig for the sling, which worked for me. Dodging the pile of droppings, I got into position, jumped, and hauled down two feet worth of line, using my weight to lower her.

My mother bounced more than I liked, and she snorted at me for my lack of grace. With a better feel for the pulley, I hauled her down, grunting at the unwanted exercise I was putting in. When she was a foot off the ground, I said, "Your turn, Hardy. Lower her slowly so she doesn't break one of her spindly legs. Expect her to bolt, leaving you with the corpses. Try not to run them through the wringer. We need the bodies as intact as possible."

The corpses seemed intact enough to endure a fall, and the hook wouldn't fit through the pulley, which gave Hardy a chance to lower them without doing extra damage to the evidence.

"You got it," the dragon rumbled, taking hold of the rope in his taloned forehands. I got out of the way, ready to grab the sling and move my mother away from her droppings.

The last thing she needed was to pick glitter or gems out of her hooves.

Five minutes later, her hooves touched the concrete floor, and she blinked out of the sling and ran for the door at a canter. Hardy grunted, but the corpses on the other end of the line only fell a foot or two before he adjusted to the weight differential. I observed my mother in bemusement, as her gallop could blow the doors off a cop car. Later, I'd ask why she wanted to deceive the police into thinking she bolted like she meant it. In reality, she'd left the scene at a rather leisurely pace.

Well, for a unicorn.

"It seems your theory was correct," my captain said, scratching his head and staring at the warehouse door. My mother bounced off the frame and hit the street, vanishing from our view. "I can't say I wouldn't have made a run for it in her situation. Do you think we can question her when she comes to pick up her belongings?"

"I have no idea, sir. I mean, you could try, but I have no idea if she'll actually answer you."

Unicorns went out of their way to keep other species from being aware of our linguistic abilities, and my specific species was no different. We ranked as sentients, but we dodged having to do annoying things like answer questions at the police station.

"Now that we've released the unicorn, who wouldn't have cooperated with us anyway because they never do, what will you have us do?"

I resisted the urge to shoot a glare in my captain's direction. "We get the bodies lowered to just over the ground, check them over per whatever the hell protocols we have for situations like this, and call in forensics to handle the rest from here." In theory, my order of things to do was correct, although I suspected we should have called forensics in earlier. "And we brace for the wrath of the forensics team because we hadn't called them before stepping foot into the warehouse."

With a rumbling chuckle, Hardy lowered the corpses to right over the floor so we could get a closer look at them. "Well done, Smithson. You got it in one. Have you been sneaking to preschool without telling anyone?"

"Not that I know of, but I've been told I walk in my sleep, so maybe I went the evening schooling route."

Captain Farthan snickered and headed to the bodies. "Lovell, call in the forensics team and ask them for containers for the droppings. We'll value everything and package it for her return. Get prints off the saddle, and let's see about identifying these vics. I'm less worried about the unicorn and more worried about who wanted these ten men dead and why."

"Is it possible to fingerprint corpses this far decayed?" I asked, pointing at the discolored fingers on the lowest corpse in the pile. "I can't say I've ever fingerprinted a corpse before."

"As a matter of fact, yes. They're still fresh enough. But we'll let the forensics team worry about that. We might mess up the evidence. Just ask Lovell about the time he messed up their evidence."

"They dragged me over coals for losing admissible evidence," the detective replied. "You're not doing badly for someone utterly wet behind the ears on investigations."

"Well, at least I can say I didn't try to lick the evidence. Why did Yvon lick the evidence, anyway?"

"He wanted to find out if purple tasted like grape. Curiosity got the better of him," Captain Farthan replied. "The evidence tasted like wet paint, and wet paint does not taste like grape. Some days, I think I need to send the entire precinct back to preschool. If one has licked the evidence, others have thought about licking the evidence."

"But *why*?" I asked, staring at my captain with wide eyes. "Why lick wet paint?"

"I think the particularities of the case may have broken something in Yvon's head. It was a rough call."

I'd dealt with some rough cases in a support role, although I doubted anything would top discovering my mother hanging from a sling with ten corpses. "Sir?"

"If you think this is bad, try to imagine a cult ritual gone south. I don't want to think about why they'd used stripper poles in their rituals, but let's just say it went terribly wrong. Each pole was a different color, and I guess curiosity got the better of him."

"So he licked a painted stripper pole?"

"It was the only one dripping with something that *wasn't* blood."

How did Precinct 153 get so many of the weird cases? Oh, wait. I understood why. Precinct 153 was where the weird and weirder got together for magic and mayhem in Cauldron City, thus leaving my fellow officers of the law to deal with the fallout.

"Which detectives should I send a sympathy card to?"

"Ollo and Francis are on that case. It's a doozy, and I expect the entire precinct will be involved with that one before it's closed. I thought Yvon would have been able to handle a few cultists with a stripper pole fixation, but I guess the bodies got to him."

"Dare I ask about the bodies?"

"Well, let's just say the stripper poles weren't for show."

I regretted having asked. "Maybe you should send Yvon to therapy rather than preschool."

"I'm sending him to both," Captain Farthan admitted, gesturing for me to head to the warehouse door. "Once the forensics team gets here, you're to accompany them through evidence gathering for your first lesson in practical investigation. I'll be back later to take you to the station. Order yourself lunch and give me the receipt, and I'll compensate you. If you spend less than fifty dollars, you're not spending enough. You've got a lot to learn, and you're not going to learn any faster with me breathing down your neck."

"What? You're going to leave me unsupervised?"

"I'm sure the forensics team, combined, is worth at least one cop in the partner tally. Try not to cause more trouble than you can handle."

Friday, April 6, 2057
Warehouse Row, Precinct 153

Cauldron City, Nebraska.

TEN HOURS AFTER LEAVING, Captain Farthan returned to rescue me from the forensics team. They'd gone over the place four times, and they viewed me as the ultimate gopher. Worse, not only was I their gopher, every member of the team took a turn lecturing me about how lazy cops ruined investigations. My head throbbed, and I learned an unfortunate truth about bodies and putrefaction.

There came a point where they got particularly ripe.

The hardened forensics team members ignored the stench. I did my best to avoid gagging. To my credit, I kept control over my stomach, but I appreciated when the coroner finally came to take the bodies to the morgue to be autopsied.

"It seems you've survived your first long shift with the forensics team," my captain said in way of greeting. "How'd he do, Hollands?"

Hollands Averies, the lead of the forensics crew, glanced up from his work extracting fibers from the steel cable, one of the last jobs left to be done before the cleanup crew took over. "You could send him out tomorrow without tempting me to exsanguinate you and ruin my evidence."

The captain chuckled. "Come on, Smithson. I'll take you to the station, then I'll take you home and have an officer pick you up in the morning. You're going to have a long day tomorrow."

When wasn't it a long day? Under normal circumstances, my shifts rarely went overtime. "Are we talking long as in number of hours or long as in frustrating?"

"Frustrating. You passed your long-hours trial by fire with flying colors, so you won't get another stress test for at least a few weeks. We try to save the long days for the weird cases."

"Like ten bodies worth of dead weight and a unicorn?"

"The strangeness of this case will probably be determined by the identity of the bodies," he admitted. "How do you feel about flying? It's faster than taking a patrol car. That plus I left my patrol car at the station."

Was Captain Farthan trying to kill me? Fortunately for my sanity, I'd done a few flights on the various dragons in the precinct, although I hadn't been invited to ride the opal dragons in charge. I'd been Hardy's first rider, supervised by his grandfather, which offered some hope of survival. "I've flown before, sir."

"Good. You piss, you clean the saddle," he warned.

Wait, he had a saddle? When I'd flown on Hardy, I hadn't gotten a saddle. Hell, none of the dragons had offered a saddle. That worried me.

Why did I need a saddle?

"Understood, sir."

"Come on. I don't have all night."

I followed the captain out of the warehouse, and he demonstrated he had advance control over his general abilities, flowing from human to draconic form in the time it took me to draw two breaths. I'd learned to stop asking how dragons, unicorns, and other species accounted for the mass differentials. Magic worked in mysterious ways, and that was all there was to it. As warned, he had a saddle and reins, although the reins were attached to a collar secured near the base of his skull.

The opal dragon lowered himself enough I could scramble onto his knee and reach the stirrup and saddle. Years of learning to ride on my parents and an unhealthy love of bucking broncos gave me the skill needed to get on his back without additional help. I secured my feet in the stirrups and took hold of the reins, which I assumed were for balance—and a last chance to keep from falling to my death.

I planned to clamp my legs to the dragon's sides in case he viewed aerial aerobics as a way to test the fortitude of his cops. Considering he'd established a requirement to clean his saddle if I pissed myself, I expected a rough flight.

"I see you've ridden a horse before."

"I also helped Hardy learn to carry a rider with his grandfather supervising. Everyone else ran faster."

"Ah. How'd he do? I stay out of the rearing of young dragons nowadays. They get cranky when I give unsolicited advice. Well, why invite me along for the flight if they didn't want advice?"

"Well, I'm not dead, nor did his grandfather have to pluck me out of the sky before I smacked into the ground. I spent the next week checking for gray hairs, though."

In reality, the flight had been a calm one, with Hardy fighting off his instinct to buck me off while battling his desire to keep the flight as smooth as possible, terrified of sending me plummeting to my death.

Captain Farthan chuckled, and he stretched out, giving a shake. He reminded me a little of my father when he wanted to buck and test my seat. When it became apparent he wasn't going to dislodge me, he launched into the sky, beating his wings to gain altitude. The rocking motion would leave my back sore, especially as I needed to maintain a tight hold with my thighs to keep from being dislodged.

Then, to my disgust, a familiar dark form winged over

and glided while Captain Farthan leveled out. "He didn't even protest?"

"He gave me a single look of utter disgust, but that was the limit of his complaints," our boss rumbled. "And your grandfather?"

Hardy lifted his head.

How lovely. The Black Dragon of New York had come to play in Cauldron City. "I don't remember volunteering to be the ball in a demented game of catch."

While my voice would never match a dragon's, their superior hearing gave them an edge when several hundred feet over the ground. In good news, if the captain managed to buck me off, they'd hear me cursing all the way down.

Hardy's grandfather laughed, a deep and rumbling sound reminiscent of dry thunder in the distance. "Would you rather merely fall?"

"Not particularly, but should I be bucked off, the pain will end quickly. Should one of you have to catch me because I got bucked off, I won't hear the end of it for at least a week."

Hardy performed a wing over, plummeted at least fifty feet, and righted himself before surging upwards. "The current precinct record is thirty-two seconds. If you beat thirty-two seconds, you will unseat Deputy Inspector Hagfield. The current standing prize for unseating him is a paid week off work, free therapy for having survived a thirty-three second ride, and the adoration of us all."

"I feel today has been one big rite of passage." As the captain wasn't yet trying to end my existence through aerobatics, I rolled my shoulders, went western style on the reins and put them in my right hand, and regretted having come to work in the first place. "The why of it is evading me, though."

"We need some new detectives, and you're in the running for a spot," Captain Farthan admitted. "But the detectives need to demonstrate a capacity for riding and a high tolerance for the unexpected. So, it is a rite of passage. Should you pass, you get a promotion, a raise, and your choice of partner. You'll have as long as you want to pick a partner. Until you do, you'll float between teams."

Damn. I'd do a lot more than give the captain a run for his money for those perks. I'd even sell some of my gemstones to head off somewhere or do something fun with the week off work. The raise would be welcome, especially as I'd avoided using my gemstones to buy a home and still lived in a small apartment. As for the choice of partner, I'd have to put in some serious thought into who I'd want.

A bunch of my co-workers filled in wherever needed, and I got along with most of them.

"And if I last a minute?" I asked, unable to keep the curiosity out of my voice.

Hardy's grandfather let loose another rumbling laugh. "You last a minute, youngling, and I'll allow you to pick a treasure from my personal hoard. And if you pull off a minute plus an extra second, I'll sing praise of your prowess to my many, many granddaughters."

The last thing I needed in my life was a dragoness out to add me to her hoard, and there were few dragons who compared to the Black Dragon of New York in most fields, including ruthlessness and number of offspring. "And two minutes?"

That got my boss joining in on the laughter. "You last two minutes, Smithson, and that old wyrm will make you date every single female in his line hoping to find your one and only."

"Plus a car, as I have seen your car, and it is precisely what I expect from a cop without his own cruiser," the Black Dragon of New York added. "Perhaps access to his own cruiser?"

I had bad news for the Black Dragon of New York. I didn't have a car. Until recently, I had owned a vaguely car-shaped object held together with chicken wire and elbow grease. The last time I'd tried to start the engine, it had gurgled at me. I'd gotten it started, where I'd taken it to a mechanic, sold it for parts, and relied on my parents and their car when I didn't have access to a cruiser.

Captain Farthan chuckled. "Detectives always get a cruiser, but I'll see if we have room in the budget to get a decent one if he lasts two minutes."

"Just remember to catch me when I get bucked off," I requested.

"Between the three of us, you'll be fine," my captain promised.

Friday, April 6, 2057
Hospital Quarter, Precinct 153
Cauldron City, Nebraska.

WHILE DRAGONS LACKED the agility of other winged species due to their size, Captain Farthan made up for his inability to pretzel himself in midair with a collection of stomach-turning, gravity defying stunts that would inevitably lead to my first on-duty concussion and a severe case of whiplash. He started easy, doing a wingover in an attempt to have gravity do the work for him. As I'd been set in the saddle with my thighs locked to his sides in a death grip, I stayed put, although I wished for longer arms so I could bonk the bastard between his horns and ears.

Once the wingover failed to dislodge me, he did a loop de loop. As I had some confidence Hardy and his grandfather would spare me from instant death, I whooped and asked him to do it again.

That lit a fire under the dragon's ass, and he decided to perform a tight spiral, attempting to fling me off through the use of gravity.

Had I been a regular human, the ploy probably would have worked, but thanks to my father's efforts to make me tolerable in the saddle, I'd dealt with worse. Keeping my heels down in the stirrups and leaning helped counter the g-forces, although I expected I'd have a concussion worth sending me off to the ER by the time the captain remembered he wasn't supposed to kill me while removing me from his back.

If he hadn't wanted me staying put, he shouldn't have given me reins, a saddle, *and* stirrups.

My persistence earned a growl from the opal dragon, who'd likely expected me to become a ball for the other dragons to catch after the spiral. He swooped up, and I made certain to keep close to his neck to mitigate the forces he subjected me to.

The next time, I would ask for goggles. As I didn't need to see what he was doing to move with him, I closed my eyes to alleviate the sting. The bastard went out of his way to give little warning of what he was going to do, anyway. As a bonus, I didn't have to watch Cauldron City's skyline go every which way.

On second thought, there wouldn't be a next time. I would shift the instant everyone took their eyes off me and run away at my fastest gallop, where I'd go to my parents' place and play at being a helpless foal in dire need of rescue.

Sometime between a corkscrew and some dizzying switchbacks coupled with a ridiculous amount of bucking, I went from coherent to having no idea how I'd gone from riding the demented slinky fueled with spite and sugar to on the ground.

A paramedic attempted to cajole me into telling her my name. I blamed her bright blue eyes on my impaired decision to give her my badge number instead.

"Ah, rejoined us, Smithson?" Captain Farthan asked, and he leaned over into my field of vision.

Right. Smithson was involved in my name somewhere, and after a few moments of thought, I identified it as my family name. "I don't know what that bucking thing you did was, but I request that I never have to deal with that again, sir."

"Is that the last thing you remember?"

"Did something happen after the bucking?"

"Five minutes of things happened after the bucking," he replied.

Wait. How long had I clung to the opal bastard's back? "I didn't die after the first minute?"

Hardy's grandfather snickered, and he joined my captain in hovering over me, holding up seven fingers. "From what I can tell, after the first two minutes, you were riding by pure instinct, and I plucked you off his back at the seven minute mark, as you went limp, probably from having your brains rattled about in your skull. You never actually fell, but the next buck would have done the job, and it was safer to pick you off. You probably have a concussion, so you're going on a nice trip with the lovely lady here for treatment and an overnight stay at the copper repair shop. As we dragons lack in common sense and should have put the brakes on the party at the three minute mark, we are splitting the bill."

I lifted my left hand and gave him a thumbs up. "Was he taking it easy on me?"

"No, and that had him spitting actual flame after I hauled your unconscious body off his back. Young Hardy recorded the entire flight. We were puzzled why you closed your eyes after a while, but after a few minutes of discussion, we realized you had no goggles. Humans don't react well to that much wind and cold in the eyes, which makes your feat even more impressive. We had no idea you knew how to ride dragons—at least not at that level."

"I ride horses," I admitted. "Nasty horses with a hatred of all things human. I've learned if I don't let the mean horses buck me off, I dodge injury. I've done my share of eight second rides."

My parents would forgive me for my commentary eventually, assuming the dragons informed them of my predicament. I rode my fair share of actual broncos, although I preferred the sentients and trained horses who enjoyed when fools instructed them to buck with the intent to injure.

One learned to ride well quickly when the horse would give painful instruction on the importance of staying in the saddle.

"You ride broncos?" my boss demanded, and his eyes narrowed.

"I have a time or two." As I didn't want to upset the paramedic, who had a rather displeased expression on her face, I added, "My name is Jace Smithson." I gave her the rest of my important information, including my insurance number, a repeat of my badge number, and my emergency contact number. I used my father, as I suspected my mother would blow a gasket as she'd seen me keeping company with at least one dragon before she'd bolted for home. "If I'd thought I would have gotten a concussion, I would have passed on a free ride back to work. Next time, I think I'll walk."

"That might be wise, Mr. Smithson. Gentlemen, if you'll excuse us, chatting will not get him to the hospital for testing and treatment."

"I'll accompany him," Hardy's grandfather stated.

"Suit yourself," the woman stated. "Just stay out of the way and keep quiet."

THREE

I wondered if I would survive the night.

Friday, April 6, 2057
Hospital Quarter, Precinct 153
Cauldron City, Nebraska.

ONE OF THE dragons must have done a favor for the local black unicorns, as an older member of their herd, a snappy bastard of a man named Erik, met us at the ER. As he was the primary doctor who worked with all the unicorns in the area, I expected my night to take a turn into nightmare territory once he notified my parents I'd been taken to the hospital.

Dr. Erik did not joke around when another unicorn showed up in his ER, and while I knew every unicorn in the precinct, he'd delivered most of them.

I wondered if I would survive the night.

The Black Dragon of New York gave the unicorn a companionable pat on his shoulder. "Thanks for coming. We got a little enthusiastic with one of the baby cops up for promotion. We're not sure how bad the concussion is, and you'll have to deal with whiplash, probable frostbite, and whatever else pesky humans suffer from when riding a dragon with something to prove."

Dr. Erik flowed from unicorn to human, dressed in scrubs and a doctor's coat. "I came because I work here, and I'm in charge of the ER tonight. Hey, Jace. Finally found something you couldn't ride?"

I waved at my fellow unicorn, who'd safeguard my secret and have me back on my feet, at least enough for desk duty, by morning. "Seven minutes on the captain, and he was trying to get me off. I really didn't want to be the ball in a game of catch among dragons."

Dr. Erik chuckled. "Still not as good as your last run on a grouchy unicorn."

"What grouchy unicorn?" the Black Dragon of New York asked.

"Jace's record is ten minutes on a red, which was the last time he got sent over to the hospital after a wild ride. That one was a three day stay, mainly trying to teach him a lesson. I see it didn't work. A pity."

"It wasn't an optional flight," I replied. "And I had two black dragons spotting me. Honestly, I don't remember a damned thing after the corkscrew, but it seems I'm damned good at riding even when unconscious."

"Nobody can ride while unconscious, Jace. You're suffering from memory loss due to a concussion," the black unicorn grumbled. "I doubt I'll be able to recover the memories, but I'll see what I can do. Grant, how was he riding?"

"Beyond having his eyes closed for most of the ride, he could teach burrs how to stay in the saddle."

"Your name is Grant?" I asked, eyeing the Black Dragon of New York with interest.

"What did you think my name was?"

"Hardy's Grandpa usually, Mr. Grimstone if I'm trying to avoid getting eaten by a dragon," I admitted. "The Black Dragon of New York when being formal. You're a dragon. I can't go wrong with formal."

Dr. Erik laughed. "That's Jace for you. I can't say he's wrong. Let's get him in and get this sorted out so I can move him into a room. I don't want him clogging up my ER all night. What do you figure the damaging maneuver was?"

Hardy's grandfather shrugged. "All of them can cause a concussion. We treat every cop who goes through the promotional ride for a concussion. Captain Farthan didn't joke around. He started tamely enough. Wingovers, loops, and so on, but after twenty seconds of the easy stunts, he realized he had to pull out the big guns to drop Jace. He didn't drop Jace. Jace passed out in the saddle, and I called the exercise to a halt and pulled him off Nathan's back. We were high enough up at that point it could have been oxygen deprivation, but we aren't sure. He was out for no more than five minutes, though."

"I was aware of a promotional flight scheduled for tonight, as I'd been put on notice to expect a cop. I hadn't known the cop would be Jace, but there you have it. Still, seven minutes is admirable. What was the previous record?"

"Thirty-two seconds. The corkscrew usually flings riders right off, but Jace had a good seat, a better hold on the reins, and more determination than one human man needs. The corkscrew might have started the concussion, though. After the corkscrew, Nathan went for a series of switchbacks."

Dr. Erik winced. "That would do it. How is your head, Jace?"

"I feel like it should hurt, but it doesn't."

The paramedic cleared her throat. "I did some work to make sure the swelling stayed down, sir."

"Excellent. Level of concussion?"

"Moderate."

"Active bleeds?"

"That I can't tell you, but judging from his mental acuity and ease of diminishing the swelling, I don't think so. Once he woke up, he regained coherency rather quickly. He did give me his badge number instead of his name once, but after the dragons talked to him, he was able to give me his information. His memory seems generally unimpaired outside of the injuring incident, and he has been coherent."

"Then it should be ten minutes on the table, a run through the scanners to confirm there are no active bleeds, and observation until morning. I'll take care of notifying his family."

"You know his family?" Hardy's grandfather asked.

"I was in the delivery room when he was born, and he came into the world stubborn and ready to give his parents a run for their money," Dr. Erik announced with a disgusting amount of pride in his voice. "Come on in the back, Grant. You can observe so you can convince the worrywarts back at the station I know what I'm doing."

Rather than make a pitstop at triage, Dr. Erik took me directly into one of the ER surgical rooms. Before I had a chance to request being present for the examination, the black unicorn brought out his magic guns and knocked my ass out, probably so he could gossip with a dragon about my flight, current work, and my lack of a life, love or otherwise.

Unicorns and dragons were assholes like that.

Whomever had set up my room had taken mercy, disabling the standard beeps so I could sleep through being observed. Dim lighting implied I'd gotten some nocturnal species as the night staff. With Dr. Erik in charge of my case, I guessed I either had a vampire, some form of nocturnal shapeshifter, or one of the more tolerant unicorns, including members of Dr. Erik's family, who used magic to be able to see.

As good cops who wanted to leave when morning came didn't test their luck, I made myself as comfortable as I could with an IV installed and dressed in exactly nothing but a hospital gown. I loathed hospital gowns, especially the ones with ties in the back that left little to the imagination if I didn't take care. As I'd rather not be hunted in packs, I took care. I also made a mental note to find real clothes at the first opportunity.

To prove my night could get worse, Dr. Erik swept into the room, beating a clipboard against his leg. "I love when sedation wears off precisely when I mean for it to. Your family is just having an interesting day."

Damn. I glanced at the door and raised a brow.

"It's safe to talk. We have a full floor of unicorns."

Nice. That saved me from being licked by excitable shapeshifters, tormented by the vampires who enjoyed teasing patients over their blood quality, or drooled over by the few demonesses who preferred the healing arts versus their other magics. "Heard about my mother hanging out at work?"

"Did I ever. She gave me an earful when I called her, as she'd seen you at work, highly amused over her misfortune."

"Well, outside of the fresh murder cases I have to deal

with because someone got creative hanging her up for a while, why *wouldn't* I be amused? She looked fine. I even preserved her latest attempt to get rich and asked them to take care of her tack. I gave her step-by-step instructions on how to navigate through the murky world of investigations without my boss realizing what I was up to."

"She mentioned you'd given her rather detailed instructions. When I told her you'd landed in the copper repair shop, she about blew a gasket, especially when I told her you were riding grouchy sentients again. I saved your life, colt. I informed her it was a scheduled promotional flight, and that *every* detective in our precinct gets a wild ride to go with the new badge. She's now preparing a celebration rather than planning your imminent demise."

"I appreciate that, Dr. Erik. Thanks."

"It would have marred my record if I'd lost a patient in my hospital to his own mother's wrath. I just thought you'd like some warning she muttered something about having brought you into this world and being capable of taking you out of it."

Yep, I was a dead man walking. "How long in observation do you think it'll take for her temper to cool down?"

"Longer than you have. It's ten now. I kept it dark in here so you wouldn't be disturbed, as your mother was concerned you've been working too hard. I'll feed you lunch in twenty minutes and bring in your uniform, which I had laundered so your mother won't panic when she sees you. I'll set you loose at noon. One of the colts offered to take you home, and he's been doing good with his riders, so you should have a smooth ride. Greg is one of the best blinkers in my herd, too, so he can keep you out of trouble. In this case, home is your parents' place, as they would like to fawn all over you."

"But will he defend me from my mother?"

"That is part of why I approved him taking you home. You can go back to work tomorrow, and you can review any evidence in the comfort of your home today, assuming your parents release you from their clutches. I can't stop the evidence from paying you a visit. I tried. You have a flock of dragons eager to check in on you. But they'll bring you dinner, so that's something. I asked your father to make sure your place was tidied for a professional visit from your boss. I expect your parents will release you before dinner is scheduled to arrive."

"And now I owe you. Thanks, Dr. Erik."

"I'll come calling when the next batch of foals are ready for their first ride."

I chuckled. "That sounds like a plan. Are you taking the dragons' wallets out back and putting them out of their misery?"

"We charged the minimum for your care. They called it in well in advance, they had two spotters, and they had no way of knowing you're a damned fine rider and would give yourself a concussion before surrendering. Honestly, the dragons were more of a problem than you. They expected mild bumps and bruises when you were caught falling off, not a moderate concussion and whiplash you'll feel tomorrow."

While most unicorns could heal many ailments, especially the blacks, they tended to conserve their strength for serious injuries. I would hurt for the next few days, but I'd be able to work. I would be reaching for painkillers, though. "And my parents, really?"

"They're proud as hell you stuck on that opal bastard's back. I believe they cashed out a few gems for you as compensation for dealing with him. Book money, because they firmly believe you're still hungry for every book you can get your hands on."

"I am," I replied with zero shame. "I will accept this offering, and I will be inconsolable if I don't get to add to my book hoard."

"Are you sure you're not actually a dragon?"

"I'm fairly sure I'm not a dragon. I just happen to really like books *and* gemstones, and I keep them close."

"Have you even sold any of your gems?"

"I've sold three," I admitted.

"What'd you buy?"

I coughed. "Books and gaming computers. I spent more on the books than the computer stuff."

"Of course you did. I'm going to get you something to eat and then kick you out of my hospital. I don't want to see you back here for a week."

"A week?"

"You'll be coming in for a checkup so your mother doesn't shove her horn up my ass."

"10-4."

Friday, April 6, 2057
Hospital Quarter, Precinct 153
Cauldron City, Nebraska.

I RODE Greg out of the hospital to increase my chances of making it without a co-worker catching me. Rather than escape the hospital without notice, Captain Farthan waited outside the front doors, startling the poor colt so badly he blinked a few feet away before remembering he couldn't flee from my boss. I soothed him, patted his neck to assure him he hadn't done anything wrong, and said, "I thought you were on dinner duty."

"I am, but word on the wire was you were being released, so I decided to come have a look-see. I was not expecting you to be riding a unicorn, however."

"He's new to having a rider and volunteered to take me home. He's a relative of one of the doctors. I've been informed I will not be driving until tomorrow at the earliest. The colt's learning how to keep his stride smooth, so it works out."

"That teleporting didn't seem all that smooth."

"It's not bad." Of course, it wasn't bad solely because of my experience with blinking at my leisure when a unicorn. "I'll be fine. That didn't even bother my back, which is the equivalent of a train wreck. If it isn't better in a day or two, I'll be back here for more treatment. Otherwise, I have a follow up in a week. Any news on the case?"

"We'll have some reports for you to go over to keep yourself amused with later. I'll send someone to pick you up tomorrow. You can book your time off then, and you have first crack at dates."

I'd take advantage of that. "And the unicorn?"

"She showed up in the wee hours of the morning with a typed note requesting her possessions. We saddled and bridled her and gave her the rest of her belongings. It turns out she produced diamonds worth several million dollars."

Damn. My mother must have been packing away the cheese and chicken for weeks for that nice of a haul. "Did she answer any of your questions?"

"No, but she met a bunch of curious cops, all of whom got a chance to pet her before she trotted off with her goods tied to her saddle. She seemed to like it, and she even managed to poke her nose in Hardy's hoard drawer. He gave her one of his coins because she turned sad eyes on him."

Damn. My mother must have worked the entire precinct to get a dragon to give up one of his coins. "He's never going to live that down."

"He's really not. She seemed pretty proud of having gotten a coin from a dragon, so we decided we'll take it easy on him just this once. Those eyes are potent."

If they ever learned they'd gotten hoodwinked by my mother, I'd be the one ribbed about it for all eternity. The idea of getting booked while a unicorn so I could charm my co-workers out of their coins appealed.

None of the dragons would miss a few coins, and I needed to one-up my mother.

To keep Greg from jumping out of his skin, I patted his neck again. "Did you drive or fly?"

The captain pointed at something behind me, and Greg took pity on me and turned so I could get a look.

The Black Dragon of New York waved from a rather nice sports car, a black beauty of a vehicle I suspected was a prized Black Wing, a brand for people with more money than sense. "I feel like I should ticket you just for being near that, sir."

He chuckled and came over, holding his hand out to Greg. After a moment of consideration, the colt cooperated, sniffing the dragon's hand before nudging him for some attention, which he received. "I'd loaned it to my granddaughter, who came calling after hearing I helped to hospitalize a cop. She's preparing to beat me within an inch of my life for being rude when I'm a visitor. I'd have her be my heir, but she keeps refusing the job."

The poor woman. I wouldn't want to be in her shoes. "Is she a human or a dragon?"

"She's a dragoness, a full shapeshifter, and can control her hybrid form as well. That's part of the reason I suggested she take over New York once I get bored of the place. Of course, that won't happen for a few thousand years at the earliest. New York is entertaining. It's also a challenge. In fact, she's in the car." The bastard waved his hand, and a dark-haired woman emerged from the vehicle out of the driver's side, dressed in a pair of tight jeans and a black blouse. She strolled over with her hands in her pockets, her eyes narrowed and looking me over head to toe.

Damn. I bet the Black Dragon of New York spent most of his time keeping suitors away from his granddaughter. She could walk down the street and set the whole place ablaze.

Having met his wife, I could understand how his children—and grandchildren—had emerged from their eggs ready and equipped to conquer men and women alike.

"Ma'am," I greeted, giving her a nod. I missed my hat, as I would've dipped the brim to be extra polite. Greg took the hint and lowered into a bow, one foreleg stretched out as he lowered his head to greet the woman. Once he rose and was stable on his hooves, I said, "Your grandfather isn't the aggressor this go around, so you don't have to beat him too harshly. He encouraged the incident, however, so you should discipline him some."

She laughed. "Finally found yourself a cop with a sense of humor, Grandpappy?"

"I can't take him home. I've already tried. He told me no. Then he threatened to claim part of my hoard if I inconvenience him—and he dared to read off the various bylaws that would allow him to make good on those threats. Why can't I have him, Nathan?"

"He said no, that's why not. And he's mine. Be content that he's one of Hardy's co-workers. That's the best you're getting."

"Alicia, since you came all this way anyway, I have a job for you. I'll even pay you for the work."

The woman heaved a sigh. "What do you want now?"

"Babysit the cop. He got his brain rattled in his skull, and while the hospital released him, you know how those human men get. They're fragile. Follow the unicorn and the cop to wherever they're going, invite yourself in, and keep an eye on him. I'll be back in time for dinner, but I have some errands I need to run."

Heaving another sigh, Alicia raised a hand to rub her temple. "I've been here less than an hour, and you're already giving me a migraine."

"It's only a temporary gig. I already called your sisters and your single aunts. Surely *one* of them will catch the cop. I will have him, Alicia."

Damned dragons.

The pair glared at each other, and in the matter of half a minute, they began to snarl, hiss, and snap their teeth at each other, a feat considering they remained in human form. "Captain, I'm going to go visit my parents, then I'm going home. Thank you for dinner in advance. What time should I expect you?"

"Call it seven. It'll take some time to get those two to stop yelling. Run while you can, and please don't get into any trouble riding the unicorn. I'll tell dispatch to ignore any reports of unusual transportation on the roads as long as you're the rider."

"Thanks." I saluted the captain and gave Greg the lightest nudge with my heels. The colt blinked for freedom, taking short but rapid hops to get away from the dragons before they noticed we'd left them to their fight.

FOUR

"You mean it's not my wonderful personality?"

Friday April 6, 2057
Willow Grove, Precinct 158
Cauldron City, Nebraska.

GREG GOT TO MY PARENTS' home without incident, although I'd acquired a police escort. A rather amused Hardy got out of his cruiser with Paul in tow. "You're looking good. I'm surprised you were willing to ride anything after yesterday," the dragon informed me.

I questioned why Hardy accompanied Lovell's partner, and curiosity ate away at me.

To keep Greg from bolting or transforming and revealing more to my co-workers than I wanted, I stayed on his back and reassured him through patting his shoulder. "The doctors wanted to make sure I made it home in one piece, and all black unicorns have medical training. Did you do a partner swap or something?"

"Just for today. Our partners are back at the station

reviewing evidence, and neither one of them wanted to deal with my grandpappy for some reason. Smart move on the doctor's part, though. Black unicorns seem somewhat sensible. Black dragons just collect shiny things and destroy whatever annoys us."

"And whatever happens to get on your back, with or without invitation," I muttered.

Hardy snickered, came over, and held his hand out to Greg. Once again, the colt's love of attention got the better of him, and the dragon went to work providing the desired petting. "So, this is where your parents live?"

My mother and father, both humans and dressed in their nicest work clothes, emerged from their home.

Paul's brows rose. "Damn, Smithson. Now I know where the hell you get it from."

I regarded my parents, attempting to determine what the man saw that I didn't. I'd come out of the parental mixing bowl with an alarming number of similarities to my father although I'd picked up a few of my mother's traits, including her hair and eye color. "I get what from them?"

"Your charm. Every dragon that has met you wants to take you home or marry you off to their daughter or granddaughter."

"You mean it's not my wonderful personality? I'm hurt." I swung my leg over Greg's back, dismounted, gathered the reins, and extracted the colt from Hardy's affection. "You can't take the unicorn home, by the way. He's too young to become the infatuation of dragons. Once he's a full adult, you may try to charm him into your hoard or secure him for one of your countless cousins, but he's not a full adult yet."

"You and your damned rules," the dragon complained.

I held the reins so Greg could take them from me. Once

he had them, I gave his shoulder a pat. "Escape while you can."

The colt blinked away and ran for the safety of home, fast enough a dragon would have to work to keep up with him.

"Damn, you're mean." Hardy grunted, and he joined Paul in staring at my parents. "I think you're right, Paul. How'd we miss such beautiful people living in our fair city?"

"They have a lot more common sense than I do," I replied, heading up the walkway to their porch, climbing the three steps to kiss my mother's cheek. "I'm sorry for worrying you, Mom."

"Once I heard it was for a promotional flight, I forgave you—mostly. You could have called."

"The captain didn't give me enough time to call, and Dr. Erik enforced good patient behavior. I can't cause trouble in his ER while unconscious."

"Well, that's true enough," she replied.

My father opened the door into the house. "Come on in and bring your friends with you. Erik asked we feed you again, as you'd devoured every scrap of food on your plate. You were too polite to ask for more, but he's onto your ravenous ways. We might have enough to feed your friends."

"One is a dragon."

"We might have enough to feed your friends, but it's questionable." My father eyed the detectives. "Please move your cruiser into the driveway, else the neighbors will be over asking what we're being arrested for. It's bad enough when my son brings his cruiser over and leaves it on the street just to make the neighbors ask questions."

I could think of a few reasons the cops might want to pay them a visit, but as I loved my parents and didn't want to deal with them at work any more than necessary, I kept quiet. My mother headed into the house in a hurry, probably to hide the coin she'd pilfered from Hardy.

It wouldn't surprise me if she also needed to hide her new stash of glitter and gemstones. She'd sell the glitter online because it amused her, and I tried not to think about what she'd use the gemstone money on. Somehow, she found a way to vex me.

"I have to be home at seven, as the dragons are convinced I will starve to death if they don't feed me. I had no idea dragons possessed such refined guilty consciences."

My father snorted. "Erik told me about the hovering dragons at the hospital last night. They were convinced they'd done permanent harm. Erik had to tell them you have rocks in your head instead of a brain. To keep the whining to a minimum, he allowed them to monitor you for a while after you'd been taken to your room. Once they figured out there was an entire herd of black unicorns working your floor, they relaxed."

"He hadn't told me that part."

"He didn't want you to worry or try to educate them on why they shouldn't be excessive." My father herded me into the house. "Make sure your mother has put everything away. I'll keep the cops busy."

I snickered but obeyed, finding my mother glaring at a gift-wrapped box on the table. "Problem, Mom?"

"I was going to give you a present of glitter for your promotion."

"Remember, I just came from a hospital loaded with unicorns. You have an easy alibi. You got it from them."

"Just don't open the package wrapped in pink inside. Everything else is okay."

I chuckled. "Are you giving me one of the prizes from your bounty?"

"It's a pink diamond, and it's a nice one."

Well, that would buy me a lot of books—or the best of the best gaming computer money could buy. And a new car. And a house—or three houses. "Are you ever going to be able to look at chicken or cheese ever again?"

"I won't have to unless I want to. I got a good white, a black, a blue, and a red diamond, too. You're getting the pink because it's larger than the others."

One day, I might understand what my mother also ate with her chicken and cheese to get the fancy diamonds. I tended to get large but clear diamonds. Granted, large, flawless, and clear white diamonds brought in a pretty penny, but sometimes, I wanted to have more diamonds with color. In reality, it didn't matter, as I hoarded my diamonds, but mine would fetch a fortune if I bothered with selling them. "Thank you, Mom."

"You've earned it. I swear, are you *sure* you're not a dragon?"

"I'm not a dragon, but if I'm not careful, I might end up married to one." I pointed over my shoulder with my thumb in the direction of the front door. "Hardy is here, and I don't know what you did to my co-workers, but you better have hidden that damned coin or I'll never hear the end of it."

"It's hidden with the rest of my gems. Don't worry. The only thing I'm worried about is the glitter I'm bequeathing you for daring to get hurt during your promotional flight."

"I lasted seven minutes, Mom. You should be praising me. I had to beat thirty-three seconds."

"That's not beating the record, Jace. That's ruthlessly

destroying it. No wonder those dragons are upset and following you around. Tell me about these dragonesses, though. The last time I introduced you to a unicorn, you used sad pony eyes on me."

In another decade or two, I would graduate from a sad pony to a proud stallion, as our species tended to grow slow and go through several adult phases. For the next while, I would resemble more of a fluffy pony than a horse, although that would change as I aged.

With a little luck, I would shed out ahead of schedule, as pony fur resisted being tamed even on a good day.

When I classified as old, I'd be the unicorn equivalent of a draft horse, standing at somewhere between nineteen to twenty-one hands at the shoulder and built like a tank. If I defied the typical age span of white unicorns, which was counted in hundreds of years, I might even crest twenty-two hands. The eldest unicorn, a mare with almost a thousand years under her belt, was twenty-four hands and rarely showed up in her equine form.

In the meantime, I would continue to use my sad pony eyes on my mother until the stunt lost its effectiveness.

"Well, when she shows up, the Black Dragon of New York asked one of his granddaughters to keep me out of trouble, and I don't know what the hell that family is doing, but she's definitely a looker—and judging from the commentary, I don't think that old bastard thinks she's the prettiest of his granddaughters and daughters. He called in the *other* single dragonesses to hunt me. In a unified pack. I'm not sure they're clear on how this whole thing is supposed to work, honestly."

My mother giggled and pushed the box my way. "Congratulations on your promotion, baby."

"I don't know if I've actually been promoted yet," I admitted.

"You've been promoted," Hardy announced from behind me. "You'll get your paperwork when you're back at the station along with your updated badge and cards. You're also scheduled to be evaluated for a new firearm. Yours is old."

"There's nothing wrong with my gun," I growled at the dragon.

"I'll make sure the boss knows you'll be carrying two guns, then. Also, are you *sure* you're not a dragon?"

I rolled my eyes. "I'm not a dragon, although I did steal some of your bad habits."

"He hardly has any bad habits. He just hoards books," my mother informed my co-worker. "Why don't you make yourself comfortable? Jace is about to pay penance for being hospitalized by having to dig through unicorn-gifted glitter to get to his real presents. Getting it out of his clothes should keep him busy."

I loved my mother, but sometimes, she took some of my suggestions a little too far.

With zero evidence he cared he was about to share my fate, Hardy sat next to me and patted the seat next to him until I joined him. "Thank you for the invitation, Mrs. Smithson. My grandfather wanted me to ask for your forgiveness. He was supposed to be overseeing the flight, and we all got a little overenthusiastic. We forgot Jace is just a human, albeit a resilient one."

Somehow, I kept from laughing in his face, as did my mother. She smiled and replied, "It's quite all right. We're friends with the unicorns who work at that hospital. He was born there, and the ER doc working last night delivered him. Jace can't resist when sentients offer him a challenge, and the unicorns ask him to get their older foals used to carrying someone in the saddle. They take good care of him there, and they usually ask him to go through another ride as payment for patching him up from the previous one."

"Which reminds me. Dr. Erik would like some help with the next batch of foals. I agreed, assuming they'll put me back together once they finished tenderizing me."

"Let's not tell the captain you put yourself in life-threatening situations for fun," Hardy suggested. "Or my grandfather. Both of them are fawning over you enough as it is right now."

"If them fawning means I don't have to worry about dinner tonight, I'm all right with that. Any idea what they're feeding me?"

"Steak and Portuguese chicken," Hardy announced. "From the good place."

Damn. I assumed the steak would be coming from the Brazilian joint next door to the Portuguese restaurant, which was a hole in the wall the entire city's cop population had learned about after someone in Precinct 115 had witnessed a knife fight outside of the place over the last batch of chicken for the day. "Who are they killing for *that*?"

"My grandpappy called and asked nicely last night."

Did the old black dragon know how to do anything nicely? I eyed my fellow detective with a raised brow. "In his terms, what is nicely?"

"He acquired the right type of chicken and offered a monetary bribe. That way, they have to cook more chicken but they don't hurt their supply. The Brazilian place just asked that he pose in front of the restaurant for a picture as a publicity stunt. He'll do that for the Portuguese place, too.

It wouldn't surprise me if he gets my cousin to pose in a more traditional sense. She likes to dance." Hardy shot a glare at me. "And not as a pole dancer."

"Miss Alicia?" I asked.

"Just call her Alicia. But yes, her. She loves to dance. She'll dance with horses, people—if it is associated with dancing, she's either learning it or has mastered it. I recommend you warn the unicorns to hide. She'll want to see how good they are at dressage."

"They're terrible at it," I informed him. "Do you really think you're going to convince a unicorn to dance to someone else's tune?"

My mother snickered and headed for the kitchen. "I'll get you a drink, Jace. Erik told us to make sure you sit and relax, so you get to pretend you're five and not feeling well again."

"Soup, crackers, ginger ale, and game shows on television?" I asked, wondering how far I'd be able to take revisiting my childhood.

"You can do all of the above if you'd like, just open your present first. I want a new couch."

Ah. I read between the lines: if I got glitter all over the couch, Dad would let Mom replace it. "Is there anything fragile in this box?"

"Not particularly, but I recommend against dumping it out over your head. Dig out the books *before* you make a mess of the dining room."

"You heard her, Hardy." I gestured to the box. "I need sharp claws to get through the tape."

While Hardy had a way to go in terms of controlling his partial transformations, he'd mastered developing sharp claws instead of nails, and he sliced open the top of the box so I could dig inside. A ridiculous amount of blue, pink, and red glitter awaited me, and as I'd be covered head to toe in it anyway, I went to town finding my promotion presents. While she'd deployed her gem-producing payload in terrible fashions, my mother had taken pity on me, providing at least six new books for my enjoyment, a package that implied I had a new video game or three to play, one that might contain a handheld console for my enjoyment, the promised pink box with my new diamond, and a box the appropriate shape and size for a new watch. After some digging, which resulted in wearing most of the glitter without having to dump it over my head, I located three gift cards and a larger manila envelope.

Then, as she would do things like tape presents to the interior of the box, I waved at Paul to join in and said, "You and Hardy can dump it over my head. Then we're going to the couch and adding to the chaos."

My father glowered at me. "Really?"

My mother scampered in from the kitchen. "He wants television time with his friends and some soup. We'll send the cops back to work shimmering. We're leaving the Smithson family mark on them."

No kidding—and in more ways than I wanted my co-workers to discover.

Hardy and Paul wasted no time dumping the glitter over my head. Sure enough, I found several more envelopes taped to the side of the box, which I claimed for my pile. "Thank you."

My father chuckled and waved off my gratitude. "You try to avoid birthday presents, but you can't refuse a promotional present you've properly earned."

Hardy stared at me. "You reject *presents*?"

Damned dragon. "They paid enough getting me to adulthood. I do not need additional prizes for surviving yet another year."

Hardy turned to our co-worker and blurted, "He needs to go back to the hospital."

Paul rolled his eyes. "He's fine. He's not a dragon, Hardy. But now I know why my partner is with your partner. Someone has to keep this chaotic mess somewhat sane."

I foresaw a great deal of trouble. "Who is keeping Lovell from taking over without proper supervision?"

"Dowdren. You know, my partner?" Hardy stared at me.

One day, I'd get Dowdren to actually say more than one word to me—anything. Half the time, the detective skulked around, working hard to make sure everyone forgot about him. Once, I'd gotten a hello out of him, which had shocked Hardy so much he'd retreated to his hoard to comfort himself.

"Lovell's going to need therapy," I predicted. "Dowdren doesn't talk *or* touch, and he'd prefer if we'd stop pestering him and handle all communication by email. I'm pretty sure he was at the warehouse, but he vanished off. I think. Or he explored without us bothering him. Lovell is going to start trouble, and Dowdren is going to stare him into submission. We're going to go back to work to a disaster."

"Dowdren was at the warehouse, but you were pretty focused on the corpses and the unicorn. He skulked around a little but otherwise kept track of the cruisers and made sure nobody messed with our evidence."

"Thank him for me. If I thank him, he might grunt at me again."

My father cleared his throat. "Boys, this is a no work zone. Go into the living room, turn on a game show, and wait to be fed soup. All three of you have obviously had a rough life and need to be tended to properly."

Apparently, my co-workers loved the idea of sitting on a couch, drinking soup, and watching cheesy game shows on television, as the pair went off in search of a place to sit. I refilled the box with as much glitter as I could in a hurry and followed them. "Replacing the carpet, too?"

"Go to town. We're going to go to the other residence while we have the place fully renovated. Your mother has decided she wants some change. Glitter forces change."

No kidding. The construction workers might need to tear the whole building down to get rid of the mess. "Okay. I'll come unwrap the presents later."

"I'll put them in another box and make sure the glitter is gone."

"Thanks."

In the living room, my co-workers had discovered there were two armchairs, a loveseat, and a couch, and they engaged in a fierce argument over where they'd sit. As I had my father's blessing, I chucked glitter over both of them. "The couch. That's the one with three cushions."

My co-workers shimmered, I smirked, and while they came to terms I'd ambushed them with glitter, I claimed the middle cushion for myself. "I recommend you hug the old, crabby black dragon once he shows up to spread the love."

"You're mean when you have a concussion," Hardy observed, and he took the seat to my right. "Are your parents really going to feed us soup and expect us to watch game shows?"

"They really are. That is my childhood, and they selfishly want to revisit it. It's tough caring for parents like mine. As concussions count as being sick, it's just easier to go along with it. It doesn't hurt I love soup. I'll be ready for painkillers around the time I go home, but I won't get any until after dinner."

"I'm going to have to give Alicia a really good birthday present to put up with this. She *hates* glitter."

"But why?" I patted Hardy's arm and showed off my shimmering hand. "Is it due to her inability to count every spec?"

"That is only the start of her problems with glitter," he replied.

"How about the rest of your cousins and sisters?"

"Inflicting things upon us that we can't count should be classified as criminal, Jace."

Huh. "So, all I have to do to dissuade your grandpappy's matchmaking is to arm myself with glitter and give it to the ladies as a present?"

Paul took the seat to my left and stared at me with wide eyes. "Wow, Jace. There is evil, and then there is cruel and unusual punishment. Where would you even get that much glitter?"

"I'd just ask the unicorns at the hospital and tell them it would be revenge for my concussion. I'm sure they'd hook me up with an offensive amount of glitter. It's not like they actually want to keep the stuff." I allowed myself a smile. "How much glitter do you think I'd need to defeat your grandpappy, Hardy?"

"More than you currently have, but I'm not sure how much more." Hardy stared at his hands, his expression a blend of fascination and horror. "I feel I should be more loyal to my family and tell you never to glitter a black dragon."

"You want me to glitter your sisters and cousins."

"I desperately want you to inflict glitter on my sisters and cousins. I want you to take out my entire family in one fell, glittery swoop. I want you to take over the entirety of my clan with the ruthlessness only a man willing to arm himself with glitter possesses. I saw your face when you chucked that box on us. There was zero evidence of remorse for your crime. You wanted us to suffer."

Yes, I had. "I'll talk to the unicorns at the hospital and inquire if it's possible to acquire their unwanted glitter." Given a week and the appropriate diet, we whites could create a staggering amount of glitter with minimal chance of gemstones. If my mother summoned every white unicorn in the area, we could fill several dump trucks in the matter of a few days.

The instant I had a chance to talk to her without any co-workers around, I would give her the job of acquiring enough glitter to defeat an entire clan of dragons. As she enjoyed toying with other races, she'd bite.

"Just a warning about my cousin," Hardy announced. "She will never forgive you for the glitter."

"I want to be forgiven for the glitter?" I widened my eyes. "But why?"

"Well, she *is* my cousin. Sure, she's not one of the models, but she's still an honorable member of my clan."

Wait. Alicia *wasn't* one of the clan's models? Were black dragons blind? Mentally impaired? Unfortunately biased? "Well, why not? No interest? A desire for a job that doesn't require she attempt to imitate a twig? Honestly, when I see most models, I have this urge to feed them cupcakes with extra icing. I dated a model once, and the urge got to be too much. On one of my days off, I made her cupcakes with homemade icing. I put various chocolate bar pieces on top.

Let's just say that by the end of the day, I had a lot of cupcakes to enjoy but no girlfriend to enjoy them with. I even made sure to stick to all her food rules. I used honey instead of sugar, I had to work some science magic to make them gluten free, and don't ask me about the chocolate bars. I'd done a great job on them, too. I run into her sometimes, and she cusses at me. Part of that is my fault. I usually tell her she should have tried one before kicking me to the curb."

Paul and Hardy shook their heads and sighed.

"I know, right? I thought I was doing something nice. I stayed home and baked. It took me hours. I put everything I knew she liked into those cupcakes. It turns out when your girlfriend is a model and values modeling above most other things, making her treats she will really like is a bad idea."

"I'm confused," Paul admitted.

"I'm also confused," Hardy stated. "Why would she get mad over *that*?"

I shrugged. "Who knows?" Leaning forward, I grabbed the remote, and I turned the television on, obeying the parental edict to watch a game show. "It seems we have a choice of species competitions in obstacle courses, price guessing, or elimination…" I squinted at the television menu. "Does that say it's a game about dragons battling for possession of an item from another dragon's hoard?"

"Oh. Alicia works for that show. She handles the negotiations for the dragons to participate. These shows are *hilarious*, especially when the 'item' is a person they're both trying to date. It's utter chaos." Hardy joined me in leaning forward to squint at the listing. "Oh, this is a rerun, but it's a good one. A black, one of my great uncles, and an opal dragon, who happens to be related to the captain, wanted the same gemstone on offer from a ruby dragon. The ruby dragon is an Italian fellow, who happens to be a really nice guy. He loves everything to do with the United States, and Cauldron City is his favorite city on the planet. So, they filmed here in Precinct 101. This is a four-hour special, so buckle in. It's a wild ride."

FIVE

"Harsh. Hilarious, but harsh."

Friday April 6, 2057
Willow Grove, Precinct 158
Cauldron City, Nebraska.

AS PROMISED, my parents fed us soup while we watched the game show special. The prized gemstone, a ruby the size of my fist, fascinated me. Every now and then, a white unicorn had the misfortune of producing a stone of unusual size. It usually resulted in a severe case of constipation and a trip to the hospital to monitor for complications. Following the successful expelling of the stone, typically through natural methods, the unicorn received a scolding from their herd and every medical professional involved with the incident.

Thus far, I'd dodged being hospitalized, although I'd pushed my luck a few times. My father had a knack for ending up in the ER so full of glitter and gemstones his eyes crossed and he could barely walk. My mother maintained her self-respect and dignity around our foe, cheese.

I had no idea how my mother managed, but one day, I would get her to teach me her secrets.

Cheese did me and my father in, resulting in a few uncomfortable days after we went on a binge and decided to transform.

As it was, I'd have to be careful, as my mother had opted to fill the soup with copious amounts of chicken and veggies good for producing mid-valued gemstones, typically sapphires. Depending on what the Black Dragon of New York fed me, I might have to skip off as a unicorn on my days off to add to my personal collection.

In what counted as pure insanity, the game show had opted to test the dragons in a myriad of ways. Their first game involved chess, except they played as dragons, the board and pieces were crafted of fragile glass, and they suffered penalties for breaking anything.

Twenty minutes into the game, Hardy's great uncle, Thebault, began using compliments on his opponent, Vincent, the captain's cousin—most of them targeting the captain's various sisters. That had resulted in the first broken piece and a fuming opal dragon.

"Has the captain seen this episode?"

"Yep," Hardy replied, shaking his head and laughing. "This first aired a few years ago. My uncle is now happily married to the captain's sister. You will *love* how this ends."

I would? "Do they brawl over the captain's sister?"

"It was broadcast live, and yes."

I snatched the remote, but Hardy stole it from me and passed it to Paul so I couldn't check if the network would allow me to fast-forward to the end. "Hey! I want to see the brawl."

"You will, in roughly three and a half hours." Paul tossed the remote onto my father's chair, transferring copious amounts of glitter in the process. "He's seen this episode, but I haven't."

As they would gang up on me, I relaxed and observed Hardy's great uncle thoroughly crush the opal dragon at chess, although skill at the game had nothing to do with his victory. It took a single suggestion of being uncertain if any opal dragon might be a suitable partner for a dragoness as glorious as Estaria to do the captain's cousin in.

"Is Estaria the captain's sister?" I asked.

"Yep," Hardy confirmed. "Opals typically join other opal clans, so my great uncle was both complimenting and insulting opal dragons at the same time."

"Harsh. Hilarious, but harsh."

"Ah," Hardy's grandfather said, and a moment later, he leaned over the couch behind me. "That episode is a good one. Introducing Jace to our family's insanity?"

Hardy nodded. "Where's Alicia?"

"Behind me, staring in horror at the trails of glitter everywhere. Where did you acquire so much glitter, and what possessed you to wear it?"

Hardy and Paul pointed at me. I pointed in the direction of the dining room. "My mother wants to renovate the house, so she trapped my promotion present with glitter, which she acquired from some unicorn, probably from the hospital. As I had already been exposed, I thought I'd share with my co-workers. As we're now infected with glitter, we get to be pampered, watch game shows, and go home after we're mystically cured thanks to some good soup and television time."

"How old are you again?" the Black Dragon of New York asked in a curious tone.

"Not old enough to skip my mother's soup and television time," I replied. "I've never seen this show before, and it's fascinating. That opal dragon shattered the chessboard because a black dragon complimented his cousin."

Alicia came around and perched on the arm of my father's chair. "This was one of the better episodes, I do have to admit. That old bastard did not bring shame to our family's name. Captain Farthan? They're watching that episode."

Damn. Before I could protest about work following me to my parents' home, the captain stepped into the living room, caught sight of the television, and laughed. "Remember that incident with the little redhead who bolted into the station wailing over how life wasn't fair, Smithson?"

I doubted I'd ever forget, as I'd only gotten settled into my role at the station before she'd come storming in. "I remember her. She ran for the public women's bathroom and spent an hour wailing over the unfairness of it all. Every time we sent one of the women in, she'd come out laughing and tell us not to worry about it. We worried about it. Then you told us to go back to work, knocked on the bathroom door, and somehow got her to come out." That incident had left me with more questions than answers, and I'd gone home questioning why I'd decided to become a cop.

"That's Estaria. She'd watched the episode live, and her future husband made an appearance in the last few minutes of the show to knock heads together. She knew I was busy, so she had a fit in the bathroom."

I did the basic math and chuckled at the idea of a dragoness becoming enamored with a black dragon after having been told all her life opals stuck with opals. "Prejudice problems?"

"Fewer than you think. It's not that we dislike other dragon types, but we rarely witness them doing something we find to be appealing. You'll understand when you get to the end of the episode."

"Let me guess. That mean old black just spends the entire episode regaling your cousin with how marvelous your sister is, tossing in a comment about one of the eligible black dragon bachelors now and then."

The captain snickered. "Good guess. The games become more and more ridiculous as it goes, too. There's a mud-based course where they needed to shift partway through. The mud keeps it acceptable for television along with some creative camera panning. I'll just apologize for your self-esteem now, boys. These dragons are fit, and by the time they get to that part of the episode, it's indecent."

As unicorns tended to indulge in similar behaviors, I could imagine how the posturing would make for some excellent ratings and heartbroken women. "Were either of these dragons single at the start of the episode?"

"No. You'll get to see their wives at the end, too."

Alicia chuckled. "This episode tends to destroy the ratings any day its played. We actually warn other networks when it's about to run, as we've determined it would be cruel to schedule it in during one of their pilots. Who is going to watch anything else when two naked dragons mud wrestling is available for the enjoyment of all? Dragons *love* this episode for some reason. I mean, they love all the episodes, but this one is special."

After the chess match, the dragons engaged in a game of tug-of-war, once again in dragon form. Hardy's great uncle decided to make use of his wicked sense of humor and the captain's sister again to claim victory, dragging the opal dragon across the ground with ease.

"I'm worried about that poor opal's self-esteem," I admitted.

"Don't. He gets payback soon enough," Alicia replied, brushing off as much of the glitter as possible from my father's chair before sitting down. "We blacks have a reputation for being ruthless, but we also tend to get comfortable in our victory before we are actually victorious. Once, I had been *so* certain my idiot grandfather would go onto the show, but no. Right before I could finalize, he threw a different dragon at me, losing me my victory."

"The prize wasn't good enough," her idiot grandfather stated.

"What do I have to do to get you to come onto the show? Put one of these cops up for grabs?"

"Actually, yes."

I bowed my head, raised my hand, and pinched the bridge of my nose. "Take the hit for the team, Paul. I just took a bunch of hits for the team, and I have a concussion to show for it."

"Oh, that was a good one," Hardy praised. "Paul, you have to respect that level of cunning. He didn't even hesitate throwing you under the bus."

"You helped them give me a concussion, so you should be up for grabs, too," I said, elbowing the black dragon. "And your grandpappy would have to give his best to defend your honor."

"He's good at this," the Black Dragon of New York

announced. I lifted my head in time to observe the black dragons engage in a glaring contest. "What's your move, my little princess? You now have two cops to work with."

"I don't remember agreeing to giving you my cops," my captain growled.

I struggled to keep my expression neutral. "And there's your second dragon, Miss Alicia. It's a rematch between the Farthan and Grimstone clans, and the starter prize is one of Grimstone's grandsons and another cop from Precinct 153, with Captain Farthan defending our precinct's honor."

The black dragoness leaned back in my father's chair and regarded her grandfather and Captain Farthan with interest. "It could work."

As I had a long way to go to stay safely out of Alicia's scheming, I said, "Hardy's single, and I'm sure Captain Farthan knows a young, beautiful opal dragoness in need of a young black dragon of good reputation."

"There are more than a few dragonesses in the branch families who might be charmed with the appropriate display." Captain Farthan eyed Hardy with interest. "It would be good publicity for our precinct."

"I'll do it under one condition," Hardy declared.

"Oh, this is going to be good," his grandpappy murmured. "What is your condition, my little prince?"

"Jace has to referee the match."

Alicia clapped. "Approved. It's perfect."

Damn. I'd almost escaped unscathed. "I have a case I need to finish first, but if it can be arranged so it doesn't interfere with my first investigation, I don't mind." With luck, I would be safe from participating. "As the referee, I can't be offered as a prize."

"Negotiable," every dragon in the room informed me.

"How is it negotiable?" I shook my head, sighed, and muttered, "Damned dragons."

Alicia grinned at me, rubbing her hands together. "As the referee, you can set the conditions of when you might be eligible to become a prize."

"But why would I want to be a prize? I'm not getting anything out of it," I reminded her.

"Ohhh," the dragons chorused.

Why me? Whenever I had to deal with a dragon, more problems flew my way. "I will referee, and you may offer a pitch—and only one pitch—near the time this show will be ready to be filmed. I will be dressed in my uniform, and I will not be put on display in any sort of mud wrestling competition. If I need to be mobile, a unicorn will be hired, and I will ride a sane sentient."

"That's reasonable. I'm sure we can find a unicorn. Any preference on color?"

"No preference. They just need to be willing to be shown off. I mean, unicorns are gorgeous. The unicorn will end up stealing the show." Aware I'd tweaked the pride of every dragon in the room, I gestured at the television. "Name the episode the Battle for Cauldron City and have the dragons fight to be the crowned champion of our city."

"Every dragon in the city will want a piece of that pie," Captain Farthan said, shaking his head.

I smirked. "That's just more episode possibilities later. A new clan can attempt to unseat the winner of the episode."

Alicia considered me with interest. "Maybe you should move up into the television business."

"I'm afraid I'll have to decline. I just moved up in the cop business, and I haven't recovered from my promotion yet. I've been promised good food for dinner tonight to go with paperwork to review. Captain, taking today off won't cause problems with the investigation, will it?"

"Not at all. We won't have the labs back until tomorrow at the earliest, and the fingerprints probably won't be done until next week. We have no eyewitnesses to work with, and we haven't identified most of the bodies. The bodies that have been identified are going to be dry leads in a lot of ways. We're gathering information now. You can go over what we've gotten from the comfort of home tomorrow. It'll be a work day, but I'll let you do it out of the station. I'd like to see your initial conclusions before the seasoned detectives train you out of creativity."

"Is that normal, Hardy?"

"It is. We all did part of our first case at home so the captain could evaluate how we think compared to everyone else. You'll be cultivated to preserve your good habits while we'll replace the bad ones with better methodology. Everyone views cases differently, so we need to see where you shine. We can't do that without throwing you in. We're going to be going over the same information you are, and we'll compare notes. We'll roll with your initial suspicions first to see what we find, and then we'll do things the old way if it doesn't pan out."

I could work with sinking or swimming for my first investigation. "Is there any indication the killer will strike again?"

"That's what we don't know," the captain admitted. "We don't have enough intel yet, and unless we can get the unicorn in for an interview, it'll be hard to figure anything out."

Having my mother go in for questioning would be problematic, but I would test the sinking or swimming theory out via a questionnaire I would give her to answer and turn in to the station. "Do we have anything on the killer?"

The captain heaved a pained sigh. "Not a damned thing. Your general knowledge proved to be accurate, especially on the motivation front. Our cruisers at the site probably scared any culprits off."

That I believed. "So, I go home and spend tomorrow reading into the case and doing research. Anything else?"

"Relax for today, as we won't have a complete set of intel for you until this evening. It'll be brought over after dinner. And Smithson?"

"Sir?"

"Take a shower before you infest the entirety of Cauldron City with that scourge."

I'd never thought about leaving glitter all throughout the city before. Could a single unicorn actually infest the entirety of Cauldron City with glitter? On my days off, I would have to find out. With the right diet, I could crank my glitter and gemstone production to something insane. As I was a kind and considerate unicorn, I'd even practice using my magic to purify the payload.

My first targets would be the dragons, with a focus on any black and opal dragons foolish enough to reveal the location of their homes to me.

"Understood, sir."

"Try not to get too many ideas watching that show, Smithson. Come on, Grant. Leave the kids to their television. This lot probably hasn't had a scrap of parental affection in at least ten minutes, and they're prone to whining."

"You can stay, Alicia. According to your father, you rejected all parental affection from the moment you were born, so it might do you some good to learn how to accept it," the Black Dragon of New York stated on his way out of the living room. "Have fun, kids."

"He is such an asshole," the dragoness muttered, but only after the front door closed and the dragons were headed down the walkway.

"Truer words have never been spoken," her cousin agreed.

FRIDAY APRIL 6, 2057
WILLOW GROVE, PRECINCT 158
CAULDRON CITY, NEBRASKA.

THE EPISODE LEFT me questioning everything about dragons, especially their physique. At one point, Alicia had left the room, her cheeks red. My mother, upon spotting the dragoness's discomfort, had come in to admire the scenery. I thought about leaving, but as Hardy and Paul endured, so did I.

My self-esteem would never be the same—or I would end up spending more time than I liked working out to match the mud-covered men who'd gone out of their way to flex and challenge each other with their muscles.

The promised brawl, which had degraded to two shirtless men fighting over who could better compliment Estaria, had been broken up by Estaria's husband-to-be, who had lifted both dragons up by the back of their pants, at the same time, and had tossed one each way to restore them to sanity.

I could no longer question the dragoness's decision to

wail about the unfairness of it all. I understood—and I had questions. "How did he even do that?" Not only had he tossed them, he'd done so while wearing a suit. Somehow, he'd showed off his might without inflicting a single wrinkle upon himself, although he'd gotten a little muddy.

I would have torn my suit trying that stunt.

"I can answer that one," Alicia said from the hallway, peeking into the living room. "Single blacks are moody, and he would head to the gym to work out his general unhappiness over being single. He's one of the ones who needs to be pampering a clutch. So far, they're an equal mix of opal and black, so everyone is happy."

"Dare I ask how many? It hasn't been *that* long," I pointed out.

"Their first clutch had six, and their second had three." Alicia shrugged, came back in, captured the remote, and turned the television off. "The last thing any of us needs to see is more posturing. The end credits were designed to cater to the women watching the show. It's a slaughter."

My mother pouted. "That seems like a poor reason to turn it off."

"I don't need a sibling, Mom. You have enough trouble dealing with me on a good day. Two of me would inevitably break you."

"Well, at least you didn't say I was too old to have any more children. That's something."

I looked her in the eyes and replied, "I'm as smart and wise as you say I am handsome, and only an idiot would call his young, beautiful mother anything other than young and beautiful. As it seems you are not feeling young and beautiful today, would you like me to take you to the spa tomorrow? I can get away with dropping you off in the morning and picking you up once you have been pampered, as it seems I am being left unattended with paperwork."

"Actually, I'd like that."

"Dad? I'm borrowing your car to take Mom to the spa tomorrow," I hollered in the general direction of his office, where he hid from the dragons and likely laughed at us.

"Have one of your cop friends drive you to your place tonight," he called back. "We're ordering in tonight. Return your mother in a better condition than when you took her out. If there are any changes of plan, I'll call."

With that out of the way, I freed myself from the couch, shed off as much glitter as possible, and headed for the front door, where I snagged the keys from the rack. Returning to the living room, I tossed the keys to Paul. "You get to drive me home."

He caught them and nodded. "I see you're wisely earning your way back into your mother's good graces. You about ready to hit the road? I know those old, grouchy dragons want to fatten you up tonight."

Fortunately for me, I didn't have to work hard to keep the extra pounds off. "Let me grab my presents. There were books in that box."

My co-workers laughed and went to work getting ready to leave. Alicia eyed me, and when I went into the dining room, she followed. "You're a book worm?"

"I am no mere worm. I am a connoisseur of fictional adventures into new and wild places. I also collect and read non-fiction, but I have a habit of trying to buy out entire bookstores when I go. I might not be a dragon, Miss Alicia, but I will whine, cry, and complain with the ferocity of one should anyone take my books from me." I claimed the new box, which my father had filled with my presents after removing most of the glitter. "Don't feel you actually have to hover, by the way. I'll quite enjoy my time at my apartment with my books and dinner, although if you know any tricks to make two guilt-ridden dragons go away faster, I'd be happy to hear them."

"My grandfather is upset you were hurt on his watch."

Damned dragons. "Make him take you out to see Cauldron City tonight while I enjoy some peace and quiet with dinner and a book. Challenge the captain and your grandfather to see who can give you a better tour. Have them take you on a second trip later, then you'll get to see everything the city has to offer."

She barked a laugh at my suggestion. "They might flatten the city if I do that."

"Make sure your phone is charged and record the whole thing. You'll make a fortune."

"You know what? I think I'll do just that."

SIX

"Dragonesses hate being protected."

FRIDAY APRIL 6, 2057
UPPER NORTH LAKE, PRECINCT 153
CAULDRON CITY, NEBRASKA.

GRANT GRIMSTONE, the Black Dragon of New York, brought six of Alicia's sisters to my apartment along with dinner, and they were dressed up as Brazilian showgirls. I questioned the outfits, my understanding of physics, and how one pair of parents could produce seven women who redefined what it meant to be dark beauties. I wished my peace of mind well on its journey, expecting to be dumped into some hell involving six women I had no real interest in dating.

Alicia dove into the fray, hissed at her sisters, and started a war on the sidewalk in front of the staircase leading up to my apartment. Hardy sighed and stayed to referee.

Paul stared at the women, and I left him to his admiration.

Hardy's grandfather followed me up, and once we were out of their striking range, he said, "That backfired rather spectacularly, I must admit. I told them I was bringing you Brazilian. I hadn't meant for them to sign up to be dinner—or have you for dinner."

"Are they aware sex doesn't actually cure headaches?" Previous girlfriends and I had tried, and as the one who tended to suffer from headaches, I'd been game to repeat the experiment despite relentless failure, although I'd never expected a changed result. "I'm not sure my doctor would be happy with me if I tried to indulge right now."

"You know what? I tried to impress that upon them, but they keep telling me to mind my own damned business. I suppose some things they'll have to learn on their own." Shaking his head, he followed me into my apartment. While tempted to shut the door and leave the dragonesses to their dispute, I left the door opened if they decided to come inside. "I wasn't going to let you be on their menu, as I was warned rather explicitly where a unicorn horn would be shoved if I set you back."

I needed to thank Dr. Erik and the rest of his herd in a few days.

The dragon angled for my table and set down two over-filled plastic bags of takeout containers. "I am sorry I got carried away with the promotion flight."

"Apology accepted. There wasn't anything to forgive, anyway. You would have had to pull my unwilling ass off his back before I'd passed out anyway. I was *not* losing to him."

"It was your victory after thirty-three seconds. After the second minute, I think he forgot you are one of his cops and wanted you off. That he took you up too high is his loss; he couldn't ditch you through his basic maneuvers." The Black

Dragon of New York sat, leaned back so he balanced on the hind legs of my chair, and eyed me with interest. "So, what do you think of my granddaughters?"

"I wouldn't survive if I went down there and tried to split them up, that's for sure. Are they the children of one of your sons or daughters?" I'd figured out early on the Grimstone clan absorbed men and women alike.

The strongest clan claimed the right of naming, always.

"They're the product of my beautiful daughter. All my daughters are beautiful, of course. They just happen to be from one of my most beautiful daughters, who loves children more than life itself, so she has brought forth many beautiful daughters of her own into the world. My sons and grandsons are outnumbered. One out of five of the brats are boys. It's better for the world that way. The girls tend to want to guard their nests, their hoards, and their men, which restrains their general inclination to take over the world. The men have different ambitions. Hardy is unusual in his tendency to want to serve the public. This game show could be good for him. He needs more confidence, especially with women. Of course, I intend on cheating. The goal is for the many women of the world to see him on television, not to hook him up with a black or an opal. Perhaps a lovely red might suit his spirit or one of the metallics. Hell, he might not even need or want a dragon. He's the protector type, and dragonesses *hate* being protected."

That I could believe. As it wouldn't do to let my dinner get cold, I investigated his offerings, discovering he'd gotten a little of everything both restaurants offered. Three whole chickens from the Portuguese place would be my holy grail of leftovers for the week. A single serving of fries demanded my immediate attention, and I crunched on them while exploring the Brazilian food.

I grabbed a plate, a steak knife, and a fork, and targeted the promised steak first. "I appreciate the leftovers. Thanks."

He chuckled. "I figured I'd make sure you're well fed tomorrow while you work from here. I've got your case research in the car, and I'll bring it up before I leave. I'll take the girls off to work some of that energy off terrorizing Cauldron City. I trust Alicia wasn't overbearing?"

"We survived any overbearing tendencies," I informed him between bites of my steak. "Try to convince the captain he's like a prized bronco. I lasted a hell of a lot longer than eight seconds, so he doesn't have to apologize. How many can say they've ridden an opal who didn't want to be ridden for that long?"

"It hasn't been done before you. I'll work to contain his guilt. So, your new car."

I raised a brow. "You were serious about that?"

"Absolutely. You earned that putting that mean old opal back in his place. Pick the make, model, and color, and I'll have the paperwork brought up in your name and bring it over for you to sign. If you don't want a sporty vehicle, pick something you're comfortable with."

"I'll think about what I'd like," I promised. It wasn't a lie. I would think about it, but I had no intention of accepting a vehicle for surviving a seven minute ride on a grouchy dragon. "Being able to take home a cruiser I don't have to coerce into working and has paint left on it will be a nice perk, though."

"Most detectives here have their own cruiser, and when they partner up, they toss the keys over to another pair as needed. I asked about that, as I thought it was strange the detectives all had their own cruisers. It turns out he allows the detectives to split up or join other pairs, so each one having their own cruiser helps. It's a strange system. In New York, a pair has a cruiser, and unless they get a special dispensation, they don't get to take the cruiser home with them. The cops I know share custody of their cruiser." The Black Dragon of New York lowered the chair back to the floor, plopped his elbows onto my table, and rested his chin on his clasped hands. "Models aren't your type, I couldn't help but notice. You spotted my beautiful granddaughters, and for a brief moment, your eyes betrayed your terror over the possibility they might invade."

As I wasn't going to let some old dragon beat me, I met his gaze, chewed until I could swallow, and said, "I have dated a model. The relationship ended over me spending hours in the kitchen making her cupcakes she could actually eat. I am not prepared for such trauma again. The cupcakes were good, too. Do you have any idea how hard it is to make gluten free cupcakes without using regular sugar? I had to perform sorcery with multiple flour types and honey."

"Why would anyone want to?"

"Well, to be fair, she couldn't have gluten. It made her sick, and I'd never feed my girlfriend something that'd make her sick. She would allow honey and fruit as sweeteners but no regular sugar. And that's not unreasonable. She didn't stop *me* from having it. But the cupcakes were the last straw. Now I run when a model looks at me," I admitted.

"I recommend against running from my granddaughters —or even my single daughters, although they are fewer in number than my single granddaughters. Running activates their predatory instincts. And once they lock onto a man, they don't surrender without a fight. I mean, we're dragons. We're the ultimate species."

I crossed my eyes at his commentary and went for another piece of my steak to buy myself time to wonder how his excessive ego had fit into my apartment. "I will endeavor to hold my ground should an entire pack of dragoness models confront me."

"I'm concerned for any dragoness who falls into your clutches, honestly. Alicia wasn't even enough to deter you, and she sends most men running for their lives after ten minutes. She has a pretty active chase instinct, so she follows, ends up disappointed he's yet another man lacking the necessary fortitude to handle a dragoness, and wallows for a few days before the cycle begins again. And since she isn't a model like most of her sisters, she gets a lot of familial flack."

"What sort of fool gives a dragoness flack over anything?"

The dragon's chuckles rumbled in his chest. "Other dragons, of course. Black dragons, as the other colors would never dare to insult one of *my* little girls."

"Mr. Grimstone, your little girls murdered an entire flock of peacocks to show their asses off to my entire apartment complex. And however lovely their asses are, you're going to end up having waging war with the entire city if you set the bar that low. After nine, the drunks come out in earnest, and around here, most of them ask for sex in as insulting a fashion as possible."

"Well, in good news for them, I don't have to do anything to defend their honor. In bad news, they'll defend their honor. Tonight will be entertaining to say the least."

I considered my headache, which had decreased to

tolerable levels thanks to my species, Dr. Erik's work, and the hospital's medications. If I left the black dragons to their own devices, would Cauldron City even exist when they finished? On second thought, I decided I wouldn't care.

If Captain Farthan hadn't wanted them romping around the city, he would have asked them to leave. "Call me if you find any unicorns hanging anywhere with corpses as dead weight, you need advice from a cop, or you want help finding a half-decent hotel. Otherwise, avoid the bars with the purple lights."

"Why?"

"Let's just say those ones get particularly rowdy, and the only time someone goes into them is if they're rather free-spirited and don't care what species or gender they're going home with. If you do decide to go to one of the bars with the purple lights, be aware you will be expected to leave with someone for a good time. Couples can go in to enjoy strip teases and other activities without being hassled."

"Let me see if I understand this. The bars with the purple lights are either for couples or if someone wants to be a couple, and *everyone* is expected to leave with someone?"

"Yes, sir."

"And they're guaranteed to find a date for a fling?"

"Yes, sir."

"Where do I find one of those bars?"

I lowered my head and sighed at my folly. What sort of fool was I to think a black dragon would view the bars and clubs as anything other than an invitation to have a good time? "Precinct 107 has most of them, but you can also find a few in Precincts 125, 134, and 159."

"Not in Precinct 169?"

"It was written specifically into their bylaws that no

lighted clubs and bars could operate there. The jokes are bad enough without help," I informed him in my most serious tone.

"In good news, my wife is here, as she escorted our granddaughters here. As such, I think we shall explore all Cauldron City has to offer."

"You can call me if you get arrested, but I'm not paying your bail."

Saturday April 7, 2057
Upper North Lake, Precinct 153
Cauldron City, Nebraska.

THE BLACK DRAGON of New York kept me company until I couldn't eat another bite, and once satisfied he'd subdued me through some of the best food Cauldron City had to offer, he put away my leftovers, sent me to bed, and promised he'd drag his granddaughters off to cause trouble elsewhere. Had I been thinking, I would have warned the captain so that the city might survive through the night.

A little after three in the morning, my cell rang, and the display informed me a G. Grimstone wished to speak with me. I considered hanging up, but as I'd given my word he could call if he got arrested, I tapped the green button, put the damned thing in the general vicinity of my ear, and mumbled, "What are the charges and how many counts?"

The dragon chuckled. "Two counts of misdemeanor mischief for me, and honestly, I lost count of the number of charges the girls picked up. My wife probably has the most, and I'm wise enough not to question her judgement when she decides she's having fun."

What had I been thinking, offering to let the old bastard call me if he got arrested? "Can you put a responsible adult on the phone? Preferably one of the cops."

A moment later, a woman said, "Sorry to bother you, Mr. Smithson, but we're hesitant to release them into the public in their current state without supervision."

"Which precinct?" I asked.

"169, sir."

Of course. I shouldn't have even bothered asking. The dragons would have opted to cause trouble in Precinct 169 given a single chance. "I'll bring my badge, a van, and transfer the menaces to Precinct 153," I promised. "Just prepare the transfer documentation. I can put in a reliable claim that they started their idiocy here."

"Sir?"

"He didn't tell you he called a cop?" I asked, forcing myself to sit up. I attempted to stifle a yawn, but it slipped out. "Sorry. I'm an officer in Precinct 153, and the dragons were visiting my apartment before going out for a night in the city. You can blame Captain Farthan for the disruptions. He's the reason they're all here."

"I see. How soon can you get them? They're singing in general holding. We've had to ask them to please stop trying to strip several times already."

"Are they still wearing feathers?"

"Most of them. One is dressed in business attire, and she looks like she wants someone to put her out of her misery. We had to detox her."

Damn it. "How bad is her intoxication?"

"We think a spiked drink at a bar, but we did a general

purge, and she seems to be recovering."

What the hell? When did they just settle with making someone throw up during a suspected drugging? "Is that a dragon thing?"

"Apparently. The one who called you thinks they need to learn from their mistakes."

"What's your name, ma'am?" I asked.

"Cindy," she replied. "You're going to come get them?"

"And I'll come armed with a dragon or two to help," I promised. I'd also come armed with a unicorn, as the last thing I needed was any one of Grimstone's granddaughters suffering from some damned street drug. "Keep them in general holding but take the one dressed in business attire and stash her in either a questioning room or someone's office until I arrive. Get her drinking a lot of water and check for dehydration. The dragons dehydrate easily."

We'd learned that the hard way with Hardy.

"Thanks for the tip. I'll start plying the rest of them with water if you think it'll help."

"It should. Ask the owner of the phone you're using. One of the women is his wife, the rest are his granddaughters. Give them a deck of cards or something to keep them amused until I can get there. The last thing any of us needs is an entire pack of dragons becoming bored while waiting for an escort out of general holding." I gave Cindy my phone number, told her I would be on my way as quickly as possible, got the station location, and dug out the captain's number, braced for some shrieking, and gave him a call.

"Smithson?" my captain answered, his tone as sleepy as mine had been a few minutes before.

"Grimstone and his pack of granddaughters are in general holding in Precinct 169 along with his wife, and I foolishly offered to escort them to our precinct before there was an incident. I can confirm they started their trouble on our turf."

"I should have known," he groaned, and a moment later, he yelped. I winced at the thump of him hitting the floor. "Damn it."

I gave him a minute to gather his wits and recover from a graceless abandonment of his bed. "Alicia may have been drugged, and they did a rudimentary detox, so I'm going to give the hospital a call and get a black unicorn and a ride to their station. The last thing we need is Grimstone sobering up and realizing someone drugged or poisoned his granddaughter."

"Good call. I'll meet you there, and I'll call the commissioner to get formal approval for the transfer. Why did Grant call you?"

"I foolishly offered to accept a call if he got arrested although I refused to pay his bail."

That got my captain laughing. "I'll meet you there."

Once off the phone with him, I called my father.

"What's wrong?"

"Remember the black dragons that followed me to your house?"

"With unfortunate and alarming clarity. The one is the undisputed ruler of New York, Jace."

"He got drunk along with his granddaughters and wife, they're in Precinct 169 in general holding, and one of the granddaughters might have been drugged. I need a unicorn willing to pick me up and deal with a bunch of drunk dragons before Grimstone realizes she's not just drunk off her ass."

"We'll be over in five, and I'll send Erik to the precinct."

My father hung up, leaving me to scramble to get changed into a clean uniform.

I was pulling on my shoes when someone knocked on the door. I opened it while waging war with my shoe to discover my father, mother, and Dr. Erik waited for me on the landing. I waved to them, hopping on one foot while fighting my clothes, winning the battle a moment later. "Thanks for coming."

"Erik's faster than we are, so you'll ride him. We'll show up to help with the detox on the easier cases," my father informed me. "How is your head?"

"Not bad, but I'm going to miss the painkillers come eight when I'm supposed to get my last one."

"You'll be fine," Dr. Erik promised, heading down the stairs and transforming. He'd long since classified as a regal stallion, although given another decade he'd head for the draft category. At eighteen hands, most used a rock or other aid to get on his back.

I vaulted into the saddle, got my shoes in the stirrups, and saluted my parents. "We'll see you at the station."

After giving them directions, I tapped Dr. Erik with my heels, the sign I was ready for whatever hell ride he decided to put me through. With a woman in need of a proper detox from an unknown drug, he went for a mix of his fastest gallop and chained blinks, dodging lights, traffic, and anything else in his way to cut across Cauldron City in record time. Two minutes after departure, we'd travelled at least fifteen miles, I needed to work to stay in the saddle, and we arrived at the precinct, where a startled cop gaped at me. I swung off Dr. Erik's back, gathered the reins, and led him up the steps, keeping an eye on his hooves to make sure he didn't slip and break a leg.

Broken legs sucked, and I'd learned to be cautious after my first one, not that it had prevented me from breaking my spindly pony legs several times over the years.

"You Detective Smithson?" the cop asked.

I showed him my badge. "My new badge is with the captain, but yes, that's me. This is Dr. Erik, and he'll have a look at the woman who needed detoxed first. Where is she?"

"The women's room. She started throwing up again."

Wasting no time, I followed the cop with Erik in tow, where a woman stood near the open door of the bathroom. "Go on in. It's just her and Cindy in there," she said.

I nodded, thanked her, and helped Erik squeeze through the tight door, moving the trash can so he'd fit. We followed the sound of retching to the appropriate stall and greeted Cindy. I took over her job of holding Alicia's hair, cramming as close to the stall wall as I could so Dr. Erik could shove his head in and start his work.

As I'd seen an unfortunate number of ulcer patients over the years, I recognized bloodied vomit contaminated with the classic coffee grinds of an older condition. "Ulcer or upper GI bleeding," I commented, wrinkling my nose. "Cindy? Contact the nearest hospital, warn them they have an active internal bleed incoming, and get a few black unicorns on the floor if you can. We'll be coming in hot with a black, but without knowing if it's just an ulcer, a drugged cocktail combined with an ulcer, or some sort of toxin, I'd rather be safe than sorry."

"Roger," Cindy replied, and she hurried out of the bathroom.

Dr. Erik bared his teeth and lightly nipped the dragoness on her shoulder. Alicia coughed and hacked, and I transferred her hair to one hand and grabbed toilet paper with the other, wiping her mouth and nose clean. "I'll ride you double with her to the nearest ER, and I'll get the cops to give the incoming whites directions to the hospital."

He released her shoulder, backed away, and bobbed his head. A moment later, he transformed into human form, dressed in his hospital scrubs, and said, "There's definitely evidence of an ulcer, but there's also some form of drug cocktail making it worse. Good call on the ER. She'd just had some water. Your advice?"

"Yeah."

"Good advice. She purged more of whatever the hell drug it is; I was able to detect the evidence of it in her throat. But the ulcer is preexisting."

Alicia panted, and judging from her glazed expression, she had no idea anyone was with her. Rather than try to coax her into doing anything, I picked her up, carried her out of the bathroom, and waited for Dr. Erik to transform in the hallway. He went down to his knees, and I mounted, careful to get Alicia settled astride in the saddle in front of me. "There are going to be two white unicorns blazing in shortly. Send them to the hospital. The unicorn confirmed she has been drugged, which has agitated an ulcer. Get a criminal report rolling and talk to the dragons about where they were at. I don't know if there's sufficient evidence in the toilet, but I didn't flush, and Dr. Erik said she'd just purged some of whatever it is."

"We'll collect a sample," Cindy promised, and she made another call and headed into the bathroom to get the ball rolling on her next task.

I nudged the black unicorn, who blinked right out of the station and moved like he meant it, another worry piled onto many.

SEVEN

I had no problems with being the sacrificial unicorn.

SATURDAY APRIL 7, 2057
LOWER RESTAURANT ROW, PRECINCT 169
CAULDRON CITY, NEBRASKA.

WHILE AT A HIGH risk of my species being exposed, the instant we got to the hospital and the ER team took Alicia, I dismounted, shifted, and followed Dr. Erik into the building. We skipped triage and headed directly into the operation room, where a team of nurses and a surgeon waited for our arrival.

Dr. Erik shifted, grabbed a pair of gloves, and snapped them on. "She has multiple open holes in her stomach, probably exasperated by whatever drug she'd been given at a bar. She's a black dragon, so we can get rough with her, but we're going to have to make sure she comes off this table unscarred. The colt here can take care of that work, and he's a good sort to help control bleeding, but he's not hospital trained. I've got two other whites and a pair of blacks on their way in, so we'll rotate them in and out as we need. I did rudimentary stabilization at the station, but she'll need a transfusion. She's vomited out at least a pint and a half from what I could tell, and I don't know if that was it."

While I had a long way to go using any of my abilities to handle internal injuries, external injuries I could handle.

Judging from his commentary, he meant to handle the situation expediently, operating to access her stomach directly, fixing the holes with his magic, and leaving me to tend to the incision. Sure enough, the staff went to work preparing Alicia for the operation. One of the nurses drew a blood sample, identified her type, and went to get bags while everyone else hooked her up to the various machines needed to keep her breathing.

She wouldn't appreciate the intubation process later, but it would keep her alive. I questioned what Dr. Erik had meant by rough, as they did all the things I expected of doctors and nurses in an emergency surgery situation. I regretted my decision to serve as the controller of external injuries, as the last thing I wanted to see was anyone's internal organs, especially not the organs of someone I knew by name.

Twenty minutes into the work, my parents showed up, and my mother had opted to arrive as a human while my father crammed his bulk into the room, stepping with care around the equipment. The two black unicorns, who I recognized from the hospital in Precinct 153, grabbed gloves, masked up, and joined the fray.

My father got to stick his nose into Alicia's abdomen several times during the operation at Dr. Erik's instruction, working on the delicate stomach lining I couldn't handle yet. Even with his experience, the black unicorn coached my father, offering suggestions to improve his general technique and checking to make sure the repairs would hold while her stomach finished healing naturally. Once he finished, I got a round, as it was my job to close the damaged blood vessels and repair all tissue between her stomach and her skin. Healing skin injuries tired me the most, but I'd developed a knack for it from an early age to the point other unicorns asked me for help whenever there was any worry of scars.

It took me forty minutes, but not only did I prevent any scar tissue from developing, I restored her skin pigmentation to its natural color.

That left the abrasions from the intubation, and to my dismay, Dr. Erik insisted I begin learning how to heal internal injuries while my father backed me.

The black would pay for testing me after I'd done the equivalent of run a magical marathon, but I did as told, pressing my nose to Alicia's throat. My father transformed, and he explained the process from the perspective of a white unicorn, as black unicorns approached abrasions in a different fashion than we did.

He described it as a sharp sting and a lingering burn, which I could detect when in contact with a patient. Sure enough, I sensed what he described, and I flicked an ear forward.

"Very gently cool those sections down until she feels pleasantly warm," my father instructed, easing around the table until he stood at my side, patting my shoulder. "You want to soothe it until everything in her throat is the same temperature."

As I'd done similar plenty of times with rug burns and similar injuries, I went to work, flattening my ears while I concentrated. After a few minutes, my father patted my shoulder again. "That'll do, colt. Go with your mother and have her wash that blood off your nose. You can explain how you got the blood on your uniform easily enough, but good luck explaining away the rest. Better yet, we'll concoct a reason we sent you off. Erik?"

"Send him to the reds for the morning to work on his headache and concussion symptoms, citing the blitz rides as an irritant. Play like you're hurt when all that's wrong is some fatigue, Jace."

I bobbed my head, sticking around until certain the staff wasn't doing anything other than prepping Alicia to go to a recovery room. I plodded after my mother, who draped her arm over my back. "And who is the best little colt on this planet?" she cooed.

"Love, he's not exposed yet, so don't you go exposing him to his co-workers."

I gave it several hours before someone at the hospital blabbed a cop had transformed into a unicorn at the ER. In good news, I'd done it at a hospital I hadn't been to before. Rather than make a fuss, I went with my mother to the nearest staff bathroom, one sized to accommodate unicorns. Whistling a merry tune, she hosed me down in the oversized shower stall and flung soap on me. I flattened my ears and snorted at her, but she ignored my posturing, purging my coat of blood. Once done, she grabbed the squeegee, which did a good job of scratching the various itches along my back and getting the water out of my coat.

Toweling me off to get rid of the excess moisture took

her an extra half an hour and fluffed my fur, and when she finally declared she was finished and led me out of the bathroom, we had an audience of unicorns in human form.

"Change of plans," Dr. Erik announced.

I lowered my head and blew air to express my general discontent over more changed plans.

"I'm going to send the colt up to monitor the dragoness while the rest of us go to detox the remaining members of her clan. None of them are feeling well now, although they're mostly sluggish and lacking in general willpower. Colt, you keep a close eye on her, and if you see something you don't like, hit one of the alarms. The floor is on alert for potential issues, but I think I got all the toxin out."

To Dr. Erik, thinking wasn't knowing, and not knowing drove him crazy. With a bunch of sick black dragons to worry about, I would keep my misgivings to myself and stay with Grimstone's granddaughter while she slept off her operation.

I wouldn't look forward to explaining anything to her later—or figuring out how to cover how I'd gone from arriving at the hospital to disappearing into thin air. Later, I would regret my choice, but I hadn't had much of a choice. I hadn't been able to help much, but I'd been able to help. That alone justified the risk of being exposed.

One of the nurses came up and offered a bowl with water and ice, and I took the time to drink, resting my nose on her shoulder in thanks when finished. "Come with me, colt. We were asked to just call you that. We're all unicorns in the ER here, but you whites are more skilled at certain things like closing incisions without scarring and treating intubation abrasions. We're generally better at the internals, but most of us don't pack much in the way of applicable magic, not like the blacks or you whites do."

I bobbed my head, as magic was individualistic, and healing was often a mix of desperation, skill, and will. The nurse led me into a single occupant room where Alicia slept on a bed. Someone had thrown down a mattress large enough to accommodate a unicorn, and I eased down on it, resting my head at the woman's side to stand watch while everyone else handled the more immediate problem of helping the sickened black dragons.

Saturday April 7, 2057
Lower Restaurant Row, Precinct 169
Cauldron City, Nebraska.

AT SOME POINT in the wee hours of the morning, my grandparents on my father's side swept into the room and interrupted my nap, and they brought a pair of chairs with them, assuming a guard position by the door. My grandparents on my mother's side plodded into the room as unicorns, eyeing me with their ears twisted back. As I'd made myself nice and cozy, I refused to move, instead flicking an ear in a refusal to budge.

Both of my grandmothers laughed, with my mother's mother whinnying her amusement.

"We're a little disappointed we didn't get to witness your first internal work in a hospital, but your father says you did a picture perfect job. He filled us in, and as he's still working, he wanted us to let you know the rest of the dragons will be fine. The toxin damaged their stomachs, too, but we were able to repair the tissue without needing to operate on anyone. We tubed two of them to be safe rather than sorry, but everyone's recovering. The older ones will be a bit slower at recovering, as they insisted on being monitored for a few hours so we have a better understanding of what is going on and why."

I lifted my head and regarded my grandmother with interest, pricking my ears forward.

"They weren't the only patients to hit the hospital tonight, and after seeing what it did to the dragons, let's just say every unicorn with any medical magic or experience has been working in the hospitals city wide."

Damn. My precinct would be dragged into the investigation as the dragons had started their evening romp at my apartment. In the only fragment of good news, I wouldn't be doing any investigating into their specific situation as I counted as a potential witness.

I wouldn't escape partial involvement with the investigation, as every cop in the city knew of the Grimstone clan, but most of the work would be moved to other people—I hoped.

My grandfather grinned at me, left his guard position, and crouched beside me, scratching my chin. "In other news, your ship is sunk, colt. Your captain came to the hospital and wanted to know where you'd gone. He managed to engage one of the fillies in a stare down, and she tattled on you. He found you catching a snooze in here, stood guard while you napped, and stayed until one of the nurses replaced him. One of the other nurses came to fetch us, as it is obvious you are wiped out and need to rest. That also means your parents' ship is also sunk. After leaving the room, he had a good laugh over your clever masking of the truth, as you played him pretty damned well. You'll be scolded, but he won't mean it. He will insist on providing work appropriate tack, as he's never seen a unicorn working as a cop before. We're usually doctors, nurses, or paramedics for some reason."

As I'd been given the go ahead to rest, I put my head back on the hospital bed beside the sleeping dragoness, although I kept my eyes open and my ears pricked forward.

"She'll be fine, but I was told to tell you they'll keep her sedated for another few hours. She'll probably wake up before you do, as nothing amuses us more than observing patients when they realize they have a unicorn napping next to them. It keeps the magic alive."

I understood. Patient morale mattered, and while unicorns could do a lot of good healing work, sometimes just being present made the most difference.

I had no problems with being the sacrificial unicorn required to nap and keep her company. Keeping her company as a human would have sent an entirely different message.

At the very least, when my unwillingness to reveal my species was brought up for discussion, I could state when it mattered the most, I'd been willing to toss the ruse for the sake of another.

Next time, I hoped helping involved less blood.

Saturday April 7, 2057
Lower Restaurant Row, Precinct 169
Cauldron City, Nebraska.

UNDER NO CIRCUMSTANCES would I admit to anyone how much I enjoyed having someone scratch behind my ears. Waking up to a good ear scratching topped the ways to conclude a nap. The attention stopped, and a warm hand rubbed my nose. I snorted and opened my eyes to discover Alicia giggling at me.

"I was told unicorns worked a lot of hospitals here, but I didn't think they let them sleep in the rooms, Grandpappy."

I lifted my head to discover the Black Dragon of New York leaning in the doorway, dressed in a suit with his arms crossed over his chest. "That specific unicorn helped with your surgery. I have decided you can take him home. You can marry him at your leisure. He's why you won't have any scars."

"Grandpappy," Alicia complained. "I don't care about any scars. They're badges of pride." She resumed rubbing my nose. "Won't the unicorn's family miss him?"

"I'm sure they will complain, especially that mother of his." The undisputed ruler of New York pushed off the door frame, stepped into the room, and sat on the mattress beside me, giving my back a companionable pat. "Word on the wire is you got rescued by a rather handsome cop after you busted three ulcers open."

Alicia gulped, and she averted her gaze. "I'm allowed to have a drink a week, and I only had one. I was getting treatment."

"I know, my little princess. I talked to your mother, who

informed me you'd been having stomach problems and was taking care with your diet. Three ulcers, though?"

"Bad luck and stress."

"Well, I called your work, and you're off for at least three weeks to recover. I talked to them about the show idea Jace pitched, and we confirmed we'd do the show as long as your health allows. That made them more willing to give you the time off."

While I'd guessed the dragon adored every last one of his children and grandchildren, understanding he'd thrown himself under a bus for her sake, without hesitation, confirmed my suspicions. He'd throw me under a bus for his family, too—and I wouldn't be able to blame him.

In his shoes, I'd do the same.

"What about Jace? He needs to agree."

The bastard snorted and patted my back again. "It turns out he was confident of his ability to wrangle unicorns for good reason, as all he had to do was go ask one of his parents. You'll referee the show, won't you, Jace?"

Busted. I heaved a sigh but nodded.

Alicia's attention turned to me, and her eyes widened. "You're Jace?"

I bobbed my head, and as I didn't want to leave her with the impression I was unhappy with her for her situation, I pricked my ears forward. Most people understood ears pricked forward meant equine interest or general contentment, although we could send other messages with our ears in that position as well.

"You helped with my surgery?"

I flattened my ears and displayed my teeth to her grandfather, hoping he received the message I would bite him if he pushed his luck. In reality, I'd snap at him but wouldn't land a hit.

"I see he's annoyed you spilled his secrets."

"Don't worry about it. He'll forgive me eventually. Anyway, while he was recovering from using his magic, shapeshifting, and bolting across Cauldron City with another unicorn, his captain kept watch. His secret is no longer secret. I'm safe from his posturing. He won't bite me because he knows I was a patient right along with you. But it made figuring out where we'd gotten hit easy; you only had one drink at one bar. You otherwise stuck to corner stores or not having anything. The coppers have already hit the bar."

I flicked an ear forward at the news the police had done a hit on the bar. The other stayed back to indicate I disliked someone had gone on a mass drugging spree.

"I'm sure your captain will go fill you in. You may as well do whatever it is unicorns need to do to get changed and dressed. Your parents are still here, and they could probably use a pair of hands."

I interpreted that to mean the old dragon wanted some quiet time with his granddaughter and escorted myself to the door, heading off to figure out where the hell I'd sent my uniform with my blitz transformation in the ER.

Saturday April 7, 2057
Upper North Lake, Precinct 153
Cauldron City, Nebraska.

TO MY ETERNAL DISGUST, I was forced to run home to get a change of clothes, as nobody in the hospital had located my bloodied uniform. Upon arrival, I needed help from my landlord, Carlen, to get in, where I discovered the missing clothes, neatly folded, right inside. My landlord, an owl-griffon shapeshifter, hooted a laugh, especially as my keys and cell were on top of the pile. "You weren't kidding about the blood, but congratulations on having teleported your clothes home. Folded, too. Is the vic okay?"

"She's fine, but it was closer than I prefer," I replied, stepping inside my apartment so I could go to my bedroom, change back into human form, and find something to wear. "Thanks for letting me in."

"You're welcome. Call me if you need anything."

"How about a ride back to the hospital?"

"I'll go get shifted, get the wife to saddle me, and be back in a few minutes. Do me a favor and call that grouchy boss of yours so he can see a proper flight demonstration."

I whinnied, went off to get shifted and changed into a t-shirt and a pair of jeans, and made myself presentable. Upon gathering my uniform, I determined it would need a lot of magic to be cleaned to my satisfaction. I dumped my belongings on the table, separated out the things I couldn't replace with ease, and decontaminated my cell before giving Captain Farthan a call.

"I see you found your phone. What's wrong?"

"Nothing's wrong, but I'm going to need a new uniform. I'm not sure magic is enough to clean this to anyone's satisfaction, especially mine."

I braced, waiting to see if my captain deemed the request to be reasonable.

He had issues when it came to touching the general budget for any reason.

"I'll put in an order. Get sized at a tailor so everything fits properly. After hearing the circumstances, bag the contaminated clothes as evidence. If you wore your vest and general gear, toss it in the bag. You're due to get new stuff anyway. Maybe there's some residue we can send over to the lab."

"I cleaned my phone and keys," I warned him.

"I'll pretend your phone, keys, and wallet were not exposed. Just so you are aware, Grant's looking for you, as are your parents."

"You can meet me outside of the hospital in about ten to fifteen minutes. I needed to go home to get clothes, so I trotted back to my place. In good news, I found my uniform."

"At home?"

"Neatly folded, too."

"Gun?"

"I'm going to be annoyed if it isn't where I left it, which is in my safe; I'd left it at home when I went to deal with a dragon's arrest."

"Well, the dragons are getting off with no charges, as it's clear they were victims of being drugged. Good work with Grant's granddaughter, by the way. He would not have handled any scarring well at all."

"I had guessed that by his commentary in the hospital room." I shook my head at the insanity of it all, wiped my wallet clean, and stuffed it into my pocket. "I'm getting ready to head out, so do be outside the general entrance if you want to see my current mode of transportation."

"You're going to do something to annoy me, aren't you?"

"I'm going to do something to annoy the black dragon, but if I happen to annoy you, that might be a bonus at this stage in my day."

My captain chuckled. "You're lucky I like you. I'm going to do you a favor, and I'm not going to tell anyone what your species is yet. However, I'm going to insist you do a test for me."

"A test?" I asked, stepping outside of my apartment and locking my door. "What sort of test?"

"The kind where stubborn unicorns who don't want their identification revealed can still provide witness information in a better fashion than bringing in a handwritten, unsigned statement. However nice the *fucking diamond* she sent in as an apology for not being helpful is, we do need a better way to question unicorns."

I rolled my eyes at my mother's antics. "A diamond, sir?"

"The unicorn requested that her hard work and pains of her labor be better dressed."

"I don't see how my choice to wear jeans and a t-shirt at this moment in time has to do with this diamond, sir."

"I am perfectly aware the unicorn in question is your mother, Detective Smithson."

My landlord meandered over from the leasing office, ringing in at fifteen feet long with a thirty foot wingspan. His head, that of a snowy owl, swiveled to keep an eye on everything as he came my way. His hind half, that of a snow leopard, served as an important reminder he would happily play with his food before eating it.

"My ride has arrived, and we should be there within ten

minutes. While you were discussing the situation with my mother, did the reasons why we're secretive come up?"

"They did, they're sensible, and we will permit a private, truth-witnessed interview should there be a trial. Next time, try not to be quite so blatant when giving witnesses instructions on how to best skirt the law."

"And here I thought I was being clever."

"You were disgustingly clever, and I am going to be spending many hours finding the best way to handle the situation, as I am barred from promoting you again for a set period."

"I am receiving mixed signals, sir."

"Get your ass over here," the dragon roared at me before hanging up.

I laughed, pocketed my phone, and hurried down the steps to get into the saddle. Once astride and confident I'd only suffer from a great deal of wind and the rare smack of feathers to the face during showy maneuvers, I said, "However much I'd love to give the old dragons a heart attack, we can't pop me off the saddle and play catch today. The one was a patient this morning, and the other is an overbearing opal who probably needs his blood pressure checked by now."

"Spiral down to a graceful halt?" my landlord suggested.

"Sure, you can even do a loop at the end of the spiral before setting down with the elegance of a butterfly. You'll probably have a frantic clan of dragons watching."

"You'll be all right with that even with the concussion?"

I considered my head and shrugged. "I probably got some tender loving care from some unicorns while I took a nap in the one patient's room. Maybe the captain is upset because one of the unicorns came in to check on me while I was sleeping off helping in the ER?"

"Yes, your father had called in to ask me to check in on you throughout the day. I wasn't expecting you to be bright eyed and swishing your tail, eager to get into your apartment because you'd lost your keys, but I'll take it." The griffon stretched his wings and gave a full body shake. "A spiral from a thousand feet down to the ground, a loop, and butterfly kisses for a landing. Posture to look good for the ladies."

I snorted. "I've done all the looking good for the ladies as I'm doing for this week. The ladies got a bloody cop with a side show of bloody unicorn."

"Blood isn't a good look on you, Jace."

"Is it a good look on anyone?"

The griffon swiveled his white head to regard me with glowing eyes. "You know, I'm simply not sure."

"How *do* you manage to talk so cleanly with that beak, anyway?"

"Magic, Jace. How else? The same way your pony mouth manages not to mangle English when you do decide to get chatty."

Right. Magic. Magic served as the primary source of mayhem in Cauldron City, although the eclectic collection of species tended to aid in our various issues. "It's been a long day. And night."

"I bet. Your father told me you got to ride Erik in a blitz to the hospital with a poisoned ulcer patient."

"The Black Dragon of New York's granddaughter at that."

"When's the wedding?"

"Get your ass in the air, Carlen. I would have done that for anyone."

"While I know that, you know that, and your parents know that but are hopeful, do the dragons know that?"

His question worried me. "Just get us to the hospital without adding another concussion to my tally, please."

"Don't be such a wuss. You know you'll get attention if I do give you a concussion."

I rolled my eyes. "Why don't you show those dragons who is better at flying *without* injuring their rider, instead?"

"We could also try for that. All I'm going to promise is to try, though."

One day, I would learn to not ask for the impossible.

EIGHT

The entirety of the black dragon clan stared at me.

Saturday April 7, 2057
Lower Restaurant Row, Precinct 169
Cauldron City, Nebraska.

CARLEN DID MORE of a dive than a spiral, though he did add a twirl or two, with his wings tucked close, to make it clear to those below he outclassed the larger dragons in aerobatics. As planned, he snapped out of the twirl, fanned his wings, and performed the equivalent of an in-flight backflip before fluttering to the ground as though he weighed nothing. As I hadn't lost my head, been dislodged, or suffered any inconveniences from the stunts, I hopped off his back, gave his chest a rub and a scratch, and asked if he wanted me to strip him of his saddle.

He shook his head, gave a shake, and launched back into the air, winging for the direction of home.

My mother planted her hands on her hips. "Again?"

I smiled, went up the steps, and kissed her cheeks. "I've ridden bumpier roller coasters."

"You're a terrible, naughty child!"

I grinned and glanced at my father, who shrugged and said, "Don't look at me, Jace. I can't resist trying that shit. You know what happens when I try it?"

"You usually end up in a lake. Nobody who knows us with wings is going to fly you over anything other than water. All you do is fall off."

"Exactly. You're on your own for that nonsense. I'll ride sensible creatures, thank you. Ones without wings."

I shot my captain a salute while he glared at me. "It would have been at least an hour if I went by ground, and griffons are faster than dragons although closer to a quarter of the size."

"You have zero fear of death."

"I have other things to worry about, including what my mother is going to do to me for pushing my luck already."

The entirety of the black dragon clan stared at me, including Alicia, who waited in a wheelchair.

"The Grimstone clan has been discharged, and as you were first responder on the scene with Miss Grimstone, we get to head to Precinct 169 to answer some questions," my captain informed me. "The dragons have been asked to remain human until their checkup two days from now unless there is an emergency. Several cruisers are coming with us. You will escort Miss Grimstone and your parents, as you have medical training."

"Understood, sir."

Before I could go take a position near the woman, her grandfather stepped up, looking me over head to toe. "What happened to your uniform?"

"It's evidence now," I replied, which reminded me I needed to give the captain my bloodied clothes. "Oh, sir? Carlton should be home within ten minutes if you want to send someone to my place to bag everything. It's on my table."

The captain retrieved his phone, placed a call, and ordered someone over to my place to retrieve my uniform.

With that out of the way, I asked, "Why aren't jeans and a t-shirt acceptable?"

According to the Black Dragon of New York's expression, I was beyond hopeless.

"Don't mind him, Grant. He's supposed to be taking a break, so casual is acceptable," my captain said, giving me a shove up the stairs. "He didn't bring his badge or his gun, and once we're done being questioned, he will be sent home via a motorized vehicle rather than a sentient charmed into serving as transportation."

As unicorns were the most charming of species inhabiting Cauldron City, I went to join Alicia rather than argue. "How are you feeling?"

"Much better. Thanks for your help. I don't really remember anything from the bathroom, but I think I saw you?"

"Yeah, you were in shock by the time I arrived. It's faster to get to the hospital by unicorn than ambulance, and Dr. Erik, one of the black unicorns, moved like he meant it. It's probably better you don't remember the ride."

"Why?"

"We blinked, and people not used to blinking find it to be rather disconcerting. You didn't have to go through triage upon arrival, either."

"I waited once for triage about my ulcers," she admitted.

"My regular doctor told me to go in. It was like eight hours. I didn't mind. The real trauma victims need to go first."

"Let's just say you left a great deal of blood in the bathroom rather than keeping it in your body where it belongs. I'm surprised they didn't want to keep you longer."

"The unicorns confirmed the bleeding has stopped, they gave me a transfusion an hour or two ago, and they want me in a more restful environment. I'll have unicorns checking up on me several times a day to make sure my vitals are good."

I glanced at her grandfather, wondering where she'd be staying. While Cauldron City had decent hotels, even the luxury ones tended to have noise, especially during the day. One day, someone would get around to better sound-proofing buildings where dragons roared and took flight often enough.

"We have a vacation home outside of the city limits that should be quiet," he explained. "I see you are a worrier."

My parents snickered.

As I wasn't in a uniform, I didn't care if my boss saw me, and my status as a unicorn had been somewhat revealed, I flipped my middle finger at those who had brought me into the world, well aware they might make me wish they'd take me out of it again by the time they finished with me.

"Bold choice, colt," my father stated, and his tone implied I was right to prepare for some form of living hell. "Anything else you'd like to add to that?"

As I had zero sense of self-preservation, I flipped my second middle finger his way.

My mother laughed. "He won that one, my darling. I'm

sure you can find some heinous way to get payback for being his typically feisty self."

"He can plan on it, and I will come for him when he least expects it." My father came up the steps, stared down his nose at me, and said, "I'm taller than you, bigger than you, and have more experience, punk. Go ahead and try me."

I smiled, and I pointed at my captain. "Come talk to me after you ride him for seven minutes."

My mother screamed her mirth, bent over, and beat the hell out of her leg. "He took you *down*."

Everyone stared at me with wide eyes.

"It was like watching a wolf go after a baby rabbit after not having eaten for a week," my captain stated.

The Black Dragon of New York's entire family opted to look elsewhere, and the old dragon said, "That was so harsh the definition of harsh is going to need an update in the dictionary."

Of his granddaughters, Alicia recovered first and asked, "Is that sort of comeback even legal?"

That was a good question. I smiled at my father and patted his shoulder. "You might be taller than me, bigger than me, and have more experience than me, but I'm the reason I'm an only child."

My captain snickered. "That was overkill, Smithson."

"I'm just giving him an opportunity to run away from home and be pampered by my mother for a while. He should be thanking me." I grinned at my father and went to my mother, kissing her cheek. "Call me when he's released from the intensive care unit for the damage to his fragile ego and pride."

My mother wiped the tears from her eyes, kissed my

cheek back, and went to claim my father, dragging him down the steps. "We'll call you eventually. Just text when you're ready to return the car. Keep it for a day or two. You can take me to the spa once we're back. He'll probably need a sporty rental to get over that defeat. Why don't we go on a road trip, my darling? We could go drive to the beach."

"The beach is halfway across the country," my father said.

"Exactly. We can go in a nice, sporty rental."

"It'd be cheaper to just buy something sporty at that point."

My mother ignored my father's complaining and dragged him in the general direction of the main street, where they'd either grab a cab or transform. It could go either way.

"I'm not even sorry for them," I admitted once they disappeared. "Captain? I'm going to need a lift home after questioning."

"I'll make sure you get back to your place promptly. Perhaps not as promptly as a flight, but you'll get there. It wouldn't do to have one of my cops crying because he couldn't get home to his leftovers."

I laughed because it was true.

Saturday April 7, 2057
Lower Restaurant Row, Precinct 169
Cauldron City, Nebraska.

MY QUESTIONING SESSION took fifteen minutes, and Precinct 169's detectives spent most of it asking questions about what it was like being a literal unicorn in the force. In the five minutes required to explain how I knew Alicia and my role in her going bar hopping with her grandfather, we'd concluded I knew nothing about the drugging. My quick arrival had made a big difference, as the word on the wire was that the dragoness might not have survived if she'd waited for an ambulance and had gotten sent through standard triage before being sent to surgery.

According to the security footage and Cindy's witness report, she'd vomited out at least three pints of poisoned blood, which had gone to the lab for analysis. The thought of her dying hadn't occurred to me until I'd been flat-out told my inclination to get her to the ER as quickly as possible had made the difference between life and death.

I'd thought about the job, what I needed to do, and went about doing it rather than thinking through the consequences of delay.

Once released back to the wilds, my captain ambushed me. "Hardy and his partner will be over in ten minutes to take you to our precinct. They have documents for you to review. Do impress upon the local unicorns that they need to present truth-verified statements if they are the victims of crimes, and that we will permit them to submit them in writing as long as someone who is *not* also a unicorn verifies the unicorn's honesty."

In good news for my species, such verifications were simple enough to acquire; we called in the eagle-griffons, who hated falsehoods to the point nobody could breathe the hint of a lie around them without them losing their shit. I supposed they'd been infected with some sort of worshipper-driven magic at the conception of their race, likely Greek in origin. The Greeks had a wide variety of species who could sniff out falsehoods with ease.

I failed to understand how the eagle-griffons differed from the other griffon species, but I tried not to think much about it.

My species shit glitter and gemstones when we did our business as unicorns, so I was in no position to talk about others.

"Understood, sir."

"And Smithson?"

"Sir?"

"As you have to be ribbed in some fashion upon promotion, and you bested me with your promotional flight, I'm afraid I'm going to have to toss you in general holding for your choice to ignore traffic signals while riding a unicorn. But due to the nature of the emergency, no charges will be pressed and it won't go onto your record. I'll even be considerate and give you a paid day off. If you're lucky, your fellow officers will let you out and feed you."

There was mean, and then there was flat-out evil, and my captain dipped his toes into evil territory. I sighed, but as there were worse fates, and he meant to keep my secret secret, I would cooperate. "Understood, sir."

"Also, you about scared the liver out of me being passed out in Miss Grimstone's room. Fortunately for my blood pressure, one of the staff explained you're basically a baby among the hospital workers, it was your first time working in the ER, and that you worked a lot of magic you don't typically work, so you passing out was expected."

"I had to do something new, too. Usually, I can see what I'm working on." Of course, I hadn't wanted to see any of

Alicia's internal organs, but I hadn't had much choice. The images would be seared into my memories for longer than I cared to think about. "Working on the abrasions from the intubation was new."

"So that black unicorn had mentioned. Still, for your age and experience level, you're one of the best for the type of work you do. Can you handle old scar tissue?"

I nodded. "It's a little harder, and it involves the business end of my horn, but I can do it."

"Let's say someone has a heavily disfigured face. Is that work you can do?"

With a grimace, I realized he likely meant the commissioner's daughter, who had been severely disfigured thanks to a drunk driver. "I'd need Dr. Erik's help, but if you can pay whatever his fee is and whatever he says my fee would be, it can be done." I dug out my phone, searched for a picture of the woman, and examined the scarring covering most of her face. "She'll need bone repair work, and that's not something I can do. You'll need to ask Dr. Erik which color could do that work. It's not just scarring. She's missing bone in her face."

"You can tell from looking at a picture?"

I showed him the image and pointed at her forehead, where the skull had been thinned from trauma. "I don't know how the rest of the bones are, but that spot is fairly obvious. Her nose is an issue, too. Did the commissioner ask about having the damage repaired?"

"The accident happened in Orlando, which is where she lives."

Unlike Cauldron City, Orlando tended to have a rather mundane permanent population, with the magical species coming to visit rather than stay. As such, the hospitals kept human staff—and most of the humans lacked the ability to do anything close to what hospitals staffed with unicorns could do. "Talk to Dr. Erik. I don't mind helping. I just can't do the underlying work. The scars? Those I can handle. You'll have to ask Dr. Erik a lot of questions, though. I don't know what the patient needs to know about the process. If we're working together and mixing colors, we can do a lot as unicorns, but we can't do *everything*. We're not even the best at healing magics. We're just more inclined to do the work for a decent paycheck."

"I have been informed you could make a lot more if you decided to work the hospital circuits."

I stared at my captain and raised a brow. "Sir, with all due respect, I can earn even more eating some quesadillas, plodding around as a unicorn for a while, and retrieving the gemstones afterwards. There's a damned good reason that criminal had left a unicorn just hanging around. If the perp had gotten away with it, that's a lot of money that registers as a natural diamond according to every scanner on the market."

"Yet you chose to be a cop?"

"Yep."

"Anyone ever tell you that you're crazy before?"

"It happens from time to time."

"You're something else, that's what you are. Stay out of trouble for a few days, you hear?"

"I'll try, sir."

"That doesn't sound like you're planning on staying out of trouble for a few days to me."

I shrugged and did my best to keep my expression neutral. "If the trouble would stop calling, I wouldn't have to engage, sir."

According to my captain's expression, I disgusted him. Fortunately for the both of us, Hardy and Dowdren arrived. Hardy's partner got out of the cruiser, opened the back door, and stared at me until I put my hands up, laughed, and escorted myself inside.

"What did I do this time, Hardy?"

"What haven't you done? You were spotted zipping off on an owl-griffon, which was called in by a concerned citizen, as word on the wire is you'd been in the ER again."

"It wasn't for *me*," I replied, closing the door and locking myself inside so Dowdren wouldn't have any additional excuses to rebuke me with his stare. "Seriously? Someone called that in?"

"Yep."

"Can someone get a concussion from rolling their eyes? I'm trying to figure out if this is possible—preferably before I do it. I've reached my limit on concussions for one week."

"I don't believe it's been studied."

I considered the possibilities, shrugged, and buckled in, grimacing at the rather uncomfortable seats meant to accommodate those in handcuffs. "I'll avoid doing any tests. Any news on the case?"

"Most of it is bad, and I expect it'll get worse once we get the toxicology reports in. The initial autopsies indicate the most common primary cause of death was internal bleeding, predominantly in the stomach."

My eyes widened. "You can't be serious."

"Unfortunately. It's not really feasible for all the victims to be ulcer patients, and there was no evidence of *Helicobacter pylori* infections in any of them. We have identified a few of the bodies, and we'll be swinging by the station to get you hooked up with everything we have, then we'll take you home. How are you feeling?"

"Like I had a very long night," I confessed.

"Well, good work on wrangling unicorns. My cousin is still alive because you're a damned good rider and got a surgeon who can handle that level of trauma to the station." After exchanging glances, the detectives switched seats and Hardy took the passenger side, buckling in and twisting around to face me through the grate separation the front from the back. "For the record, this case is cruel and unusual punishment to toss a green detective on, and I wish you the best of luck compiling your report."

"What did I do to deserve this?"

"You were stupid enough to show the captain you're smart enough for the job," he informed me in a solemn tone. "But at least you'll get a raise. That's something, right?"

"Right," I replied, allowing my doubt to come out in my voice.

"You'll survive. You might not like it, but you'll survive."

NINE

"Yep. Now I get to claim you're part of my hoard."

Saturday April 7, 2057
Lower North Lakes, Precinct 153
Cauldron City, Nebraska.

WHEN WE ARRIVED at our station, located in the southeast section of Precinct 153, our co-workers had opted to host a party. Upon my arrival, I got blasted with an obscene amount of confetti, which included large pieces of glitter. I'd have to thank Captain Farthan for banning small or powdery glitter in the station.

His foresight spared me from a fate worse than death, especially as someone had gotten hold of a absurd number of silly string cans. While most cops were proficient with their firearm, I'd learned in the academy that the wise were masters at silly string, canned cheese, and anything else that might be harmlessly sprayed at an adversary.

I counted my blessings someone hadn't gotten a hold of the cheese.

I made a show of removing the mess from my face. “Thanks, I think.”

Wynonna, our resident magicker with a knack for hearing the truth, gave her can of silly string another shake and applied it to my hair. “You’re welcome. 169’s dispatch gave me a ring when you headed to the ER covered in blood. We’re celebrating because it wasn’t *your* blood. We had not known that at the time.”

Ah. Everything became clear. We had a rule in the precinct, although it wasn’t written down anywhere. Those who worried their co-workers without a prompt call-in were ambushed in a celebratory greeting. As I had no grounds to stand on, hadn’t called, and would otherwise get ribbed for a few weeks over it, I dropped to my knees and held my hands up to our lead dispatcher. “Forgiveness, Lady Wynonna, Controller of the Radios.”

Hardy snickered, held out his hands, and caught an incoming can of silly string. “We’ll forgive you, but you should clean this mess up.”

Damn. The word on the wire must have gotten crossed —or someone had opted to misinterpret the situation. I collapsed onto the floor and flung my arm over my eyes. “Such cruelty.”

Wynonna snickered, crouched beside me, and patted my arm. “Poor baby. Was the captain hard on you for your promotional flight?”

“I won that round, so I’m pretty happy with it overall. I also won a concussion. Sacrifices had to be made. I *crushed* the record.”

“That’s why we held the cheese,” she admitted. “And you don’t have to clean it up. I already volunteered. Of course, I’m volunteering because I bothered to get the details once the dust settled. Good work. The last thing we need is the Grimstone clan taking over Cauldron City to secure vengeance over the loss of one of the younglings. Which one was the vic?"

"My cousin," Hardy grumbled.

I ignored Hardy and replied, "Alicia. I think she's a television producer. If she's not, she does something important for television." I lowered my arm from my eyes, sat up, and went to work shedding glitter and silly string off my chest and lap. "Since you're the one cleaning up, I won't do a dance all the way to my desk."

She chuckled and lifted off some of the silly string from my head. "Next time, you'll call, especially when you go into the ER covered in blood. Where did the blood come from?"

"Alicia burst three ulcers. She lost a lot of blood, and I had a unicorn and was willing to use him. The unicorn in question? Dr. Erik."

"And that solves the mystery. We had no idea where you'd gotten a unicorn, why you were riding him, and why you got dragged into the ER. That's where we got confused."

"I accompanied Alicia," I replied, grateful it was the truth. "The last thing we wanted was for her to wake up in a hospital without any of her family around. It turned out all of them needed a trip to the ER. The others were coherent, so treating them was easier. Alicia was in shock and relatively incoherent when I arrived. They didn't even have a chance to get an ambulance to the station when I arrived. I'd made an unfortunate offer to that old black bastard for him to call me if he needed bail. They all got drugged at a bar and were arrested. The charges were tossed from my understanding of the situation."

"This is a case of not charging vics for a situation they wouldn't have gotten into without some serious drugs being tossed at them. Dragons aren't exactly lightweights, and none of them had nearly enough to be that much trouble," Wynonna informed me, and after she stripped me of silly string and wiped off most of the glitter, she helped me to my feet. "Patricia is getting you some coffee, which she'll bring to your new office. She's too nice to do anything rude to it. Travis offered, but he would have given you coffee with extras, and we all would have faced the captain's wrath, especially if the extra was hot sauce and you painted your new office with it."

"Wait, office?" I stared at the dispatcher with wide eyes. "What office?"

"You know the detectives get offices, Jace," she scolded, pushing me in the direction of the elevator. "The first floor is for the baby cops who need a reminder of how hard the world is. The second floor is for the toddlers. You're no longer a toddler, so you get to go up to the third floor. The babies are lucky we aren't making them clean this mess up."

While I'd understood we had various floors at our station for the cops, it hadn't occurred to me I would be leaving my comfortable desk in the open space for an office a floor up. "But Hardy is still downstairs? I like my desk. Nobody told me I'd be losing my desk."

"All the detectives who have been loitering on the second floor are moving to the third floor where they belong," she declared.

Hardy ran in the direction of the elevators, backpedaled, grabbed me, and dragged me along with him. For a moment, the dragon and magicker used me as a rope in their game of tug-of-war. Dowdren grunted, hooked his arm around my chest, and hauled me along, taking the woman along for the ride.

"You all are moving. Today. That is the captain's orders."

"No!"

The battle continued until the elevator arrived and we made it to the second floor. Only when we reached my desk did Hardy release me, whipping out his cuffs. While Dowdren kept me from running off, Hardy cuffed my ankle to the desk leg. Considering the damned thing was bolted to the floor in case a rowdy civilian tried to flip it, I had no hope of getting out unless he unlocked me or I found a matching key.

I made a mental reminder to keep a set of cuff keys with my apartment keys so I could escape without requiring someone else's help.

I sat on my chair, shedding more of the large-sized glitter. I leaned over to stare at my foot. "You did that knowing I don't have my keys."

"Yep. Now I get to claim you're part of my hoard."

I would miss Hardy when his grandfather got a hold of him. "I belong to no dragon, Hardy. Go to your desk and cuff yourself to it. Dowdren?"

Hardy's partner whipped out two pairs of cuffs, glared at Hardy, and waited until the black dragon cooperated before cuffing him. To my amusement, he then went to his desk, which was next to Hardy's, and made certain he wouldn't be going anywhere, either.

"I think your partner likes you and doesn't want you to be murdered by your grandpappy. I volunteer to take on the case if it gets to that, though. He'll probably bludgeon you to death with your own hoard."

"He would, too," Hardy complained.

"I'd what?" asked the Black Dragon of New York.

Hardy wailed, twisted around, and said, "Who let you in here?"

I twisted around as well, discovering the entire Grimstone family had come over, including a rather tired and worn Alicia. Wynonna intercepted the woman and led her away, probably to the questionable comfort of the break room.

A rather displeased Captain Farthan stood beside Grimstone with his hands on his hips. "Do I need to send you three to preschool?"

Patricia, who worked dispatch off the non-emergency line, brought me a travel mug filled with coffee. "Thanks, by the way."

"For?"

"I bet you'd protest being moved up a floor. Everyone else assumed you would go upstairs as told."

Everyone else deserved to lose their money to Patricia. "I brought this desk up from the first floor, and so help me, this desk comes up with me to the third floor." I pointed at the bolts, which I had helped install. "They bought this desk because there wasn't one for me. I am not leaving my desk behind."

"Seriously, Smithson?" our captain asked, shaking his head and likely questioning why he'd hired me in the first place. "It's a standard desk. You can bond with the new one."

I engaged him in a staring contest, narrowing my eyes. After considering my options, I settled with shaking my head. If I said a word, he'd find some way to deny me the ownership of my desk. I'd been present for all but one scratch, and the culprit, a certain black dragon, had brought me coffee for a week as an apology for damaging my baby.

Hardy's grandfather laughed, came over, and perched on the edge of my desk. "If that mean old captain won't help you take it upstairs, I'll help. We'll get those pesky other detectives and their desks moved up, too. Do you have a big enough office for four detectives to share? You can't separate the children, Nathan. The whining would be most severe. I'm sure we could have all three desks upstairs in an hour." He leaned over to examine the bolts holding my desk in place. "Two, if we have to bolt the desks upstairs, too."

"They'll have to be bolted, but the holes are already in place." Our captain heaved a sigh. "Fine. All three of you are going upstairs, and you have to move the desks in your spots down here."

I turned my staring contest to the elder black dragon.

"I'll help get the old ones down, too. That's a small price to pay to get three of your detectives on the right floor. Schedule the moves for in a few days, and we'll make a pizza party out of it. All the cops who help get pizza."

A few whoops indicated we'd have all the help we needed to get the desks upstairs. "Thank you, sir."

The Black Dragon of New York ruffled my hair, shedding more glitter onto my desk. He plucked out some more silly string, depositing the pieces onto the floor. "I see you were viciously waylaid. Get those cuffs off. I'll give him the keys to my car, load up the trunk, and send him home so he can get to work."

"Why are you here, anyway? You were supposed to be questioned."

"Alicia's still not feeling well, and the good captain here suggested he could handle the questioning over the next few days. Your parents would have offered to let her spend the night with them, but your mother said your place might be quieter. Having been to both, your place *is* quiet. I'm imposing."

Imposing was one way to put it, but I wouldn't refuse the woman, especially if her grandfather wanted her somewhere quiet to rest. More importantly, when I wasn't home, I would ask my neighbors and landlord to keep an eye on her.

I'd pay my mother back for her recommendation later. While I'd been set up, Alicia would be safe while she healed. If she needed some fresh air, neighboring Precinct 154 consisted of a massive park, the precinct's headquarters, a few restaurants, a gift shop, and a parking lot. As such, few vehicles passed near the apartment, and my landlord had done a good job of soundproofing the place. When I wanted to escape the city for a while, I crossed the street, went into Precinct 154 through one of the pedestrian gates, and spent some time in one of the groves offering some privacy for those seeking an escape.

With so many parks in Cauldron, while Precinct 154 could handle tens of thousands of people a day without issue, most stayed close to their home.

"I'm fine with her imposing," I replied. "It doesn't get much quieter than at my place around here." Well, I could think of one place quieter, and few liked venturing into North Lake Memorial Park and Cemetery located in the south of the precinct. As the dragons had built a necropolis beneath the cemetery, urban myths had already cropped up, and nobody wanted to find out if any of them were true.

As a cadet, I'd been forced to do numerous trial patrols of the cemetery, accompanied by some of the songbirds, who could fly off if I needed assistance and report my performance to my superiors. Worse, I could never tell the difference between the sentient avians and the rest of the wildlife.

Well, unless one decided to get chatty with me. My final patrol, I'd gotten a chatterbox of a hummingbird who was determined to give me his entire life story, beginning from the day he'd hatched. By the time I'd escaped, I'd learned everything about Billy Bob's life, including the hummingbird ladies he liked to visit, his track record of being a champion breeder, and how he checked on every nest he held responsibility for.

I'd survived the experience, barely.

Unlike mundane hummingbirds, Billy Bob was a present and talkative parent. I still saw Billy Bob from time to time, although the bird had slowed down and faced a retirement to continue being a doting parent until his dying day.

"Excellent." The Black Dragon of New York tossed me a set of car keys. "Drive her home in that. If any of the papers don't fit in the trunk, I'm sure someone can bring them over."

I caught the keys and set them on my desk. "Thank you, sir."

"No, thank you. I'll take the rest of the girls to a hotel, and they can sleep off their adventure there. They'll be fighting with each other by morning, and Alicia is not up for that nonsense."

That I could readily believe. "What should I feed her?"

"Your mother spoke with the doctors and decided to delay her trip to the beach to prepare meals for her and keep an eye on things. She figured you'd be stressed enough without trying to add more to your plate. I'll send over some more Portuguese chicken for you along with some steak. I'm sure you'll be fine on the food front."

Heaving a patience-worn sigh, Captain Farthan came to my desk, crouched, and removed the handcuffs from my ankle and desk. "Go home, take the woman with you, and bring her back when she's able to be questioned better. We've gotten the little information we could out of her, but she's not able to tell us much of anything else right now. That might change, but we're not holding our breath."

"Shock can do a lot to damage memory," I replied, aware of the courses I'd taken on witness reliability, especially when injured. "Did someone have her play Tetris after she woke up?"

I would end up playing for a while on my phone as soon as I got a few spare minutes of peace and quiet. I didn't understand how the game could help prevent PTSD in some people, nor did I know if I was one of the people the game helped, but I would try the trick anyway.

"Correct. And yes, she did. Hardy, you and your partner go up to the third floor and sort out where you'll be working. As you will surely whine if Smithson isn't in close proximity, figure out where he'll be put. I don't care if you move the physical desks up there, but all three of you are moving up there within a week. Got it?"

Hardy saluted. "Yes, sir."

"Smithson, get out of here. Don't even bother loading up the car. Just go before one of these damned dragons starts crying about you leaving. Take the travel mug with you, and anyone who has a complaint about it can come to my office to discuss it later."

"I'll bring it back when I'm in uniform," I promised.

"Out of my station!" Captain Farthan barked at me.

I grabbed the keys, anything I needed, and snagged my favorite pen before bolting for the break room. As suspected, Wynonna had taken Alicia there and kept her company.

"Ready to roll, Alicia?" I asked. "I'm your ride out of this madhouse."

According to Wynonna's relieved expression, she would have preferred if I'd rescued the black dragoness a few minutes ago.

Alicia nodded, got up, and staggered in my direction. I narrowed my eyes, looking over her pale appearance. I snagged my cell out of my pocket, sent Dr. Erik a text, and asked for him to meet us at my apartment. A moment later, he acknowledged me, and he promised to bring over one of his fillies just in case. Once she got close, I offered her my arm, which she took.

"Come with us to the car, Wynonna?"

"You got it. I'll tell Patricia I'll be on my break a little longer than expected." She bolted off, and I let Alicia set the pace.

As I wouldn't belittle the woman's determination to keep up with everyone when she should have been resting, I asked, "You're having a rough day, aren't you?"

"That's one way to put it. They have me on some hefty painkillers. I like the lack of pain, but my head is full of cotton balls."

That would do it. I still worried about a missed internal bleed, but if there was something amiss, Dr. Erik and his filly would find and take care of it. If Alicia needed another trip to the hospital, there was a good one a few miles from my apartment. By unicorn, it wouldn't take long to get her there, especially if I cut through the neighborhood backyards and gardens—or I hitched a lift on Dr. Erik while he ran like he meant it.

If I felt she needed to get there faster than either of us unicorns could run, I'd barge in on my landlord and ask him to take her. I wouldn't like tying her to the saddle, but he could fly. We couldn't.

The elevator ride down to the first floor went without incident, and I breathed a relieved sigh.

"You'll be able to get some rest at my place." I showed her the keys. "Know which vehicle these belong to?"

"Ah. Those go to his Black Wing." Alicia lifted her head, considered the police station, and pointed in the direction of the front doors. "I think he parked by those doors, just down the way. There were a few cruisers lined up there along with an ambulance."

"That would be the dispatch waiting area. We keep a few cop pairs here for emergencies. It's an office day that might be interrupted if it's busy," I explained, walking her out of the building. I refused to tell her the ambulance was probably on standby if she needed it. Sure enough, the ambulance was parked behind the black sports car, which had probably cost her grandfather at least half a million dollars. I accompanied her to the passenger side, unlocked the vehicle with the fob, and held the door open for her. Before I had a chance to help, she buckled in.

"I'll just be a moment, all right?"

She nodded, reclined the seat, and sighed.

I went around the back of the vehicle, saluting the driver, one of my favorite wolf shifters who worked in our precinct, who slid out of his ambulance. Once certain Alicia wouldn't hear me, I said, "I've got her from here if you're here about the dragoness."

"We were asked to be accessible," Mac replied, eyeing the car. "Give me a ring if you have any problems, but in that beaut, you can get to the hospital faster that I can if you need."

"Ah, but you have the medical gear I don't. I have a black unicorn going to meet us at my place, where she'll be resting for a while. Got a spare blood pressure cuff?"

"When we heard about the patient, we brought an extra. You want it?"

"Yep. Yell at my captain about how I ran off with it and grab the spare from the station if you need it. Give me anything else you think I need to monitor her."

"We packed an extra kit just in case. I'll register you as checking it out."

That would work. Within three minutes and one signature later, I carried a small duffle to the car, got behind the wheel, and chuckled at Alicia's surly expression. "Mind holding this for me?"

She nodded and held out her hands, and I gave her the gear. "What is this?"

"It's a blood oxygen meter, a blood pressure cuff, and other stuff the ambulance guys had for me. It's your get out of hospital free card unless you need to go."

That got her smiling. "You did that for me?"

Ah, my need to be honest when I wasn't hiding things from everyone would get me killed one day. "One part yes. The other part? I don't want your grandfather to murder me for not taking care of you properly." Before I had a chance to get the car started, Captain Farthan strolled out of the station and waved at me. "What now?" Groaning, I started the engine, rolled down the window, and leaned out the vehicle. "Problem, sir?"

"I'm giving you a siren and lights." Before I could protest about the magnets possibly hurting the sports car, he slapped the bulb lights on the roof. He handed over the remote. "Dispatch is calling in that you're headed home in a hurry, so run your lights and sirens and practice getting through traffic like you mean it. Alicia, call your grandfather when you get to his place. We'll be timing him."

I hated my life, but I loved that I'd be able to put the Black Wing through its paces. "Understood, sir."

"If you don't make her gasp at least once, you're not doing it right," the captain said, thumped the roof, and got out of the way. "I'll give you a ten second buffer to get on the road."

"Give me a few extra seconds to check where everything is, sir. It's my first time in anything this nice."

"Ah. Right. I'll give you ten seconds after you leave your spot."

I saluted him, rolled up the window, and rubbed my hands together. "Ready to have some fun, Alicia?"

"It's just a car. It's not that fun."

I smiled, as there was only one thing I did better than ride cranky dragons and unicorns, and that was drive cars in ways the manufacturers likely wished I wouldn't. "Oh, it can be, Alicia. It can be."

TEN

That old, mean black dragon didn't need his car, did he?

Saturday April 7, 2057
Upper North Lake, Precinct 153
Cauldron City, Nebraska.

I WAITED for the green to turn on the sirens and lights and put the Black Dragon of New York's car through its paces. As burning rubber would lose me valuable momentum, I eased the vehicle from a standstill until the tires caught and pushed its acceleration to get a feel for the car.

It drove as though it had aspirations to catch an owl-griffon in a sprint, it handled with the same agility of a hummingbird determined to show off, and it made me question my initial plan to refuse any gifts from a dragon.

That old, mean black dragon didn't need his car, did he? I would take much better care of her.

While I could have taken a straight run from the station to my apartment, I decided I'd give Alicia a tour of Precinct 153, zipping through one of the nicer residential areas nearby before heading north through an area where elegant corporate offices faced off against some of the pricier apartment complexes. As I wanted to reach my place sometime today, I cut westbound to dodge North Lake Shopping Center, which created traffic snarls on a good day and turned the streets into a parking lot the rest of the time.

I got three gasps out of her, and they involved a light tapping of the brake before darting through red lights.

We had, as a general rule, done a good job of training the residents to make way when anyone ran their lights and sirens. I considered zooming by the police station closer to my home, but as I would miss the feud between the two opal dragon captains, I resisted the urge, instead taking a more direct route, passing the small park near my complex. "You can call him," I announced, glancing at the time.

In eight minutes, I'd gone roughly eleven miles, which amused me. When I drove in, I expected at least thirty to get across town, and that was if I stuck to the residential streets and took the quieter routes. Alicia dialed on her phone and put it to her ear while I searched for a place to park. Partially due to having barely beat rush hour, the main complex lot had a few spaces available, which spared me having to park the Black Wing on the street with my parents' car.

I killed the sirens and lights, turned the Black Wing off, and retrieved the contraption from the roof, checking to make sure the captain hadn't damaged the paint. Fortunately for my sanity, the car had emerged from its adventure unscathed.

"Hey, Grandpappy. We've arrived. He just parked." Alicia stared at me with wide eyes. "He's a better driver than you are."

Yep. I would die at the hands of a black dragon. The only question was which one? Would Alicia kill me for having given her a few gray hairs and making her gasp and squeak? Would her grandfather get tired of me besting him? Would Hardy snap and murder me for being the reason he would be forced to go up to the third floor? I chuckled, tucked the lights and siren assembly and its remote under my arm, circled the vehicle, and opened the door for her. I held out my free arm, which she accepted to get out.

"I'll call you back. We have to go up the steps, and I'd rather not lose control of my feet or drop my phone." She hung up, stashed her phone in her pocket, and grabbed the first aid bag. "Is there anything you can't do?"

"Fly without having to abuse some other sentient," I admitted. "I lack wings. I'm also nowhere near as fast as the black unicorns, although I give most whites a run for their money. If you like gemstones, I'll show you my hoard."

"You have a hoard?"

"I certainly do. I've only sold a few of my stones. I am happy to dig out my hoard, get you curled up on the couch unless you want to take a nap, and give you full access to the coffee table so you can play with my gemstones."

"But why keep most of them?"

I guided her towards my apartment, pausing long enough to lock her grandfather's car. "I like earning my keep, I enjoy my job, and I also enjoy knowing I don't *have* to do my job. I work because I want to. By not cashing out the stones, I feel like I need to go to work even on the days I would rather go back to bed."

"Like this morning?"

"That would imply I realistically got to stay in bed until morning," I replied, grinning at her. "Today has been quite the adventure, and after I get some work done, I plan on crashing out. My house rules are quite simple. The visiting lady decides where everyone sleeps."

"Is your bed large enough for two?"

"I have a queen, so it's a little cozy but plenty spacious for two."

"I dislike the idea of either of us being uncomfortable."

She might change her mind once she met my couch, which I'd spent an unholy amount of money on due to its ridiculous level of comfort. "I'm fine with that."

"I'm sorry my grandfather foisted me off on you."

"I'm not." I guided her to the stairwell and gestured for her to go up the steps first. "I can transform into a very heavy unicorn at my whim, so if you fall, I'd rather be behind you. The last thing you need is a tumble, and it's easy to fall when on heavy painkillers." I claimed the first aid bag, which she'd clutched. "There's no shame in using the rail, and I expect the doctor will be here soon."

A snort behind me informed me the doctor had arrived. "Shameful, Jace. I came up right behind you without you noticing," Dr. Erik said. I twisted around to discover his daughter had caught a ride on her father's back.

With a smile, I held my arms out for the woman to help her down, as she had two right feet and zero skill mounting or dismounting. "Thank you for coming, Gloria. Alicia, this is Gloria, Dr. Erik's daughter. She's training to be a trauma surgeon like her father, so this is good practice for her."

The instant Gloria's feet touched the ground, she pounced, wrapped an arm around Alicia, and insisted on helping the dragoness up the stairs. "We'll have you feeling better in no time, and you can enjoy the scenery while you rest and recover. Daddy wants Jace to stay put for a few days, and if he's taking care of you, he won't be trying to ride anyone who'll let him."

"That makes me sound like a pervert," I complained, following the pair of women up the stairs. "I haven't gotten her grandfather to put on a saddle yet, but I got Hardy's first flight with a live body, but we didn't use a saddle."

"That implies my cousin learned with a dead body," Alicia replied.

"We used sandbags tied to his back. They move enough to mimic bodies so he wouldn't kill somebody. I didn't ride Hardy until he stopped attacking the sandbags. He was a fairly slow learner, but once he got up with a rider, he did well."

"Grandpappy really trusted you with Hardy's first ride?"

"It was rather harrowing, but yes. I often get first crack at riding the local sentients. For some reason, they are less inclined to kill me."

"Too pretty to kill?" Gloria suggested.

"Too good at riding to be bucked off," I countered.

"That, too."

I pursued them up the stairs, tense until Alicia was safely on the landing. I unlocked the door and let them in, handing off the first aid bag to Dr. Erik when he shifted and came up, dressed in a fresh set of scrubs. "Were you the one who arranged for the ambulance?"

"I was. She wanted out of the hospital, we didn't have a good reason to keep her with the treatments we'd done, and the quiet will do her good. I'm still worried. The poisoning issue was severe."

"She's pale."

"She's healing, so it's to be expected. The painkillers are a factor, too." Dr. Erik went in and took over, sending Alicia to my bedroom, asking her to make herself comfortable so he could tend to her.

I read between the lines: Alicia would be taking a nap within twenty minutes, leaving me to do my work in the relative peace and quiet to follow. I peeked through the open doorway, and sure enough, within five minutes, he had her out like a light and tucked into my bed. "It's easier when the patients can't talk back?"

"Understatement of the year. Come on in. You may as well learn something while we handle this. She won't wake for at least a few hours. And if she does, you can feed her, which will probably knock her back out again. I'll cut to the chase since you got a close look at the damage. While she had three ulcers prior to her going to the ER, they were healing. She had been careful to take her medication, she was working at eating a better diet, and her medical records showed improvement of her condition. By the time she had arrived at the ER, her condition had degraded significantly —far worse than when she'd been diagnosed."

"Because of the toxin."

"That's right. I'm going to use magic to check in on the ulcers, make sure the tissue is still sound, and monitor her for an hour for any signs of internal bleeding. Should I find anything, I'll have you start learning how to treat it. You may be in a situation on the street when you need to use your magic—while you're a human."

Ack. I stared at him with wide eyes. "I can barely do the work while a unicorn, Dr. Erik."

"That is a mental block more than an actual handicap. You're a unicorn in either form. You're just wearing human clothing right now. You're old enough to learn the trick of it. Being a unicorn makes the work more potent and easier, but you might not be able to transform—or you might require fingers to hold pieces of your patient together while you mend the damaged tissue."

I turned to Gloria in hopes of rescue from her father's plan to add more complexity to my life.

She smiled, came over, and kissed my cheek. "Sorry, Jace. You stepped into the ER where he could watch you work, now you have to pay the piper. You'll be okay. From all accounts, you have a better knack for it than your parents. You won't ever be an ER surgeon or a nurse. We all know that. But we *can* help you become an excellent first responder, which means you can assist victims you come across while you do your job. You joined the force to make a difference. We're just going to change how much of a difference you can make."

Damn it. I couldn't argue when she presented it that way. "I have no idea when I'm going to find the time to learn this."

Dr. Erik chuckled, went into my kitchen, and grabbed one of my chairs and hauled it into my bedroom. He sat, leaned over Alicia, and pressed his fingers to her throat. "Gloria and I will come tutor you on your days off. Give us an hour a night, and we'll have you in tolerable shape to do the basics within a month or two. Once we're done with you, we'll run you through an official first responder course and get you a low-level certification. We can put you in the queue to volunteer in the ER to learn more of the ropes, too. It'll let you practice wound closure, and as it's volunteer work, the patient isn't charged for your work by the hospital. You *can* invoice once you have the right certification, but you don't need to."

"I'm not changing career fields," I reminded him.

"It was a good try, Dad." Gloria sat on the edge of my bed and regarded the sleeping dragoness with a frown. "Her blood pressure dropped since she was discharged."

"It has. That's not entirely unexpected, but I want to see if there's another bleed or if it's a matter of draconic biology. The dragons usually go to the hospital in Precinct 101. That's their roost. We're all about the unicorns in 153, and 169 just wishes they were as good as we are."

"Which is why they let you trot in like you own the place," she replied.

I rolled my eyes at the general insanity and ego of black unicorns out to prove they were the best at their art. They were, but I never understood why they felt the need to tell everyone about it. "They let him in because he'd already seen the patient, had done basic work on her in the station, and didn't want to change up the staffing when she had an active bleed."

Dr. Erik sighed and shook his head. "You got into Yale and did what?"

"Acquired a Master of Studies in Law. You know that."

"You could have been a lawyer, making a killing defending every unicorn against idiot malpractice suits, and you picked *that*?" Erik grunted, narrowed his eyes, and went to work on the dragoness. A time or two, he betrayed his annoyance with a light tap on the woman's throat.

I couldn't tell if her condition or my disregard for his desire for me to be an attorney had gotten to him. Rather than agitate him further, I crept for my kitchen to investigate the documentation waiting for me before the next batch of papers arrived.

"I'm not done with you yet, colt."

"Is she bleeding?"

"She's not actively bleeding, but there is membrane irritation, likely something we missed during the toxin purge. It'll be good practice for you. We'll see if you can handle it while a human, and if not, you can shift and give it a whirl that way."

Gloria got up, captured my hand in hers, and dragged me to the bed. "We really can do much of the same work while human, Jace. We just shift when we want perfection or we need extra magic at our disposal. Membrane irritation will be easy for you."

Dr. Erik got up, gestured to the chair, and hovered until I sat. "All right. What do I need to do?"

"We'll start with her throat. The work you did for the tube held, but after your treatment, the toxin did more tissue damage."

"Ah. Thus the painkillers?"

"Yes. We purged remnants of the toxin after you left in the morning, so I suspect that's the source of the issue. She could also be suffering from hypotension; pain and other conditions can raise blood pressure, and she's in a calmer, relaxed environment."

"I would hardly call the past day relaxing."

"Ah, but right now, she's safe and sound, she knows she's safe and sound, and she has had a lot of stress unexpectedly removed. She doesn't have to work, and while being poisoned was painful and stressful, she's healing. We'll monitor it, but as long as her blood pressure stabilizes or increases, she'll be fine. She's on the lower end of normal. Once she's awake, I'll have you use the blood pressure cuff to confirm it. I'll show you how to do it correctly with Gloria."

"You're going to abandon me to the dragons, aren't you?"

Dr. Erik chuckled and nodded. "I am. Now, rest your hand on her throat. Remember how it felt when you worked in the hospital?"

I nodded.

"It will be like that, but fainter. You'll be less sensitive than you're used to. You'll want to cool the heat down to be the same temperature as the surrounding tissue. Go ahead and give it a try. We'll be observing, and we can stop you from doing anything harmful."

I did as told, and sure enough, I could sense the heat he described. Having the awareness he'd prevent me from injuring her further, I did my best to mimic what I'd done at the hospital. While the temperature decreased beneath my hand, the process took longer than I remembered. By the time the heat faded, I panted as though I'd run a race.

Dr. Erik clasped my shoulder. "See? Harder to do and takes longer but still as effective. It is tiring, though. You're not done yet, colt. Now you get to check her stomach. I'll help you with the work this time, though. Some of this I'm better at, but I'll have you help lower the overall irritation."

As though sensing I'd struggle figuring out how to touch the woman appropriately, Erik took my hand and pressed my palm to the blanket covering her and applied pressure. "You can work through cloth. You don't need to touch her skin. Your prudish ways won't bar you from helping victims. Just be aware it's a horrible and painful process to remove cloth that has healed into flesh."

I winced at the thought of such a procedure being necessary. "Let's avoid that."

Gloria snickered. "Well, unless you make her eat your blanket, I think she'll be fine."

"As I rather like my blanket, I think I will pass on feeding it to her. I might share some of my chicken, though."

"Now that is a true sacrifice."

"Children," Erik scolded. "Do you feel the three hotter points in her abdomen, Jace?"

I concentrated, and sure enough, three spots burned under my hand compared to the rest, which was hotter than her throat. "It's a lot warmer, and yes, I can feel the three hotter spots."

"The toxin did most of its damage in her stomach. It's roughly the same as when she was discharged, which is good. But that irritation is being masked by her painkillers, and the painkiller we gave her doesn't spike blood pressure, which is part of why we picked it. If the dosage the hospital in Precinct 101 gave us is accurate for her height, weight, and species, she'll metabolize it within the next three hours. So, I'm going to handle the ulcers, which are the hotter spots you're detecting. The way I work differs from you, but I'm going to lower the temperature to your senses to what I want you to match. The stomach should register warmer than other parts of her body to you. That's due to the stomach acids. We don't want to neutralize the acids completely, as she would not be happy with us around the time of her next meal."

"But wouldn't she have been taking antacids to help her ulcers heal?"

"There is a difference between lowering acid levels and neutralizing the acids completely," he replied.

Right. "That makes sense. Okay, I'm ready."

"You'll probably want to close your eyes for this, as

you'll start sensing my activity, and it can be disconcerting, especially when what you see doesn't match what your hand feels."

I obeyed. "This isn't disconcerting, not at all, Dr. Erik."

Gloria giggled. "He's in good form today, Dad."

The longer I held my hand over Alicia's stomach, the stronger the general discomfort became. The three stronger points of heat bothered me the most, but I became aware of something cooling them down, icy on the edge of my awareness. I resisted the urge to flinch away from the chill. When the sensation receded, I took note of the difference in temperature of the three spots compared to the rest of the area my hand covered.

They were cooler, but not by much. I frowned and worked to spread the same temperature from the cooler spots to the rest, halting my work where the temperature dropped more than expected and outside of where Erik had worked. When I finished, I rolled my shoulders, lifted my hands, and grimaced at the ache in my back. "Does it feel like you ran a race every time you do that?"

"It's easier on us blacks than you whites, but you're a great deal gentler and your healing restores tissue better than mine. Your thoughts, Gloria?"

"He'd be a god in the ER, but only for one operation. Then he'd be useless for days. At that point, he might as well be three-legged and sent out to pasture until he fell over to be disposed of."

I cracked open an eye and glared at Dr. Erik's daughter. "Don't send me out to pasture or put me down for being lamed. Come on. That's just mean."

She grinned, came over, and gave me a hug. "To make up for my mean ways, I'll go warm you up something while you get to work. You do *not* want to take a nap right now. You'd regret it. You need to move around, eat and drink, and do whatever it is you cops do when working from home."

I hugged her back. "Sort and read papers, I think. And try to make sense of what I'm reading. I'm not confident in any of that right now."

"Reading is a good activity. Are you going to stick around, Dad?"

"For at least an hour. I want to monitor her vitals, but I think she'll be fine. After that work, she shouldn't need any painkillers, either. We can probably head off then without worrying about them. The colt can handle himself for the most part. He's starting to get leggy, and he's easing out of that sweet pony face, so he'll be a proper stallion soon enough."

As the last thing I needed was Dr. Erik telling every mare and older filly I might classify as a proper stallion sooner than later, I asked, "Did her condition worsen after she was in the ER?"

"Yes. We didn't get the toxin completely removed until later, so this is just the additional damage. The ulcers would have taken a little longer to heal, but it should have been fine to heal on its own. We did the work after you left, and it didn't take that long. I needed a breather almost as much as you did after that. Now, I want you to stay up until ten tonight. That should give you a good night's sleep without screwing up your sleep schedule."

I resisted the urge to roll my eyes at his demand. As he would come over and scold me if I went to bed even a minute before ten, I said, "I'll do my best."

Gloria headed for my kitchen. "I'll make you some

coffee. That should keep you up long enough to dodge Dad's wrath. I'll take care of your parents. I mean, I'm going to tell them you have some chick over at your place and you're sleeping with her, but I'm sure you can handle it."

"What did I do to you to deserve *that*?"

"Two words: Black Wing."

Of course. She wanted a ride in the car. "I will ask if Grimstone doesn't mind me taking you for a ride in it before he leaves, but there will be no lights or siren used. The only reason I got away with that today was because Captain Farthan probably realized we'd have a city-wide emergency if the Black Dragon of New York thought one of his little princesses wasn't doing well—and he knew I'd call in your dad."

"It's true," Dr. Erik agreed. "I actually got called by a cop and was told the colt would be running his lights and siren, and they notified the other stations a Black Wing was on the move. Think you can land me a ride in it, too?"

I laughed. "I can't promise anything, but I'll try. If we're really lucky, Grimstone will let us take it to the track and see what it can really do."

All three of us sighed at the thought of taking the car out for a spin where speed limits were not a factor.

"You pull that off, colt, and I'll let you ride me during one of those police parades," Dr. Erik offered.

"If I pull that off, you're going to let me ride you during a game show where I might have to referee a bunch of dragons fighting over everyone they see."

Dr. Erik snickered. Gloria shook her head, excused herself, and headed for my kitchen.

"I don't think she believes me."

"Trust me, it's for the better."

"Why?"

Dr. Erik pointed at Alicia. "Because ever since that damned episode aired, my daughter watches it once a week while sighing and wishing something *nearly* as interesting might happen to her."

Interesting. "How would she feel about becoming the prize in a fight between dragons?"

"She'd worship the ground you walked on, especially if either of the dragons are single."

"Well, how about the parent or grandparent of many single and beautiful male dragons? That's how these families operate, Erik."

The black unicorn frowned, considered me, and then stared at Alicia for a while. "What do you think the odds of that are?"

"That depends on if I tell her grandfather she helped with the treatments."

"And I see I'm the one who is about to be put out to pasture with only three legs. What are you going to ask for for *that* sort of favor?"

"What will you give me? Because honestly, I would have done it for free."

"A free ticket out of jail when you get your ass handed to you by a sentient you shouldn't have been riding," he offered.

"Sold. But think about it this way, Dr. Erik. I won't be able to hold *that* favor over your head for too long."

"Are you sure you're actually a unicorn?"

"My tendency to shit glitter and gemstones indicates I'm probably a unicorn."

"But are you sure?"

"I don't know. You're the doctor who was in the delivery room. You tell me."

Dr. Erik eyed me. "I'm going to steal some of your blood and have it DNA tested. You have to be part dragon."

I flung my hands up in the air. "Just because I collect certain shiny things does not mean I'm a dragon."

"But are you sure?"

I realized the unicorn screwed with me because he could, and spitting curses at him, I retreated to my kitchen table so I could begin work on the dead weight case determined to drive me to the edge of my sanity.

ELEVEN

"I'm guilty and request a lessened sentence."

SUNDAY APRIL 8, 2057
UPPER NORTH LAKE, PRECINCT 153
CAULDRON CITY, NEBRASKA.

SOMETIME AFTER MIDNIGHT but before two in the morning, I crashed out while reading over a ridiculous amount of information on the warehouse where we'd found the bodies, how people could access it, and why people accessed it. I'd meant to go to bed, but my couch had eaten me. The evidence of my wrongdoing somehow remained in my hand.

A rather insistent individual cleared his throat at me.

I thought about throwing the papers at my captain, but I thought better of it. I did, however, lift the stapled sheets and covered my face. "I'm guilty and request a lessened sentence."

"Well, you're certainly guilty of sleeping on the job. Do you know what time it is?"

"Time to get my ass to the shower, get cleaned up, and pretend I'm a law-abiding member of the force?"

"Correct on getting up, taking a shower, and getting cleaned up, but incorrect on pretending to be a law-abiding member of the force. It's your day off."

I got days off? I thought about it, realized I usually got Sunday and Monday off, and I'd almost made a mistake. "I wasn't working on my day off."

"The papers in your hand indicate you were, actually, working on your day off."

"I may have worked a little after midnight. The tyrant said I had to stay up until ten."

In my mind, a little over an hour counted as a little.

Somewhere nearby, Alicia laughed. "Sorry, Jace. I was going to let you sleep when I saw you'd passed out on the couch while working, but your phone kept ringing. I ignored it, but then a cop knocked on the door. The woman saw me and requested backup. I'm not sure why."

My father made an appearance, and he laughed at me. "That's because the last time Jace dated a woman, she was a model, and every cop around here is worried she'll try to shove him down some steps because of the cupcakes."

Damn it. "I really thought she'd love them. I worked for hours on those damned things. And since she got mad and left, I ate them all, and they were pretty damned good despite being weird as hell to make. Her culinary rules were awful. How many times is that story going to make the rounds?"

"We'll keep spreading it until the woman in question no longer hisses at you," Dad replied. "Are you really sure that's all that happened? She hates you."

"Well, I didn't save her one after she broke up with me.

And I don't see why I should have. She told me off. I wasn't wasting those cupcakes." I considered it, and then I shrugged. "I also didn't give her any diamonds."

"She doesn't know your species, Jace," my father reminded me.

"But what if she does?"

That earned me the stares of everyone in my apartment, which included Alicia's grandfather. He wielded a takeout box from the Portuguese place, which he brought to me. "Eat while it's hot. My granddaughter is on her third bird. I'd only brought four, so that one is yours. I called Hardy and asked him to fly over to see if he can get a few more. Food tastes better when eating doesn't hurt her stomach, apparently. I had not planned for a three-bird slaughter."

No shit. I dumped the papers onto the pile, cleaned off some room on the coffee table through shoving everything onto the floor, and opened the container to reveal still-steaming chicken covered with extra of oily sauce. "Thank you, sir." I hesitated, staring at my captain. "Why are you here?"

"The local cops were worried the model had showed up for some payback, and you weren't anywhere to be seen. They called me. I tried to convince them your ex wasn't going to try to kill you but failed at that, so I came over. I took a picture of you passed out on your couch, sent it over to the whiners, and then took a picture of Miss Grimstone attempting to be domestic."

"It did not go well," Alicia's grandfather whispered. "I'll replace your eggs and anything else she managed to destroy. I think your stove survived, but I contacted your father, as I have no idea who around here is your landlord and thought he might know."

"Which I did," my father added, also whispering. "Her grandfather ate the eggs, and we're concerned he might end up in the ER. He gave her the chicken, which she's been savoring."

"I will be sending her to cooking courses, as I fear the reason she got the ulcers involved her trying to eat food she made." The Black Dragon of New York glanced in the direction of my kitchen. "She used your hot pepper sauce, your blue cheese, and raisins."

"And you *ate* it?" I breathed, afraid of the woman's wrath if she heard us discussing the culinary horror that had been born in my kitchen.

"Please tell me you had blue cheese in there on purpose. Please."

"I did, but it was for salad, not scrambled eggs. Did she murder the bacon?"

"She tried to scramble the bacon into the eggs. She understood the bacon needed to be cooked, but she hasn't cooked bacon before. I have failed my family."

At a complete loss of how a dragoness had gotten so far through life without cooking bacon, I plucked out a chicken leg from the box and took a bite, chewing and staring at the old dragon with wide eyes.

"It gets worse," my father confessed. "She added frozen peas in the last minute or so of cooking."

I kept chewing, trying to comprehend why anyone might cook raisins, peas, hot sauce, and my poor blue cheese in eggs. When my first swallow didn't provide any insight, I took another bite. "Peas?" I whispered.

"Just don't ask what she did with your pesto."

Somehow, I swallowed without gagging. "My poor pesto. I'd just made that."

"It's excellent pesto, I must admit. I was able to enjoy bites of just the pesto between forkfuls of those eggs," the traumatized dragon whispered. "Would you share the recipe with me?"

"I'll teach your granddaughter how to make it, and I won't let her leave until she is not a food poisoning risk in the kitchen. Did you throw up?"

"If she catches me, she will cry." He swallowed several times and took a deep breath.

"Tell her you want to check on the car, which is parked in the complex lot." I gave him directions to the landlord's apartment. "Tell him you need to use his bathroom, and let me take him on a ride in your car, and he won't even care if he has to clean after you. But if you let that raw bacon digest, you're going to be sick." I turned to Captain Farthan. "Call Dr. Erik and ask him to send a foal who can handle food poisoning. How long ago did he eat that?"

"Only fifteen minutes or so."

"Maybe it's not too late." I hoped. "If you perish, can I have your car, Grimstone?"

"Unicorns are mean, Farthan," the old dragon complained, but he headed into the kitchen to do as I suggested.

"That was pretty mean," my captain agreed. "Well played but mean."

"If she wants to know why we're whispering, we're discussing the dead weight case and didn't want her to overhear the descriptions of putrefaction." I set my leg down, licked my fingers, and wiped the grease off on a tissue before palming through the papers left on my coffee table until I found one of the autopsy overviews. "Here, hold this and look convincing."

My captain obeyed, and he grimaced after reading the sheet. "Yeah, these reports are pretty gruesome. Definitely not a good breakfast discussion."

"Do you think he'll be all right?"

My father shrugged. "I watched while he ate, and he devoured everything on his plate while hissing at us as though he'd kill us if we stole even a bite. The only thing that saved us was the fact she'd used all your eggs feeding her grandfather. If he doesn't make it, I respect his dedication to his family."

I could understand the blue cheese. Everything else she'd added made me question everything I thought I knew about life. "Dad, maybe you should follow him. Act like you're dying to see the Black Wing."

"Right. What should I tell her?"

"That we're grossing you out about putrefaction and you want to see the car. Don't make me show you pictures of corpses, Dad."

He fled.

I turned my attention to my captain. "Am I allowed to work today or not, sir?"

"I'm allowing it, and I brought more paperwork, but I'm expecting you to take a four-day weekend to make up for working now. When I gave the commissioner a heads up about the poisoning and the autopsy report, he ordered me to prioritize it. We've already taken a look for anything obvious, and we don't have anything actionable beyond interviewing the friends and family of the deceased, of which we have none at this point in time."

"You get to train me with the bonus of the trained detectives having had a good look at the case?"

"Precisely."

"How much can Alicia see?"

"I'm sure you can find a way to keep her amused without her seeing sensitive material. Perhaps recommend a book? I can't help but notice I have entered the lair of a book dragon. Can you fit more books into this apartment?"

I pointed at the tops of the bookshelves, which held knick-knacks rather than books. "I can make some sacrifices for the cause if necessary." I also pointed at the ceiling. "I'm thinking about a suspended bookcase. I bet I could convince my landlord to let me hang some books from there."

"Are you sure you're actually a unicorn?"

"I'm actually a unicorn. I just like to read."

"It explains a lot, including why nobody sees you much outside of work. When you aren't reading, you're riding other sentients wherever the unicorns hide to make sure nobody else knows they're unicorns." My captain considered me through narrowed eyes. "Except the blacks. They're not shy."

As he said nothing but the truth, I shrugged. "I visit my parents, and I do some other things. But you're not wrong. I have some new books to read, too. If nobody hears from me on my days off, I'm either reading, at the bookstore getting new books to read, reading, or figuring out how to fit more books in here without having to move. As for the blacks, nobody tends to screw around with unicorns who are intimately familiar with how to take you apart and put you back together again—and if you annoy them, they may not be inclined to put you back together again."

"That is a fair point I hadn't considered before. Once your father and Grant are back, I'll take my leave and report the woman is supposed to be here so everyone else stops having a heart attack. Are you sure this individual is not going to be a problem in the future?"

"You mean Marci?" I snorted, shook my head, and wondered how our dispute over cupcakes had resulted in the woman hating me for life. "It's not like we see each other often. Although it wouldn't surprise me if she showed up after hearing about the latest visit to the ER. She *does* tend to verify I haven't died for some reason. And yes, I changed the locks."

"I'm concerned."

I pointed in the direction of my kitchen. "There is a black dragon in my apartment. I'm confident that she can take out a human model."

"What sort of human are we talking about here?"

"Human. She has some magicker skills, but not enough to classify as a magicker. When we were together, she was about as offensive as a cotton ball. She has some decent shielding abilities, though, but not enough to handle a dragon."

As we'd graduated from whispers, our talk lured Alicia into my living room, and to my amusement, she carried a plate of chicken with her. I guessed she had maybe two pieces with any meat left. I made space on the couch, moved my breakfast aside, and waved for her to join us.

"What's this about someone who can't handle a dragon?"

"My ex. The fuss is all because someone decided to do a wellness check, saw you, thought you were my ex, and ran to get backup. I suspect they think my ex is completely off her rocker because she dumped me over making her cupcakes that met every last one of her dietary restrictions."

Alicia sat, grabbed her last remaining drumstick, and gnawed on it, staring at me with wide eyes.

"It's worth mentioning my ex is a model, and she could learn more than a few things from you."

That earned me a raised brow, although the woman refused to give up her chicken. I couldn't blame her for that. I joined her, grabbing a piece of chicken with zero care of how much of it got all over my hands and face.

In my apartment, I did not abide by polite eating rules, and I didn't want to find out if she'd take me on to get my chicken.

I could only hope Hardy came to the rescue with more chicken.

"That's very nice of you to say, Jace."

My captain dug out his cell phone, narrowed his eyes, and tapped on the screen. "Marci Thallen?"

"Yeah. That's her."

His brows went up, and he turned his phone to show the screen to Alicia. Of all the pictures to find, he'd located one of her in a barely there swimsuit, showing off her assets in such a way nobody had any doubts regarding her general flexibility. I'd tried the posture once and could not figure out how someone with a chest as large as hers could stand with her ass in the air, contort so her chest was in full view of the camera, and appear as though she wasn't about to topple over.

I'd fallen over most times I'd tried it, and I'd sprained something in my back. My mouth had gotten me in trouble, too, as I asked her if she needed anything, including a back rub, foot rub, and a rub anywhere she wanted to make up for people asking her to do horribly painful things for the sake of fashion.

Had I been wiser and a little less young, I would have realized then she worshipped at the altar of beauty. I didn't, nor did I understand the sacrifices models made. In my view, I'd always respected her limits. I'd never taken her out for anything she couldn't eat. I made certain her schedule was kept to the second, and the few times I'd rolled in a few minutes late because of work, she'd forgiven me readily enough.

I'd even gone shopping with her on demand, hauling around her new clothes.

Alicia's eyes widened even more, and she stared at Marci's picture before swallowing, placing her semi-consumed drumstick down, and licking her fingers. She blinked, reminding me of my landlord when he got caught off guard. "You think I'm prettier than *her*?"

"I mean, she is pretty, don't get me wrong. And I got into shit for asking in a roundabout way if she needed a chiropractor after that. I survived upon her realizing I was volunteering to be the chiropractor."

"You have zero sense with women," my captain informed me. "I see the concerns are accurate, as you have a severe case of foot in mouth disease. I'll look into a treatment plan for you."

I scarfed my current piece of chicken, sucked the spice off the bones, and went for my next one, aware I couldn't say a word without compounding my troubles.

Then, because things could get worse, someone knocked at the door.

As my mother would shove her hooves up my ass if she found out I'd talked with food in my mouth, I swallowed and said, "With my luck, that's the ex. For the record, she's not a terrible person. She just hates me because I'm a terrible person who made her cupcakes? Or something."

Alicia got up, laughed, and replied, "You have no idea why she dumped you."

"You would be correct."

"I'll answer the door, so you keep eating. Grandpappy said you'd need a lot of calories to make up for the past few days."

"Appreciated."

"I'm not moving because I'm your bodyguard right now," Captain Farthan informed me. "I'll leave after the rest of the adult supervision arrives."

"I don't need a bodyguard."

"Hardy's here with a tail," Alicia announced, and she came back into my living room with two carry out containers, one of which she handed to me. "He brought an entire flock of chickens, and he will put the rest of our meal in the kitchen. He is trying to remove the tail."

"Why would he remove his tail?" As I had more chicken to eat, probably piping hot knowing Hardy and his enjoyment of zipping across Cauldron City whenever he had an excuse, I went to work getting my first batch into my stomach where it belonged.

"Well, he had several tails. Your father is back, and he's not happy."

"She actually showed up?" I whispered, resisting the urge to twist around, as the kitchen was behind me down a short hallway.

"Mr. Smithson," my ex crooned in her sweetest voice, and judging from my father's grunt, she'd gone in for the kill, jumping on him and wrapping her legs around him so he couldn't refuse her affection. I bowed my head, sighed, and debated where I might be able to hide.

Captain Farthan took a few steps to the side, and his brows crept up. "How is she even doing that?"

"Those legs are lethal, her muscles are probably made of steel, and she can hang off anyone or anything as long as she can hook her ankles together," I muttered between desperate bites of my chicken.

If she stuck around, I'd feel compelled to feed my ex, as she rarely indulged in anything and the Portuguese chicken was something she could have.

"She's taken your father hostage."

"She adores my parents," I confessed. "That's usually what gets her coming around. Her parents are not ideal people, and they never think she's doing enough. Mine? Well, you've met them."

"They couldn't be nicer people if they tried," Alicia whispered. "Right. So, she's mad because she can't have your parents, but you did things she couldn't stand, probably like encouraging her to eat and put on a few pounds, finding ways around the rules she made. You meant well, but she was probably terrified of not being thin enough for the runway. It's an issue on television, too. The actors and actresses are horrified if they think the camera will add ten extra pounds."

I sighed, stared at my second container of chicken, and surrendered to the inevitable. I put my share aside, grabbed it, and went into the kitchen. A pale Hardy crammed himself into the corner, his gaze fixed on my ex. I set the takeout container down, snagged my ex around her waist, and tugged. "You may as well eat some chicken and catch up. He won't escape you at the table."

The instant my ex twisted to face me, my father informed me, through silent mouthing of the words, that I was a traitor and would pay.

After a moment, she released him and dropped her feet to the floor. I dragged her to the nearest chair, made her sit, and gave her the box of chicken. "If you use utensils, it might escape. It's from the Portuguese place."

She gasped something out, which I assumed was some expression of gratitude, and attacked the whole bird as though she'd never eaten a thing in her life. As always, I worried about when she had last eaten.

I could only hope the containers Hardy held would keep the women from turning their hunger on us men. When I counted bags, I realized he'd probably bought out the entire restaurant.

I might end up with a second bird all to myself. I helped him set the bags on the counter. "Thanks for coming over."

"Are you going to be okay?" he whispered in my ear.

"I hope so. Guard my dad?"

"You got it. Make sure you eat. Grandfather demanded you eat at least three. I'll make sure the woman eats that whole bird. She looks like she needs it."

I nodded, and on my way by, I patted my ex's shoulder, hoping she interpreted it as a gesture of welcome. While I had zero desire to reenter a relationship with her, I'd never wished her harm—and I could count her ribs. My father sat next to her, and with no sign of having been tossed to the sharks, began filling her in on how I'd ended up visiting the ER because I'd gotten a promotion.

She lifted her hand, and I froze, wondering which gesture she'd give me. Then, to my amusement, she graced me with a thumbs up to show her approval. I responded with a salute before fleeing to the living room.

"Call Dr. Erik and ask him to look her over," I mouthed to my captain.

He nodded.

There was a lot we couldn't do as law enforcement, including wellness checks without justification. The successful models, like my ex, toed the line and often suffered from eating disorders. She hadn't showed active signs of one while dating me, but I'd been there monitoring and watching for trouble, making certain she always had access to low calorie but nutritious food she could eat without guilt.

In some ways, I'd worried that had been the ultimate cause of our breakup.

I sat next to Alicia, and she nudged me with her elbow. "You fed her, didn't you?"

"Yep."

"How often do you feed her when she drops by and you two are bickering?"

I thought about it, realized I had a bad habit of feeding my ex, and heaved a sigh. "Often."

"Eating disorder?" she whispered.

Captain Farthan waved his phone to indicate he was taking care of that concern.

"Not as far as I am aware."

"Good. Does she do television?"

"I honestly have no idea."

Alicia twisted around and attempted to get a view into the kitchen. With narrowed eyes, she picked up her chicken and bounced off to join the fray.

"I'm doomed," I predicted. "Captain, please give me a

good burial and console my parents when I reach my end at the hands of two women. There is no good that can come of this."

The captain sat beside me, shaking his head and making disapproving sounds. "So, when you aren't feeding her, she's yelling at you?"

"It's more looks of utter loathing, which I return."

Another knock at the door tested my patience, but my captain waved his hand, got up, and investigated. A moment later, he returned and said, "Dr. Erik is here with Alicia's grandfather. They're joining the battle in the kitchen."

"Is my apartment going to survive? Am I going to survive?"

"I hope so. I'd hate to have to promote another cop. Pretend everyone is part of the gossip posse at the station. You can work through that, so you should be able to work through this, too."

"If you keep an eye on that disaster, I'll try to get some work done. That way, at least I can have at least attempted to be a detective before I reach the end of my rope."

TWELVE

Magic couldn't cure everything.

Sunday, April 8, 2057
Upper North Lake, Precinct 153
Cauldron City, Nebraska.

THE AUTOPSY REPORTS, which had been finished in the early afternoon, told a troubling story of mutilation and organ theft. I'd expected some parts to have been carved off the victims, as ten men rarely averaged 134 pounds each. The coroners, which had been split across numerous morgues around the city, had taken the time to contact each other, evaluate the cuts on the bodies, and determine it was probable the same person had operated on the victims.

Five of the victims had already been identified from missing persons records. Their families had been notified, and several pairs of detectives, including Hardy and Dowdren, had begun questioning those who'd known the deceased.

To my dismay, the families were reported as not caring

their relative had been murdered, although they'd been willing to answer questions.

Of those identified, Julian Cane had suffered the most mutilation, with all organs in his chest and abdomen missing. Skin, muscle, and fat had been shoved back into the open cavity and secured in a cheesecloth bag. Grabbing a notebook and my favorite pen, I made a note to investigate the cheesecloth bag, where someone might get something like it in Cauldron City, and why someone would have used that type of bag to secure the scraps of muscle, skin, and fat inside the victim.

In life, Julian Cane had been the kind of person few would miss. Even his family, according to the initial interviews, showed no surprised someone had taken offense to his existence. His rap sheet included numerous counts of sexual misconduct and sexual assault, assault and battery, petty theft, grand theft auto, and harassment. Unfortunately, that meant he had a long list of people with motive to get rid of him.

Cane's four outstanding warrants would further complicate the investigation, as I would have to look up those cases and determine if his living victims might be inclined to carve him open, remove most of his organs, and hang him up to rot while profiting off my mother.

My mother's statement, which she'd assembled using a mix of fonts designed to mimic newspaper clippings, detailed how she'd gotten nabbed after giving my father a lift to a local clinic so he could get in some volunteer work. I questioned why he hadn't trotted over on his own, but I tried not to worry about it. Most likely, she'd wanted to go to a nearby store.

The note included a step by step guide on getting the

most money from the blue diamond she'd donated as compensation for not being more helpful. The file on my mother also informed me a pair of detectives would be handling the details of her kidnapping, leaving me to handle the dead weight case.

I put a reminder in my phone to talk to the detectives in Precinct 154 on Tuesday, as they were given the case due to my mother having been kidnapped in their precinct rather than ours. As the junior detective, I would be making the trip to see them on their schedule, although I doubted they'd give me a hard time. Captain Farthan had a reputation, as did Hardy. With news traveling around that Hardy's grandfather prowled the area, I expected the precincts would play nice with each other for a while.

Several hours into my research, which involved a great deal of reading and puzzling out how and why someone had carved up Julian Cane and the other victims, my favorite pen died. I gave it a funeral, threw it away, and braved the kitchen long enough to fetch a new one from my junk drawer.

A rather heated game of Uno kept everyone occupied, with my father, Dr. Erik, and the Black Dragon of New York standing around the table while everyone else had a seat, crammed together worse than sardines in a can. With my replacement pen in hand, I got out of the way and observed my ex take on the Black Dragon of New York and crush him with a ruthlessness Alicia and Hardy adored. By the end of the day, Marci would charm them all.

I left them to their card game, returning to the fray to see what else I could learn about the case.

To get a better idea of the scale of mutilation the victims had suffered through, I organized the autopsy reports based on the status of the corpse. Julian Cane remained the undisputed victor, having lost all his organs in his chest and abdomen to the killer. An unidentified corpse came in a close second, with all his organs damaged or removed. The coroner made a note the heart had been dissected and examined before most of it had been discarded in a cheesecloth bag inside the body. The rest of the organs had been stolen. Robert Richards, with a set of seven outstanding warrants for his arrest across three precincts, all valid statewide, came in a close third. Unlike John Doe number one, the culprit had opted to take pieces of Richard's organs, leaving enough behind to be identified but little else.

I recognized the next victim, James McDonald. In the warehouse, his face had been mangled beyond the point of recognition. I'd arrested him several times over the years, mostly for indecent exposure, although I'd busted him once for vehicular hijacking.

Well, the captain had done the busting. I'd been the first officer to arrive after the dragon had brought the vehicle to a rather destructive halt. At the time, the man had been wanted for numerous counts of sexual assault, which had put the woman he'd kidnapped at high risk.

Captain Farthan had opinions about rapists, and we worked to make sure he wasn't the one who handled the arrests. Rapists stirred his ire, and angry dragons became violent dragons. Breathing tended to provoke the opal when it was the rapist performing the offensive act.

McDonald had served a month in prison before being released on good behavior. He'd gone on to earn two outstanding warrants in Precinct 140 for armed robbery.

There were gaps in his record indicating that McDonald

didn't live in Cauldron City, but nowhere knew where he'd come from or why he kept coming back.

I checked the other identified victims and identified several trends: all had been convicted or were wanted for sexual misconduct, sexual assault, rape, armed robbery, or theft. With bad reputations among law enforcement and the general public, the five were the kind of people nobody would miss.

One entry caught my attention, and my brows rose at the twenty outstanding warrants and Leo Ferguson's status as wanted dead or alive. With six charges of murdering law enforcement officers, nine charges of murder in a mass shooting in Boston, and a mix of sexual assault, rape, and armed robbery tossed in for good measure, I suspected I'd be battling a complete lack of interest in securing justice for the deceased.

The other cases would also trip the triggers of a few too many cops, which would put me in the uncomfortable position of doing a job nobody wanted me to succeed at. With the other victims having followed a trend, I made a note to check the missing persons registries across the country for similar men who might make good targets for the killer, primarily focusing on Cauldron City.

With luck, narrowing the missing persons list down to people with outstanding warrants would bag me the identities of the remaining corpses.

The last of the identified victims, Adam Gill, only had two outstanding warrants for petty theft and armed robbery, although his rap sheet included sexual assault, rape, and murder.

I compared what I knew of the deceased men with the coroner's records, compared their ages, and came to several conclusions. All the victims were white males in their thirties with a known history of violent crimes. They also shared the same blood type, O-positive, something that caught my attention.

Universal donors were wanted for more than their blood, with many hospitals hoping and praying for organ donations from universal donor patients. With the advancements of magic and medicine, organ donations had steadily decreased, leaving a lot of people in need of transplants with nobody to get the organs from. Even accounting for campaigns to increase organ donors, fewer died after accidents, leaving those waiting for organs often in dire straits.

Magic couldn't cure everything, although unicorns and the other healing types did their best without the needed donations.

While not all the bodies had been stripped of their organs, I could readily believe someone might have taken an organ or two to make use of an underground surgeon for an illegal transplant.

The possibility chilled me.

"Hey, Dr. Erik?" I called, leaning back and tilting my head to see if I could summon the black unicorn.

After a few moments, he emerged from my kitchen. "What do you need?"

"Come look at this." I showed him the autopsy reports, pointed at the victims' blood type, the damage to the various organs, and the cheesecloth bags. "Organ theft?"

He pointed at the corpses of Leo Ferguson, Robert Richards, James McDonald, Julian Cane, and two other victims. "Those are candidates for organ theft." He pointed at the photographs of Leo Ferguson's corpse, which had been pieced back together to show the murderer's incisions, tapping where the man's heart should have been. "See those cut lines?"

"I do."

"Had his heart been in the appropriate place or the surgeon more skilled, that would have been the appropriate incision point for cracking the chest to access the heart for a transplant." Erik shuffled through the images, picking out a few and setting them aside. "This man has dextrocardia; his heart isn't in the correct location. This variant is situs inversus totalis, so everything is flipped around. He likely had no idea he had the condition, but you can see where they prepared to do the incisions and discovered the heart was not in the anticipated position." He took a closer look at the partial heart images, scoffing. "A hack surgeon did this work, literally. He knew just enough to make the attempt, realized he couldn't do anything with the organ, and stopped working. His heart *could* have been used in a transplant if the surgeon knew what to do, but there are extra steps required to attach the vessels in the correct placement."

I pointed at the other corpses with either damage to the heart or the heart missing altogether. "And these?"

Erik pointed at Julian Cane's corpse. "That one is a potential multi-organ donor. The incisions are clean, the body was cleaned out, and there's minimal damage to the tissue surrounding the organs." After a moment, he pointed at the body of James McDonald. "This man is a likely candidate, too. I'd say the odds the organs were harvested from these bodies, potentially for transplant purposes, are pretty high." He picked up the autopsy report, made a satisfied sound, and pointed at a line. "See this notation?"

I nodded, although the string of letters and numbers made no sense to me. "What does that mean?"

"That's a shorthand reference to the corpse possibly being suitable for organ donation at time of death. That means there's no evidence the victims were in poor health, and what the coroner could see of the body was in good health at time of death." Erik narrowed his eyes, shuffling through the images. "What do we have here?" He picked up a picture, which I realized was that of a dissected stomach. "I've seen this damage before."

He had? I peeked, not sure what I was looking at. "What is it?"

"That's the same exact tissue damage I saw from the Grimstone clan in the hospital." Erik picked up the coroner report associated with Julian Cane's body, got out his cell phone, and dialed a number. "Is this Dr. Jemmel? Excellent. I'm Dr. Erik Shrenville. I was asked to help review an autopsy report of a probable organ theft case. Yes, that's the one. Contact the main hospital in Precinct 169 and request their toxicology report from the Grimstone case. I was the lead surgeon on the incident, and the damage on the victim's stomach tissue seems similar. Yes, please, and thank you." He hung up.

"Good news? Bad news? No news?" I asked.

"Well, the stomach condition was driving Dr. Jemmel more than a little insane, as he hadn't seen anything quite like it. It reminded him of decomposing ulcer damage, except there was no actual evidence of an ulcer and the damage had spread throughout the entire organ. And while NSAIDs and similar drugs can cause stomach bleeding, this damage isn't consistent with drug use. He'll get samples tested for the toxin. He'd done a full toxicology report, internal and external, of the corpses, so hopefully you'll get a positive or a negative sooner than later."

"I wasn't losing my mind, then? About the organ theft possibility?"

"It's nice to see you're putting your education to good use. Yes, it's definitely a possibility in the bodies I showed you. The rest appear to be more haphazard mutilation, likely to ditch weight from the corpses to hang them up."

I made a face. "Disgusting."

"That it is. Anything else you need?"

"Pepto," I complained, sorting through the mess of images and putting them back into their appropriate places. "Thanks for the help."

"You're welcome. I shall go back to refereeing in the kitchen, else it might come to blows."

"What are they playing?"

"Monopoly."

My eyes widened. "Are any of you planning on leaving today?"

"Maybe, but quite possibly not. Grant's ordering in dinner. Oh, and your ex is fine. She's lean, but she's healthy. She's not even at risk of an ulcer right now. Apparently, her work wants her to gain five to ten pounds to advertise to women a size up. I checked the internet, and her popularity has been skyrocketing as she's been adding on a little weight and curves."

Because it was Marci, she was adding them in all the right places, busting ass to maintain her form. "Okay, good. Thank you for checking."

"You're welcome. Stop angering the women in your life, though. It's bad for my blood pressure."

"No promises, but I'll try."

Monday, April 9, 2057
Upper North Lake, Precinct 153
Cauldron City, Nebraska.

AT ONE IN THE MORNING, I hovered in my kitchen and tapped my foot so they'd finish their damned game of Monopoly. The instant the Black Dragon of New York swept in and stole victory from my father, I evicted everyone except Alicia. On her way out, Marci stared at the black dragoness, turned her gaze to me, and leered. I braced for the worst, as nothing good came out of her mouth once she decided she was doing something perverted at my expense.

"He's hung like a horse and aspires to be a perpetual motion machine," she declared before closing the door behind her, speaking loud enough I had zero doubt everyone else leaving had heard every word.

The muffled howl of laughter confirmed Hardy would never let me forget it.

"Well, that was an overshare," Alicia stated, peeking out my peephole in an effort to spy on those outside my apartment. "She has no idea how right she is or why about the first part, and no woman alive wouldn't be curious about the second part."

Yep. I gave it a day at most before word spread throughout the entire precinct about my supposed prowess. Worse, I couldn't tell if Marci was trying to help or hinder. "When we first met, she complained her previous partners were five minute wonders. Absolutely spectacular for those five minutes, but if she wasn't done before then, that was it.

She was not getting a repeat performance—not for a while at least. The real problem was the failure for them to be bothered with her after their five minutes. I learned from their mistakes. Sure, I wasn't a great boyfriend, but I got *some* things right." As there was no use being embarrassed over it, I shrugged and added, "Unlike mundane equines, I am not a whore, I stick with the woman I'm dating, and I do my best to be considerate. For some reason, I kept getting girlfriends who had been burned by idiots. And I don't mean dragons losing their temper."

"Literal burns are a unique peril of dating a dragon," Alicia informed me. "May I ask how long you two have been separated?"

"I'd say about a year now. Even after the cupcake incident, I told her to come see me if there was a problem."

"Have you tried being friends with her?"

I blinked. "I mean, we have a functional relationship founded on utter loathing and hatred with some disgust mingled in."

"Jace, she's trying to friend zone you."

"You mean she's trying to friend zone my parents."

"They're just a bonus. If she was just after your parents, she'd show up so *they* feed her rather than *you*. She's just awkward. You're dense."

"I'm not disputing the dense part, but where did you get the idea she wants to be my *friend*?"

"I asked."

Oh. I blinked. "Okay. But I have a condition."

"She has to eat one of your cupcakes?"

I scowled. "How did you guess?"

"She clued in she'd broken your heart after getting upset over the cupcakes. You were working every time we looked in on you, and you didn't seem to notice a damned thing outside your work. She was five pounds over, hadn't told you she was over, and you basically had made the holy grail of cupcakes for her. She clued in you two are romantically incompatible because you will never understand her career choice—and you put her over her job, and that is tough on a model."

"How dare I see the person rather than the model," I muttered. "I was dating her because of *her*, not her ass!"

"Yes, how dare you? You have brought this upon yourself, being a nice person. She does feel bad about overreacting, though. And yes, that confused the hell out of her. Her ass is spectacular, on that we're all agreed, and you were all interested in her personality. She was not ready for that."

I shrugged. "I wasn't *that* heartbroken over the cupcakes."

"You were about to cry, she knows it, and will hold it against you if you try to deny it."

Damn that woman. "Are you convinced she isn't going to push me down the stairs now?"

"As long as you keep feeding her, yes."

"Wait, I have to keep feeding her?"

"It's in the friendship contract. When you cook as well as you do, food is required. I *try*, but I'm pretty sure I almost killed my grandpappy today. I don't know how he ate that. I panicked, then I kept making it worse. And then he ordered groceries to replace everything I destroyed. I'm sorry about that. I just wanted to be helpful."

"I'm not upset, but I'm afraid I'm taking you into custody until you are not a danger to everyone around you should you step into a kitchen."

"I'm hopeless," she warned.

"I'm sure I can come up with a training program that will make you less hopeless. I'm going to start with teaching you how to make pesto."

"I'd noticed my grandfather kept licking the fork whenever he got to the pesto. I couldn't figure out why at first. Then I realized it was the only actually edible thing on his plate. Do you think I killed my grandpappy?"

"Dr. Erik was here. Your grandfather will be fine. He is a doctor."

"Do you think even a unicorn can save him from my cooking? I don't know if I cooked the bacon right."

She hadn't, but I wasn't going to hurt her feelings when she wore her remorse on her face. "Tomorrow, I will teach you how to render bacon. I will also teach you how to cook eggs. Anything ruined will be disposed of, and we'll try again until you've made something we can consume. After breakfast, you'll have to deal with me going over these cases, but we will resume your kitchen training at lunchtime. I'll let you play with my hoard when I'm working. You can count my books and gemstones to your heart's content."

The delight on her face warned me I might end up losing part of my hoard to her. Then, some of the remorse returned, and she said, "We may have cleaned your fridge out of leftovers. We'll replace everything."

"If he doesn't, I'm selecting his Black Wing as a prize I will take from his hoard. I'm confident I will take much better care of her than he ever could."

Alicia narrowed her eyes, grabbed her phone, and eyed the screen. "You don't want that Black Wing."

"I don't? Why? She's *marvelous*."

"She's the cheapest Black Wing money can buy because my grandfather gives it to us grandchildren as a loaner when we've been good. He had it brought to Cauldron City for the visit, understanding he would have an entire pack of his grandchildren around, and since I'm the most responsible of my sisters, I got to have the keys. We flew in like sensible beings."

"Plane or self-transportation?"

She raised a brow. "As we're sensible, plane. That's a long flight, Jace."

"If I could get the time off, I'd cross the country on the hoof," I admitted. I'd also stop at every single fast food place on the way, overdose on all things cheese, and court a hospital visit due to overindulgence in meals capable of producing quality gemstones. "I think about it from time to time."

"May I ask why she blurted that before leaving, by the way?"

I shrugged. "She likes you and hates me?"

"She basically shouted about your prowess for the world to hear."

"Do you know what's going to happen the instant I go back to work on Tuesday morning?"

"What?"

"If my desk isn't covered with pictures of my ex-girlfriend modeling, prescriptions for various medications, and requests to date the sisters or cousins of my co-workers, I will be shocked. And if word spreads to the other stations and precincts and the dragons find out? I'm doomed."

"I'm pretty sure the dragons will know by morning. My grandpappy and Hardy will start fighting over you again. Then my sisters will get involved because there's nothing black dragons love more than a good fight. Do you need me to come into work and protect you?"

"Actually, yes. Does protection come with help carrying filing boxes back into the station?"

"I think I can manage that much. According to my father, I've never worked a real day in my life, so if you can get a picture of me carrying boxes, that would be helpful. Don't ask what my mother says."

I thought about the various ways a pair of evil parents might tease their daughter. "That your father should be proud you've never worked a corner in your life?"

"Close. She asked if she should take me out and help me start working the corners. My mother was a stripper and a private entertainer when she met my father. She lured him into her lair and decided to keep him."

My eyes widened. "Your mother was a prostitute?"

"She's a Grimstone. She is exactly what she wants to be. But she prefers being called a private entertainer, as that sounds classy—and she charged him a thousand per fifteen minutes. My father made a few key mistakes. He asked her if she charged a thousand per fifteen minutes if he took her out for dinner and coffee first, if she accepted cash, credit, or other forms of payment, what her rules were, and requested precise instructions on what he needed to do, as *he was a virgin and knew nothing about women.*"

I blinked. "Your father is both a bold and a brave man."

"He was also desperate, had *no* idea who she was at the time, and couldn't understand how someone so beautiful was *only* charging a thousand per fifteen minutes. It gets better."

"How?"

"She thought he was cute and shy, so she'd actually pitched him below her normal rate. But then he kept trying to tack on ridiculous things, like if he could be charged for the time it took them to reach a location appropriate for their business, because there was no way someone as beautiful as her was worth that little. He didn't realize she's a Grimstone, Jace."

"But isn't he a black dragon, too?"

"He's a black, but he's actually the son of a red and a blue. It's rare, but when you have mixed colors, you can get any color in the heritage or even have a new line start. He's the first and only black of his line. He'd never seen another black dragon in his life. He just saw a pretty woman working a corner, thought she deserved better, and wanted to make a difference. He had never been to New York City before, had gotten rather lost, and had no idea he'd stepped into our territory." Alicia giggled, and she turned her attention to her phone, showing me a picture of a black dragon chained to the wall of a lair. "That's Dad when she decided he was not leaving her lair. She just added him to her hoard and sent a letter informing his family he was now a Grimstone."

"How long did it take him to decide he was okay being a Grimstone?"

"I'm pretty sure he was okay with it about five minutes after he got my mother out of her shirt and she started training him." She shrugged. "She didn't know he was a black dragon until he went to leave and she asked if he wanted a ride anywhere. He accepted, but only if she'd charge him for the time. She went to the street, transformed, and told him to get on. Ask me what happened next."

I went to my couch, sat down, and patted the cushion until she joined me. "Now I need to know. Tell me, else I might perish from curiosity."

"Are feet allowed on the paperwork?"

"Absolutely. I have to sort through everything later, so I don't care." To prove it was fine, I put my feet up to relax.

Once she made herself comfortable, she said, "Mom says his eyes got all sorts of wide, and he asked if he could touch her muzzle, like he'd never seen a black dragon before. He'd seen dragons before, but never a *black* dragon. It was his first confirmation he wasn't actually some genetic freak and that there were really other dragons like him out there. He cried, which alarmed my mother so much she shifted back, not sure what was wrong. He had a total meltdown. For a dragon, while adult, he was really young, so she took him to her actual home, showed him her lair, and he *lost his shit* when he saw her hoard. Transformed, started rolling in it like the freshly hatched tend to do when introduced to gold for the first time. Turns out, that *was* his first introduction to gold, as his parents aren't all that wealthy. They hoarded natural and interesting rocks, but not gold."

"Your mother must have freaked."

"Definitely, because our family thought they knew all the black dragons, and she had a young, charmed male rolling around her hoard like he's never seen gold before—and that's because he hadn't!" Alicia giggled. "She called my grandfather and asked for a clue because she wasn't sure. He told her to keep him if she liked him and that he'd smooth over any of the feathers. She got a chain, mounted it to the wall, chained him up, and kept him in her hoard. Then she was having fun with her new dragon and decided to give up her professional private entertainment ways, as she much preferred having her own trainable male and more hatchlings than is sensible."

"How many siblings do you have?"

"I have twenty-six sisters and three brothers."

"Your poor brothers must feel like they are under siege."

"They are. Constantly. Every brood in the United States keeps putting offers up for them, like my mother would actually sell one. They're just like my father, although not quite *that* innocent. They grew up hearing the story, and they're absolutely charmed by the idea of being trained by the dragoness lucky enough to win them. My grandpappy finds it hysterical. So, I have three virgin brothers, and I'm the only girl of the lot who didn't pick up private entertainment as at least a hobby. I came out of the egg disgustingly monogamous, or so says my mother."

"Ah, you're like your father?"

"To enough of a degree, my mother asks me if I would prefer being addressed as a male." Alicia rolled her eyes. "I am just like my sisters, except I don't want to test drive my men before agreeing to date them—and I don't want to charge them for dates, either. I make plenty of money without having to take advantage of men half-blind with lust. And then I'd have to join the competition, and I don't think so!"

How did women compete when it came to picking up men for pay? "Competition? How do you even compete about something like that?"

"His size, stamina, monetary offers, if he comes back for a repeat performance, and if he asks if he can bring a friend. Things like that. My sisters have no shame, and if one of the men performs well enough, my sisters share him —without charge. There's a soft-spoken blue my sisters are currently fighting over. They've progressed from paid nights to squabbling over who gets to date him. So far, the eldest of my single sisters has won, and she's been on three dates with him. If she emerges from this single, I'll be very surprised.

My grandpappy's already given his approval, and my dad likes him, too—he's partial to the blues for some reason."

"It couldn't *possibly* be because he's half blue," I replied in my wryest tone.

"I'm sure that's only a small factor in his approval. He's genuinely nice. And taming one of my sisters through being nice? That takes true skill. That he got them all fighting over him? Magnificent, really."

"Now I'm curious how you escaped his charms."

Alicia wrinkled her nose. "He breaks the spines of his books when he reads and recycles them when he's done."

I scratched my temple, debating how best to inform her I lost my shit if I spotted someone breaking the spine of a book. "And your sisters are okay with this?"

"The one currently dating him tolerates it. By tolerates, I mean smoke trails out of her ears and she about loses her shit. She'll train him, I'm sure. And if he doesn't change his ways, well, would anyone actually convict us for his brutal murder?"

Her question made me blink, and I stared at the piles of papers under our feet. "Can I ask a really odd question, Alicia?"

"Go for it."

"If you were a cop, a judge, or anyone in law enforcement, and a killer murdered a bunch of people who did things far worse than break book spines, would you be serious about pursuing the case?"

"It depends on what the crimes were. I'll admit, I'm not the perfect person, and I'd definitely think twice about certain things. If a serial killer went after pedophiles, I'd work on something else."

"How about rapists?"

"I'd be guilty of working on something else."

"So, let me ask you another question."

"Go for it."

"If you were a killer trying to get away with murder, where would you find rapists to murder?"

"Sex offender registries. They're public. I'd also check the news for any information on confirmed rapists. Once I had my target, I'd isolate when they could be found alone or when they hunt for their next victim. I'd then enjoy the murder more than I should."

I smiled, wrote a reminder to check out her ideas later, and said, "That's actually helpful. Thanks. I have spare pajamas, but you'll probably swim in them, and ladies always get first crack at the tub. I have no idea what my bad sleeping habits are, as if I have them, none of my girlfriends complained."

"I shall find out soon enough. I will warn you I have numerous bad sleeping habits. You'll find about them soon enough. It's more fun that way."

THIRTEEN

The poor recruit looked like he wanted to throw up.

MONDAY, APRIL 9, 2057
UPPER NORTH LAKE, PRECINCT 153
CAULDRON CITY, NEBRASKA.

SOMEONE KNOCKING WOKE ME, but Alicia's decision to use me as her bed prevented me from answering the door. I assumed claiming anyone and anything within her vicinity as part of her hoard counted as a bad sleeping habit. She mumbled something and rolled enough I could escape. I almost made it out of bed when she snagged hold of my waist and refused to let go.

With the choice of waking my neighbors at the unholy hour of six in the morning or dragging a draconic attachment across my apartment, I headed for the door.

Alicia thumped to the floor, and while she lost her hold on my waist, she reattached to my left leg, which made the journey tedious but manageable. I opened the door, debated cursing at the unwanted visitor, and ended up glaring at a police officer, a green recruit with a badge so new he hadn't scuffed it yet. "Detective Smithson?"

In good news for him, he worked at the station near my apartment. In bad news for him, it was six in the morning, I wanted to go back to bed, and he'd woken me up just late enough I wouldn't fall back asleep even if I wanted to. "That's me. What can I do for you?"

The poor recruit looked like he wanted to throw up. "I'm supposed to do a wellness check."

Somehow, I kept from rolling my eyes. "On which one of us?" I pointed at my attachment, who had snuggled up to my foot. To my dismay, she drooled. "If you want to take her, you can. Just approach the first black dragon you spot, dump her off, and call it a day."

"You, sir. There were concerns you might have been eaten alive or…" The cop's face flushed.

Bastards. I would begin my revenge with eating myself into a cheese stupor to crank my glitter production through the roof, and I'd take every damned diamond I produced and buy even more glitter, and I would leave tons of glitter on their doorsteps for them to clean up. "Take a picture of my attachment, give that to whomever sent you out, and remind them I'm friends with Dr. Erik and they aren't." The absurdity of it did me in, and I laughed and shook my head. "They're hazing you, and they're just giving me a hard time because they can. We all get shit calls early in our tour of duty. Try not to worry about it." As I'd left my badge on the stand by the door, I grabbed it and displayed the shiny new declaration I'd been promoted. "Well, it's one part hazing, one part fucking with me, and one part dragons being dragons. Do yourself a favor. If you can, pretend nobody around you is a pervert. They won't test you as much. And if the ladies at the other station find out you're easily embarrassed, you're going to be their dinner. If you think the guys are bad, they're worse once they decide you're fair game."

His eyes widened. "I can take a picture of her? She's gorgeous."

I glanced down, confirmed my pajamas covered everything important, and nodded. "I'm not sure how she did not wake up through falling off the bed, though." To demonstrate her determination to keep hold of me, I attempted to extract my leg from her clutches with no success. "If she hadn't wanted her picture taken, she would have stayed in bed."

I'd let him decide for himself what we'd been doing. In reality, we'd talked before taking separate showers, getting ready for bed, and then going to sleep. When I'd dropped off, she'd been on the other side of the bed, having passed out with enviable speed. I'd found her snore to be soft and pleasant, unlike most of my exes, who mimicked trains or some form of natural disaster.

The cop took a few pictures, apologized for bothering me, and fled. An older cop waited at the bottom of the stairs, a man I recognized from my various forays to the local hospital where cops of different stations tended to run into each other. I waved. "Hey, Oliver. Anything interesting on the wire that doesn't involve me?"

"It's been quiet tonight. How are you feeling?"

"Not as rested as I would like. It being six in the morning has something to do with that."

He chuckled. "The captain wanted to make sure you got out of bed at a reasonable hour, else the other stations might get involved." Then, with a raised brow, his gaze dropped to Alicia. "We were asked to make sure you woke first."

She would never live down her defeat of her grandfather with eggs, uncooked bacon, and other crimes against breakfast. No matter what I said, I lost, so I shot the man a salute, dragged the black dragoness into my apartment, and closed the door. As I wouldn't be falling back to sleep, I headed into the kitchen and investigated the fridge. My guests had done more than just replace the food that had fallen to Alicia's experiments, they'd filled the entire damned thing. I got out some eggs and bacon, setting them onto the counter. Once I had the fry pan on the stove, I attempted to shake the woman off my leg.

She clung to me, but after a brief but fierce battle, I jostled her enough she snorted and blinked.

"Time to make breakfast," I informed her, extracting my leg from her clutches. "We are starting with making bacon. Wash your hands."

She sat up, blinked again, and rubbed at her eyes. "This isn't bed."

"My asshole co-workers did a wellness check. I had to answer the door, and you decided you were coming with me. Up, up. It's time to make breakfast. I am not dealing with being awake this early on an empty stomach."

"What time is it?"

"A little after six. There's now photographic evidence you took a hostage in your sleep. I expect every cop in the city will know you have bad bed habits within the hour."

"Damn it!" She got off the floor, her cheeks flushing. "I'm so sorry. I didn't do anything else, did I?"

"You snore, but it's soft."

"I didn't sleepwalk?"

Would I sleep again knowing she might go wandering off without having a clue what she was doing or where she was going? "You stayed in bed until someone knocked at the door."

"I didn't talk or anything?"

"If you did, I wasn't awake when you did it, and you didn't wake me by talking."

"I slept on you, didn't I?"

"I may have woken up with an extra blanket this morning, and when I went to answer the door, you may have fallen out of bed and attached yourself to my leg, which is why you're now here."

"Damn it!" She bowed her head. "I am so sorry."

"I'm not worried about it, but as I couldn't get you off, the cop who did a wellness check has photographic evidence we're alive and well. In good news for you, the photo will be used against me rather than you. If it makes you feel better, you didn't wake me up when you decided you wanted to visit my side of the bed."

"They really did a wellness check on you?"

"It's promotion hazing. They like to rib the newbies after promotion, and they had a green recruit who needed some experience doing wellness checks. They probably wanted to make sure I was actually all right, too. Opals are worry warts, especially the older ones. All the police chiefs in this precinct are opals."

"Why?"

"Opals rule this specific roost. Each precinct is controlled by a color, and the clans of the appropriate color tend to have a lot of law enforcement. Since this precinct is controlled by opals, the opals are promoted to be captains." As she'd had a rough enough morning, I gave her the important job of operating my coffee maker so we would be able to function. "While you tame the coffee maker, I'm going to show you how bacon is cooked. Then I'm going to show you how to add bacon to eggs with some cheese in a basic omelet. I'm assuming you were attempting to make an omelet yesterday."

"I have no idea what I was doing yesterday."

"For the sake of your esteem, you were making an omelet, and I will teach you how to master making omelets." As I didn't mind her company, I added, "I may not allow you to venture away from my apartment until I am confident you can prepare the three major meals of the day plus snacks. Snacks are important."

"Jace, I think you underestimate just how bad I am at cooking."

Allowing myself a wicked grin, I replied, "Perhaps you should call in a wellness check on your grandfather. Have the dispatcher notify him that you have been taken into protective custody until you learn to cook. Use the non-emergency line for my station, ask for Patricia, and inform her of the situation. She's usually working this shift. If you tell her what you put in the eggs, she'll understand the severity of the situation. I'm sure the captain knows where your grandfather roosted for the night."

"He's probably in Precinct 101; we're not supposed to shift for a week, which makes getting up to the ridge house problematic. He likes the hotel there. It caters to dragons, and they have family suites."

When the dragons had built Cauldron City, they'd done so through creating an entire mountain range shielding the city from the frequent storms plaguing the area. Rather than requiring tornado sirens, the mountains blocked the storm systems and diverted them. There were sirens in the rural areas surrounding the city, but the mountains did their jobs—and the dragons kept watch on the farms nearby.

With a little magic, the dragons could divert any stray funnel clouds away from the crops and people who grew them.

I wondered what it was like to be the king of the hill—especially when the hill was an entire city.

I gave her the number for the non-emergency line. "You can also pass along we survived the wellness check if you feel like it."

Alicia giggled, and she retrieved her phone from my bedroom, wandering back while tapping at the screen. She held her cell to her ear, waited, and then said, "Good morning. Is there any chance I can speak to Patricia, please? Yes, the dispatcher. Thank you." With a pleased grin, she sat at my table, placing herself to face me. "Good morning, Patricia. It's Alicia Grimstone. Yes. I'm feeling much better, thank you. Well, mostly. Someone had a wellness check done on Jace, so he's having a rough morning. He's going to attempt to teach me how to make breakfast, but I'm afraid. I almost killed my grandfather yesterday with eggs. I was wondering if you might inquire if he's doing well? Jace told me you might be able to help. And he told me to tell you what I did to the eggs. It's really bad."

I fought my urge to laugh, failed, and did my best to keep my snickering quiet.

"Yes, that's Jace. It's fair game to laugh. I ruined a lot of his food, making my family go replace everything. I started with eggs, and I figured out how to make the pan hot, but then I thought my grandpappy might want some bacon. I cut it up and tossed it into the eggs. Then I added some peas I found. You know what? Let's just say I made a lot of mistakes, and the only thing I got right was adding pesto on top, as my grandpappy liked that. He's probably at that fancy hotel in Precinct 101. Maybe you could check to make sure he's feeling well while I learn how to never do this again? Jace has threatened to make me stay here until I'm capable of cooking something for breakfast, lunch, and dinner. I also have to be able to make at least one snack. I'm worse. I cook by calling someone competent to feed me." Alicia grimaced. "That's the only thing I can do, honestly. Thank you very much. Of course. Yes, Jace looks fine. He's laughing at me. Earned, I promise. I'm not mad he's laughing. It would be strange if he *wasn't* laughing. I put raw bacon in eggs I fed to my grandpappy. Will I be arrested if he gets sick or dies?"

I bit my knuckle so I wouldn't chortle at the thought of the Black Dragon of New York being felled by nightmare eggs.

Alicia hung up. "It's okay to laugh, Jace. Patricia was laughing so hard I think she was crying. She said she'd find someone to check in on my grandpappy, though—and she'd send a doctor along just to be certain. Do you really think you can teach me how to cook?"

"I hope so, else you're going to end up living here. I don't think this apartment is big enough for a dragoness and her hoard plus a unicorn and his hoard."

The black dragoness eyed my apartment with interest. "Well, it would definitely be a challenge, that's for certain."

"Do I want to know what you hoard?"

"Anything I want."

"Good answer. So, before you start actually cooking, there are some things you need to know."

"Like what?"

"All foods have a minimum safe cooking temperature. This means you have to cook it to that temperature before you can feed it to someone. The minimum safe cooking temperature of bacon is either soft but bordering on crisp, crisp, or fringing on burned without being burned," I informed her.

"That's not a temperature, that's a state."

"Bacon is a state of mind. It's an art made of food."

"I see you like bacon."

"I do." I pointed at my stove. "Bacon is best rendered over low heat. You want the fat to melt off, and then the remaining meat will cook to the desired level of crispiness. In bad news, this takes time. Good bacon is worth waiting for."

"So, thirty seconds in runny eggs isn't enough time to reach bacon's minimum temperature."

"You would be right."

Alicia got up, came over, and eyed my frying pan. "Okay. How do I turn this on to the right temperature? I did not do it right, so I want to start this from the very beginning."

Chuckling, I introduced her to my stove, how it worked, and the types of pans I owned. From there, I gave her a basic guide to what temperatures were best for eggs and bacon. I slapped the package of bacon in front of her, gave her a knife to open it, and stepped out of the way. "Put the bacon in the pan, turn the pan on, and observe true magic."

"Marci wouldn't eat bacon, would she?" Alicia followed my directions, turned the stove on to the correct temperature, washed her hands, and went to work plopping pieces of bacon into the pan. Then she washed her hands again and engaged my cooking utensils in a staring contest. "You have steel ones, wooden ones, and plastic ones. Which one do I use?"

"This is a non-stick pan, so you want either the wooden flipper or the plastic flipper. I usually use the wooden one. I like it better."

She selected it, held it like most would wield a knife, and eyed the pan. "Should I move the bacon around or something?"

"You put it in the pan okay, so you can leave it for a while. Do you think your grandfather is going to end up trying to reclaim you before you're taught how to cook?"

"He might bring a ball and chain to make sure I stay," she admitted, keeping a close eye on the bacon. "You're really not supposed to do this at high heat?"

"You cooked the eggs on high heat?"

"I did."

"While you can cook eggs at high heat, you need to take care doing it. I don't recommend it. Will he take you back if I demand a Black Wing? If that's the low end one, I would sell some of my gems for one."

"Where would you park it?"

"A parking spot?"

"On the street?"

"Well, yes."

"You can't *do* that to a car that nice, Jace."

I shot a glare at the woman. "Well, where am I supposed to park it, then?"

"In an indoor parking garage. Hail happens here sometimes. Hail would destroy your car. You'll just have to move to somewhere with an indoor parking garage."

As she understood I could produce diamonds on my whim, she wouldn't let me get away with stating I couldn't afford it. "Are there places like that? With indoor parking that won't wipe me out of my hoard? I like my hoard where it's at, in my possession."

Alicia glared at the bacon. "Why isn't this done yet? I'd rather look at real estate than this."

"And this is why you're terrible at cooking."

"Can I watch you cook? Then you can test me on it later. Maybe if I can tell you I know how to cook, and I only have to do it when mandatory, that will be acceptable? I only need to know enough not to kill someone, right?"

I worried for my sanity—and her grandfather's stomach. "Maybe I should have started you on grilled cheese."

"Is it faster than bacon? It doesn't look like anything is happening."

"Grilled cheese is faster than bacon," I confirmed. After some consideration, I rescued my wooden spatula from her. "Go to my bedroom, look under the bed, and retrieve the small pink box and the orange shoebox. There's also a black rectangular pan. Dump the boxes into the pan on the table."

Alicia skipped off, and I shook my head. I leaned against the counter, kept an eye on our breakfast, and waited for the moment when I introduced the dragoness to only part of my diamond collection. As instructed, she made herself at home at my table, set the pan down, and poured out the larger shoe box first. Diamond after diamond spilled out, all uncut and ranging in size from shards to pebbles to large stones jewelers might kill to have.

Her eyes widened, and she ran her hands through the stones. "These are your diamonds?"

"Some of them."

"Some?" Her attention focused on the stones, all of

which were H to D on the diamond color scale. With amusing efficiency, she began sorting them by size. "You're okay with me looking at these?"

"I'm even okay with you touching, but you would have to pitch a pretty good deal my way to get me to think about letting you keep any of them. The pink box has the one my mother gave me for my promotion, so I haven't seen that one yet."

"You've counted, categorized, and graded them all, haven't you?"

"I even have an appraiser's license," I confessed. "I got bored when at college, so I took lessons on how to appraise cut and uncut gemstones. I even know how to cut them, but I'm not practiced, and I'd have to eat a bunch of foods I don't like to get practice stones. Or buy them."

"The disgust in your tone at the mere *thought* of buying a stone," she teased. "These are all colorless grades of diamonds for the most part." She made a pleased noise, locating one of the H stones. "H?"

Damn. Dragons had a reputation of being able to eye up gemstones and judge their worth, but I'd never seen one do it before. "That box only has my H to D stones."

"What about your Zs?"

I huffed, shot her a glare, checked my bacon to make sure I could leave it unattended for a while, and went to my bed to retrieve the rest of my diamonds. It took three trips, but I set the collection of boxes onto the table, sorted through them by color grade, and handed over the box with the Zs in them. "I don't produce much in the way of fancy diamonds. That's more of my mother's thing. My father does produce diamonds, but not nearly as often as I do. My mother aims for fancy diamonds, because one good red can set her for life. She's produced several good reds over the years."

"And people pay the same rate for your diamonds as natural ones?"

"They pay more," I admitted. "My mother has a production rate of about one red per five thousand stones, and it can take her years to produce that many stones. That includes her shards."

"There are thousands of stones here." Alicia shoved the better color grades to the far side of my sorting pan and dumped out the Zs, and I swore the woman purred, running her fingers through the collection of yellow diamonds. "Have you produced any fancy diamonds?"

I pointed at the dark blue jewelry box I'd hauled out with the rest. The stone existed to vex me, as I'd been after a good, colorless diamond to fund my book buying ways. Alicia abandoned the rest of my diamonds, snatched the box, and popped it open.

At the size of a golf ball, the damned thing had about landed me in the hospital. Blacker than even the dragons plaguing Cauldron City, I expected to put up a fight to keep it—or be coerced into accepting a ridiculous amount of money for it.

Judging from the way Alicia's eyes widened, I may as well have presented the keys to every castle on the planet along with the entirety of the earth's money. "Do you have any idea how much this is worth, Jace?"

I did, as I'd gotten it double appraised; I hadn't believed its price tag when I'd calculated its uncut value. I'd taken it to a trustworthy appraiser, a unicorn who lived up in Montana, to give me a second official appraisal.

We'd both valued the damned thing at almost thirty

million dollars. Blacks typically came in industrial grade rather than gem grade, and the black I'd produced fell into the top percentile of gem grade stones. Most needed to enhance the diamond to get the pitch black color desired by collectors. Mine couldn't get any darker if anyone tried while still preserving its translucence. The light test had cranked the stone's value through the roof.

Under a bright light, not a single flaw could be spotted. To show off the stone, I grabbed one of the test lights, adjusted how she held the diamond, and directed the beam through the smooth surface.

"Holy fucking shit," she whispered.

"We've estimated it to be worth about thirty million. The estimated cut carat size should be around a hundred and fifty carats, maybe a little larger. Usually, there's a lot of unusable material around the edges." I pointed at the smooth surface of the stone, which set the diamond apart from ones dug out of the ground. "Our larger diamonds have better surface material, so we can get more out of the cut."

Alicia set the stone on her palm and gave it a few bounces. "Two hundred and fifty carats, roughly?"

I nodded. "On the nose. For the record, that stone about killed me." I snorted, shook my head, and reclaimed the diamond, holding it up for a better look. "This thing was a literal pain in my ass."

"Is it your largest?"

I grunted, gave her the diamond back, and pointed at a different jewelry box, a red one. "No, that bastard is. I got lucky on that one. The casing was thin. That run got me in other ways, though."

"Glitter?"

"I could deal with glitter. No, I'd gotten an undercooked chicken sandwich from a restaurant, so I was dealing with salmonella poisoning at the same time I was producing stones. Unlike regular equines, unicorns *can* vomit, it's hugely unpleasant, and I spent a week sick as hell. That was right before I applied to join the academy and became a cop."

Alicia set the black diamond down and went for the red box.

At a little over three hundred carats, the colorless, flawless diamond would produce a cut stone well over a hundred carats, possibly over two hundred in the hands of a skilled cutter and a fancy cut. The dragoness narrowed her eyes, examining every face of the stone. "D, flawless. There isn't even a scratch on the surface, Jace. What did it appraise at?"

"It appraises at a number high enough I get sick thinking about it. That stone is *mine*. I suffered for that stone, and you can take it out of my cold, dead hands."

She raised a brow. "How else did you suffer?"

"I got sick eating chicken at a questionable restaurant. That's suffering enough. Do you know what I did after?"

"You produced a record-shattering diamond of unparalleled quality."

"I mean beyond that." I wrinkled my nose, pointing at a green box. "The first week I had off work as a cop, I spent the week leading up eating a diet exclusively of chicken and cheese. Then, because I hate myself, I ate undercooked chicken on purpose to see what would happen. That stone happened."

Alicia placed the large diamond in front of her with care and picked up the green jewelry box, popping it open. Like my prized stone, my second largest diamond was top grade and flawless, although it had been shaped like an egg, which had made my work significantly easier. She picked it up, examined it, and giggled. "You produce better diamonds when sick with salmonella poisoning?"

"Apparently."

"What's the value of this one?"

"A little less than its big brother. For the record, I did not attempt that experiment a third time. When I went back to work, I was still sick, and I stayed sick for a week after. We do not tell my parents about the salmonella experiments."

"They don't know about these stones, do they?"

"They don't know about them."

"Have you appraised all of these stones?"

"Only the ones over a hundred raw carats," I admitted, although I skirted the truth. The insurance company accepted my base appraisals for the smaller stones, and anything over a hundred raw carats was double appraised. "I haven't sold off many of them, and when I did, they were all smaller ones, and I had my father take care of the details. I just wanted the money to buy books and upgrade my computer." I returned to the stove to monitor the bacon, flipping it over to continue the rendering process. "Honestly, I don't sell them because I don't want to stop working."

"You can have wealth and keep working because you want to, Jace. My entire family has mastered this art. But if you're going to kidnap me until I demonstrate I'm good at cooking, we're going to have to do something about this apartment. My book hoard will not fit. We could have the book hoard house for when you're not working and this apartment for when you're working. We can move books in and out of the book hoard home."

I realized the sneaky woman had abandoned learning

how to cook so she could stick around. "Are you going to protect me from Marci?"

"You don't need to be protected from your ex. You need to give her hugs now and then when she's having a bad day and feed her things she can eat without worry. She wants to be your *friend*, not your executioner."

"I do not get the eating without worry problem," I complained, hopping up and sitting on the limited section of counter without overhead cabinets. "Why is this even an issue?"

"It's a matter of respect. She knows you will respect any limitations she has without question. You don't need some doctor telling you she has to avoid gluten. You accept what she can or can't have at face value and take her seriously."

"This should not even be an issue," I grumbled.

"That is because you're a unicorn among men."

"There is a reason for that."

"I meant the kind of nice guy that doesn't show up every day. She does feel bad about how she dumped you, though."

I shrugged. "I'm over it, except I've been waiting for her to murder me over those cupcakes."

"That really was her trying to figure out a way to ask you to make her a batch, Jace. It was a miscommunication. And it wasn't really your fault."

"It wasn't really her fault, either," I pointed out. "We both had horses in that race."

"Well, she had a horse, you had a unicorn, and she didn't know it."

"She respected me for working hard to be a cop. She wouldn't have understood why I worked if I didn't have to."

The dragoness smiled, and she returned my two large

diamonds and my black diamond to their boxes. "Let's cut a deal."

I recognized I courted trouble, but I saw no way out of the trouble I'd created opening my mouth and threatening to keep the woman until she learned how to cook without running risk of killing somebody. "What deal?"

She gestured at my lower grade diamonds. "Let me pick a stone from these color grades. Just one. I will sell it, and I will procure a home for our books. We'll have competing book hoards."

"You're going to win that," I warned her. "All I have is what is in this apartment."

Her expression changed, a mixture of resignation, regret, and something else I couldn't quite read but unsettled me. "I've worked a lot and haven't read nearly as much as I want to, so my hoard is not nearly as impressive as you might think."

I considered my diamonds, went to my box of K stones, and rummaged until I found one ringing in at a hundred and seventy carats. "You may sell this one. I've already appraised it, so I have a rough idea of its value. I am not going to tell you its original appraisal amount. If you sell the stone for over the original appraisal amount, I'll go along with your scheme and buy a house with the funds. It has to be in Precinct 153, and it needs to be the same distance or closer to my work. If you sell the stone for below the original appraisal amount, you may look into larger apartments that have a mystical indoor parking spot—and you have to hoodwink your grandpappy out of a Black Wing for me. And I get the change."

She narrowed her eyes. "That's sneaky. Can you verify the appraisal?"

"The appraisal certificate is dated, and there are pictures of the diamond from all angles with its precise measurements." I pointed at one of my bookcases. "There's a false book in there with the appraisals. I'll play fair, that much I can promise."

Alicia smiled. "I'll play fairly, as in I will break no laws while making sure I squeeze every penny out of this stone."

Dragons. Pleased I'd found some way to keep her amused while I worked, I returned to making breakfast, wondering what sort of chaos she would create using one of my diamonds.

FOURTEEN

Only a fool left a hoard of diamonds with a dragon.

TUESDAY, APRIL 10, 2057
LOWER NORTH LAKES, PRECINCT 153
CAULDRON CITY, NEBRASKA.

ONLY A FOOL LEFT a hoard of diamonds with a dragon, but I needed to head to work and Alicia refused to leave without counting and appraising each one. Losing the battle might win me the war, assuming I could figure out the victory conditions. Did I want her to leave? Did I want her to stay? What would I do with a *dragon*?

No, what would I do with a headstrong dragoness on a mission? Her current mission would win me a larger home of some sort, something I'd been too busy and career-oriented to pursue. As her mission would give me more space for books, I meant to look the other way and observe the chaos she created.

If she struggled to find a buyer, I'd recommend she pick a fight with her grandfather over the stone.

Five minutes before the start of my shift, I parked my parents' car in the parking garage at the station, grabbed the filing box with the most important info I'd gathered on the murders, and hauled it inside. Hardy intercepted me at the elevator. "We've been moved to the third floor," he complained.

"We knew it was happening. Did you get to keep your desk?"

"We all did, but we were forced to accept new chairs." The black dragon shrugged at that. "Alicia didn't come with you?"

"Alicia is at my place, counting my book hoard or something." While the captain knew my species, I believed when he said he would keep it a secret. In time, Hardy would learn from one of his family members, but he would keep my secret, too. "I tried to get her to come in after I fed her breakfast, but I lost that one. She dug in her heels. I had a choice of being late or leaving her there."

"And how goes the plan to teach her how to cook?"

"I think I've taught her basic food safety, but she has the patience of a hummingbird right along with their general attention span."

"Hey," one of the station's hummingbirds complained, a young male who'd barely learned to fly and had a long way to go before helping with any investigations. I held up my finger, and Mikhal landed. *"We're not all that bad."*

The magic giving them the ability to speak, which translated their natural noises into something I could understand, always impressed me. While I used something similar while a unicorn, I accepted I would never comprehend how it actually worked. "No, you're not—but she certainly is."

"The pretty black dragon? The sickly one?"

"Yes, that's her. How are your flight lessons going?"

"Terribly." The hummingbird anxiety preened his feathers. *"I tire quickly."*

"Don't let it drag you down, Mikhal. You're well ahead of the curve on talking. Why don't you ask to keep a detective company? If your stamina is behind but you're ahead of the curve on communication, you might fit there." To make it clear I didn't think less of the little fellow for his shortcomings, I stroked his chest with a finger. "Workout day today?"

"I did two hours, and it hurts to fly now."

I transferred Mikhal to my shoulder. "You can hide on the third floor today. I'm scheduled to make use of my brain today as far as I know."

"We are. Paul and Dowdren are headed out on some calls with Lovell. I got assigned to serve as your sounding board today."

"Are you being rewarded or punished?"

"Both. I have to go get lunch for you and my cousin today. And since she is at your place, I'll have to make an extra stop."

I laughed. "Chicken again?"

"Anything to make sure Alicia eats. When my grandpappy says I have to make sure, I make sure."

"Trust me, she's eating. A lot. I'm already out of eggs again, the bacon didn't last long, and I've cleaned out half the fridge taming that stomach of hers. I'll have to go grocery shopping tonight to feed her dinner. This time, I'll be prepared, though."

"Dr. Erik swung by an hour ago to talk to me about her ulcers. I'm on general feeding duty, as the rest of the family is still feeling under the weather. She's going to be eating more than a horse."

As a proud representative of the equine community, I could readily verify she ate far more than I did at my worst. "It's fine, Hardy. Just text her asking what she wants, order it in for her and have it sent to my apartment, and we'll do the same here. Then you're rewarded rather than having to try to compete against half the city for chicken."

"Mercy? From you?"

I laughed. "I am going to make my ex those cupcakes to try to restore general peace and prevent the neighborhood cops from fretting if she's going to do me in this time. I'll also feed them to your cousin. I will not be defeated by their stomachs."

"Brave but foolish man," Hardy muttered.

"You can't win against a female stomach," the hummingbird informed me. *"It can't be done."*

I rewarded Mikhal with another petting of his chest, and the hummingbird rubbed his head against my hand. "Wise men try, else the females find some other way to conquer."

"That's good advice," Hardy admitted. "You're getting your own office, which will be next door to an office I'm sharing with Dowdren. Lovell and Paul are next to me. You're at the end of the row. The captain has decided you're batting solo for a while. Yvon's going to be in preschool for a while, and he doesn't want to have to investigate his murder if he tries to pair you up with someone who licked purple paint to see if it tasted like grape."

"I wouldn't kill him, but I'd escort him to the nearest shrink."

"That was discussed, too. Feeling better?"

"Yeah, I am. I forgot I had gotten my brain rattled in my

skull. The autopsy reports might give me nightmares, though."

"What's your base conclusion?"

"Organ theft by either an inexperienced surgeon or someone trying to cover their tracks. I asked Dr. Erik to review some of the pictures, and he confirmed many of the incisions were consistent with how organs are removed from donors. I'm going to have to do a lot of reading into organ theft now, and I'm not even sure where to start."

"Ask the captain. He's got our primary reference list, and he can put you in touch with the doctors who can help with the specialty work. Organ theft is more common than you think—but this would definitely be the most elaborate form we've seen. It does make sense, though. Getting an organ is hard enough. Paying an underground surgeon is expensive. The last time we busted an op like that, the surgeon was charging two mil to use a stolen organ. Let's just say that case was messy. The surgeon is still loose."

"Could it be the same guy?"

"Not a chance in hell. The surgeon in question is smart, methodical, and hates messy cuts. He's pretty distinctive. We checked for that while you were doing your work—but excellent question. You're scoring full points for what you've figured out so far. Anything else?"

"They're all the same blood type, and they were all in good health at the time of death, or so the coroners stated in the report."

"Which supports your theory of them being taken and killed for their organs." Hardy headed for the elevator that would take us to the third floor, pressing the button once and only once.

Those who tested their luck and hit the button

numerous times might not get an elevator at all depending on the whims of the elevator gods. According to the high-pitched whine from behind the doors, the elevator gods liked us. "I need to figure out how to compare the sex offender registry against the missing persons lists, as all the identified victims have a reputation of violent sexual assault and other crimes. They're the kind of people most wouldn't miss."

"And you just won me a hundred bucks out of the captain's pocket, and I will repay you with picking up your lunch for a week."

"I'll bring cash to make it easier," I promised, grateful the dragon would save me from going out to get lunch. "What were you betting over?"

Half the time, I played the betting game with the other cops, making a point of keeping my bets low to maintain the appearance I spent most of my earnings on books. While I expected people would be playing a guessing game of my species soon enough, Hardy would be the one least likely to spill my secrets.

The dragon wanted me as part of his hoard, and that had been before I'd let his cousin know I collected diamonds with wild abandon.

I expected she'd send me packing off to a new home in a nicer neighborhood of the precinct using a single diamond, which she would offer up to her grandfather to keep my secret as safe as possible.

Hardy and Alicia battling over me would be my real problem. Add in their grandfather, and I'd be at my wit's end within a week.

"He said you wouldn't find the connection for at least three days after coming back to work. I bet you'd be ready to pursue the connection within five hours of coming in."

The elevator dinged and opened, and we both stepped inside before it changed its mind about being functional. Hardy pressed the button for the third floor before saying, "I feel like we're making many poor choices today."

"It's only a poor choice if either of you had Indian before getting into the elevator," Mikhal announced.

As hummingbirds were notorious about forgetting most details about human life, I rewarded the youngster with another petting. "That was a good one."

"It really was. We're good on that front. I had cheap Mexican for breakfast."

We ran a high risk of dying if the elevator broke and we were stuck inside.

Mikhal whined, soft and pitiable enough I continued to shower him with attention. *"That is worse than Indian. Will we perish in here?"*

Maybe Mikhal struggled with the endurance flying of his training, but someone had taught him the unfortunate realities of humans and spicy food.

Hardy chuckled. "I took antacids before indulging. We should be all right—this time."

"A lesson to be learned, Mikhal. Ask Hardy what he ate before agreeing to get into an elevator with him."

"An important lesson," Mikhal zipped off my shoulder and waited for the doors to open, darting to and fro.

The elevator cooperated and set us free on the third floor, and the hummingbird zoomed to safety, checking out the cops working on the open section where most mingled when working on something they wanted input on. As a general rule, everyone had access to an office, but most set up second desks in the shared space to aid in their efficiency.

They would have to drag me out of my office kicking

and screaming before I consented to being set loose into an open space again. I liked being able to hear myself think without contemplating throwing things at my co-workers.

"Your office is this way." Hardy dodged the chaos of the open space, which had most of the station's detectives bustling around and chatting up a storm. Within twenty minutes, everyone would settle in to get work done, but I'd learned early on those who hadn't been called out tended to get their gossiping in early. We skipped past the first row of offices, and Hardy pointed at one on the end. "You not only get your own office, but you also get windows."

"That's going to annoy the other detectives," I muttered. "Will I survive long before I'm killed off for my office?"

"You'll be fine. Everyone okayed it after hearing you gave the captain a real run for his money. You're the precinct's hero right now. Having your own office is a small price for having the joy of hearing the captain can be defeated in a man-vs-dragon battle."

"You're sure?"

"We're sure. And nobody minds Dowdren and I are sharing an office next to you along with our other neighbors. We have a reputation of working well together, and we stayed downstairs to keep you company. Paul and Lovell office swapped with someone else to be close to us. And now that they know my cousin is staying at your place, and that it's a probable hostage situation, well, we must take care of our own. We just aren't sure if we're supposed to be helping you leave your apartment safely or handcuffing you and dumping you there for Alicia's entertainment."

"There's no way I'm living this down, is there?"

"I'm afraid not."

Well, shit. "Alicia's pretty smart," I commented, cracking

open the door to discover several wrapped gifts on my desk, which had been hauled upstairs as promised. "Presents?"

"Consolation prizes for dealing with the captain, helping my clan out, and otherwise being an upstanding officer of the law. There are more in the captain's office. He said we had to ease you into accepting gifts."

"I don't refuse earned presents, and I earned these." I headed for the waiting rewards, sat down in my new chair, which still had its store tag on it, and decided the move up to the third floor, while stressful, came with perks. "I'm expecting these to be trapped, but it's an office day as far as I know, so that's fine." I tore into the smallest one, which proved to be a sizable jewelry box. I lifted it to my ear and gave a gentle shake. Keys jangled within. "Is this from your grandfather?"

"Probably."

I lowered the box and popped it open to discover a set of car keys, rather familiar as I'd driven Alicia to my apartment in the vehicle they belonged to. A note inside declared for however long I kept his pretty little granddaughter, I would get to keep the keys to the Black Wing. "Alicia has dug her heels in and refuses to learn how to cook, and her grandfather is encouraging it."

I showed him the note.

Hardy cackled. "He takes his debts seriously, and he's determined if you're taking care of her, he has one less granddaughter to worry about. No is an allowed answer."

"Doesn't no just make dragons try even harder to lure someone into saying yes?"

"I won't deny our tendency to find a new way to make potential partners tell us no, but we always respect the thing we're told no about. It's a rule. A Grimstone marries a willing partner—but we keep score to see who finds the most stubborn mate. In good news, dragons are compatible with all humanoid species, so you're considered to be prime male stock. We're also compatible with the equines, griffons, and anything else capable of assuming a humanoid shape. Do us all a favor. Tell Alicia a whole bunch of maybes, sprinkle in a no here and there, and let us observe the fireworks. I am concerned about her refusal to learn how to cook, though. Our grandfather is at the hotel wishing he loved his clan a little less right now. Good call on the wellness check, by the way. He's sick as hell, and the medical team in Precinct 101 called Dr. Erik to assist with his care."

Damn it. "We hide that from Alicia unless she directly asks. She won't take it well."

"She really won't. Her sisters are keeping him company, as is my grandmother, so he'll be fine. He's just going to have a rough few days."

"Especially considering that toxin."

"So, about that."

I claimed the Black Wing's keys and put them in my pocket. "That doesn't sound promising. What's wrong?"

"Your corpses all tested positive for the substance. Captain Farthan put in the request with toxicology, and a magicker did the scans on them all. One of your bodies is odd."

"How so?"

"The poison was *on* the body rather than *in* the body."

Hello, hello, hello. "How interesting."

"All of the organs tested from the other bodies were damaged by the poison, and it's probable the poison, except for the one body, is the primary cause of death."

I came to several different conclusions, all of which

would complicate the case. Using the poison to hide the organ theft came to mind, although I could also see an enterprising surgeon making the most of the situation, studying the toxin on live subjects while hacking apart the final victim for an illegal organ transplant. Other possibilities existed, including the one body having been the control for the experiment. "One corpse for organ theft or as a control, nine corpses for testing?"

Hardy nodded. "That's our current theory."

"That's going to make a mess of my investigation, isn't it?"

"Well, it's certainly complicated the situation. Good notice on the rap sheets. Do you want me to go swing by the captain's office to get information on how best to compare the databases?"

"Please."

"You got it. The Black Wing is in the garage, and I'll drive your car home."

"It's my parents' car."

"I'm sure I can figure out where it needs to go safe and sound. How fond are they of the car?"

"That depends on who is asking."

"My grandfather."

"He'd have to ask them. I'm sure they'd love having some black dragons following them around." I snickered, made a mental note to warn my parents the dragons were coming, and opened the next present, discovering an air fryer. "Maybe I can teach Alicia to use this thing." I investigated my new toy, lifted the box, and discovered it to be suspiciously light. "Do you know what this is, Hardy? I can promise it is not an appliance."

"Disappointment, apparently. I'll make sure my grandpappy knows you are interested in having an air fryer, though." Hardy grinned and waited for me to open the box.

I took care with opening, peeking inside to discover an old, worn stuffed dragon, a black one that had seen years of love. I lifted it out and burst out laughing when I saw it had a collar with Alicia's name on it. "Is this why she ended up sleeping on me?"

"Very probably. Our grandfather realized she hadn't brought it with her and asked her father to retrieve it. He hadn't expected to be here for more than a few days. We get downright crabby without our stuffies."

"Your family is quite strange, Hardy."

"It really is. But, while he can be ruthless, he keeps an eye on us kids. My stuffed dragon, for the record, is blue, and I get mean if I forget him when I travel. Alicia's dad gave it to me when I was three. My previous dragon had experienced a rather unfortunate accident. We all have a stuffed dragon."

"Including your grandfather?"

"He's the one who started it. He got a black one for my grandmother so she would have a dragon to keep her company when he needed to go out of town. She insisted he have one, too. Yes, they take them almost everywhere. We're hoarders. We can't help it."

That I could believe. "I'll take it to her tonight. I am questioning why it's a present for *me*, though."

"Well, she won't be in a hurry to leave if she has her stuffy."

The Grimstone clan might drive me crazy. "Hardy, I've already made the mistake of telling her she wasn't leaving until she wasn't a risk to anyone sharing the same kitchen with her. I now have a live-in dragoness, and I have no idea what I'm going to do with her. Well, beyond feed her at the appropriate intervals. Do you know what my apartment isn't large enough for? Two book hoarders."

"She's trying to find you a new apartment, isn't she?"

"It's either that or we're going to be sleeping on our books," I muttered.

"Entry-level detectives don't make *that* much. I'll make sure Alicia knows she can't bankrupt you. She's the most likely of us to forget not everyone can be as marvelous as a dragon."

Damned dragons. "Riddle me this. Why do we make a distinction between a dragon and a dragoness, but when we're talking about dragons generally, you're just dragons?"

"It is too many extra words to distinguish, and when we use dragoness, we are usually trying to escape a sketchy situation alive."

Hmm. I could buy into that theory. "So the males are just all lumped together, and the females rule the roost and have a special title?"

"I don't think that's why it initially started, but that's now my story, and I plan to stick to it. I'm more likely to survive the wrath of the next dragoness to cross my path that way. Also, dragonesses is a pain in the ass to say. Thus, we use dragons."

"Now *that* is a solid theory. I like it. How hard do you think it's going to be to cross-reference the sex offender registry and the missing persons lists?"

"That's a good question. I can't remember having ever done it before. I'll go get on that while you get settled in your office. Are the rest of the files still at your apartment?"

"They are."

"I'll wing over with some extra hands and pick everything up to limit the amount of temptation surrounding my cousin. I love her, don't get me wrong, but she has even more issues than I do."

"I find that difficult to believe."

"You'll understand the first time you see her around something bright and shiny."

"Like glitter?" I snickered.

"Wrong type of bright and shiny." Hardy wrinkled his nose at me, waved his fist, and left my new office.

I doubted I would ever understand dragons. I grabbed my cell, texted Alicia, and warned her she might have company bringing her lunch at some point, and if she could return my hoard to its appropriate place, I would appreciate it.

Her reply came a few moments later with a photograph of my cleaned kitchen table with a pile of books on it, a tablet, and a notepad with one of my preferred pens.

I worried she would take over my life and steal my books by the time she finished with me, but rather than question her, I put my phone in a drawer along with my keys, cracked my knuckles, and went to work delving deeper into the case of the dead weight. The question of who had kidnapped my mother would go to somebody else, as we tried to minimize personal involvement.

In reality, if we kept the personal involvement rules intact in Cauldron City, no cases would get solved. If someone didn't know somebody else, chances were they shared some form of relation or association.

Ten minutes later, Hardy returned with Captain Farthan in tow. I leaned back in my new chair, propped my feet up on my desk, and waved. "Good morning, sir."

"If Grant annoys you too much with his hints, let me

know, and I'll rein him in. Hardy told me about the Black Wing keys."

"I could use it as my cruiser for a while. Just slap the lights and siren on and wait for the next incident of gun violence. With my luck, the car will end up with more holes than intact paint."

The opal dragon snorted. "No. Your actual cruiser will be set up and ready to go by the end of the week. Unless we get leads on where to look into your case, you're sticking around the station. That's doctor's orders, by the way."

"If any doctor thinks benching me for a week is going to stop me from riding willing sentients, they need a doctor," I replied.

That got my captain laughing. "No, that's not the issue. Erik is just concerned you were exposed to a lot of healing magic the past few days and wants you to settle into your new role in a calmer environment. This case has a lot of paperwork and financials to go through, so it works out well. Tomorrow, you'll start sitting in on questioning sessions to learn the ropes. So far, the questioning sessions have been fruitless. The families of the victims haven't communicated with them in years and display zero evidence they have wanted to, which is a whole lot of wasted man hours and no leads to follow."

"I disagree. It supports the theory that the killer is deliberately picking people nobody will miss—people who have a bad reputation. Probably to prevent us, as police officers, from looking too closely at their crimes. The unicorn was unscathed, probably sedated when nabbed, and that's that—it's common practice if somebody thinks they can profit from a unicorn."

"Unicorns should be put into protective custody," my

captain muttered. Hardy snickered, waved, and abandoned my office to go to work. With the black dragon out of the way, my boss stepped in, closed the door, and said, "I had your office soundproofed. What are your thoughts about the unicorn?"

"She was likely a source of funding to pay for an organ transplant or a red herring to have a surface reason for the dead weight. The toxicology reports complicate the situation. It could be someone who isn't aware of how autopsies work or assumed we wouldn't investigate the full causes of death. It *could* also be a lack of understanding it's possible for us to detect new toxins during the evaluation process."

"All that is generally sound. Good. Erik came over to deliver the intel on the poison himself before he headed over to take care of Grant. We've gotten a sample bumped up to be evaluated and compared to other instances in the nation, but so far, it seems to be unique to here. That's a problem. If this toxin gets spread into the general population, the medical system will collapse. There just aren't enough people who can treat it, and we don't have any drugs capable of countering the poison's damage. Erik has given samples to his more promising researchers, but developing a new antidote takes time. The only good news is that the black dragons, except for Alicia, would have survived with minimal care. Grant remained untreated long enough for them to observe how he metabolized the poison. What does that information lead you to think?"

My brows rose at that, as Cauldron City had one of the most robust medical systems in the world, with most precincts having at least one major hospital and several clinics. Most clinics served those who didn't want or need care at a hospital and were willing to pay a set rate for their appointments. While expensive specialty clinics existed, they were few and far between, typically serving dragons and species with more money than sense.

Unicorns went to the hospitals to be cared for by other unicorns as a general rule—or made a phone call and got someone to do a home visit.

"We're fucked," I informed him. "The victims were all non-shifting humans, and they all died from the poison except the probable organ donor." I dug through the box to retrieve the autopsy report. "Which vic hadn't been poisoned internally?"

"James McDonald."

I checked, and sure enough, the body with the best odds of having been used as an unwilling organ donor matched the vic who hadn't been poisoned. "That's the one. He had his heart and kidneys removed, clean incisions, professionally done in the same way a surgeon would have for an organ donation. The coroner had made a note about the removal, and Dr. Erik evaluated the photographs."

"And as Erik has done many organ transplants, he would know what the incisions should look like." The captain sat in the new seat across from my desk. "I have four pairs plus you working on this case. With the identification of several of the victims being rather high profile, the poisoning of the Grimstone clan, and the kidnapping of a unicorn, the commissioner wants this solved sooner than later. He also wants the local unicorns, especially the whites, to be on guard or being watched, as that might lead us to the killer." Something about the intensity of the captain's gaze worried me.

Piece by piece, it clicked on what he wanted me to do.

"You want me to eat cheese, wander around, and lure the killer out."

"The killer obviously understands the value of white unicorns. She was treated well beyond a tranquilizer dart to the ass, which would make anybody grumpy. Even the sling had been specially designed to do as little harm to her as possible. I had the whole rig evaluated, and your guess about putrefaction seems to be spot on. We're not sure if the unicorn would have actually bolted without you making such commentary, however."

I snickered. "She totally would have stuck around to dig out her gems. She must have been working on those for several weeks at a minimum. Whites get downright pissy when they can't get their gems."

"Like a dragon's hoard."

"Most unicorns sell off their gems," I admitted. "Often fairly early, and they keep the money in a series of different accounts with different banks, usually having a home in every city they have a banking account to separate their assets. My parents have their fancy property in Chicago, and they visit it several times a year. The Chicago herd uses the place for hosting guests and parties in exchange for keeping it maintained. As I opted to stay here, because here is where I was born, my parents keep their primary residence in Willow Grove. They bought the property shortly before I was born and before Cauldron City boomed, so it's worth a lot more now compared to what they paid for it."

"And you live in that small apartment why?"

"I've been told it's too small for a unicorn and a dragon to share hoards, so Alicia is amusing herself with real estate searching here. I gave her the restrictions of equidistant to work and still in Precinct 153. I then gave her something to sell and told her if she got more for it than its appraisal value, she could pick any property she can pay for with the proceeds. If she gets less than its appraisal value, she has to find an apartment with an indoor garage to park my Black Wing."

"I see you're taking Grant's car."

"Oh, no. Remember that nonsense about what would happen if I beat you at a ride? I'm demanding a Black Wing of my own. It's his fault. If he hadn't wanted to get me a Black Wing, he wouldn't have let me drive his. I was going to ask for a low-key cheap car until I got behind the wheel of that beaut."

Captain Farthan chuckled. "May I ask how much the appraisal is for?"

"Six and a half million."

The opal dragon whistled. "That'll get you a nice place not far from here. Hell, for that much, you could convince just about anyone to move out. You could almost buy something in the core precincts for that much. Please tell me everything in your apartment is insured."

I snickered. "Everything is photographed, insured, and tracked. I'll have to update the trackers on the stone I gave her to finalize the sale, too. I pay ten thousand a year for the insurance policies, but the tracking helps. I have a deal with the insurance company; I permit them to train magickers on how to track diamonds, and I run a test on them yearly. Otherwise, the policy is five times as much for what I have."

"What else have you neglected to tell me?"

I got my phone out of the drawer, pulled up my degree from Yale, and handed it over. The captain raised a brow, scrolling through the details associated with my degree.

"I told the commissioner we needed to make those fields

non-optional. Why did you opt against putting in your education?" After handing my phone back, he regarded me with interest.

I'd expected some anger, and I breathed a relieved sigh he displayed no signs of irritation. "I didn't want special treatment, and having the degree doesn't mean I was qualified to be a cop or a detective right out of the gate. I wanted to learn from scratch." I patted my desk. "I earned being here, and that's what I wanted. The degree was to help make sure I could be the best I can be. And my species? I'll be in the prime of life for hundreds of years if I decide to stay a cop. So far, I have no desire to change fields."

"You're playing the long game. I *had* wondered about your physical results; you'd come to the academy late, but the report put you at the same physical level as someone years younger. Your reports haven't budged since joining the force, either. Do you even go to the gym?"

"I exercise, though not usually at the gym. I'm often helping the younglings get used to riders, which is a lot of work. They don't mean to buck, but they can't help it. By the time I'm done with them, they're able to handle regular non-shifters."

"And most unicorns work in health care in some capacity. So, you're the black sheep of the whites. What do your parents do?"

"They do light hospital and clinic work, usually for those with poor insurance policies. Whites do a lot of the volunteer work. We don't *need* to earn the money, so they'll call us in when somebody needs health care they can't afford," I admitted. "Mom also does secretarial work. She likes it. Dad does whatever catches his eye, often on a temporary level. They want the freedom to wander off. They sometimes take long-term work, but honestly? I don't pay much attention to what they're doing unless they wander off long enough to worry me."

"That explains why you weren't concerned in the warehouse."

"I'm not old enough to be targeted. People who know anything about whites tend to go after the fully grown ones. They leave the shaggy little ponies alone because behind every shaggy little pony is a pair of angry grown unicorns who absolutely will kill anyone who touches their foal. Once the shaggy ponies grow out, they're fair game, although the younger stallions and mares will bring out the cranky older unicorns. Whites are targeted more often than other colors, but they're all targeted for *something*."

"So, shaggy ponies aren't likely to be grabbed?"

"Only by those with a death wish or haven't researched unicorns enough," I replied. As I could see the opal dragon using me as bait, I considered him with narrowed eyes. "A pair of clippers can temporarily turn a shaggy pony into something almost resembling a young stallion. Someone who isn't a unicorn or isn't that well versed about them wouldn't be able to tell the difference."

"If I wanted you to play bait, and we got some clippers, it might work?"

"It'd work a lot better if you dropped the other unicorns a line somebody is stalking the shaggy pony around and snap a few photos. The problem would cease being a problem, and unicorns tend to leave their victims in dire need of going to the ER but still alive." While laws on kidnapping sentients varied, unicorns tended to have better protections than other races, dragons included. Dragons got certain leeway when declining a kidnapping invitation. Unicorns tended to gather in herds and take a rather violent approach when pushed.

Having a sharp and dangerous weapon attached to our heads helped with our acts of violence.

"Is this a case of unicorns knowing how to put people back together, so they're equally skilled at taking their victims apart?"

"Something like that."

"In your opinion, how long would a unicorn need to prepare before being considered a viable target?"

"Two to three weeks. If you expect the unicorn to be targeted, they would be found at places serving high quantities of chicken and cheese."

"How would you feel about three weeks of daily Portuguese chicken for breakfast, lunch, and dinner on Grant's dime?"

I glared at him. "Constipated, sir. And cranky. If you make me do that, know revenge *will* be coming, and you and everything you own will sparkle by the time I finish with you. I will load up an entire dump truck with glitter and pour it into your home."

The opal dragon spent a disconcertingly long time considering my threat. "What sort of cheese produces the best result?"

I groaned and bowed my head. "The Cheesecake Factory." After my last stint with cheese and chicken, I'd sworn off cheesecake despite it being effective at the job. "Fresh mozzarella is good for the job, too."

"Cheesecake? Are you seriously telling me unicorns run on chicken and cheesecake?"

"Unicorn biology is fairly unique. Eat chicken and cheese as a human for several weeks, with evening stints as a unicorn, and several weeks down the road, the chicken and the cheese become diamonds. I blame humanity's fascination with cheese and shitty jokes about chickens crossing the street, personally."

"An interesting theory. But if we wanted to prep you to be a target, we'd need two to three weeks for you to be in your prime for being grabbed?"

"Approximately."

"And if you were to streamline your diet, how much would your diamonds be valued at?"

"An amount I will never reveal to a dragon, as I don't want to be the next item to be hoarded," I replied, raising a brow.

"I will not claim you as part of my hoard as a result of the value."

"My last chicken and cheese bender, which was two and a half weeks of living hell plus a stint with salmonella poisoning, was valued at a little over fifty million dollars."

"Excuse me. I need to go to my office and cry now," he said, rising from his seat. "I am concerned this killer will try to grab another unicorn and leave more dead weight hanging around for us to find."

"I'll inquire where my mother has been getting her chicken and cheese from and haunt those roosts, but I'll probably want to ditch the badge and the uniform when on those outings."

"And the Black Wing. I'll be back with a tracker for you to install on your bridle and saddle. You find out where to get your hits of chicken and cheese for the next few weeks and gather some intel off the streets. Somehow, the culprit knew enough to hunt for unicorns eating the right diet.

Have her show you her haunts—and make sure the local unicorns know you're eating the appropriate diet."

"Shouldn't we be trying to find this stuff out through financial reports rather than hanging me out to dry?"

The captain snorted and waved his hand. "I've been on the force long enough to recognize this might be a hell of a lot more successful *and* faster. I want this case solved and the killer off the streets, and I want it solved *now*."

"I am protesting," I muttered.

"Just protest quietly, preferably alone and to yourself. Unless you want everyone knowing your dirty little secret?"

I waved my fist at the opal dragon, who laughed at me and left my office, closing the door behind him.

FIFTEEN

"Are we in mass murderer or serial killer territory?"

TUESDAY, APRIL 10, 2057
WAREHOUSE ROW, PRECINCT 153
CAULDRON CITY, NEBRASKA.

THANKS TO A CALL reporting yet another incident in Warehouse Row, I went with Hardy to investigate. Hardy's partner stayed at the station to help handle questioning some distant connections to the victims. I'd spent most of my morning reviewing the interview tapes, which involved my fellow detectives uncovering that nobody knew anything.

While he handled the driving, I made use of the cruiser's laptop to check into the frequency of incidents at Warehouse Row. At an average of one a day, I questioned everything I thought I'd known about patrolling the area. On second thought, we could patrol and not notice anything going on inside the building.

"You look grumpy," Hardy stated in a neutral tone.

"I am grumpy. I don't want any more bodies added to

my current pile of bodies. Do you know what I'm expecting?"

"More bodies."

"Precisely. I'm expecting more bodies. If we find more bodies, we'll be headed home at an offensively late hour." I hesitated before adding, "We could just call forensics right away and run once they arrive. We could call in a patrol pair while we flee, leaving them to deal with this."

The black dragon chuckled. "That is a valid tactic, but I would call in forensics, wait for them to arrive, and then do a sweep for evidence while they're present so we don't ruin anything. Then we flee. They'll gather everything we miss, and they'll be happy we didn't mess up their crime scene. We'd still call in a patrol, but only to keep an eye on the area while the forensics team works."

I eyed him. "Can we get away with that?"

"Jace, they want us out as bad as we want to be out. Our job is to evaluate the evidence and find where to get more evidence. Their job is to make sure our evidence is admissible in court. If we let them do their job, then we get more and better admissible evidence. It's a partnership. They might tolerate you around, because you stayed out of the way and learned at your first stint here. But your time is better spent letting them do their job and going back to the station to do yours."

I could work with that. "Do questioning sessions often result in so little information?" I asked.

"Those sessions basically confirmed your one theory is sound. The perp picked people that wouldn't be missed, not by anybody. More importantly, they picked targets with a list of people who might want them dead, too. The questioning sessions will become more intense as we weed out those who would have motive to make one or more of the vics disappear. The perp's primary mistake was killing readily identified people. They're relying on people hating these criminals enough to hamper or stop the investigation. In reality, we have a killer capable of taking out violent criminals, which we don't want on our streets. Sure, some of us might agree with what this bastard is doing, but none of us can afford to let this killer go." Hardy shrugged. "This criminal isn't precisely stupid so far, but you'll learn quickly enough how many are absolutely lacking in sense, common or otherwise."

"Are we in mass murderer or serial killer territory?"

"It depends on a lot of factors," Hardy admitted, parking the cruiser not far from where Captain Farthan had taken me when we'd discovered my mother hung up with dead weight in the form of ten mutilated corpses. "If the bodies in here are killed the same way, we have *something*, but it might not be a serial killer or a mass murderer."

I tried to think through the other options but drew out a blank. If my professors at Yale learned I'd forgotten half of what they'd tried to teach me, they'd hang me up to dry. If they ever learned my species, they'd feed me chicken and cheese first and run with the money. "I don't get it."

"Organ theft leading to death would be classified as standard murder. It's just a case of multiple counts. Mass murder tends to require the victims dying at the same time rather than at intervals. Like a shooting at a bar. Serial killers have a different style and motive. We may be looking more at organ theft leading to death, so standard murders, except the killer is racking up the body count—and hoping we'll look the other way because of who the victims are. It's an important distinction because it changes the nature of the investigation."

I closed the work laptop, turned my head, and banged my head into the window. "Now I feel stupid. That's obvious."

"You're learning. If it makes you feel better, we get district attorneys who fail to clue in on the distinction, too. Most think of it as serial killer versus mass murderer, forgetting multiple counts of murder of any degree or manslaughter exist. It's a knee-jerk reaction, because those are the types of slayings that tend to make headlines. A serial killer sounds more impressive than an organ thief with twenty counts of murder."

"Honestly, I'd be more curious about the organ thief. It's different." I hesitated. "And I can understand why they'd do it, too."

When desperate, people were capable of doing terrible things to each other—including sacrifice a stranger's life—for someone they loved.

Hardy nodded. "I get it. Organ donors have become rare as have circumstances allowing organ donation, which means there are fewer organs for those who need them, so people get desperate and use the black market to get organs. Organ theft has been on the rise globally, but it's something a lot of people don't talk about."

Sometimes, society made me question everything I knew about what it meant to be human—or at least acting like one. I understood the bitter truth; I'd been born with a hefty number of advantages over non-shifting humans. I'd grown up with security; with a little chicken and cheese and some patience, I would never have to worry about money. If money did, for some reason I couldn't fathom, become an issue, I could live off the land without shifting back to human. Grass, bark, and other vegetation ranked low on my list of favorite foods, but I could survive without help from anyone. Non-shifting humans came dead last in terms of survivability and prospects, although most races valued them for their versatility and persistence. Dragons adored the plainest of humans, and ones like the Black Dragon of New York went out of the way to bring them into their family lines. "You think they would."

Hardy shrugged. "Magic and medicine have come a long way, and because of it, there are fewer people dying of injuries, thus fewer people donating organs after death. This is something we've been aware of for a while—and we've all had to deal with a few cases dealing with organ theft leading to death."

"How long had you been in the force before dealing with your first organ theft case?"

"Ten years. Dragons tend to promote slower, so I was still with the newbies on the first floor when I accompanied a pair of detectives on the case. That was when I got bumped up to the second floor. You made working the lower floors fun, so I dug my heels in when it was time for my promotion to detective."

"Weren't you a detective when I graduated from the academy?"

Hardy snickered, got out of his cruiser, and gestured for me to hurry it up. "I'd been so wet behind the ears then that the captain sent me back to preschool for two weeks after I flubbed my first case. Then he made me stick around on the second floor until I grew up a little. I'm fairly young for the force. Usually, the academy doesn't take dragons until seventy and they have good flight experience. I do tend to be tossed with the more senior detectives because I have connections that can help with investigations."

That explained a lot. I got out of the cruiser, checked over my weapon, shoved the laptop under the seat, and questioned why my friend had become so talkative. "I can't help but notice you're a lot chattier about your experience in the force today than normal."

"I didn't want to scare you off. This stuff washes out a lot of people, and since you handled the start of the case, you can handle the rest. We try not to drive people out of the force, and those who need to be eased in get more training, like Yvon."

I raised a brow, still amazed our fellow cop had licked wet paint. "Since you're being so chatty, care to explain why we only have six female detectives? And while we're at it, why are all our support staff women?"

"Dragons are insane," Hardy informed me.

"While true, I don't see what it has to do with our odd staffing."

"Twenty years ago, Captain Farthan got into a dispute with Captain Dupont. The commissioner declared Dupont would have six men working the streets at her station and the women would rule that roost, and Captain Farthan would get six women while men ruled our roost. It's been working so well that it's stayed even after the period ended. The rest of the stations in our precinct are staffed normally."

"But *why*?"

"Captain Farthan opened his idiotic mouth and claimed a station of exclusive women couldn't handle the streets. Captain Dupont disagreed and said all us men did was make a mess of things. The commissioner demanded that all stations have at least one pair of the opposite gender on shift at all times. The stations were also required to send cops back and forth as needed. Then they did a street test to see which one of them was correct. It turned out gender makes zero difference on the general effectiveness of police officers. And we've been doing it for so long that we have a friendly rivalry—and several of our cops have married several of their cops, and thus everyone lives happily ever after."

"You have got to be kidding me."

"You know that crabby red dragon who works in accounting?" Hardy asked.

I raised a brow. "Who doesn't know the crabby red in accounting? Do you know what he does if you don't have his receipts in perfect order?"

"Beyond blowing steam out his nose because he can't light us on fire? He's married to a detective, and according to the station gossips, they have a betting pool on who will marry who between the two stations."

With so many dragons working in law enforcement, such things were inevitable. "How is that going for them? Most of us are single."

"Most of them are single, too."

I gave up attempting to make sense of it. "I think I'd rather add more bodies to my pile. Let's get to work before this gives me a migraine."

"Good call."

Tuesday, April 10, 2057

Warehouse Row, Precinct 153
Cauldron City, Nebraska.

INSTEAD OF A UNICORN, the dead weight held up a cage containing a pair of infant falcon griffons and a red unicorn foal. All three were muzzled, bound worse than a calf at a rodeo, and couldn't have been left unattended for long. Three bodies, stripped nude, showed the same evidence of damage as the last batch, and they hadn't been dead for long. I took a long look at the cage, cursed, and eyed the assembly. "This is not good."

"That is an understatement. I'll call it in and get a rope. Think you can get a line on that cage? It's a miracle those griffons can breathe bound like that."

"I can get a line on them, and with that little weight, I can get them down easily enough. Call for Dr. Erik and have him phone my landlord. Ask if there are any missing adult reds in the area. They obviously don't expect a red foal to produce stones." I followed Hardy out, took the rope and grapple from the trunk, and began the process of setting up the line. While my hands worked the knots, I considered the distressed younglings.

Kidnapping my mother made sense; she had produced a fortune of diamonds. Outside of the illegal markets, where anything or anyone might be sold, the griffons and foal would bring hell down on the head of the killer.

The killer had done the equivalent of suicide. Once word spread a foal had been targeted, every unicorn in the city would join the hunt. With two griffon chicks also stolen from their nest? I would race time, not against the killer hunting for their next victims, but against most shifters in the city out for blood. If the unicorns got a hold of the killer, there'd be nothing left by the time they finished—and justice would not be served, not in a conventional sense. If the griffons got a hold of the kidnapper, the poor bastard would be a long time dying before they stopped playing with their living, screaming toy.

Two minutes later, determined to make sure none of the little ones suffocated, I hauled the cage down, waiting long enough for Hardy to take over the line as a dragon. I started with the griffons, as the muzzles came dangerously close to their nares. Once I got the muzzles off, the babies shrieked for their parents, and they panted. I took a moment to scratch both between their eyes, something they found to be comforting. To my relief, both quieted, buying me the time needed to work the muzzle off the foal.

While the griffons had been secured, the culprit had put a little more work into binding the foal. A brief check informed me she was a filly, and judging from her size and development, she was no older than six or eight months old.

Fuckers.

Once I had the muzzles off, I picked the babies up and removed them from the cage so I had more room to work. As the filly would be easier to contain, I started with her, whipping up a rope halter to make sure she wouldn't run off on me.

She wouldn't start blinking for a few more years. While she couldn't blink, she did her best to escape, pulling on the line, which I'd tied to my wrist to keep her from staging an escape.

"Well, the foal is lively."

At roughly forty pounds, she put a great deal of pressure on my arm, but I kept her contained while I worked with the griffons. "She's a filly. She should be all right. She hasn't been without care for long, although she's young enough she probably can't shift without her parents giving her a nudge." I had no memory of being her age, but my parents had told me they made me practice shapeshifting even through infancy. It gave them a break from shitty diapers while also giving me time in my natural form.

I had no reason to believe the filly's parents were any different from mine.

"Why isn't she just darting off now that her hooves are on the ground?"

Damn it. I couldn't justify ignoring Hardy's question, and it would be a matter of time before the black dragon realized why I knew so much about unicorns. Knowing him, once he learned, he'd escort my shaggy pony ass to general holding and yell at me for hours for ruining his belief I was a very interesting regular, run of the mill human. "She's a baby, Hardy. A literal baby."

"Fuck."

No kidding. "Get an ambulance here for them. The griffons can't be older than a few months, too. If their parents show up and we don't have medical staff here, we're gonna need medical staff."

"Dr. Erik is on the way. One of my cousins is flying him."

That would help, although the dragon would have to fly several miles to reach us. Unlike the filly, who wanted to leave and run on home, likely without any idea of where to go, the griffons went for the closest source of comfort: me.

One day, I might understand why griffons liked me so damned much. I soothed them both, resigned myself to the fact I would need to hold the feathered babies until help arrived. Once they settled on my lap and chirped rather than whined and hissed, I began the tedious process of checking their stubby, underdeveloped wings for signs of damage.

Fortunately, their captor had taken care with binding them, and beyond a single broken baby feather, they'd emerged unscathed.

The baby feather would molt out soon enough without causing any lasting harm.

Once the filly realized she wouldn't be escaping me and her fellow prisoners had accepted me as a safe haven, she gave up her efforts to flee and wobbled closer, making distressed sounds and blowing air.

"Come here, baby girl," I whispered, holding out my arm so she could tuck herself in to my side. It took some coaxing, but she caved, pressed against me, and trembled. I cooed to her, and I guided her nose to mine, breathing on her until she clued in to breathe in my scent.

Her ears pricked forward.

I took turns stroking the babies, making sure I could reach my firearm if anyone showed up and tried to take the little ones from me.

They'd leave in a body bag, and if the firearm didn't render immediate results, my co-workers would become enlightened on my species along with enduring a demonstration on what an infuriated unicorn could do to someone.

Within ten minutes, Dr. Erik arrived with one of Alicia's sisters and her grandfather, and both squeezed into the warehouse as dragons. The black unicorn crouched beside me and checked the filly over first.

"Do you know her?"

"I do. She was taken this morning out of Precinct 184, some six or so hours ago. Her parents were shot with poisoned darts. I don't think the shooter realized they had a foal around. Witnesses state he didn't get out of the vehicle, a gray van, until spotting her. Then he just grabbed her by the head, dragged her inside, and drove off." Erik cursed, grabbed his phone, and handed it to me. "Call my daughter, tell her to get her ass to the hospital, and get a status report on her parents."

"What sort of poisoned dart?"

"The same shit they hit the black dragons with."

Both of the black dragons snorted, and smoke coiled from their nostrils. I glared at both of them. "Don't you wreck any of my evidence. If you can't stand there without messing up my evidence, go to my apartment and check in on Alicia."

The dragons exchanged looks, and the Black Dragon of New York let out a low growl. "Make sure your sister eats, and if she's up for it, go get her nails painted, offer a haircut, and do anything she wants. Just don't let her find out they targeted children. There have been sufficient murders for one day. No hostile takeovers of the city. I have to draw a line at taking over the city in any fashion. I've already decided I'm taking it over. I need to rule over the cops."

Alicia's sister bobbed her head, bumped noses with Hardy, and fled the warehouse.

"Grandpappy, we're not available for you to hoard. Could you please stop for ten minutes?"

"I'd offer better pay," the Black Dragon of New York replied.

Even Hardy had a hard time complaining about better pay, and the dragons settled into glaring at each other.

Rather than call Erik's daughter, I sent a text, informed her the one black dragon with me wasn't aware I sported hooves and a horn and asked her to get in touch with the griffons to see if their parents could be identified. Once done with that task, I dug through my pockets for my new work phone, which had been given to me because of its advanced camera features and ability to text evidence to the captain. I took pictures of the filly and griffons, sent them over, and informed them the filly's parents had been poisoned with the same toxin.

Twenty seconds later, my phone rang. The filly whinnied and shoved her head against me, and I did my best to soothe her.

Two full sets of baby griffon claws dug into my leg.

In a pained voice, I answered, "Smithson."

"You have got to be fucking kidding me. Also, what's wrong?"

"The griffons were startled by the phone, so my legs have been punctured by tiny claws. I'll be fine. Dr. Erik is here checking over the little ones. His daughter is finding out the status of the filly's parents, and we're trying to locate the parents of the griffons. This time, there are three corpses, and the killer didn't bother with clothing them to hide the mutilation. Hardy already called for forensics. How do you want me to handle the babies?"

"I'll send another pair to help with the forensics work, call in one of our social workers to help make certain the little ones are appropriately cared for until we find their families, and play it by ear. The babies are healthy?"

"They seem to be healthy."

"That's something. I'll make sure forensics knows I want every pit of dust in that warehouse tested. Same rig as the last time?"

"A cage to hold the little ones instead of a sling, but he

used the same assembly. We have witnesses this go around and a description of a van."

"Excellent. That might finally get us making good progress. Who is with you?"

"Hardy, his grandfather, and Dr. Erik," I reported.

"Grant showed up?"

"He was being seen when we called about having the babies checked."

"If he pukes on my evidence, I'm drowning him in the lake," the captain growled. "And you can tell him that."

"Mr. Grimstone, I've been asked to formally notify you that should you expel anything or do anything that wrecks the evidence, Captain Farthan is going to drown you in the lake," I relayed.

The old black dragon chuckled. "I'll be fine. Erik drugged me to keep the symptoms at bay, and he thinks I'll be back to normal tomorrow. We dragons have robust digestive systems—and the only reason I'm sick is because my stomach is still crabby from that poison."

I informed my captain the black dragon would behave before saying, "How do you want to handle the jurisdiction issue? The filly was kidnapped in Precinct 184."

"I'll take care of it. You game to handle dual investigations? If not, I'll give the kidnapping portion over to Hardy and Dowdren. And it's no black mark against you if you don't want to tackle both."

"They're related, and it makes more sense if one person is working everything. There's obviously a reason why they're doing this, and we need to figure out what that reason is. I won't say no to having help, though."

"Good. Tell Hardy that he's your bitch for the case, and that he's to get Dowdren on the move. I'll warn 184 that he'll be on the way, that we've recovered the filly, and we'll end up with primary jurisdiction." He hung up, and I sighed.

Once Captain Farthan decided we were getting jurisdiction on something, he typically got it. While the opal dragons didn't control as much of Cauldron City compared to other colors, the precincts they monitored tended to have higher solve rates.

Opals got stubborn, and once an opal got stubborn, nothing dissuaded them.

"That doesn't sound promising," Hardy said, considering me through narrowed eyes.

"You're my bitch for this case, and you need to get Dowdren to head to Precinct 184 to talk to the cops about the filly's kidnapping. He's claiming jurisdiction, and the kidnappings are being grouped with the dead weight cases."

"Logical and centralizes the investigation, so that works. Our current cases are mostly cold, and what isn't cold we're waiting for labs and fingerprints on, so it's good timing. I'll get Dowdren on the move. Now you know why detectives all get their own cruiser, so we can do this."

"Make sure he takes someone or a pair and an extra with him. He might need the backup to help control the unicorns and griffons once word spreads about this. It's one thing to snatch a grown mare, but to take a filly? They're going to show you the business end of their horns, and it won't be pretty. And don't ask about griffon claws."

"I don't have to ask. I've had a few cases where idiots too stupid to live tried to sell a griffon hatchling. We needed shovels to pick up what was left of them."

That I could believe. "See if you can get some blues in to referee the reds. That *might* stop the bloodshed before it starts." I glanced at the filly, who Dr. Erik continued to check. Her antics, which involved bouncing around, slowed the examination. He'd wisely left my temporary halter in place, which kept her from running around the entire warehouse unchecked. "Maybe, if we're exceptionally lucky."

"It'd definitely be safer for this nitwit if we arrested him and tossed him in prison, that's for sure."

"And if the unicorns or griffons kill him before we can get him, we might not be able to find out who is after the organs and why." I resisted the urge to curse, taking several deep breaths to calm my temper. "We had nothing for the first portion of the case. Why blow what might have been the perfect crime?"

"That is a very good question. I propose we find out." Hardy turned his attention to his grandfather. "Think you can protect us from a bunch of angry griffons?"

"I know I can."

"Without eating them."

The old dragon's chuckle rumbled in his chest. "I can manage. It will be easier if I can convince the little ones to trust me. Even griffons think twice about taking on an elderly black."

I snorted at his comment. "Among dragons, elderly means more likely to play with their food before eating it, like a cat but worse. Come try to make friends with the griffons. Their claws can't tear through your scales, and I'd rather check the holes in my legs before I might do something unfortunate. Like bleed to death."

"I'm sure you'll be fine."

SIXTEEN

I hated when history repeated itself.

Tuesday, April 10, 2057
Hospital Quarter, Precinct 153
Cauldron City, Nebraska.

THANKS TO A GRIFFON claw a little too close to a rather important artery for Dr. Erik's comfort, I earned yet another trip to the hospital. Upon arrival, a pair of irritated unicorns, one red and the other green, spent thirty minutes reminding me why it was a bad idea to put baby predators on my lap. I accepted the scolding with good grace, and once Hardy was out of sight and being distracted by his grandfather, I offered to handle the work to patch myself up. It took an offer of allowed criticism and more scolding to win their cooperation.

An hour later, they released me back to the wilds with a clean bill of health and yet another reminder to be more careful around beings with claws and wings. The ER entrance reminded me of a zoo, and a pair of wobbly red unicorns nuzzled their foal. An entire herd of black unicorns, all in human form, monitored the pair.

One griffon, in even worse shape than the unicorns, curled around the hatchlings while even more black unicorns attended to her.

The Black Dragon of New York, in human form, strode over and clapped my shoulder. "They're giving the male griffon a fifty-fifty chance of survival at this point. The reds refused to settle upon finding out you'd found their filly, so they were brought over by ambulance. The griffons were already here. Erik suggested you try to help the male. He's already in the operation room, and he could use the help with the tissue damage. Everyone else is wiped out, and they're afraid they'll lose the next patients to come in inflicted with this damned poison."

"Who do I talk to about going to help?"

He pointed at a nurse observing the female griffon, and I headed to her, introduced myself, and volunteered to work with the father. She sent me to the back, giving directions whispered in my ear to transform so I could work more efficiently.

I hated when history repeated itself, and I could only hope we could make the difference for the griffon.

Five minutes later, sporting a fur coat, hooves, and a horn, I picked my way through the crowded operating room. That they treated the griffon in his natural form and struggled to keep him alive worried me. An exhausted Dr. Erik waved me over and gestured to the griffon's midsection. "This is way over your pay grade, colt, but he's one mass hemorrhage at this point, and if we don't get some of these holes plugged, we'll lose him. I can only work so fast and everyone else is too wiped out to do the work. You're the only white I've got with any experience at all doing this sort of healing. And you only have it because of the black dragons. The other colors tried, but they can't touch this damage. They're describing it as though they're bouncing off whatever the hell this poison is doing. You don't bounce. I don't bounce, either, but my working isn't as good at this as yours is."

"Mine's better? I don't understand."

"Trust me, we don't either. The other whites are bouncing, too."

Fuck. "And you're not?"

"Barely."

"Is it different from the previous poisoning?"

"No. This has just metabolized. We got to the black dragons faster, and they're naturally more resilient. The unicorns might recover without intervention. Their bleeding started healing naturally. The female griffon did better; she metabolized it slower. He wasn't as lucky. Check his head first, then work your way down. I'm addressing the most critical bleeding, but it's like someone figured out how to create a poison that mimics Ebola. In good news, such as it is, it's only internal. Well, so far."

Great. The last thing we needed was a bunch of people falling over dead from internal bleeding. With a dying griffon to worry about, I cast my work worries aside, moved to the griffon's head, and touched my nose to his beak, closing my eyes so I could concentrate. A few warm spots in his brain worried me, and I began the slow and tedious process of cooling the hot spots down to match the uninjured sections. Once close enough, I worked my way to his neck, which burned from a mix of damage from the tube they'd shoved down his throat and something in the throat tissues. It reminded me of pond scum, clinging to him. I understood what Erik meant by bouncing, as the scummy feeling resisted my efforts to cool it down and bring relief.

I snorted, and rather than attempt to continue cooling, I applied a soothing heat, which helped to break down the foul substance. Cooling then worked.

Residue remained, but I found I could shove it along the tube to his beak and expel it onto the table.

I opened my eyes and regarded a dark green, oily substance on the stainless surface. "Dr. Erik?"

The black unicorn came over, wrinkled his nose, and said, "What in fucking hell is *that*?"

"It was all in his throat. Cooling didn't work, so I warmed it up, then it came off and I could push it out."

"Not a tactic I would try, but that's because I'm classically trained, and you are not. Think you can repeat that in his stomach?"

"Maybe if we can take the tube out?"

"Once that tube is gone, we have ten minutes, and that's it. That's the limit we can keep him alive without it," he warned. "His lungs are in bad shape. We might be able to take the tube in and out if necessary, though."

"What temperature should his lungs be?"

Erik looked over the griffon's body, then he pressed his hand to the feathered and furred shoulder. "This temperature. If you can get his lungs functional, he has a chance."

So much for fifty-fifty. I pressed my nose to the griffon to get a feel for it, and once I had a good sense of what I was supposed to do, I went in search of hot spots where I thought the griffon's lungs should be. Then, bracing for the reality of fighting death in a war I had no business waging in the first place, I dove in.

Wednesday, April 11, 2057
Hospital Quarter, Precinct 153
Cauldron City, Nebraska.

TWELVE HOURS and sixteen minutes after stepping into the operating room, a haggard Dr. Erik announced we'd done everything we could.

The griffon would live or die, and we had nothing left to give him. I observed, tense while the nurses, fresh from a shift change, eased the tube out of his throat. Every gaze focused on the monitoring equipment as the life support system went offline, leaving the poisoning victim to breathe on his own.

While his vitals changed, his heart continued to beat, his lungs labored but did their job, and we sighed our relief.

I had one last job to do, which involved easing the discomfort from the tube that had kept him holding on while Erik handled the brunt of the work and I'd helped push out a bucket worth of the oily substance, which someone had taken off to be examined in a lab.

After twelve hours of continuous practice, I soothed the inflamed tissues in two minutes flat, although the effort sapped the little energy I had left. "What's next?"

One by one, the staff changed shifts, with Dr. Erik and I keeping a close eye on the griffon's vitals. Within twenty minutes, the fresh crew would take him into a recovery room to monitor, freeing the operating room for somebody else.

"For you, nothing. One of the staff will give your coat a

good cleaning, make sure you're detoxed, get you something to drink, and draw a blood sample to make sure you weren't contaminated. It'll take twenty minutes to check the blood sample, but you're cleared to go home after that. Don't transform until you're home, at your bed, and can flop into bed without having to do anything."

"You are aware I have a woman staying at my apartment, right?"

"Ask her nicely to not peek." Dr. Erik snickered at me. "Will she resist? Probably not, Mr. Hung Like a Horse." Damn it. While the nurses and other doctors laughed, I snapped my teeth at the black unicorn. Rather than be properly cowed, he petted my nose. "Oh, should I have called you Mr. Perpetual Motion Machine instead?"

"What did I do to deserve this?" I complained.

"You did my job better than I did, and my professional pride is offended. And I can't even demand you change job fields, because you do an important job. Please apprehend the asshole behind this quickly. If we get many more of these cases, we will lose the patients on the table, and there won't be anything we can do about it. You won't be able to help with that sort of work again for at least a week, and I'm going to have to explain to your boss why you might not be available tomorrow."

"Come on, colt," one of the nurses said, patting my shoulder. "I'll take care of getting your coat cleaned and combed out. Don't you worry about that mean old black stallion. You did good work. I'll even plait your mane and tail and make you beautiful for the ladies."

"He has a black dragoness over at his place," Dr. Erik stated. "If you do all that work making him pretty, maybe we won't have to worry about him as much."

"It is much easier to romance the dragons when they're aware of how pretty we are," the nurse agreed. "And you're a pretty little colt. You're starting to get leggy, and you're losing some of that shaggy pony look. In a year or two, and you'll be prancing around in parade gear showing off your manliness."

I flicked an ear back, wondering how much of her commentary was her yanking on my chain versus serious. Unicorns tended to hit up other cities to find a single unicorn, often of the same color. "Am I supposed to be romancing a dragoness now?"

"Yes," everyone chorused.

Jackasses, all of them. I snorted, lifted my head, and attempted to mimic my mother's lethal glare.

Dr. Erik snickered, came around, and patted my shoulder. "That was an excellent attempt at the stink eye, but that isn't going to work on us, colt. Go get prettied up for your guest. Annabella, I'm sure we can find some black ribbon around here somewhere. We can entertain ourselves with the colt while we wait to make sure the patient gets settled and we don't need to do more work."

As I'd get in the way, I plodded out of the operating room, and once in the hallway, I resisted the urge to shake my coat out, which would splatter blood and other fluids everywhere. In good news for the cleaning staff, everything had dried into my coat.

I didn't envy Annabella or anyone else who helped restore me to a pristine state.

At the end of the hallway, a rather miffed Captain Farthan accompanied Hardy and his grandfather. As I refused to be scolded, I bared my teeth and flattened my ears at the dragons, and then I stomped and blew air. My defiance earned me a thump on the shoulder from Dr. Erik, and he grabbed hold of my mane and tugged.

"Behave."

As snapping my teeth at the stallion would earn me a living hell, I settled with a few more snorts and another defiant stomp of my hoof.

"Don't mind the colt. He's grouchy, needs a bath, dinner, and some quiet time," Dr. Erik said. "We all do."

"How is the patient?" Captain Farthan asked, coming closer and looking me over nose to tail. "Judging from appearances, things have not gone well."

"He should survive. It was touchy for a while there, but between the two of us, we were able to keep ahead of the hemorrhaging. The colt here has a knack for reversing that sort of tissue damage. Since he isn't formally trained, he doesn't come bundled with preconceived ideas of how to approach problems. So, while most of us were bouncing off the damage, he was just nosing his way through it and figuring out how to work around the poison. Once the toxin metabolizes, it's difficult to address. The key is getting to the patients before they start metabolizing the poison. Once it spreads beyond the stomach, it gets into the bloodstream and attacks everything. I suspect there's a magical component at play. We have samples to test and study, but it'll take time to work with."

The captain nodded, prowled around me, and grunted. "Why is he wearing the patient?"

I huffed and cast a desperate glance at Annabella, who shooed Dr. Erik out of the way, patted my shoulder, and gestured towards the staff showers. "Unicorns work better when in physical contact, and the colt here is inexperienced, so he took a nose-on approach. There was a significant amount of discharge, which I'm going to clean up."

Dr. Erik sighed and made space for us to pass. "You can help, but understand we're tired and need to wait until we're sure we don't need to resume care on the patient."

Hardy eyed me with interest. "I'll help. This is a novelty." The young black dragon shot me a glare. "I had no idea I was sitting right next to a unicorn all this time, and I feel like I'm going to find a creative and cruel way to get revenge. But your secret is safe. Dowdren knows only because he's a telepath and will pluck it out of my head like it or not, as I will think about how I can't believe you're actually a unicorn. A unicorn!"

I read between the lines: by the end of the day, everyone in the station would know my species, but nobody would say a word unless I brought it up. Swishing my tail, I followed after Annabella, and as I passed Hardy, I kicked a hoof in his direction.

He yelped and dodged. "Hey! What did I do?"

"You don't have to do anything to get a white to try to kick you into next week when they're that tired. They're not all glitter and sunshine," Dr. Erik informed my fellow detective. "You can work your way into his good graces with the squeegee."

"With the *what*?"

"Squeegee. We use them to get water out of our coats, and shaggy little colts like Jace have a thick layer of fur. Nothing sucks more than baby fluff becoming moldy. If he molds, he'll get sick, end up in the hospital for treatments, and have to be shaved. A shaved unicorn is a grouchy unicorn—and one prone to getting sicker. Give him a few years, and he'll be a sleek beauty of a stallion."

"And that little filly? She looked like a young horse filly —not a pony."

"That's the starter stage for unicorns. We resemble horse fillies. As young children, they grow to be spunky little ponies. Then you have Jace here, who is a colt about to grow out to be a proper stallion. As he ages, he'll bulk up into a draft. If you see a draft unicorn, be wary. That's a very old unicorn, and they only look big and slow."

"I'll keep that in mind." Hardy held open the door into the cleaning room with the equipment necessary to clean a unicorn. I stood in the special shower stall and made use of the scratching pole installed to help remove the gunk caked to my neck and head. "What is he doing?"

"The bristles on that are really good at working into the fur, especially on the younger unicorns. His fur is probably matted, and that isn't comfortable."

"What would happen if he shifted back to human?"

"It wouldn't end all that well," Dr. Erik admitted, grabbing one of the nozzles and turning on the shower. "See that sprayer? That's soap. After I get him wet, you get his coat so bubbly you can't see him under it. With luck, we'll get everything out first try. If not, expect a few hours of hell."

Tuesday, April 10, 2057
Lower North Lakes, Precinct 153
Cauldron City, Nebraska.

THREE HOURS after finishing in the operating room, Captain Farthan decided I would pay the piper. After earning a kick for fucking around with my hoof without permission and fiddling with the frog in a rather painful fashion, he bridled me, using a soft bit that would drive me crazy within ten minutes, and dragged me to the station, where he tossed me into general holding. To keep me from blinking away and going home, he borrowed a nasty bracelet meant to disrupt unicorns from teleporting, worn around the ankle over the hoof so it couldn't be slipped off.

In addition to preventing teleportation, it disrupted my ability to shapeshift to human.

Dr. Erik would pay for providing the bracelet.

Stomping on the concrete won me zero sympathy, and snorting, blowing air, and whinnying earned me a glare and an order to quiet down. When it became obvious I would be stuck at work but unable to do my job, I picked a corner, eased down to the ground, and took a nap.

A shoe to the shoulder woke me up, and Dr. Erik's daughter grinned down at me. "I've been given the honor of bailing you out, colt. Dad says you should be rested enough you might not try to bite or stomp on anyone who annoys you, touch your hooves in inappropriate ways, or otherwise push your buttons. While I'm sure Captain Farthan deserved to be kicked for messing with your hooves without warning you, Dad had to wrangle you so you wouldn't bite him, too."

I flattened my ears, and because I could, I rolled onto my back and pawed my hoof at her, waving the bracelet at her. Then I snorted in a promise to rain hell down on those who'd stuffed me into general holding.

Somehow, the captain would pay—and I'd make Hardy and his evil grandfather pay, too.

I wouldn't hold the ache in my hoof against Captain Farthan. Dragons struggled with controlling their curiosity, and I'd tolerated his investigation of my legs. Had he known how easily he could damage the frog and create a painful mess, he wouldn't have fiddled with my hoof with clawed hands.

As I had kicked him across the room with the intent of stomping and biting him for the stab of pain, I deserved some time in general holding. I would even forgive Hardy for his enthusiasm.

He found the idea of arresting a unicorn to be hilarious. In an effort to put me at ease, the bastards had promised they wouldn't press charges.

I would spend the next few days considering pressing charges for the damage done to my pride and dignity.

"I know, I know. The captain had no idea how sensitive that part of the hoof is, and he was poking with his claws because that's how those pesky dragons investigate magical things. Dad gave me the code to get the bracelet off, but you can't bite the captain today."

I rolled to my hooves, braced, and shook off. After being washed and dried, my fur stood every which way. Heaving a sigh, I regarded my fluffy coat, twisting my ears back. Gloria reached into her purse and pulled out a curry comb, giving my coat a test stroke.

My fur crackled with static.

She grimaced. "Okay. I see mistakes were made regarding the care of your coat. It'll settle down. Eventually."

The eventually would drive me crazy, as my fur's situation would directly translate to my hair in human form, resulting in me transforming into a demented poodle. I plodded to the open door, careful to keep from limping, heaved another sigh, and turned my saddest eyes on her.

"Okay, you can't use sad pony eyes on me, sir! Those should be registered as dangerous weapons."

"They really should be," Deputy Inspector Hagfield said, coming over. He touched my coat and got a jolt. "I had no idea unicorns were electrified."

Damned touchy-feely dragons, worse than any elephant. As biting the ringleader of our station's circus would get me tossed back into general holding, I sighed and continued to stare at Gloria.

She ignored my silent plea for mercy, although she petted my nose.

"We aren't. He's still in his baby coat, and when we blow dry the babies without using the right conditioners, the static electricity is a nightmare. And he'll shift with his hair sticking up on end, so don't be surprised if he refuses to shift until he goes home. Then he might claim he's horribly ill until he gets his hair to behave. We unicorns are perfection, but that perfection sometimes accompanies a certain amount of vanity."

The ruler of the station snickered, and he dug his fingers into my thick coat behind my ear. As he did something I liked, I turned my head in his general direction, careful not to hit him with my horn.

"And how do we care for a young unicorn? We aren't participating in child labor, are we?"

"Oh, no. He's an adult in human form, and we judge maturity in our human shape. Our unicorn forms are tied closer to our natural lifespan, although he's growing into his adult form a little ahead of the curve," Gloria informed him. "He'll probably transition to his early adult form his next shed. His head will resemble a horse's more than a pony's, and he'll lose some of that pony cuteness. Instead, you'll want to put him in parade gear and have him show off."

As the opal dragon, who kept his rank and stayed at our station by choice, would toss me in parade gear and show me off unless I did *something* to escape my fate as the latest circus attraction, I swung my head around, bumped Gloria with my nose, lifted my aching hoof, and pawed at the air to indicate she needed to pay attention to me.

She raised a brow, rolled her eyes, and positioned herself so she could trap my foreleg and get a good look at my hoof. A moment later, she cursed. "And that explains everything. Damn it, why didn't my father check your hoof?"

I shook my head and neck, as I had no idea why her father had opted to rescue the pesky opal dragon rather than check my abused hoof.

"Is something the matter?"

"Captain Farthan accidentally punctured the frog. You want to torture a unicorn? Injure this part of the frog. Our hooves aren't magically resistant, and they heal slower and take a lot of work to repair—and if we don't do it right, we make it hurt just as bad as the initial injury. I'm so sorry, Jace. I hadn't realized your frog had gotten injured. Deputy Inspector, can you get some form of antibiotic cream for me? Preferably something with a numbing agent? I'll ask Dad to send someone over to his place to treat it, and I'll get someone to bring a van so he can ride home that way. We have vans that can handle the ponies so we don't need a trailer."

The opal dragon nodded and went off to do as she asked.

"Seriously, I'm sorry, Jace. I had no idea he hadn't checked your hoof. I guess it's because the blacks have been exceptionally gentle, even when they had their claws out. He probably thought you'd gotten tickled, and he's almost as tired as you are. You did great work on that griffon. He's recovering, and he should escape without any permanent impairments, although he will be staying with us for a while. We were able to get him moved into a roost room, so he's with his mate and chicks, which will help."

I breathed a relieved sigh. "This killer made a pretty big mistake targeting a foal. Add in those chicks? The entire city is going to be hunting for him."

Deputy Inspector Hagfield returned with a tube of ointment, which he tossed to Gloria. "You're right about the city-wide hunt. Unicorns of all colors have shown up at police stations, wearing bridles and saddles, asking if they could help. We've accepted offers of transportations from them and the owl-griffons, we lost count of the falcon-griffons wanting a piece of the pie, and the eagle-griffons are so infuriated they're not talking to anybody. We're sending cops out with melons so they can bite fruit rather than trees or people."

"Melons?" I asked, snorting and turning my head towards him, flicking an ear forward.

"Mostly honey dews, as that's what the grocery store had on sale. Mini watermelons are going to be endangered for the next while, too. Anything with a thick rind and was on sale got picked up. We learned that trick the last time someone thought it was a good idea to kidnap a griffon chick. Toss the adults a melon, give them a chance to work out their nerves, and *then* approach to talk to them. Sometimes it takes two or three, but once the griffon settles down enough to chew on the rinds, it's safe to approach and get information."

Gloria adjusted her hold on my leg, squirted the ointment onto the frog of my hoof, and began poking at it. I flattened my ears, but as she worked to fix the problem, I resisted the urge to kick and bite.

"He looks ready to take a piece out of you," the deputy inspector stated in an amused tone.

"What I'm doing hurts. He won't actually kick or bite me unless I hit the nerve. And then? He won't be doing it on purpose. He'll buck, and it won't be because he wants to buck. He'll be bucking because it feels like having a hot nail through the foot."

The deputy inspector took hold of my bridle and petted my nose. "And unicorns appreciate comfort like horses?"

"We're attention whores," Gloria confirmed. "If his pappy or momma were around, they'd have him standing pretty as a picture no matter how many hot nails went into his hooves, but he's not used to having me do the work. He's also shy, so he likes keeping his dirty secrets to himself. My father usually does his hoof work. Stones *hurt*, and we're just as prone to them as horses. If anything, we're more sensitive to them. Jace has a history of picking up stones, probably because he's more inclined to go exploring while a unicorn. He doesn't shift as often as most of us, but when he does, he finds *some* way to get into trouble. Also, don't ride him."

"Don't? Why not?"

"He doesn't tend to accept riders. He did the base work to graduate from basic riding education, but he bucks his riders off within ten seconds of the end of the lesson. If they didn't get off him at the set time, he got them off. I don't know anyone who has completed an eight second ride on him. He *will* do a flip in the air and land on his back. When he says he's had enough, he's had enough."

I snorted. "I don't always flip in the air and break my saddle. Saddles are expensive."

"No, you'll blink into the nearest body of water and smash the rider into the wall. We've set how many broken bones because of you?"

I tilted my head enough I could stare at her. "Why wouldn't I? I let them ride. I just don't let them ride beyond the permitted ride time. If they didn't want to be bucked off, they would dismount properly. They're given warning."

"Why do you even bother with a bridle or saddle?" she muttered, giving my hoof another poke.

It hurt, but the pain began to ease as she worked her magic. Within a few minutes, the discomfort eased to a minor annoyance which would finish healing within a few days.

"I'm beautiful in my bridle and saddle," I informed her. "I got these when I joined the force, and I got them because they make me look great even in my pony coat."

Gloria released my leg, straightened, and laughed. "You do look stunning, it is true. And this specific bridle makes those sad pony eyes all the more effective. Take it easy on your hoof, no riders, and for fuck's sake, nobody cares about your hair."

I turned my ears back. "I care about my hair."

"That pretty little black dragoness he has waiting at home for him might care about his hair," the deputy inspector added. "It's not every day a unicorn manages to lure a dragoness out from her clan and gets her all to himself. He's the envy of every single male dragon right now."

I turned my glare to the ringmaster of the station. "That implies the single male dragons know."

"Oh, they know. Word spread like wildfire about the baby white who has worked the ER twice now, saving a dragon and a griffon from this toxin. Dr. Erik backed the rumors, saying you'd done good work despite being wet behind the ears. He spoke to me after you'd kicked Nathan. Nathan doesn't even mind he'd gotten kicked. After giving you a concussion, he thought he'd earned it. It does mean you're busted. I had to approve tossing you into general holding until your temper cooled. Oh, Gloria?"

"Sir?"

The deputy inspector pointed at my hoof. "Can you put a wrap or something on that so people have a visual to know he's got an injury? I didn't think to bring any booties with me. I'll bring in a set for him in case that's a while healing. I'd rather none of his touchy-feely co-workers end up also being kicked or bitten."

"You're into horses?" she asked, and she dug into her purse before pulling out a roll of self-adhesive bandage. As she would not leave me alone until I did what she wanted, I lifted my hoof for her. I doubted the bandage would last long, especially as she wrapped my entire hoof in it, but walking around with the equivalent of one horseshoe on would remind me to pay the injured hoof more attention than normal.

"I love them. I've a farm in the foothills. I raise quarters and paints. I also run a mustang rescue, although most of those just run free and get corralled a few times a year for health checks. They may as well be wild, but they have a fenced area so they don't go wandering off. I pay good money for the mustangs, and when the government plans to get rid of a herd, they give me a call first. So instead of shooting them from their damned helicopters, they use the helicopters to drive them my way and my clan drives them to their new home."

"Any good broncos?" I asked, unable to keep my interest out of my tone.

"Now that I know what you do in your spare time, no."

I gave him a dose of my saddest pony eyes.

He did his best, but after a minute or so, he heaved a sigh. "I'll consider testing you with one of my broncos if you do your best not to bite or kick anyone for the rest of the day."

"Only if you tell me why the Farthan dragons tend to be captains while the Hagfields tend to be in the upper ranks. And is the commissioner a dragon?"

The deputy inspector chuckled. "The commissioner is not a dragon, but he's married to an opal. He's a magicker, a rather long-lived one, much to my clan's relief. His first wife passed away, and one of my cousins fell for him. And thus, a sad and lonely Miami cop got wrangled by an opal and brought to Cauldron City, where he worked his way up the ladder and became the commissioner. His daughter is from his first marriage, and she stays in Miami because she's worried her scars will wreck his reputation."

"And the other clans are okay with a magicker bossing everyone around?"

"It's better than having a dragon bossing the other dragons around. And having an opal for a wife doesn't mean the opals get jack shit out of the deal. What do we get? A harder time of it. How dare we disappoint them?

How dare we not be demonstrably better than the other colors?" The deputy inspector laughed. "Right now, we're all about to get lined up and whipped if we don't make good progress on this case. Which means I need to get you brought up to speed and working with the other detectives. But right now? We have a whole lot of nothing beyond the sex offender registry and the violent crimes registry to work with. Good idea on comparing the various databases against the missing persons lists. We have a disturbing list of potential victims to work with now. I have a spare uniform for you in your office, and I can go find Sophie and ask her to help tame your mane. If she can't, nobody can."

Sophie, one of the six women who worked on the top floor and handled the touchiest cases along with her partner, Denice, had curly hair with a tendency to frizz at a moment's notice. I eyed the deputy inspector. "Maybe."

"Go introduce yourself to your co-workers properly. The bastards raided the nearest grocery store to get you some treats. Dr. Erik sent a list of your favorites, so you should at least get a good snack for putting up with us. The breakroom near the daycare might never be the same. If fresh coconut shavings and coconut milk is not an actual favorite, I might be tempted to teach that unicorn a thing or two."

My ears pricked forward, and I headed for the breakroom on the other side of the floor, which was located where the cadets and green cops learned the trade while the more experienced supervised them. I poked my head in, and sure enough, several coconuts had fallen prey to some of my co-workers, including a giggling Patricia, who held a knife and eyed her foe.

The rest were new recruits I hadn't worked with before, fresh from the academy and likely trying to win some favor with their supervisors while playing nice with the detectives. I'd learned that lesson early on.

Recruits who played nice with the detectives got help from the detectives when the going got tough.

Judging from the mess, the coconut had put up quite the fight. I plodded over, sidestepping bits of coconut shell. I investigated a bowl, which contained fresh coconut milk. Before I could dunk my nose in and get to work drinking the bounty, the dispatcher put down her knife, strolled over, and patted my neck.

I behaved, and I lipped at her fingers to indicate she held my favor.

"You won me so many bets," she informed me. "Last year, we betted on your species, and we had tossed in a hundred a pop on all the floors over what you might be, and I'd been the one to say you were obviously a unicorn among men. You got dumped by a super model for being too damned nice." She reached over, grabbed a chunk of coconut, and held it out for me to eat. "Nobody else thought anyone with your general temper could possibly be a unicorn."

I plucked my prize out of her hand and settled in for the serious business of enjoying my treat. After I took my time to enjoy and swallowed, I asked, "My temper?"

"Steadfast, tolerant, and unflappable. Most of us have seen enough unicorns to understand unexpected horn honking sends them blinking off, spooked and possibly never to be seen again."

Right. My species had cultivated being flighty except for the medical staff on duty, who couldn't be fazed by something as minor as a horn being honked. "I am dignified."

She laughed and fed me another piece of coconut

before picking up the bowl and holding it out for me to drink from. "So it seems. You've also been very busy. Good work with the griffon. Better work for kicking the captain. We're all sure he did *something* to deserve it."

"Yeah, he did," Gloria announced from the doorway. "He poked a hole in Jace's hoof, and it'll be an uncomfortable week healing. Expect a limp for the next few days in any form. If you could spread the word he's to do as much of his job seated as he can for at least two days, I'd appreciate it."

"Sure, I can do that. Is it really okay to feed him all this coconut?"

"Just wait until you start feeding him the pineapples and mangoes. Just don't let anyone sneak a ride on his back. He bucks, and he'll hurt his hoof more if he gets too energetic."

"10-4."

As I had no reason to contribute to the conversation, I went to work drinking my coconut milk and devouring the shredded flesh so I could get to the pineapple and mango portion of my day. Perhaps the circumstances leading to being ousted at work sucked, but I would cope.

I always did.

SEVENTEEN

"Warning noted and respected."

WEDNESDAY, APRIL 12, 2057
UPPER NORTH LAKE, PRECINCT 153
CAULDRON CITY, NEBRASKA.

ONE COCONUT, pineapple, and mango binge later, Captain Farthan concocted several good threats to get me to shift back to human. Sophie took pity on me, and with the help of some products, a comb, and an hour, she tamed my hair before sending me home. As I'd come in well after midnight, I beelined for my couch, flopped onto it, and conked out, leaving the tagalong co-workers to see themselves out after confirming I made it inside without incident.

I woke to a slender finger poking my cheek. "Jace?"

Right. I had a dragoness living in my apartment with me, and if I didn't feed her, she might try to feed me. Before I could say something stupid, my phone rang. I grunted and reached out for the device.

Alicia laughed and put it in my hand. After a bleary-eyed battle, I figured out how to answer and put the damned thing near my ear. "What?"

"It's upside down," the black dragoness informed me.

Damn it. I flipped the phone. "What?"

Captain Farthan laughed at me. "I would have let you sleep in a little longer, but we need you to come be the brains of our operation for a while. We have evidence."

Maybe he had evidence, but I had a cracked pot theory, and if it bought me five more minutes of sleep, I'd fling it out with zero care of the consequences. "The killer was hired, and the hiring entity wants every unicorn and griffon in the city to destroy him, thus removing the evidence chain and limiting the chances of being arrested. Cash payments because the hire is too smart to write his crimes down. The killer-turned-kidnapper is either desperate, stupid, or both—or knows nothing about unicorns or griffons and just did as told. Can I go back to bed now?"

"You can't go back to bed," he replied.

I held the phone out to Alicia, who took it. "Tell him I'm going back to bed." To make it clear I would not be moved from my couch, I grabbed the nearest object, which proved to be some papers, and shoved them over my head.

"Hello? Oh, Captain Farthan. Jace just threw papers over his head. I've been trying to get him up, but I don't know if he's going to be moving anytime soon. Where's a good place to order breakfast? I paid just enough attention to his first cooking lesson to understand I will poison us both if I try right now. It would have been better to learn that before I had poisoned my grandpappy, but at least I've learned."

There was a pause, and the black dragoness giggled. "No, he didn't even make it to the bed. He's on his couch. I tried to lure him to his bed, but all I've gotten out of him is a groan and some handwaving. No, he isn't running a temperature. He's just tired. That *could* be because someone kept him at work until after midnight. You want me to check his what?"

I snorted, and as the worrywart opal dragon wouldn't be leaving me alone until I checked my damned foot, I rolled, lifted my leg, and checked the heel of my foot, which was where the magic tended to associate frog damage when in human form. Judging from the scab, it would be raw but serviceable by the end of the day. "Sore, scabbed over, but otherwise fine. I'll be walking okay by the end of the day, probably."

She relayed my message, and a few moments later, she hung up. "A pair is coming over to pick you up in half an hour. They need you at work. Take a shower. You'll feel better. What happened to your foot?"

"Captain Farthan got a little too touchy-feely while I was a unicorn and accidentally pierced my frog. That's part of the hoof, and it's pretty sensitive. I thought my sleep-deprived suggestion was a good one, though."

"It was a good one. He praised your sleep-deprived suggestion once he was talking to me. But he still needs you at work. He did let you sleep in, though. And he's paying you for sleeping in, and he's also paying you for having been the station's evening entertainment." Alicia stole the papers off my head. "Will you be able to manage getting down the steps?"

"I will bitterly complain, but I can manage." As the dragoness wasn't letting me go back to bed, I got up, grumbled over the rumpled state of my uniform, and limped to my bedroom. I discovered my gemstone collection in their boxes decorating the dresser, and stacks of papers were piled on top of them. "Did you have fun with the collection yesterday?"

"We had a marvelous time, and I've gotten some excellent offers for the gemstone. I notified a dragon this morning that the stone was produced by the same unicorn who helped that poor griffon in the ER. It just happens the news had spread about said unicorn. And once news spread you are the unicorn who volunteered and stayed in the operating room for twelve hours, I had a bid war going between a bunch of griffons, unicorns, and dragons."

Well, shit. With a bid war going on, she might even get more than the appraisal value for the rock. "That was ruthless, cunning, and brilliant. Want to come in to work with me today? You can take over my office. You can guard me from anyone trying to get a look at me, the unicorn." I allowed my shoulders to slump. "I'd lasted so long without anyone knowing, now everyone knows."

"That depends. Can I bring the diamond with me? I should have it sold by the end of the day."

"You can even meet the buyer in the station lobby, as that's public space. Just call Captain Farthan back and tell him you're going to be a guest today. He'll let the pair coming know. He'll probably send a K9 SUV so we don't have to deal with shit seats. Most of our cruisers have backseats designed to accommodate people in cuffs."

"I will come protect you. And if you take a nap in your office, I'll make sure you can get some sleep in. I was only trying to get you up so I could feed you—and not with something I was making!" Alicia pulled her phone from her pocket. "Go take a shower and try to get yourself together. I'll make sure the captain knows I will be accompanying you. And for the record, I would never poke holes in your hooves because of curiosity."

"But you'll poke holes in my hooves for other reasons?"

"Well, if I ever have to peel information out of a unicorn, I know where to start now."

With wide eyes, I decided I needed to get on the move before she targeted my feet. "Warning noted and respected."

She laughed at me. "I'm sure I won't have any information I need to peel out of you. I have other contacts willing to talk about you in front of you and behind your back."

"Using my parents against me like that is an act of pure evil," I informed her.

"There is a time and a place for me to be good, and I've decided the only way I'm getting what I want is if I'm bad. You'll survive." She shot a wicked smirk my way. "Probably."

I fled to the bathroom while I could.

Wednesday, April 12, 2057
Upper North Lake, Precinct 153
Cauldron City, Nebraska.

I TOOK A BATH, as showering wasn't happening with my foot throbbing every time I thought about using it. Reapplying the ointment and bandaging helped a little although I still limped, taking care to keep any pressure off my heel. While I'd gotten dressed, I failed to finish my workday preparations before someone knocked at the door. Alicia let them in, and she said, "He's grooming in the bathroom. I've learned he doesn't handle life without his morning grooming very well."

For fuck's sake. I removed the toothbrush from my mouth, popped open the bathroom door, and said, "I'm brushing my teeth, not prancing in front of the mirror. This is mandatory."

I'd already handled my hair to the best of my ability, but I gave it an hour before I ran to find Sophie and beg for her help again.

Pony fluff did not surrender easily.

"Sure, sure," the black dragoness teased. "Do come in while he finishes getting ready. His foot hurts, so he's moving at a hobble, which surely slowed him down." She bounced to the bathroom and stared at my feet, which were covered in dark socks. "You did wrap your foot? And not just with a sock."

"I treated it and bandaged it," I informed her before resuming the tedious work of brushing my teeth so I wouldn't alarm my co-workers with my morning breath. As cutting corners resulted in extra dentist visits, I made them wait until my teeth passed my scrutiny before limping over to see who had come calling.

Patricia and Wynonna waved from my living room when they caught sight of me.

"The captain let you escape?"

Wynonna laughed, and she grabbed my keys, my holster, and the other work stuff I kept near the door. "Get your gun. We'll carry the rest of your kit. The new recruits are working dispatch with Janice, and Captain Farthan is listening in to see if we can work in a few extra bodies on each shift. He'd rather kill our budget with extra staff than kill his staff."

I raised a brow. "Dare I ask?"

"He's selling that pretty diamond that unicorn gave to us for some strange and unknown reason, and the sale value of said pretty diamond is enough to get a bunch of new staff in, and once we have them in, it'll be hard for the commissioner to make us get rid of them, especially when our dispatch is top-notch. But for some *strange and unknown reason*, certain detectives are getting new uniforms."

"Our dispatch is already top-notch," I replied. "I have no idea what you're talking about regarding new uniforms. I am innocent. Where is your evidence I have anything to do with new uniforms?"

"Spoken like a proper detective. You can make it down the steps, right? Because if you start oozing blood out of your shoes being stubborn, I *will* call dispatch," Wynonna warned me.

She would, too. Without hesitation or remorse. "It was a puncture wound, not a gash."

"Remember Paul with the nail?" she countered.

I wished I could forget Paul and the damned nail. Back when I'd been a fresh recruit, he'd managed to ram a nail into the bottom of his foot during a pursuit, resulting in a horrifying amount of blood gushing out. I'd been given the dubious job of elevating his foot over his head so he wouldn't bleed out, as in typical Paul fashion, he'd dislodged the offending rusty object.

He'd needed a trip to the ER and a tetanus shot. I'd needed a new uniform and therapy, as I disliked wearing the blood of people I knew.

Some things never changed.

"I don't like wearing my co-workers' blood. That it hasn't been isolated to a singular event doesn't thrill me." I grabbed my shoes, sat on my couch, and loosened the laces as much as possible, attempting to work my foot into it without causing more harm to myself. It worked, and while I winced, I managed to limp to the front door. "On the one hand, I want to make progress on this case, but on the other, I do not want to leave my office today."

"Considering I just watched you change colors putting your shoe on, I hope you don't have to leave the office." Wynonna made shooing gestures at Patricia. "Bring the SUV as close as possible. He really might perish if he has to walk on that foot long. And call dispatch and tell at them to yell at Dr. Erik."

Patricia pattered out of my apartment and headed down the steps.

"You're going to get me into trouble."

She snorted, grabbed everything from my end table, and asked, "Is that everything?"

Alicia gave me my phone, and I limped into my bedroom to retrieve my gun from my safe. "If you have my wallet, keys, and badge, I'm ready."

"I have them. Please be careful on the steps."

"I'll go first," the black dragoness offered. "I can shift and keep him from falling if he starts to tumble. Of course, he won't like getting a face full of scales, but he won't tumble down the steps. Do these manly cops always need us women to rescue them?"

"Always. You know what happens at our sister station?"

"Beyond it being a self-rescuing princess society and a heaven for independent women?"

Wynonna cackled her delight over Alicia's question.

"Oh, it's even better. The men love being rescued. They try to avoid it, but once the women swoop in to save them, they're kings of the castle for a day or two. Of course, the women will only rescue them when they're in trouble due to some heroic act, but they have a lot more fun than we do. We just get cases like Jace."

I scowled. "Hey, what did I do? I thought I was doing all right."

"You're independent," Wynonna muttered, heading down the steps.

"I don't see the problem. I don't want to bother anyone. Why is being independent a problem? Come on, Wynonna. That isn't fair."

"Confident?" Alicia guessed, joining the dispatcher outside of my apartment.

"Oh, the confidence just oozes out of him. It's absolutely disgusting, really."

Women. I would never understand them. "If we're going to do this, can I at least have a good quality, as it seems independent confidence is no longer acceptable? I thought you women liked when a man can cook and clean after himself."

Alicia snickered. "Your fluffy pony hair."

"Your sad pony eyes," Wynonna added.

Evil women. "What did I do to deserve that? Those aren't good qualities. They're a bane of my existence." The sad pony eyes often worked, but I waved goodbye to my pride and dignity every time I made use of them. With a little luck, I would grow out of the sad pony vibe and more into an elegant stallion.

Sure, elegant stallions didn't get choice bits of coconut, pineapple, or mango, but they benefited in other fashions.

As for the fluffy pony hair, I would not miss the need to recruit help to become presentable.

Wynonna turned to face me, and Alicia moved out of the way so she wouldn't obstruct the dispatcher's view. "You kicked the captain when we weren't able to watch and enjoy the show."

All right. I could understand how that would upset almost everyone in the station. "He'd just shoved his claw right up my hoof. The only reason I didn't bite him and poke holes in him is because Dr. Erik stopped me. He's lucky all I did was kick him across the room. That *hurt*."

Wynonna shook her head and clucked her tongue. "A most memorable 10-10, and nobody called it in."

"I would have won," I muttered.

That got both of them snickering, and I scowled. The instant they noticed my expression, they howled their laughter and headed down to the sidewalk. I limped after them, careful to keep a firm grip on the rail. "Come on. I could have taken him."

"According to eyewitnesses, he did land a good kick. Maybe we should credit him for that much." Wynonna shrugged before engaging me in a stare down. "Nobody who isn't also a dragon just takes on a dragon with any expectation of winning, Jace. When he transforms to his full size, he can eat you in a few bites."

"He wouldn't, but he could," Alicia said, grinning at me and waiting for me at the bottom of the steps. "The opals are a little more inclined to play fair. And Jace did have the jump on him. It *is* possible. That's better than most."

The dispatcher considered the black dragoness's words and nodded. "It's true. That *is* better than most."

I thought about transforming and giving the women a

hefty dose of my sad pony eyes. Instead, I inched down the stairs and made my way to the SUV Patricia brought up to the sidewalk.

Wynonna beat me to the vehicle and ordered me into the front seat. "We'll never hear the end of it if you don't get the prime spot. I'll take care of your lovely princess in the back."

Princess? I supposed her grandfather may as well have been dubbed a king, as he controlled New York with a black claw. "Mine?"

"Well, you did lure her into your apartment, you set rules, and the dragons have accepted your rules are law. She can't leave until you declare she's capable of feeding herself and others without risk of food poisoning," the dispatcher replied, taking her position in the seat behind me. "Honestly, we're impressed you beat the dragons at their own game."

"It is really impressive," Alicia agreed. "I think I've passed the prerequisite course. I identified it was not safe for me to attempt trying to cook this morning."

"That might count as a quiz, but I'm not sure I can say you've passed any preliminary or prerequisite courses yet. You need to understand all the basic tools of the kitchen before you have covered all the preliminaries," I informed her.

"Crap," the dragoness muttered while Patricia and Wynonna snickered.

"I'm not sure if we're looking at a two year, four year, or eight year program, but we'll find out soon enough," I teased. "Or not."

"Just give him the point," Wynonna advised. "There's just no winning that one. Jace has gone in for the kill.

Fighting back now will just do more damage to your pride. But if you want to see him strut, try to beat him. He probably has a whole chain of comebacks ready for use. Jace does not play when it comes to taking someone down."

I really didn't.

The granddaughter of the Black Dragon of New York laughed long and hard. "He got his father so badly his parents fled the city. My grandpappy doesn't even know where they went. After Jace absolutely destroyed his father, they weren't seen again. His mother left a note on her door informing any would-be thieves she knows some dragons, her son is a cop, and if anyone touches any of her stuff, they will *pay*. I don't think anyone is going to be touching her stuff."

"How did you find that out?" I asked, twisting around in my seat to better talk to the woman.

"My grandpappy sent one of my sisters over to check in on your parents. She took a picture of the note and sent it to the family chat. He was trying to get some intel on their preferred cars so he could give their beater a beating."

I snickered at the chaos the Black Dragon of New York would inevitably create. "They're luxury sedan folks when they're in town, but they're always skinflints because they don't advertise they're white unicorns. They can afford their own car."

"Ah, but it's now a matter of pride, as you haven't gone for my grandfather's hoard or his pride yet. You've taken Captain Farthan down twice now, which has riled up every dragon in the city. My grandfather's actually concerned the killer might target you next. If he targets you, the entire city is going to pitch a fit. The dragons are becoming cranky over the babies. The little red filly did him in. His paternal instincts are in overdrive, and they've targeted three babies so far." Alicia's eyes narrowed. "Grandpappy promised I can have my turn if I keep an eye on you. I'm cleared to shapeshift only for emergencies, and he wanted to make sure I'm ready for any emergencies."

Well, so much for not telling Alicia the killer had targeted kids, and I wondered what had happened since I'd last seen her grandfather. "I'd like to get this guy alive."

"That's why grandpappy asked me to gift wrap his still-living body for your arresting pleasures."

Under no circumstances could I tell my parents that the black dragons were arranging to bring in the killer specifically so I could arrest him. I struggled with the reality of the dragons dragging the killer to the brink of death and toying with him versus my enjoyment of the idea of being the arresting officer.

Patricia cackled. "He's going to need a few minutes to process that. He's positively dense when it comes to women. He's going to end up blurting a proposal. We've learned the dense men in our station end up blurting out their proposals, sometimes before even inviting the subject of his affection on a date."

I wondered who in our station had blurted a proposal, and I decided I'd go ask Hardy after I escaped from the women. "I'm smart enough to know blurting a proposal is probably not a good idea under those circumstances, but would anyone actually blame me?" I heaved a sigh. "I'm pretty sure everyone in the precinct wants to see this bastard go down. I'm concerned I'm the only one who wants to make sure he gets his day in court."

"You're going to have to work fast if you want that," Wynonna warned me. "Lethal force has already been approved if there's any indication this guy is preparing to strike again. And we're already making bets on how long it takes for her to convince you to propose—and how long she's going to run you around first."

"Do unicorns and dragons even pair up?" I asked, raising a brow. "I thought dragons tended to stick with other dragons, magickers, or non-shifters."

"They do now," Alicia informed me. "There's no dragon anywhere stupid enough to tell a Grimstone who she may or may not drag to her lair. I make allowances for the other races. They need to learn about the superiority of dragons."

Goodness. She could give a unicorn a run for their money in the ego department. I only knew one thing for certain.

It was going to be a long day.

EIGHTEEN

"The dragoness comes with me. The rest of you are horrible traitors."

Wednesday, April 12, 2057
Lower North Lakes, Precinct 153
Cauldron City, Nebraska.

CHAOS WAITED for me at work, and I regretted having come into the station. Janice, armed with a pair of crutches, intercepted me in the parking garage. I accepted the blow to my dignity in exchange for relief from the pain, thanked her, and went through the hassle of adjusting them to be the appropriate height. "Figure I'll get hazard pay for this?"

"No," everyone chorused, including Alicia.

My attempt to make use of my sad pony eyes ability while a human earned me a bunch of laughs and zero sympathy. Huffing over my failure to rein in my co-workers or the dragoness, I made use of the crutches and headed for the elevator, as I doubted I could handle going up the steps even if I wanted to. "The dragoness comes with me. The rest of you are horrible traitors."

Wynonna laughed, patted my back, and beat me to the elevator, pressing the up button. "We're just realists. The captain is feeling guilty over your foot, though, so expect some hovering. Dr. Erik should already be here, and he'll check how much damage was actually done. Alicia, you're also being seen, as the last thing we need is your grandfather razing the city. I happen to like living here."

"As I seem to be living here until I learn to cook, I agree with you. I can't promise my grandpappy won't take the city over, but he doesn't tend to destroy the places he's ruling. It's bad for business."

The thought of the old black dragon taking over another city chilled me, and I shuddered at the realization if he ruled over Cauldron City, he might concoct a hundred and one reasons to pay me a visit. As he doted on his family, I'd have to deal with him often enough. Having the keys to his Black Wing would help to make coping with the visits easier.

While waiting for the elevator, I glared at my foot, cursing how the injury would realistically sideline me from driving until confident a stab of pain wouldn't prevent me from maneuvering the vehicle safely.

"Realized you can't drive with your foot like that?" Patricia asked.

Startled, I lifted my head to stare at her, widening my eyes. "How did you know?"

"A man only looks that despondent if the love of his life left him, he has a nice car he can't drive, or the girl he wishes he could date is dating someone else. Or there's a puppy he wasn't allowed to pet, but that's universal. Who wouldn't become despondent under those circumstances?"

"I would be heartbroken for the rest of the day," Alicia

announced. "I heard there are K9s, but I'm guessing I'm not allowed to pet them."

Wynonna snickered. "You can pet them. Later in the day, when the shifts are changing, I'll run you down to the kennel and introduce you to some of the friendlier pooches. If the fuzzy little unicorn needs some quiet time to work, I can take you over to see the dogs in action. I'm sure the captain won't mind you observing. He probably won't let you be the target for a takedown, not until Dr. Erik fully clears you, but it's fun to watch."

"I'd like that."

"Consider it to be a date, then," the dispatcher replied, gracing the dragoness with a smile. "Jace gets a bit irritable if we interrupt him too much while he's trying to work, so if he starts posturing, come on down to dispatch."

Alicia narrowed her eyes. "What kind of posturing are we talking about?"

"If he's taking his shirt off, don't leave, take pictures, and enjoy the show. But if he starts huffing and puffing, flee."

"I do not huff, nor do I puff." Before I could get myself into more trouble, the elevator pinged and opened. As I couldn't fend off the door should it get ideas about when to close, the ladies herded me in first and trapped me in the corner. "Alicia can stay in my office unless I'm working on something sensitive. However, if I can get someone to fetch us lunch today, that'd be great."

"Tired of chicken?" Wynonna asked, raising a brow before pressing the button for the third floor.

Aware that the captain wanted me to fuel up on chicken and cheese, I feigned disgust over her question and replied, "Never. But today, I think I want my chicken in quesadilla format."

“I bet that chicken would make killer quesadilla filling,” Alicia muttered, her eyes still narrowed. “One of my sisters uses this thingie that she closes the lid, and after she works some time-based sorcery, she opens it, and there is a perfectly formed quesadilla within.”

While I lacked one of the grills she talked about, I’d been tempted by them more than a few times. “If someone can run to the store to pick up the right kind of grill, someone else gets the chicken, and yet someone else fetches us cheese and toppings, I could probably make those quesadillas happen.”

“On it,” Patricia announced. “I’m accepting a payment of one quesadilla to go to the store and get the grill. Wynonna? Herd dragons. One of them can get us enough chicken. Alicia, don’t let the unicorn escape. Our quesadillas are on the line.”

The dragoness saluted. “I will make certain he does not escape our clutches.”

“If you’re expecting me to cook for a bunch of people, I’m going to need more than one grill, Patricia.”

“I’ll get two, and I’ll make the captain pay for them. I’ll tell him it’s part of his penance for hurting your foot—then the second floor can have a grill in the kitchen.”

“Just get one for every floor if you’re going that route,” I replied, shaking my head at the insanity. “And tell him I’ll even make him a quesadilla if he goes along with it. Just make certain to get hot sauce—and forget to get any milk. I want to enjoy the suffering of my fellow cops.”

Wednesday, April 12, 2057
Warehouse Row, Precinct 153
Cauldron City, Nebraska.

WITHIN TWENTY MINUTES of making it to my desk, a call to dispatch resulted in Hardy and Dowdren invading my office and dragging me out to handle the incident. To prevent whining, Captain Farthan sent us out in one of the K9 SUVs. I got to share the back seat with Mamma Mia, one of the station's grumpier animals. According to her handler, she'd gotten her name on her first shift, as the man she took down had screamed the phrase before she'd gotten him to the ground and sat on him. As she was more than a little wolf, if she didn't want to move, she didn't move.

The instant I was buckled in, Mamma Mia did as she wanted, which involved cramming as much of her bulk onto my lap as possible. As she would get grumpy if I didn't convince her I loved her best, I petted her, scratched behind her ears, and praised her for being such a good wolf.

"He really is one of the brightest of us," Hardy muttered, getting comfortable behind the wheel. "Do you know what happens when I have to sit back there with her?"

"She growls at you. You're scared of her, and she knows it, so she puts you in your place with well-timed growls," I replied, grinning at how the wolf-dog took and maintained her authority. "She knows growling won't win her anything with me. She's learned if she's nice to me, she will be treated well and shown affection. It doesn't hurt I make a point of going down with a choice bone once a week to make her like me. Speaking of which, tomorrow is bone day. What's the deal with this call?"

"It's another dead weight case, but this time there aren't

any other victims other than the corpses hanging around for us to pick up. We have two larger gentlemen on one side and three smaller ones on the other to contend with. The captain wants to make sure you're present for the initial analysis. He's also fiddling around in your office while we're gone."

Damn it. "What is he doing to my poor office?"

"You're getting a digital murder board. You're going to need it to organize the data. You're also getting a standard whiteboard so you can continue to think on your board and drive us crazy with squeaky markers before you input the data. The commissioner wants this solved yesterday, and if giving you a digital murder board makes you more efficient, he'll get you three of them."

I raised a brow and continued to appease Mamma Mia, who huffed and settled on my lap to take a hard-earned nap. "That's not going to settle well with the other detectives."

"It's settling just fine, Mr. Unicorn."

Damn it. "I'm going to be ribbed forever over this, aren't I?"

"Only if you don't show up in your fur coat every now and then for our enjoyment."

Why had I wanted to be become a cop? Heaving a sigh, I asked, "What do you want, Hardy?"

"Honestly, I just want to make sure you have good intentions with Alicia."

"Seriously?" Given five more minutes, the black dragon would inflict a skull-splitting migraine upon me with zero remorse. "For starters, I'm going to make sure she has basic survival skills before she leaves. And I don't mean *her* survival, but the survival of those around her. She almost took out the Black Dragon of New York with eggs, Hardy."

"When you phrase it like that, I feel like we should all be chipping in from our hoards to pay for her stay with you."

"I'm not concerned. I have the money. I'm annoyed I'll have to move to have space for a dragoness and her hoard. She's nice company, I don't mind having a roommate, and it seems to me she needs a safe space. I'm happy to provide that." I glared at Hardy, and because I knew Dowdren would find some way to cause me trouble, I gave him a dose, too. "I'm a cop because I want to be a cop."

Hardy snorted. "That's how you end up married to a black dragon, Jace. Don't say I didn't warn you later. My grandpappy *will* kidnap you if he thinks you're trying to run away from Alicia. While he spoils all us grandkids, she's the jewel of his long life. As for you being a cop, trust me, we all know. We figured you had a side job of some sort. That the side job happens to be shitting glitter and gemstones is a little weird, but hey? If you're happy pawing through your own shit to earn money, I'm not going to stop you."

Well, that was a unique way of viewing the situation. "It's not just money, it's a filthy amount of money. I have my own hoard, and I like it as it generally is: in my possession. I did give Alicia one stone to sell so we can have our hoards under the same roof without much overlap. And honestly, I'm due to move. The books have taken over, and I refuse to unload any of my books."

"Spoken like a true dragon. I did want to warn you, however. Grandpappy *adores* Alicia."

The last thing I needed was dealing with the Black Dragon of New York hunting those who had hurt his favorite granddaughter. "Could you please suggest to the angry dragons and other beings that I would like the killer alive? I can't interview a corpse, Hardy. I know everyone's angry because of the babies, but the babies weren't hurt. Their parents? They're lucky to be alive. But if we kill this guy off, we've done the hire's work for him. The killer seems to have some morals. Outside of not really understanding how best to secure the babies, he rigged the cages so they'd be safe. That tells me he's got some strong motive to be doing this work. The organ theft lead is a strong one. He could have a wife, child, or parent in need of an organ—or he could be the one in need of an organ. But he doesn't want to hurt the babies. Had he, he wouldn't have grabbed the filly."

Everything about what we'd heard about the filly's kidnapping bothered me. From top to bottom, I got the feeling her kidnapping hadn't been planned. I frowned.

Dowdren grunted, and then to my astonishment, he said, "We did come to that conclusion this morning. You're not wrong. Can we convince the dragons, however? I just don't know. It'll take some work. Also, you should share that thought with Hardy. It's a good one."

Damned telepaths. "How long have you known I'm a unicorn, Dowdren?"

"About five minutes after you showed up at the Academy. I was helping to monitor the preschoolers, I hadn't been introduced to you yet, and you were questioning what the hell a unicorn was doing wanting to be a cop, and then becoming rather determined because you didn't pay for an education at *Yale* just to give up because the other students reminded you of alley cat riff-raff fresh off a catnip bender."

Fuck. "Thank you for not telling anyone, Dowdren. Also, why are you so chatty today? I'm pretty sure this is the most I've ever heard you say since being hired."

"Your species matters. I have some abilities that can cause problems for the unwary, and so I try not to say too much. As I didn't want to blow your status as a unicorn, one of the species immune to my abilities, I kept quiet. I'll still keep quiet around most—dragons, unicorns, and a few others are immune, but it's better to be safe than sorry."

I winced, as the prevalence of magic often resulted in inconvenient abilities cropping up from time to time. "Sorry."

"You have nothing to be sorry about. You're just not receptive to telepathy, so I can't just fling thoughts at you at my whim. Hardy's able to decide who can reach him, where you have the equivalent of a brick wall blocking telepathy. I can read you with some work, but I can't reach you. That's actually handy. Sure, your thoughts aren't private around a telepath with skill, but you're not going to get taken over."

Ah. Right. As telepaths weren't much of a threat to unicorns unless deliberately snooping, I tended to forget that they could do a lot of nasty tricks, including take someone over. "Do you have to work to hear my thoughts?"

"Yep, and it's highly irritating. I only listen in if I think something is wrong or you're holding back a juicy tidbit—like what you should tell Hardy."

"You mean about the filly's kidnapping not being planned?"

"Yes."

I shrugged, and I petted Mamma Mia, taking the time to better organize my thoughts. "That poison is definitely lethal, that much we know. The killer knows what he's doing when he's targeting the adults, but the fact he kidnapped the filly after noticing her worries me. Is the toxin meant to be contagious or spreadable with contact in the early stages?" I hadn't been contaminated, nor had the other unicorns, but we were unicorns. Handling that sort of thing was par for our course. "Could the killer be doing species testing on this toxin?"

Dowdren grunted, which I translated to mean general satisfaction with my speech.

Heaving a sigh, Hardy replied, "I just don't know. When we all got in this morning, we had a talk about it. Honestly, this is way over your pay grade, but the captain wants to see if you can shine. He's also worried you're going to be targeted."

"Because I'm a unicorn?"

"In part but mostly because news has spread on the wire that you're the unicorn that has kept the death count low. Thanks to your general descriptions of how you've been handling it, other whites have been able to do the same work—and the blacks are starting to figure it out. Even one of the greens gave it a shot and had results."

Wait. One of the *greens* had tried it?

Greens were not renowned for their healing abilities.

"All the colors are trying?"

"Even the ones who don't have good healing abilities. It turns out when desperate times call for desperate measures, all unicorns can struggle through and help mitigate the damage, even the species with no general healing abilities. There was another group of cases last night, but the ER was able to handle them with minimal loss of life. There were two magickers and four human shapeshifters who died. The toxin really hits humans hard. Magickers have an easier time surviving, but their survivability is really low. There's one straight-up human in critical, and she's only alive because there's a rotation of six unicorns trying to reverse her organ failure. We should know if she'll make it by tonight."

Damn it. "Spiked alcohol?" I guessed.

"We think someone contaminated a buffet this time. The toxin seems to be colorless and tasteless as far as we can tell. We're waiting for toxicology reports from the lab to determine what had been the source of the toxin," Hardy replied. He drove us in the direction of the warehouse, huffing and puffing every now and then. As we pulled up to the front, he finally said, "It's like the killer is warming up the hospitals by giving us a bunch of cases so we *can* treat them as they come in. Had we had yesterday's batch the first go around, there would have been a lot more deaths."

Great. We had a methodical hire and a killer with morals. Between the two, I'd develop gray hair, shed out my pony coat in record time, and go on a chicken and cheese bender due to anxiety rather than any desire to lure the bastards out for arrest. Depending on the circumstances, I might even spend the earnings from my choice of diet on gaining viable leads from the public.

Unfortunately, greed tended to make such propositions sketchy at best. Every rare once in a while, we got a viable lead, but more often than not, offering rewards resulted in wasted hours of manpower as we struggled to determine who wanted a quick buck earned through lies and the genuine informants. If I could convince the dragons, unicorns, and griffons to keep their murderous tendencies to themselves and bring the culprit in alive, we might get somewhere with the case.

If not, I would have to hope the killer or hire made a mistake.

I joined Hardy in huffing and puffing.

The black dragon parked the cruiser in front of the warehouse, shaking his head. "What pisses me off is that we're barred from installing security cameras around this place. The owners of the buildings nearby do not want their activities monitored."

"I wonder why," I muttered in my wryest tone. "They may as well have taped a bullseye onto their backs while wearing a sign informing the world they're engaging in illegal activities. All they're doing is making sure we're going to start watching them more closely. And I will, because this whole thing is starting to irritate me."

"Irritated unicorns kick opal dragons and attempt to skewer them," Dowdren stated. "They only look fluffy and sweet."

"I do not look sweet."

Both of my co-workers burst into laughter.

"Assholes," I muttered. Once Hardy had the SUV in park, I made certain Mamma Mia's leash was secure on her collar, woke her up, and gave her the order to be on guard. While I needed a lot more training to handle a K9, I knew just enough to get us into trouble—and contain her until needed.

If I let her off her leash, all hell would break loose, but I doubted I'd need to let her off her leash. As she looked far more like a wolf than a dog and her back came up to my waist, most decided against trying the animal.

Her bark terrified people, and her bite was far worse than her bark.

I adored Mamma Mia, even when she did a good job of convincing me she'd rip my face off if I pushed her. "Remind me again why we have a wolf?"

"She's only 95.2% wolf," Hardy replied.

"And the rest is clearly rage incarnate," Dowdren added. "I don't know what sorcery you performed on that menace, but please keep doing it until after we're done in here."

"Dog bones once a week, Dowdren. I already said that." Secretly loving the animal helped. I bet she could smell fear and pushed the buttons of the cops who couldn't stand up to her and her wicked ways. "Are we alone on this one?"

"No. After hearing about your daring exploits, we have been graced with a team of the ladies."

I wondered if I could manage a crutch, a wolf, and at least two of the women from our rival station. "Just get it out. How does it get worse?"

Hardy snickered. "It doesn't. Don't forget your crutch, try to contain Mamma Mia, and keep an eye out."

I'd struggle with all three tasks, but when Hardy turned the corner to the main entrance to the warehouse, I discovered our rival station had sent three cruisers. "We're outnumbered. Six of them, three of us."

"And they're probably all single," Dowdren muttered.

The last thing I needed was more complications added to my already complicated life. "I am already attempting to teach a black dragoness how to cook. I cannot handle additional women in my life, no matter what her species may be."

"Don't get in the way of whatever they're planning, Jace. They're ruthless," Hardy reminded me. "If we mixed stations at this point, they'd take over. Worse, we'd let them take over. We're ruled by the women at our station as it is, and they're the support staff!"

"Hardy, the support staff *always* rule the roost, even when we try to deny it. Without them, we flounder and look like idiots," I reminded him. "We better get everyone flowers. It's about time. And chocolates, treats, and whatever else they like. I'll even let you all hitch me to a wagon this once for the deliveries, but only after my foot heals."

"Do it," Dowdren ordered.

"And I guess I will start putting that together as soon as we're back at the station. Anything else, Mr. Fluffy Pony?"

"I'd like my dignity returned."

"That ship sailed long ago," my friend replied.

"Not quite a week is not long ago." Wrinkling my nose, I waited for Hardy to get parked in the lineup of cruisers. Dowdren hurried out to open the door for me, and after some conferring with our queen and ruler, Mamma Mia, I handed over her leash long enough to get out and grab one of the crutches. Once stable on my foot, I took her leash back, ordered her to heel, and hobbled in the direction of the doors.

Within thirty seconds, I regretted my decision to go to work, as the captain of the rival station poked her head out of the door and looked me over. At a hair under three hundred years old, Captain Maria Fernandez counted as the city's reigning cougar out for the blood and a bed of young, eligible men. As a proud opal dragoness, she didn't go on the prowl often, ruled over her station with a steadfast claw, and tolerated zero crap from anybody, especially other dragons. "Farthan got you good, didn't he?"

"Yes, ma'am, he did," I replied, taking care to keep Mamma Mia on a short leash and watch my stride so I wouldn't embarrass myself further. "I got some payback. I kicked him, and if the pesky doctors hadn't of stopped me, I would have stabbed him a few times, too."

She grinned at me and snapped a salute. "I heard. Well done putting that mean old dragon back in his place. First, you rode him, and then you kicked him into next week. As word on the wire is he managed to put a claw right up your hoof, we volunteered to serve as backup because we're strangely light on cases in our sector. For whatever reason, you're getting the lion's share. That's putting us all on edge." Captain Fernandez gestured for me to follow her into the warehouse. "And who is your lovely partner?"

"This is Mamma Mia. She's one part wolf, one part rage. I have bribed my way into her affections with bones offered at consistent intervals." To keep the animal happy, I praised her for good behavior, scratched her behind an ear, reinforced the command to heel, and followed the captain inside. "I'm not sure why Captain Farthan sent us with Mamma Mia, but if anyone gets any ideas, I'm one of the best armed members of the force in our precinct right now."

"Likely for that reason, especially when you're on a crutch. Those usually come in pairs."

"The other one is in the SUV, where it does me no good but allows me to pretend I can control my K9 partner."

She chuckled. "Between us dragons and the rest of the crew, I'm sure you'll be fine. So, your bodies are interesting."

When a seasoned cop viewed a body as interesting, I worried. "How so?"

"They were doused with the toxin after being hung up. The substance is all over the place, but I've got a few good magickers around who were able to get a glow on it."

Once inside, I eyed where the other bodies had been hung up, and sure enough, the vics dripped various fluids of different colors, one dark, one yellow, and another resembling water. As promised, one of the magickers had gotten the substance on the floor to glow, which did a good job of warning everyone what to avoid. "Which fluid is our culprit?"

"The clear one is the toxin, and we successfully got some samples."

How strange. "Interesting is one way to put it. The other two?"

"We don't know, but I think the killer had lines crossed and is trying to either expose the hire *or* wants us to be able to develop an antidote. We got clean samples of everything." Captain Fernandez pointed at the top of the rig, and I spotted three plastic bags, the kind I often saw attached to IVs in hospitals, which proved to be the source of the fluid. "You probably can't make it out from here, but there are several more bags just like those behind the corpses, and they haven't been punctured. As soon as we figure out how to get them down without damaging them, those will be going to the lab to be studied."

I eyed the rig. "Hardy, I'm going to need some rope and a black dragon."

My co-worker sighed. "Again? Why are you asking me?"

"Do we have another black dragon I can make pull on the rope after I get it set up?"

"Well, no, but we have an opal dragoness. She'd handle the task with far more beauty and grace."

I snorted, well aware Hardy and Captain Fernandez would consider murder if left alone in the same room for too long. The captain preferred quiet young dragons. Hardy pushed his luck because his grandfather was the Black Dragon of New York. "While you're not wrong, I don't want to have to hide two bodies, and while you're young, your grandfather probably taught you more than a few of his tricks. I have no interest in nursing either of you to good health, so I'd have to go with the next plan, which involves hiding your bodies."

While Hardy glared at me, the opal dragoness snickered. "Is your foot bothering you, Detective Smithson?"

"It's tolerable. Why?"

"You just informed your friend that you would hide his body."

I snorted. "It's the least I can do. If I hide your bodies, I'll keep the black dragons occupied for at least ten minutes. And then your fellow opals would get involved, and then there'd be chaos. I might even get away with it. Even if I don't get away with it, I'd be highly entertained until both colors turned on me for cleaning up after you."

She held up a hand, blinked, and furrowed her brows.

Hardy relaxed enough to laugh. "It's infuriating, isn't it? When you think it through, he presents a really good point. If he hid our bodies after we killed each other, our families would descend into chaos. And he's generally innocent of all wrongdoing, so nobody would ever actually suspect *him*."

As long as I took care with leaving DNA-based evidence, I'd be able to get away with it thanks to my ability to wipe my fingerprints off most surfaces. "And I'd be entertained the entire time. Who would win? The opals or the blacks?"

Hardy glared at me. "It's bad enough you've gotten my grandpappy involved in another episode of that show. Don't make it worse. Don't encourage it."

"I have to help referee that train wreck, Hardy. It's already worse, and I may as well make others suffer with me. Now, let's get back to work. You two can't kill each other, so I won't have to hide your bodies, and even if you *did* kill each other, there are simply too many witnesses around to let me get away with hiding your bodies."

"I'll help," every single woman in the warehouse announced.

Dowdren came into the warehouse, sighed, and grunted before gracing me with a curt nod, which I translated to mean he'd help with the disposal of the two dragons.

"Just watch your step, don't mess up the evidence, and get me a rope, Hardy. Then put your scaled rump to work hauling the bodies down so we can get the evidence without anyone getting poisoned."

NINETEEN

"What's the bad news?"

THURSDAY, APRIL 13, 2057
LOWER NORTH LAKES, PRECINCT 153
CAULDRON CITY, NEBRASKA.

AT A LITTLE AFTER two in the morning, we made it back to the station. Instead of staying in our evidence containers like we wanted, the substances had decided to replicate, creating mayhem and generalized destruction in the warehouse. With one substance known to be dangerous, we treated the others as though they were in the same class: lethal if not handled with care.

My foot throbbed right along with my head, and I resisted the urge to shift, sit down, and refuse to move. As though sensing I was on my last leg, Mamma Mia kept close to my side, bumped my hand with her nose, and often pressed close as though offering to let me lean on her. Handling crutches and the wolf took work, but she cooperated, which made it manageable.

Dr. Erik waited for me in my office, took one look at me, and shook his head while clucking his tongue. "I sent your woman to your apartment to rest, where she's being doted on by her loving grandpappy. She blew steam at around eight when she realized you would not be coming back to the station today. In good news, she sold that gem of yours."

I hobbled in, made it to my chair, and flopped down, groaning my relief at getting off my poor foot. Mamma Mia somehow crammed herself under my desk and took up residence. Somehow, I got away with using her as a footrest, although she claimed my good foot as her pillow. As promised, a shiny new digital murder board took up an obscene amount of space along the nearby wall, and I couldn't wait for a chance to put it to good use. "What's the bad news?"

"She sold that gem of yours."

"That was the entire point of giving it to her. Since you know it was mine and that it sold, know what she got for it?"

"Seventy-five million to her mother, who is planning to give it to her father as a present so he can have his very own precious diamond for his hoard."

Aware that Alicia's father was a shy black who'd never seen gold before meeting her mother, I laughed. "Her father is going to be rolling all around his hoard with that diamond, especially if it's his first."

"I see you have been educated on her father's tendencies."

I nodded. "I think it's sweet. I'll pick out a few extra diamonds for him if that's really his first."

"He's a weird black. He doesn't go out and buy things for his hoard. He only adds gifts to it. He has the smallest hoard of any black dragon, but every item in it is a prize."

I chuckled at the thought of a humble black dragon. "I've plenty of stones I can give him so the diamond doesn't feel lonely. I'll have Alicia pick one out for him every time she learns something new in my kitchen. My supply can probably handle it." I lowered my voice and muttered, "We will not tell her she's a slow learner."

"We know, Jace. We know. Good idea. But you got seventy-five million for the stone, her father knows he's being gifted with it, and he's flying over as we speak. He'll be here within two hours, but her grandfather is going to intercept him and take him to Precinct 1 until tomorrow. That means her mother is coming, as she is jealous of her black dragon. He is utterly innocent." Dr. Erik came over, seized the back of my neck, and leaned over to regard the wolf under my desk. "What's your move now, punk?"

"I'm going to sit very still so you don't move your thumb and knock me into next week," I replied, well aware the black unicorn could do just that if he wanted. "I did not get contaminated with any of the substances, I had lunch and dinner, but you're going to be pissed when you find out what I've been eating."

"You had lunch and dinner delivered, made with your new grill." With his free hand, Dr. Erik pointed at a nearby cabinet. "It's in there, cleaned and ready for your leisure. Chicken and cheese, with extra cheese and chicken. Are you trying to end up in my ER again?"

"Apparently."

While he gave my neck a warning squeeze, he did not knock my lights out to put me back in my place. "Explain the chicken and cheese bender, Jace. Now."

A wise man, when in a life-threatening situation, did as

told and hoped for mercy. "A cute little pony disguised to look like a stallion will be showing up at my mother's chicken and cheese roosts to lure out the killer. He clearly understands whites are useful for gem production. Given a pair of clippers and an hour, and I'll resemble a proper stallion rather than a fluffy young pony with a doting mare and stallion nearby keeping guard. Assuming this asshole keeps evading us, after two weeks of this, we should have a solid lead."

While Dr. Erik snorted, he released me, sat on my desk, and gave me a dose of stink eye. "I'll handle the clipping part of the work, and I'll monitor you during your experiment with chicken and cheese. I'm only going with this because your mother came to no harm, it was clear they were after her stones, and the killer knows just enough about unicorns not to mess with the ponies. Even clipped, unicorns will recognize you're a pony, so if you are targeted in public, they'll act. Add in the fact you're a cop who does work the ER, and it'll just take some word on the grapevine to get the bastard alive. Tenderized but alive."

As having an ally beat trying to dodge the doctor while causing trouble, I relaxed. "I'm exhausted, so if we can get through this in a hurry so I can go home and make friends with my couch, that'd be great."

"After the week you've had, exhausted is an understatement. I already told the captain if he wants you in tomorrow, it is a desk day, otherwise, you need to work from home or not work at all. Unless you check out worse than I anticipate, you'll be in the office. If there is another dead weight incident, you'll be looped in by phone and video. Get your foot up here so I can have a look at it."

Careful not to anger Mamma Mia, which involved cooing to her, giving her the petting she was owed, and gently extricating my foot from beneath her head, I turned in my seat and thumped my feet onto my desk beside him. "I'm literally too tired to take my shoes off, doc."

"If I hadn't started checking you over when I had my hand on your neck, I would accuse you of exaggerating, but you're really wiped out." Dr. Erik stripped my shoe off and peeled away my sock to discover my bandage had held, but sometime along the day, the puncture had decided to bleed on me.

In unison, we both sighed.

"First, I apologize for not having noticed he'd pierced your frog. In bad news, an infection is starting, so I'm going to have to clean this mess up. In good news, I can do the work here, but it's going to hurt like hell and you're going to regret it."

I gestured at the phone on my desk. "You're going to have to get someone to fetch Mamma Mia, because I'm not sure we should have a literal wolf in here while participating in a blood bath."

Rather than make use of my phone, Dr. Erik grabbed his cell and shot off a text. Within five minutes, which was spent poking and prodding my foot to get a reading on what hurt the worst, one of the K9 supervisors poked his head into my office, caught sight of my foot, and whistled. "That looks less than pleasant."

"Hey, Martino. If you think it looks less than pleasant, you should feel it. Mamma Mia did great today, and she's getting the biggest bone I can find her tomorrow. I don't know how you reward the dogs, but she needs to be rewarded. Who takes this beautiful lady home with them?"

"She's mine when she's off duty. I'll make sure there's a good cow leg in the fridge marked for you to give her tomorrow. That'll save you a trip to the butcher. There's one on my way in, and if I give her a small treat at the butcher, she'll assume I bought people food while there. You can pay me back for it later."

"Perfect. Ham this mess up, would you? Tomorrow, assuming Dr. Erik lets me in here, I want to make friends with the digital board. I can't do that if I'm having to babysit Captain Fernandez and her beautiful crew of pirates."

"I heard that, Smithson," the dragoness in question hollered. "Did you forget I tailed you here?"

Damn it. I used my saddest pony eyes on Dr. Erik.

The black unicorn laughed at me, turned, and hollered back, "Forget implies he noticed in the first place, Maria. He's got an infection in his foot and it hurts like hell, so give him a break this once, if you don't mind."

The woman poked her head into my office, took one look at my foot, and grimaced. "All right, I'll let that one slide, but I'm telling all the ladies you think we're beautiful."

"Will that help me live a little longer?" I asked.

"It sure will. You'll get a free hero of the day card for later claiming. That's the damage Farthan did, Erik?"

"Sure is. Come on in and have a look. If he were to shift right now, his hoof would be pretty bad, he'd be lamed, and we'd probably have to put him down." Dr. Erik shot a glare my way. "I'm not sure how much of a loss that would be today."

"You will not be putting me down even if I can't stand on all four hooves. I will just lie down until it heals. Alternatively, you can put me in a sling and deal with hearing me complain for the duration of my recovery." As the state of my foot had made a seasoned captain grimace, I decided against trying to get a look at the damage. "Honestly, can I use my hero for a day card to get some help for Alicia? We made a wager, I've lost, and she may need someone to escort her around the precinct in search of a bachelor pad suitable for parking a Black Wing. I'm clearly not going to be walking anywhere for a few days. My bachelor pad should probably have space for a black dragoness and her hoard. I am an idiot when I start talking, and I laid down some strict rules. She does not leave until she's no longer a hazard to her and her family. She almost killed the Black Dragon of New York, ma'am."

Captain Fernandez chuckled. "I can help you with your problem, sure, and you can keep your card for later. I've a niece who is a real estate agent, and I'll tell her that you're going to be the owner. How many parking spots?"

"How many can I get in this town? I've never looked at houses."

"Up to four typically," she replied. "I'm assuming you're paying cash in what she got for the rock, so you'll be able to get whatever you want in the precinct. Most aren't going to hesitate about moving out if you offer them ten million plus a fair value for the home—and that little dragoness is not above doing that. You aren't the luxury kind, so I'll have her showcase some things more up your alley."

I stared into the captain's eyes and said, "I am absolutely the luxury kind if it means more space for my books."

Dr. Erik snickered. "They're both book hoarders, I'm afraid."

"There is nothing wrong with hoarding books," I replied in my most dignified tone.

The doctor shot me yet another disgusted glare. "There is when you barely have room for your bed and clothes."

Determined to maintain some of my pride, I stated, "That is why I tricked a dragoness into selling a diamond on a wager to force me to move. Obviously, I need more space for my hoard. I just needed an excuse to move. It turns out the excuse is approximately human sized some of the time and has a hoard of her own that needs to share space with mine."

"You're a damned opportunist," Dr. Erik complained. "Since I have you here, Captain, get a good hold on his leg. What I'm about to do hurts like hell, and I'd rather not have to do this twice. With luck, he'll pass out. If not, expect some whining, possibly a few screams, and more curses than you probably expect coming from him."

Captain Fernandez took hold of my ankle, grimaced, and said, "I'm sorry about this, Jace. He tricked me into helping."

"I'll probably forgive you both sometime tomorrow," I replied, bracing for the worst. "Try not to kill me, please. I can't go to work if dead."

Friday, April 14, 2057
Upper North Lake, Precinct 153
Cauldron City, Nebraska.

THANKS to generalized exhaustion and a sleeping pill slipped to me by a cunning and evil doctor, I missed the entirety of Thursday. Either aware the cops of Precinct 153 were hot on his heels or the killer had it out for me, Thursday proved to be a quiet day. As the labs weren't ready, no new evidence came to light, and nobody had any brilliant ideas on how to crack the case, missing work changed little. On Dr. Erik's recommendation, I worked from the comfort of home, my foot elevated while I read through the lives of those who'd been stripped of their organs and dignity after death.

The mountain of crimes I uncovered, some only confirmed due to newly acquired DNA samples, would close many chapters in the lives of victims and their families. In the upcoming weeks, many of the notifications would fall to me. For those local to Cauldron City, I'd pay them a visit, knock on their doors, and finish telling the tale of their loved ones and the demise of those who'd caused them so much suffering and grief.

Resolution wouldn't bring back the dead, but it would allow some to move beyond their losses.

Still battling off the remnants of the sedative, I took notes, debated going back to bed, and questioned my choice to become a cop in the first place.

When someone knocked on my door, I put in some serious thought to defenestrating myself to escape whatever horrors had come calling. Instead, I said, "Come in."

If anyone yelled at me for shouting, I'd fling my clipboard at them and hope I had good aim.

Captain Farthan and Captain Fernandez entered my apartment.

When two opals came calling, trouble followed on their heels. As throwing my clipboard at my boss would get me fired, I resisted the urge. "There's only one thing more worrisome than a captain making a personal visit, and that's two captains making a personal visit. What's wrong?"

"I like how he assumed there's something wrong," Captain Fernandez stated, and she grinned at me. "There's nothing wrong, Jace, so don't worry. We just came out of a meeting with the commissioner, and Nathan wanted to check in with you. I asked to come along for the ride. How are you feeling?"

"Better, although it's still sore." I expected Dr. Erik would pay a visit after dinner to finish restoring my foot to rights—at least enough I could walk without crutches. "Right now, I'm just compiling data to input on the board when I get back to the station. I have at least twenty follow-ups I'll have to do regarding old cases, but some of these have been cold for ten or more years, so letting them sit for another twenty-four hours probably won't hurt anything. If you give me leave, I'll do the rounds and final interviews over my weekend."

"I can authorize the overtime, but you need to take time off work, Jace. I know this case is important, but you do need rest—and not the kind that is enforced by Dr. Erik's iron hoof. That tyrant wouldn't even let us up the stairs yesterday," my captain complained. "If you're game, I'll assign you to half-days for the next few weeks so you can work daily but still get time off. You'll be allowed to call in if you need a breather. I'm going to be borrowing a few of Maria's ladies for this case, as it's clear we don't have the manpower needed to handle the complexity of this case."

Half-days would work until we made more progress, especially as that would free up sufficient time to prepare to move. "I can work with that. Right now, I'm rather hating how much of a favor this killer has done us as a whole; every single victim has a rap sheet a mile long, and most of it involves murder or rape. Mostly rape. I'll give the hire credit; he picked his vics well." While Alicia's thought on the sexual-offender registry made a great deal of sense, another possibility worried me. "Could the hire be a cop?"

"That is a very uncomfortable question we've been asking all morning, Jace," my captain replied, and he plopped down on the couch beside me. At a wave of his hand, Captain Fernandez took the other side, trapping me between them. "So far, all the vics are on public registries, which makes it hard to tell. Nothing we've seen so far indicates private database data has been used to track the vics. Hell, a bunch of them have been on our wanted list for years. I'm betting these bastards are trusting that the crimes of the vics outweigh their crimes."

"It doesn't, especially not since they're poisoning innocent people."

"Had this toxin not been introduced into the mix, I can guarantee most would not be so eager to get this killer brought to justice. We want them alive, but dead is fine if there's no other recourse. Word got spread you'd like to see them actually face justice rather than get the easy way out. Once a few reminders that death counted as an easy way out for this lot, there has been a general change of heart among most. If possible, you'll get them alive. Will it be possible? That I can't tell you."

"It beats worrying about if I have to beat entire herds of angry unicorns and flocks of fuming dragons to the chase," I replied, and I leaned forward to dump my current files onto my coffee table and retrieve the more disturbing cases, all of which involved children. "I did find something interesting we might want to look into. There were a few bodies that didn't match blood type and organ damage, so I think we either have a clue or the killer has gone against the hire's wishes for some vigilante justice. All these cases are dealing with kids, and none of the vics match the blood type and organ removal scenarios. Looking at the pictures, it appears the killer mimicked what the surgeon was doing to potentially add to the mess."

I handed half the stack to each captain, leaned back, and waited for them to go through the files. Once they had a chance to review everything, I said, "We could have a copycat, but I suspect it's a network or several people working together. There are bodies originating from as far as San Francisco in this mess." I went through the pile and pulled out one for a Donald Havenport. "This vic was just released from prison two weeks ago, and according to the court records, he was under house arrest outside of the city. The bracelet stopped recording his location roughly ten hours before the estimated time of death."

"You think someone went and got him, bringing him here before killing him."

"All that would be needed to pull it off would be a plane, and considering how many bodies are turning up, the hire likely has the resources to have a plane—or hired a charter who doesn't ask questions." Another possibility loomed, and aware I might irritate both dragons into roaring and possibly leveling my home with their wrath, I added, "A dragon could easily carry a body from the San Francisco area to here in ten hours."

Captain Fernandez scowled, but my captain nodded. "While it's not something I would participate in, not all dragons are law-abiding, and these cases would be sufficient to stoke rage in most of my kin. An enraged dragon is not against flying a screaming victim upside down for a few hours to speed him to a painful demise. How fast could you make that flight, Maria?"

"Six hours," she replied. "I'd be wiped out afterwards, but I could do it in six hours if I had a damned good reason, was well-rested, and wanted to bury the bastard I had to haul. There are faster dragons."

"But not many. I'd make the flight in eight. I'm bulkier, far lazier, and prone to gliding as much as possible."

"You are also relentlessly male," Captain Fernandez muttered.

Captain Farthan grinned. "It's a crime I have yet been charged for however much it's true. The blacks would be the slowest of the lot, likely. They only move like they mean it if their target's vic happened to be a loved one, member of their brood, or friend. Any evidence of that, Jace?"

I shook my head. "New York hasn't had any vics pop up yet that I've seen. I don't know the other black clans all that well or where they live."

"The hire may be well aware of how dragons operate, then." Narrowing her eyes, Captain Fernandez grabbed the whole lot of unusual cases, flipping through them. "Most metropolis areas have vics from somewhere. New York is an odd exclusion. That implies the hire or killer does not want the Black Dragon of New York involved."

"That is a dragon who will eat obviously poisoned eggs for his granddaughter's sake," I reminded her. "Nobody wants that old terror involved in something like this. If he's given motive, he *will* tear this city apart, and that would likely ruin whatever plan the hire has."

"Except they became involved when poisoned," Captain Farthan pointed out.

"I think that was an accident," I confessed, and I pointed at the pile of papers containing information on the mass poisonings. "We've gotten a trace on the alcohol bottles, and they were seeded three or four weeks before the incident. It was a game of chance. I don't think anyone was targeted. I think that the manufacturer of the poison wanted to do a large-scale test in the city to see what would happen. We *do* have a lead in there possibly, though. If we can find out where those bottles originated from, we might be able to figure out who seeded them and why."

Both dragons grunted their displeasure over my comment. When neither said a word, I continued, "If we evaluate the poisonings as a separate issue from the organ theft cases, I would guess someone is doing a random test to see who is most likely to die from exposure to the toxin—and how our medical system will handle a mass influx of patients. According to Dr. Erik, after the initial wave and general understanding of how the toxin worked, the hospitals here can handle no more than two hundred of these cases at a time, and that is only if they code for an emergency and bring in all staff plus volunteers. The current rate of cases is two or three per hospital at a time, which is manageable. Rough, but manageable. That still leaves some ER space for standard trauma and emergency patients. The hospitals aren't currently coding for an emergency right now. If the killer is a doctor and wants to trim down the population in a way that doesn't crash the medical system completely, the number of poisonings will stabilize to that number across the city."

Captain Farthan pulled out an envelope from his work

vest and handed it to me. "This is your bonus check for your promotion plus your updated employment letter. You might need the employment letter for home insurance purposes and whatever nefarious things that dragoness has planned for you. Speaking of which, where is the dragoness?"

One day, I might get used to having someone sharing space with me. While I'd missed the entirety of Thursday, Alicia had greeted me when I'd gotten home, proudly presented the fresh pizza she'd ordered in for me because it was the only place still open in the neighborhood at that hour, and had made sure I'd made it to bed. While I wouldn't admit it to anyone, I'd enjoyed her presence. "Alicia is house hunting. Her daddy is here, and I underestimated how much her daddy loves her. I think I'm lucky to be alive, as I haven't met him yet. The Black Dragon of New York intervened. He took her out of my apartment before I got out of bed, telling me I'd have to live without my comfort pillow for a while."

That got both opals snickering, and my captain asked, "Comfort pillow?"

"I had rolled over, and poor Alicia got to deal with me half sprawled on her. I had been alone in my bed when I'd gone to sleep, so the inclusion of a dragoness in my sleeping plans hadn't been anticipated. I have no idea how that old bastard had gotten into the apartment, but he probably saved my life. I doubt I would have made it if Alicia's daddy had been the one to come calling."

"And Alicia's reaction to being used as a pillow?" Captain Fernandez raised a brow at me, and she smirked.

"She gave me another pillow, told her grandfather to stop being mean, and made sure I was properly tucked in. I went back to bed, because why make a fuss when I'm being told to go back to bed? I've been short on sleep, so I wasn't saying no to a few extra hours of rest."

She favored me with a satisfied nod. "Sensible. Good. Farthan and I have already discussed this, but until further notice, you'll have jurisdiction throughout the entirety of Cauldron City. It's the only way we can keep this investigation consistent and thorough. In bad news, it means you'll have to meet with all the captains in the city, which is going to test your patience. I'm hoping we'll be able to do it by precinct, but we'll see." With a wince, she stated, "Take the half-day offer but also take a day off a week at a minimum. Half-days are useful sometimes, but you'll burn out if you do them for too long."

"What is the probability we'll get anywhere on this case between now and Monday?" I asked, beginning the tedious work of organizing my paperwork. "If we are still waiting for labs, prints to be run, and so on, I'll just take a long weekend and resume work on Tuesday."

"Resume work on Tuesday," my captain stated. "If there are any new incidents, I'll give you a call, but you need the rest and a chance for your foot to heal—and you need to make sure you haven't overexerted your magic working in the ER. Dr. Erik was worried about that."

"Dr. Erik worries about everything," I muttered. "But he's right to worry about my foot."

"I have learned my lesson. Human hands only when examining unicorn hooves. Dr. Erik kicked me in the face when I came over yesterday. He was a human when he did it, but he promised I would enjoy a hoof to the face if he caught wind of me inappropriately using my claws to examine living unicorns."

I doubted my captain would like what I was about to tell

him, but I replied, "He can't call you out on poking and prodding corpses, as a part of our medical training when a unicorn is to dissect dead unicorns. Most of us volunteer to be used as medical training specimens after death."

"You're serious."

I nodded. "I am not currently signed up, but that's mostly due to my career field. Autopsies make it difficult to be used for medical training, and if I were to die in the line of duty or elsewhere, my corpse would need to be available for autopsy. The medical training does involve autopsies, but in an environment where it's unlikely any evidence would be admissible in court." I shrugged, as unicorns were one of the few species who practiced donating our bodies to science before burial or cremation. "We don't particularly care what happens to us after we're dead and gone, and medical students need bodies of the non-living variety to practice on."

"Well, I learned something more than a little disturbing today," Captain Fernandez announced. "It also explains a lot. We've noticed a lot of unicorns work in the medical field. You're the only unicorn in the entire city working in law enforcement. Why is that?"

"I wanted to help others, but I didn't want to just become yet another unicorn in the ER. I'll do it when needed, and I enjoy some of the work, but I've always been interested in law enforcement. I figured I'd be an awful doctor if I didn't actually want to be a doctor. I like being a cop, and I wanted to be one since I was little. I don't remember why." I finished organizing my papers back into their neat piles, making a mental note to review my journal notes before going through everything one last time to see if I missed something. "No one warned me, before I'd become a cop, just how slow investigations can be—and how little good we can do in the long run. Nobody warned me there is never enough manpower to follow up with every crime, and that thieves often get away with their crimes because we simply can't take the time to look into every robbery. And nobody warned me more murderers walk than face justice."

"What would you have done had you known?" my captain asked.

"I would have fast-tracked my schooling and applied to the academy earlier," I admitted. "I'll pursue training as a first responder, but I doubt I'll ever work the ERs, not like my parents or most of the other unicorns will. While rare, some of us do break the mold."

"I think I'll be pushing to have most of our staff take first responder courses. We have some basic training, but we can always do better," Captain Farthan stated, and he got up from my couch. "Now that we've delivered your paperwork, we must go wrangle our stations. Try to stay out of trouble until Tuesday, okay?"

Well, I'd stay out of as much trouble as possible when deliberately setting myself up for a diamond run, following my mother's cheesy example, and inviting myself to be kidnapped for my gemstones. "I'll do my best, sir."

Both opals sighed.

"Are all of your boys like this one, Nathan?" Captain Fernandez inquired.

"Unfortunately. Worse, he's the leader of the pack for trying his best and failing miserably at staying out of trouble."

The dragoness patted my captain's arm. "Why don't you come with me to my station? We'll make you a coffee and delay your return for a little while."

"You know what? I think I shall."

I waited for the dragons to escort themselves out and close the door before rolling my eyes at the absurdity of my life. Then, as a wise man took a nap when opportunity allowed, I cleaned up my work, put everything away, and went to pay my bed a visit.

TWENTY

Hardy would live or die, and there was nothing I could do about it.

SATURDAY, April 15, 2057
Dragon's Heart, Precinct 1
Cauldron City, Nebraska.

I WANTED to find the bastard who had named the center of Precinct 1 "Dragon's Heart" and kick them into next week. Everything about the place got on my last nerve, but the plethora of dragons took top prize for annoying me. The sole tolerable dragon proved to be Hardy, as he stayed human and did his best to shield me from the chaos that was his family.

Due to the sheer number of them, we'd taken over one of the precinct's parks. The presence of the Black Dragon of New York had done a good job of drawing a lot of attention. To keep anyone from bothering his family, he postured, answered questions from the other dragons in attendance, and played with the young children brave enough to approach him.

I regretted having only a cane instead of crutches, as standing around did me zero good. I did my best to stay off my injured foot or make use of my toes to spare my heel, but I would pay for my foolishness in the next few days.

Sleeping through Thursday and staying home Friday had helped, but Dr. Erik wanted my foot to heal naturally for another few days before finishing the work he'd started. Had I gotten my way, I would have been in my apartment reading a book rather than meeting more dragons than I cared to think about.

Hardy's father snorted and eyed his son. "What's this I'm hearing about a game show?"

I would miss Hardy after his father ate him. As I wasn't dumb enough to get between an irritated black dragon and the subject of his displeasure, I moved a few feet away. Rather than draw attention through wishing my co-worker luck, I remained silent.

Hardy would live or die, and there was nothing I could do about it.

"Well?"

"I agreed to be put up on auction for Alicia's game show to keep our grandpappy from destroying Cauldron City," Hardy replied without evidence of fear. "Jace will be our referee, and Dr. Erik will probably be serving as Jace's mount. He's the black unicorn that treated her. We might have a line on a young black unicorn mare, too. I don't know if we can talk him into it, but if we can get Jace to offer up one of his diamonds, it'll top the other episode. Since Alicia can't go back to work for at least a month, she really needs the episode to do well." Hardy placed his hands on his hips and glared at his father. "My contribution is to be taken on dates with eligible bachelorettes. The opals are offering up one of their dragons, too. I suggested there be a prize for each challenge to up the stakes."

Alicia, who was in her dragon form, cuddled with her parents, who took turns nuzzling her and treating her like a prized treasure. Her sisters and brothers, also in dragon form, crowded around for a turn. I wondered if the killer or hire realized how close to death they'd come.

Had Alicia perished, the black dragons would have torn the entire city apart, building by building, until those behind her death had been torn into a million pieces.

"And this Jace is good for that spot why?"

"He saved Grandpappy's life from Alicia's cooking, and he is the white unicorn that got her to the hospital in a timely fashion. He's currently a local hero. It doesn't get much better than that for publicity for her show." With a low, rather evil snicker, Hardy gestured my way. "He's also one of the hottest cops in our precinct if the ladies at our rival station are to be believed. I've learned it's wise to listen to the ladies when they make declarations like that. I'd add him to my hoard. He wouldn't bring my collection of beautiful things shame."

"You cannot take home your co-workers, Hardy. We've discussed this before. Single, eligible, and willing women? Yes. Co-workers? No." Heaving a sigh, Hardy's father turned his attention to me. "I hear that clumsy opal is the reason you're short a foot?"

While tempted to correct him regarding the state of my foot, I inclined my head and hoped the dragon understood I meant to be respectful. "Yes, sir."

"You are also the young man who has decided my little niece will not be leaving your home until she can cook?"

"Yes, sir."

"And her grandpappy has approved of this?"

"He keeps bringing her back to my apartment and leaving her there, so I assume he's fine with it. I also have the keys to his Black Wing right now."

"Uncle!" Hardy hollered, waving at Alicia's father. "Come show Dad your diamond."

While Alicia's father rumbled complaints over leaving his daughter, he got up and wandered over. The instant his spot cleared, her sisters and brothers squabbled over the right to claim the space. He transformed into a tall, dark-haired man wearing a suit, and he dug into his pocket to show off the diamond I'd given to Alicia.

His expression reminded me of a hopeful puppy seeking approval.

Hardy's father's body language relaxed, and he stretched out his neck to examine my stone. "My first diamond was two carats cut, slightly included, with a strong yellow tint. It was the first stone I bought with my own money. This stone is far more precious of a jewel than any cut stone I have ever held within my hoard."

Well, Alicia's father would float through the rest of the day, judging from his delighted expression. "I don't know anything about diamonds. What makes this one special?"

I questioned how a black dragon, the uncontested hoarders of dragon society, had escaped for so long without learning the basics about diamonds. I suspected it had something to do with Alicia's mother, who delighted in her mate's general innocence and his reactions to new things.

Teaching him the value of the stone might add to the

chaos, but I decided to do it anyway. "It's unicorn produced, which increases its perceived value." Hobbling closer, I gestured to the clear surface of the stone. "When cutting a diamond, it's not uncommon to lose thirty percent of the total stone's weight. My stones tend to be unusually clear and without surface imperfections, which means more of the stone's base material can be used should it be cut. While this one has more color than most collectors prefer, it's a hundred and seventy carats. That's a good-sized stone. The stone's clarity means you can make use of most of the material, losing little compared to most cuts."

"That's true? You, uh, produce diamonds when you eat certain foods?"

Nodding, I pointed at the stone's largest face. "Unicorn-produced diamonds tend to have smooth exteriors due to our digestive systems. We also produce glitter when we're producing diamonds. The glitter is actually mica, and something about our magic and digestive systems color it in a myriad of shades. Unlike natural mica, ours doesn't tend to emit dust, so it's generally safe to handle and be around. I suppose someone enterprising could turn the mica into cosmetics if they wanted to try to sort it by color. I wish them the best of luck with that. White unicorns can end up in the hospital when producing diamonds, as we can suffer through blockages. Generally, larger stones like this are trouble. If you see a cross-eyed white unicorn waddling into an ER, you can bet there was a complication with gemstone production. We don't just produce diamonds."

"There are other gemstone types?"

Aware I likely led Alicia's father into temptation, I nodded again. "If you're interested in having your friends and family offer you unicorn-produced stones, I can tell

Alicia what we can produce. I might offer her some other stones if she learns how to handle kitchen tasks without poisoning someone."

Alicia's father bowed his head and sighed. "We've tried teaching her, but she has no attention span for food. She has no strong desire to eat, and she views it as a boring and tedious task. She doesn't understand why she should learn when she can hire someone to make her much better food. And then she reminds me that by doing that, she helps someone else have a livelihood. It becomes quite difficult to argue with her."

I somehow managed to keep from laughing at the despair in his tone. "I'll help make certain she understands the difference between supporting a livelihood and killing off her family and friends with unsafe cooking." I almost called her method a technique but decided against it.

She'd committed an act of biological warfare in my kitchen, one capable of bringing ancient black dragons low. Under no circumstances could I encourage anyone to attempt to replicate her method.

Alicia's father twisted around and called out, "Darling?"

Much like a puppy when called, Alicia's mother left the pile, abandoned her daughter to her sisters and brothers, and sauntered over. She transformed into an older version of Alicia, with longer hair and wearing a formfitting, ankle-length black dress. "What's the matter?"

Alicia's father pointed at me. "How do we add the unicorn to our hoard?"

With a laugh, Alicia's mother shook her head. "We can't add the unicorn to our hoard, I'm afraid. A good idea, and I'm proud of your initiative, but we have to leave the little pony to his parents for a few more years. Your best chance is to act like you disapprove so Alicia is encouraged to be defiant and keep the unicorn. Then she will bring him home for holidays, and you can act like he is a part of our hoard. If we are lucky, they will bring little dragons and unicorns with them when they visit. I've been checking in on the unicorn foals, and they're adorable. I found one instance of a unicorn ensnaring a dragon, and half their children are unicorns. The other half are dragons. There were no cases of hybridization in their herd of twenty."

As far as plans went, I admired the woman's cunning. "Knowing what I know about black dragons, I feel that is a rather ruthless suggestion, one that might end with me haltered in some dragon's hoard."

Alicia's mother laughed before kissing her husband on the cheek. "Alicia told you about the day we met?"

I nodded.

Alicia's father sighed. "I'm never outliving that, am I?"

"You about broke your brain rolling around in my hoard, love. At that point, I had to keep you. I'm not at all sorry about your tendencies, because I love them and wish to preserve them. Just pretend like you're unsure about some unicorn being near your little princess, and your little princess will do what she does best. I won't promise she won't drive us all insane by the time she's done posturing and questing to prove unicorns absolutely *are* the equal of dragons. For now, be content that we have her out of the family roost. A unicorn with cooking skills will keep her out of trouble, and if they don't hit it off and have many little children together, she will at least know how to cook."

Alicia's father stared at his new diamond, and then he regarded me with wide eyes. "I feel like I should give this back to help pay for teaching my daughter."

I laughed at the despair in his tone. "It's okay, Mr. Grimstone. I would have helped her regardless. She needs time for her ulcers to heal, and it sounds like she needs a few months off work, too. She can stay with me. With the busybodies around, *someone* will be able to keep an eye on her. I don't need paid, but if you drop hints to that mean old Black Dragon of New York that we should be gifted with good chicken at least once a week, I won't complain."

"We could buy the restaurant," Alicia's father suggested. "Then we can make certain our supply of good chicken is never threatened. But we'd have to fly here fairly often."

"We have wings. Flying over is not an issue. And if we want to be lazy, planes have wings and can fly for us."

How had prim and proper Alicia come from such insane people? I should have been warned through the family stories, but I'd underestimated the amount of crazy within the Grimstone family. Then again, the Black Dragon of New York had willfully eaten poisoned eggs to spare his granddaughter from suffering through hurt feelings.

Maybe I could get the entire clan therapy for Christmas.

Aware the dragons might buy the entire restaurant, I eyed Alicia's father and said, "If you do buy the restaurant, I will pay out one stone a year, with a minimum size of twenty carats, to have weekly access to their chicken."

"You want to accept that offer, love," Alicia's mother prompted. "It's a good way to build your hoard. Do give him interesting stones, Officer Smithson. He's so excited over his new prize."

Alicia's father pocketed his new diamond and picked up his phone, tapping at the screen. "How much do you think they'd sell the restaurant for?"

"If you offer them fifteen million, I'm sure they'd love to

keep working and making chicken, especially if you offer them fifty an hour each to do the work plus pay the invoices for their food supplies." Alicia's mother peered at his phone and pointed at something. "You can use that investment account for your chicken project. Alicia likes it enough she *will* eat it every day if we let her. We'll let her, obviously, as finding food she will eat is a problem." With a sly smile, the dragoness added, "You can reinvest all the earnings from the restaurant to build a new account."

"Do you think there'll actually be profit if I'm paying all the staff fifty an hour plus all expenses?"

"You'll buy the building so you won't have rent to worry about. I've seen the lines. You can likely expand the operation to have more staff. I went over, and it's a family operation, and not all of them had room to work. They had a willingness to work, but the space is too small. It won't be much to buy them more space. The shop next to them was empty."

Well, I could explain that mystery to them. "That used to be a laundromat, but the complexes that used them installed their own, so they ran out of clients. They moved to a different precinct."

"See, love? You can make this your new project."

"This is something I am good at," Alicia's father acknowledged, his eyes narrowing. "Are you going to be upset if our family is around often, Officer Smithson?"

Yep, the Grimstone family needed therapy. Rather than tell him that, I maintained my composure and considered my reply. Only one answer stood out as appropriate: the truth.

"Why would I get upset over that?" I gestured in the direction of his daughter. "I certainly can't handle her without reinforcements. She about took out the Black Dragon of New York!"

Alicia's mother giggled, came over, and gave me a hug. "You're such a breath of fresh air. The other dragon colors grimace if we ask such a question. She's a handful, but I promise she won't be underfoot much once she's returning to work. She'll probably be in New York most of the time, although she might fly back here when she isn't producing her latest show."

I wasn't sure if that was a good thing or not. "I'm not sure a few weeks will be enough time to teach her how to fend for herself in a kitchen."

"We better lay down the law, babe," Alicia's father murmured, most of his attention on his phone. "Will your father help?"

"That mean old bastard would love to help convince her that she can work remotely and over video calls. Maybe she almost took him out with eggs, but he owns New York. They'll dance to his tune. I'll handle contacting her work and making it clear they will not stress my baby into having another ulcer. You handle the restaurant acquisition and find us a nice house somewhere in the city. Make sure we're a safe distance from our children, that way, we can get into trouble without an audience."

Alicia's father chuckled. "This house counts as part of my hoard."

"One day, I will teach you that you do not need a house for every single piece of your hoard. You can store your hoard in one location!"

"But I like having houses. Would it help if I went out and hunted some new rocks for my collection? There are opals on the west coast, and there are diamonds in Arkansas, but they're not nearly as nice as mine."

"Are any diamonds nicer than that one?" Alicia's mother asked in an amused tone.

"Absolutely not. You gave it to me."

When Alicia had told me about her parents, I had not expected a ridiculous amount of sweetness and innocence on her father's part, nor had I anticipated her mother's nurturing nature when it came to her father. Then again, what else should I have expected?

He'd tried to pay her more for her company, she'd tried to give him a good deal, and they'd made themselves a happily ever after. Their happily ever after also involved more children than I could count, as the entire park was filled with black dragons vying for Alicia's attention.

She basked in the glow of their affection.

"Let me see if I understand this, Mr. Grimstone. You have a small dragon hoard, but you have a house for every piece in your hoard?"

"That's right, son." Alicia's father grinned at me, winked, and said, "I treasure experiences more than treasure, so I make a big deal about my hoard. I use my new acquisitions as excuses to get a new house. Before you worry yourself, most of my houses cost less than fifty thousand, and when the little ones have been bad, we make them do renovation work on the places. When I get bored of fixing up the house, I sell it. I then take that money and invest it. I do buy things for hoards… just not *my* hoard. I spend a lot of what other dragons would view as my hoard money giving my parents a hoard."

"He sneaks over to their house and seeds something new in their hoards once a week," Alicia's mother stated, and she grinned at her husband. "Sometimes every other week but multiple pieces if he thinks he'll be caught in the act. They're modest dragons, and their nature is to go out and find rocks. We just let them find some slightly fancier rocks, uncut and natural, in their collection."

"They still have no idea where the opals came from. I'm quite proud of that. I buried those *deep*. I did put them in a box to protect them. I'm sure they'll catch me in the act one day."

"They aren't black dragons, and they don't understand black dragons, which is why Oliver gets away with so much. He couldn't be more of a black dragon if he tried. If I lose track of him, I just check my hoard. Most times, he'll be down there rolling away in the gold pile. Half the reason he doesn't make his own hoard is because he visits mine."

"I'm part of your hoard, so I can go roll in your gold if I want to," he replied, and he engaged his wife in a staring contest.

She growled.

He narrowed his eyes and issued the softest of huffs.

I eased away from the dragons, and as I had some common sense left, I sought out the Black Dragon of New York. If he couldn't protect me from his family, no one could.

Saturday, April 15, 2057
Dragon's Heart, Precinct 1
Cauldron City, Nebraska.

A RUSTY WHITE van pulled up in front of the Black Dragon of New York, the side door opened, and someone in dark clothing tossed out a large, wiggling bundle. The vehicle sped away.

Fortunately for me, I'd had my phone in my hand to take pictures of the crowd of dragons and others milling around to meet the menace plaguing the city, which made it easy to get good shots of the vehicle, the license plate, and the latest addition to my work woes. A red dragon reached the bag first, and with a slash of a single claw, opened it to reveal a green unicorn foal. The colt snorted his alarm, and the bag tangled around his legs did a good job of keeping him prone.

With the exception of Alicia's mother and father, the entirety of the Grimstone clan were in their dragon form, and I worried the entire lot of them would transform the van and its occupants into confetti. Their focus fixed on the colt, which bought the van some time to attempt escape.

No mere van could outrun hunting dragons, and the dragons knew it.

Heaving a sigh, I dialed Dr. Erik, and when he answered, I said, "We have another one, and this time it's a green colt."

"We don't actually have another one, fortunately for our sanity. The colt got grabbed this morning by someone in a white van; he'd escaped his parents and run out to play, and before they could catch him, the van showed up. Where are you?"

"Precinct 1, and they'd shoved him into a bag and dumped him in front of the Dragon of New York. Yes, it was a white van." Aware the old dragon might take offense, I hollered, "One of you may follow the van but you may not destroy the van or its occupants. Please detain and capture them alive."

I'd get into shit later for my directions, but with the number of species who could detect the truth, the dragons would be cleared of wrongdoing and the little colt and his parents would see justice done.

More dragons than I cared to count took to the skies. I'd get into trouble for suggesting they take part, but at least it beat them tearing the van and its occupants apart. My way might let everyone escape the incident alive.

Dr. Erik grumbled something before asking, "Which part of Precinct 1? I'll hitch a lift from someone."

"We're at one of the parks near the hotel. You can't miss the flock of black dragons. They're everywhere. Let me check on the colt. They tossed him out of the truck fairly hard. Right now, a bunch of angry dragons are freeing him from confinement."

"Call me if you need advice," he ordered before hanging up.

The fastest way to comfort the foal would be to show up as a unicorn, so I abandoned my cane, shifted, and hobbled over, lowering myself to the asphalt and nuzzling the colt to help calm him. Upon realization there was another unicorn nearby, the colt did his best to wiggle to me, which helped the dragons untangle him from the oversized bag. As far as I could tell, the little one had escaped mostly unscathed. I nosed the colt until he crowded against my side, checking him over the best I could.

Outside suffering from the fright of his young life and having a scrape or two, he passed my visual checks. While Dr. Erik would yell at me later about it, assuming he found out, I made use of my magic to check for any sign of the toxin, finding none. "He seems okay," I reported, not sure who I notified. With an entire crowd of infuriated dragons around, I could only hope knowing the colt hadn't come to any lasting harm might keep them contained.

A rather inquisitive Black Dragon of New York eyed my injured hoof before turning his head away and snorting smoke. "Alicia, defend your unicorn. Hardy, I want those things from that van. Alive is preferable, but I'll accept in pieces."

With so many black dragons around, I'd forgotten about my co-worker. "Roger," Hardy replied, and he leaped into the air, pumped his wings, and followed the rest of the dragons hunting for the bastards responsible for the latest mess.

Alicia approached, showed off her teeth to the nearest dragons, and waited for them to clear off before circling me and the foal, picking her favorite spot and curling around us, shielding us from the sun with a wing. The low growl she issued did an excellent job of convincing the other dragons to retreat out of her biting range.

The colt shivered, and I nuzzled his neck to reassure him. "Miss Alicia is a friend. Black dragons like unicorns, and not as snacks." I fought to keep my tone calm and soothing, as the last thing the little one needed was hearing my fury. "Your parents will be here soon, okay?"

The colt pressed as close to me as he could, and I settled in to wait, wondering if the incident was connected to the murders, and if so, what it meant for the unicorns of the city.

TWENTY-ONE

I was a free and wild spirit.

Saturday, April 15, 2057
Upper North Lake, Precinct 153
Cauldron City, Nebraska.

WHEN DR. ERIK came to confirm that the colt, Vinny, hadn't come to harm, the little one squealed and showed distress whenever anyone tried to separate him from me. As such, Dr. Erik arranged for Vinny's parents to meet us at my apartment while I got to ride in the back of an ambulance with the baby glued to my side. It worked out, as I got a treatment of my hoof, which did wonders for my mood and general ability to handle life.

Alicia, as a human, rode with us, and I opted to abuse my pony eyes and used her lap as a pillow for a nap.

Upon arrival, she woke me through flicking my ears and saying, "I'm not sure how you're going to get out of here. It was a miracle you fit in the first place."

The removal of the gurney had helped with the fitting

problem. As I lacked clothes thanks to my magic teleporting them home, I'd have to ease out and hope my abused hoof held. "It's not as bad as you think. Getting the colt out will be easier. He's small enough to pick up."

"If Vinny lets anyone pick him up. He's been positively spooked, the poor little baby."

"It'll be all right," I promised. I nosed the colt until he gave me some space and lurched to my hooves. My injured frog twinged, but beyond a sharp reminder to be careful and a lingering ache, it went better than expected.

Dr. Erik opened the back, and a man and woman waited with him.

Vinny squealed, bolted for the end of the ambulance, and jumped for the man, who I presumed was his father. Every adult in range reached for the baby, resulting in a pile of arms, legs, and bodies with the colt on top. Vinny squealed, kicked his feet, managed a few bucks, flopped onto the pile, and writhed in equine bliss.

I turned, kept an eye on my position so I wouldn't damage anything in the ambulance, and took the cautious approach to exiting the ambulance, dropping my front quarters out first before easing my uninjured hoof to the ground. Once stable on three legs, I finished my exit with less grace than I preferred but without falling over. I plodded to the pile of people, nabbed the colt by the nape of his neck, and gave a single tug.

His parents had taught him well, as he stopped writhing, untangled himself from the people pile, and stood still on the ground. I nuzzled him, nosing him until he waited at my side. Once I had him where I wanted, I kept a stern eye on him.

Vinny behaved, although he pranced in place, bucking

every now and then when his general excitement got the better of him.

Once everyone extricated themselves from the pile, Vinny's parents crouched beside him and performed a nose to tail check while cooing to him. Dr. Erik hovered as he tended to do when the little ones were involved.

As my keys, wallet, and phone were likely locked in my apartment, I went to Alicia and gave her a dose of my saddest pony eyes.

"Want to shift?" she asked, gesturing in the direction of my apartment.

I tossed my head in the air and shuffled into a trot.

"A walk, Officer Smithson," Dr. Erik ordered.

Tired of the restraints, I decided to take a page out of the colt's book and bucked, kicked my hooves, and squealed my defiance over his rules. To make it clear I was a free and wild spirit, I bucked a few extra times before launching into my best high-stepped trot.

His healing held, and beyond a twinge, my hoof decided against complaining about my abuse. Once I reached the steps, I exercised some caution so I wouldn't fall and break my neck.

Behind me, Alicia laughed. "I think he's feeling better, Dr. Erik."

"Well, if his hoof wasn't going to hold, he would have been spurting blood, so I guess that's good enough. Try to take it easy for the rest of the day, Jace. Let Alicia show you some homes on the internet."

"That's a good idea. I found some nice places on the market, and when word spread you were house hunting, some homeowners preparing to put their places up for sale messaged our agent so you have first chance at their places."

Alicia pulled keys out of her purse, unlocked my apartment, and giggled. "Your things are in here, folded in the middle of the floor."

I peeked into my apartment, and sure enough, I'd teleported everything to the middle of the floor, directly in the way of getting into the place.

Alicia scooped everything up and relocated it to the kitchen table before opening the door so I could get inside without breaking anything. "I'll go outside and play referee. My grandfather and parents just landed, so they'll be trouble. They're always trouble."

That they were. "I'll be out shortly."

"I recommend you sit on the couch for five minutes. If you stay awake, come on out. If not, you're taking a well-deserved nap. Your hoof is okay?"

"I think so."

She chuckled. "Just like a black dragon. The fastest way to get you to do something is to order you not to do it. You're just better at hiding your tendencies—well, usually."

I bobbed my head, whinnied a laugh, and headed into my bedroom to get changed.

Saturday, April 15, 2057
Upper North Lake, Precinct 153
Cauldron City, Nebraska.

RATHER THAN TAKE a breather on my couch, I spent the five minutes tidying up and making certain I had nothing confidential out in the open. Once done, I emerged from my apartment, rejoiced in the general lack of pain, and joined the congregation of unicorns, dragons, and griffons outside. Alicia's father had his new diamond out, showing it to anyone who'd spare him even a second of their time.

His enthusiasm amused me.

To my dismay, my parents showed up, and they angled for me, their expressions portraying open disapproval. I made warding gestures against evil, which did nothing to stop them.

"What's this I hear about your frog?" my father demanded.

Well, if that was all, I would throw my captain under the bus and show him why nobody messed with sad-eyed ponies. "Captain Farthan did it. I'm innocent. I would have rid the Earth of him, but Dr. Erik stopped me. I landed a good kick, and I was going to stab him a few times with my horn to teach him to be gentle."

My mother turned to the black unicorn, and she snorted a warning, which drew everyone's attention. "What's this about stopping Jace from teaching that stubborn opal his manners?"

The black unicorn sighed. "Jace can't kill his boss, Maria."

"You're also a Maria?" Hardy asked, still in his dragon form. "Jace, your mom is a Maria?"

"We are surrounded with Marias," I confirmed. "Unicorns like having at least one daughter in every generation named Maria. If Mom and Dad decide to inflict another Smithson foal upon the world, and they toss a filly, she'll inevitably be named Maria."

"It's true," my mother informed Hardy, and with zero care he had big teeth and a willingness to use them, she went over and patted his nose. "And aren't you just the cutest little black dragon? Perhaps I should take you home with me, then you can play with Jace whenever you want."

"Mom, you can't adopt or steal my co-workers."

"I can afford him."

I rolled my eyes. "He's not for sale."

Alicia's father snickered and said, "I'm sure his parents would be willing to sell him off if the price is right. I mean, he's a black dragon who works under an opal. That has to be some sort of crime."

I snickered. "Alicia?"

"Don't look at me, Jace. He does menial tasks for an *opal*. They're cordial about it, at least." Alicia huffed before shrugging. "There should be laws about how far a black dragon should fall before he's bleached to be some other color."

Hardy heaved a sigh. "What did I do now?"

"You let your captain stab Jace in the frog. You helped to cripple him. They put the lame unicorns down, you know."

"We really don't," my father muttered.

Alicia pretended she hadn't heard him, and she stated, "It's your fault they're going to put down one of the sanest creatures in Cauldron City."

I eyed Dr. Erik, wondering if he'd slipped the woman some heavy-duty painkillers.

"Don't look at me like that, Jace. Black dragons are, with limited exception, born mean and ready to conquer the world. Just because she happens to be one of the nicer black dragons does not mean her father's exceptionally gentle genes made it through her eggshell. Neither of his parents are black. Their temperaments somehow infected him from before birth." Dr. Erik heaved a chain of sighs, and he attempted to use sad pony eyes on my mother. "What's your excuse?"

"You are way too old to be using those eyes on me, sir," my mother replied, and she gave him a dose of her worst stink eye. "I don't need an excuse for having birthed one of the most noble of unicorns. Sure, he's a little strange, but he's good at what he does. Just look at him. He's not even out of his pony coat yet, and he's already a detective. He's doing just fine, thank you."

Given ten minutes, and the dragons would get a show as most of the present unicorns settled in for a brawl. "If you get into a fight, do not come into my apartment looking for help or sympathy. Alicia, let's go look at larger homes. If the greens weren't involved with the other case, it's not my problem. I'm just a hapless witness. They can question me later."

I expected to be questioned the instant I stepped into the station. The possibility of the kidnapping linking to the dead weight case bothered me, but I needed to pick my battles. If anyone found evidence the cases were connected, I'd be told.

If the cases were connected, I pitied the killer-turned-kidnapper.

Two counts of kidnapping had riled up the entire city. The third would be the final strike. With luck, the city's denizens would bring the perp in alive to face justice.

Another possibility existed, which bothered me. What if the killer wanted to rile the city up? Ethical killers happened, where they'd be hired for a job and complete the job, but along the way, their lines would be crossed. As far as I was concerned, the true culprit behind the cases had crossed lines even hardened criminals disliked.

Could the killer be trying to sink the hire's ship?

"That's quite the expression," Alicia commented.

My parents let out twin snorts, and my father said, "That's his thinking face, and he's chewing on something leaving a sour taste in his mouth. Aren't you off work due to hoof problems today?"

"I don't even know anymore," I admitted. "What is a schedule? Mine seems to have been flipped around on me. Hardy? When do I go back to work?"

"Tuesday," my co-worker replied. "You're working Tuesday through Saturday right now. We aren't supposed to switch our shifts until May. We're putting in our bids for shifts next week."

"Please don't let me forget to bid on my shift," I begged.

"I'll try to remind you," he promised. "Escape while you can. Are you tired of chicken yet?"

"No. And bring extra cheese. Mom, I want to know where your best cheese joints are."

"You're going to regret that later," she warned.

"I want quality cheese to partner with my regrets," I informed her in a solemn tone.

"It's your tummy. You're an adult, if you want torture yourself, I'm not going to stop you. I'll text you with my favorite stops."

As I tried to be a good son, I detoured long enough to give my mother a kiss on her cheeks and exchange hugs with my father before fleeing back to the relative safety of my apartment.

TWENTY-TWO

"And you're sure it's for sale?"

SUNDAY, APRIL 15, 2057
UPPER NORTH LAKE, PRECINCT 153
CAULDRON CITY, NEBRASKA.

ALICIA FOUND a three-story home near River Lakes Park perfect for our needs. The price, however, did me in. I could buy at least seven great homes in expensive cities with money left over for the price of the place. The diamond Alicia had sold to her mother would cover all the fees with plenty left over, but I balked at the price tag.

The library, which took up most of an entire floor, convinced me I hated money but wanted to live in the library. There was even an adjacent bathroom, which would let me retreat to my heaven of books without having to leave often. Food would be a problem, but I could adventure to the kitchen now and then to resolve any hunger issues.

The library featured floor-to-ceiling shelving, plenty of space for comfortable chairs near one of its three fireplaces, matching floor-to-ceiling bookcases serving to break up the space, room for tables or desks as we saw fit, and no windows.

A hallway surrounded the entire library, buffering the books from harmful natural light.

"And you're sure it's for sale?" I asked her for the third time, paging through the pictures of the place.

It met all my base requirements, although I'd have a slightly longer commute to work.

I could live with a longer commute when I got to go home to the perfect library.

"It's really for sale, and the seller reached out to give us a chance to put in an offer first. The family would rather avoid a bid war, and they're moving to the San Francisco area for work. The grapevine worked in our favor. They're dragons."

That tracked. Most of the dragons had grabbed up the best lots when the city was being formed, and the home's status as one of the original estates built when Cauldron City was founded factored into the insane price tag. "And the historical landmark rules?"

"It's always been private property, so you don't have to register the home as a landmark unless you want to. If you do, and you allow people to view the exterior grounds once a month, you dodge property taxes."

I could live in the perfect library and dodge property taxes just from allowing people to view the *exterior* of my home? "I can flex my landscaper's skills and dodge property taxes?"

"Yes."

With one diamond, I'd have the perfect house, no property taxes, and six indoor spots to park cars, one of which would be the Black Wing I would steal from Alicia's grandfather. "I'm not giving the Black Wing back," I warned her.

She laughed. "How about I steal it from my grandpappy and make him buy you one of your own? This one can be my vehicle while I'm in Cauldron City, and then we don't have to share when I'm around. What you do with it when I'm not around is up to you."

That could work. "This seems more than a little excessive."

"Library," she informed me, and she came over, reached around me, and showcased the premier picture of the library, which featured the largest of the fireplaces and a cozy reading nook designed for two. "They're also willing to sell the furniture if you don't want to deal with finding enough to fill the spaces."

"Wait. I can buy the house, and for a little extra, I don't have to go furniture shopping?"

"The finished but empty basement is more than sufficient for storing everything in this apartment about six times over. We can convert the space into prisons for guests."

"Prisons?"

"The nice guests get one of the four guest bedrooms, and that's on top of the seven family bedrooms. The basement can also be converted to be bedrooms for younger clutches. Most dragons never have more than seven clutches underfoot at one time. They wait until the oldest clutch moves out before having another. Just be glad this place was designed with dragons in mind. Dragons prefer to stay close to their clutch siblings, so each bedroom is meant to handle an entire clutch."

"I was wondering why the one bedroom had six beds," I admitted.

"That was their largest clutch, and all their babies have since flown wild and free to cause trouble as adults. We should probably buy out all the furniture and then donate the extra beds to charities. Unless you have a reason to think we're going to need twenty-five extra beds."

Well, as Alicia showed no sign of discomfort over the situation, I replied, "Unicorns tend to have one foal at a time, as unicorns are troublesome. I present the situation with that green foal as evidence. Foals *will* run off and do whatever they want if their parents stop monitoring them for even a second. Most unicorns recoil in horror at the thought of trying to contain more than one foal at a time. Especially colts. The colts are the *worst*."

"You're talking confidently from experience, I see. Hatchlings are also troublesome, but they can be contained with boxes and leashes."

"Dragons leash their children?" I blurted. "With boxes?"

"It's the only way to ever sleep for dragon parents. The leashes are magicked to prevent hatchlings from running away and causing trouble. Hatchlings are put into boxes when in time out with a parent observing. Once, I was so bad that I got put into a box. My parents put on and secured the lid, delivering me to my grandpappy to deal with. My grandpappy did not return me for three weeks. I came back even more troublesome than before I left, apparently. Fortunately for my parents, I outgrew it by the time I turned six."

I could not imagine her father shoving her into a box and handing her off. I eyed her with open suspicion. "Your father, who is so happy he received his first diamond, put you in a box?"

"I am the reason I have an entire clutch of younger

siblings. They shoved me into a box, handed me over, and sent off the rest of the clutch, too. And they decided they needed an entire extra clutch of eggs."

Well, when put that way, I could understand her father's decision to send off the kids. "I mean, your mom worked the streets and trained him from scratch. He probably has a very happy evening life. I can't blame him for doing as your mother says under those circumstances. I'm not sure if my father hasn't been sufficiently charming or if I am just *that* much trouble, honestly. I'm certainly old enough for them to have decided to have another foal by now."

Alicia giggled. "I think they're concerned you're *too* responsible."

"Remind me to call my parents and tell them to go have another foal already. I need a sibling to use as a distraction method." I returned to staring at pictures of the house. "And all we'd have to do to have this house is offer money?"

"Yes, that's right. And my mother took me to the bank to transfer the money to my accounts, so the cash is already accessible from the sale of your diamond. We could have this place closed in record time. The owners aren't living there. They were about to stage it, but then they heard you're in the market for a library."

"Well, they're definitely selling a library that also happens to have nearby living spaces." I returned to the picture with the main fireplace, and I pointed at a section of the floor. "I like reading on the floor sometimes with blankets."

"You're going to fall asleep in front of the fireplace if you do that."

Yes, I would. "Does anything sound better than falling

asleep while reading a book in front of a fireplace while wrapped in your favorite blanket, Alicia?"

"I can't think of anything offhand," she admitted.

"Do we actually have to look at it in person?"

"That's usually how it works. We do need to have it inspected."

"Can the diamond afford to cover literally any repairs that need done?"

"You could demolish the lot and build an entirely new home and have money left over, Jace. It's not selling for *that* much."

"Eighteen million is too much for a home with *no* books also being sold with the property."

She laughed. "Do you want to buy it?"

"Desperately." I pointed at the fireplace. "But it has to include that fireplace. It can't escape."

"The fireplace is a permanent part of the home, but I'll make sure they have all the certificates for the fireplaces and the inspection done. It seems fair since you provided the diamond that I handle the paperwork."

"When my general hatred of excess paperwork is considered, it's probable I picked a poor field for myself," I groused, shaking my head over the inevitable mountain of documentation I'd have to deal with. "How does this work? Are we co-owners?"

She shook her head. "It's your house. I'm just free-loading in it. The diamond is yours, as is all the money from it, so the property will be fully in your name. I sold the diamond on your behalf without commission."

"You should probably get a commission. We usually do five percent when unicorns sell diamonds for other unicorns.

Fix the paperwork to account for a commission. Five percent is more than fair."

"For selling it to my *mother*?"

I bowed my head and snickered, and when I failed to regain my composure, I allowed myself to fully laugh. "I should give you a bonus for being clever and abusing your parents like that. Your dad is over the moon about his new diamond."

"He really is. He's utterly charmed by the whole idea that unicorns can eat chicken and cheese and produce priceless diamonds. Is it true that you can produce other stones? You haven't shown me any."

I got up, went to my bedroom, and dug through my closet for the collection of other stones I'd produced from the moment I'd developed enough to start tossing gemstones and glitter instead of standard manure. I hauled the lot to the table, gathered my laptop, and set it in a safe place. "I mostly produce diamonds when I'm not shitting schist. Mica is the most common schist I produce, which is the case with most whites. Some of us have the misfortune of shitting shale or slate instead of schist. Schist, well, is easier to expel."

"And you still have that coating that somewhat resembles manure?"

"We have a high digestion rate, which is why that is. We convert almost everything to some form of stone. The outer casing is more of a clay than anything else. There are some unicorns that gather the casing material and use it to create pottery."

Alicia's eyes widened. "You shit *clay*?"

I grinned at her expression. "Trust me, finding out the

rest of my life would involve being wanted for my *shit* was quite the eye-opener. Then my asshole father thought the best way to learn about the unfortunate nature of unicorns involved feeding me everything needed to produce semi-precious stones. Most of these stones were from when I was a teen and young adult. I started producing diamonds consistently when I hit twenty-five. Now, I rarely produce the other stones unless I eat nothing but what is needed to produce them. But when I do, I get really nice stones." I took care dumping the collection of stones onto my table, most of which were contained in plastic bags to keep like with like. "I am a little strange compared to other whites. I don't produce much in the way of fancy diamonds, but I get the unusual colors of other stones. I have a theory it has something to do with my tendency to do things a little differently."

I grabbed my collection of garnets, which came in various shades of red, purple-red, orange, green, peach, and pink. Most viewed the green, pink, or peach garnets as the rarest, and I tended to produce more than my fair share of those colors. I started with my largest one, a peach beauty that could fetch a million on the market if I waited for a good time. I had a more valuable green, but I liked the peach better, and the peach had it beat in size by fifteen carats. "This is a garnet, and she weighs almost two hundred carats."

"Did you end up naming her after you gave birth? Because it looks like you suffered for that one."

Laughing over the idea of naming my gemstones after suffering through epic constipation, I shook my head. "The glitter volume is a lot lower when I produce semi-precious stones compared to diamonds, so I could, in theory, produce a five hundred carat monster of a garnet with less suffering than the stone you sold."

Her brows rose at that. "Should I tell my father that diamond has a name?"

With a shake of my head, I sorted through the stones in search of my favorite, a rather stunning ametrine, split into three equal sections. When cut, the ends would be a rich purple while the center would be fire yellow. "I want to get this one cut and keep it as part of my hoard. I can be an honorary dragon with a hoard, right?"

"If you are captured or hoarded by a dragon, you automatically get hoarding rights. May I?"

I handed her the stone.

She dug out her phone, snapped a few pictures, and made a phone call. "Grandpappy, take a look at the photo I sent you. That's an ametrine. Jace wants it cut for his new hoard. He has decided he needs to have a hoard of cut stones, and that's his favorite. Can you wrangle a cutter for him and get a good deal?"

Dragons would forever confuse me, but if Alicia wanted to put her grandfather to work hunting for a good cutter for my stone, I would not complain.

After giggling, Alicia pulled the phone from her ear and asked, "Do you have an odd stone you can sell to my grandpappy to give to my father? He wants to make sure my father has a starter kit for his own gemstone hoard."

I could do him one better, and I replied, "Sure, I can sell a mix of stones. My mother and father produce really nice semi-precious stones, and they *love* selling theirs. He could get a good collection just from talking with them. And if he's clever, he'll get my parents talking to *their* parents. All four of my grandparents are alive, and they're producers, too. I even have some great-grandparents kickin' around."

And their parents were around, as were their parents—my eldest living direct ancestor was just over eight hundred, and she'd tossed her last foal shortly before I'd been born. Her beloved, my second eldest living ancestor, was only ten years younger than her.

They'd abandoned husband and wife for beloved, which came across to me as more meaningful.

They'd spent the entirety of their long lives together.

We read the writing on the wall, too: when one passed, so would the other.

"Grandpappy, Jace says you should talk to his parents, but he's willing to sell some of his semi-precious stones. Try offering him some rare books. It can be a gift exchange. We found a place, and while the price tag is lethal, it would have gone for a lot higher if it'd gone to the open market. He doesn't like the paperwork, so I'm going to handle most everything and involve him only when he needs to sign. No, he didn't want to see it in person. I think his current aspiration in life is to take his favorite blanket, go to the big fireplace in the library, and read in front of it while curled on the floor until he falls asleep. It's a good plan. He's also requested I take a commission, and he proposed the rate unicorns pay for the sale of their stones. I don't think he's going to accept no for an answer on the commission."

"That's correct. I am not accepting no for an answer on the commission."

"Did you hear him? Okay, good. I'm claiming the Black Wing. It's mine now, grandpappy. His garage has six spots. You may fill one and only one of his spots with a Black

Wing of his own, per your wager for putting that mean old opal in his place. Any news on that poor little foal?"

Considering it took her grandpappy almost ten minutes to finish talking, something must have happened in the city while I'd taken the time to investigate the housing situation, decide I had zero respect for money, and had opted to behave more like a unicorn than a trash panda. After he finished, she informed him she did actually love him but would have to repay him later before hanging up. "The city has become disturbingly peaceful since yesterday. The van's occupants managed to escape although the van is in police custody. The vehicle had been reported stolen the day before the foal was snatched. I'm going to guess that there have been no new leads or labs back on what you're working on, as my grandpappy has Hardy in his custody along with Hardy's partner. Apparently, he is going to take over Cauldron City through adopting all the police officers."

"He doesn't have to adopt his own grandson," I pointed out.

"I could hear Hardy in the background stating he was not adoptable, as he loves his parents, who are still alive." Alicia grinned, set her phone out of the way, and rubbed her hands. "Can I look through these?"

"You absolutely may. Pick your ten favorite stones. You can earn them for conquering basic tasks in the kitchen. Then you can sell them to your mother and buy books. I don't think either of us have nearly enough books to fit into that library."

"I think you're right. I better find out how many books that library can fit. Grandpappy says until I graduate from your cooking program, I'm not allowed to live unattended. It seems I will be staying with him or my parents in New

York or I'll be inviting someone to keep an eye on me. I am not to be trusted."

I could understand that, and in her family's shoes, I would be making similar edicts. "Just think about it this way. You're a conquering queen, and they are part of your hoard until they set you free."

"You know what, Jace? I like the way you think."

TWENTY-THREE

Well, that answered a few questions.

TUESDAY, APRIL 17, 2057
LOWER NORTH LAKES, PRECINCT 153
CAULDRON CITY, NEBRASKA.

MY QUESTIONING SESSION regarding the kidnapping and recovering of the green foal took all of ten minutes, most of which Captain Farthan spent praising me for containing the furious black dragons who would have torn the van and city apart had I not given them direction. As part of his thanks and his quest to make certain I became the next kidnapping victim, he made it known Hardy would be braving the wilds of the city to fetch me all the Portuguese chicken my heart desired.

I would hate myself within a week, but my future kidnappers would love the haul.

As my mother loved me and wanted me to be rich, she texted me the complete list of her favorite haunts, and she included a helpful guide on which places ran the highest risk of salmonella poisoning. Her notation indicated that when she flirted with bacteria-based disaster, she produced rare-colored diamonds, and I too might enjoy such benefits. To add a little extra spice, she also indicated that spicy chicken served with cheese could increase her carat size by up to a quarter.

Well, that answered a few questions.

Aware I would likely end up in the hospital, I texted Dr. Erik with a warning I flirted with spicy chicken and cheese death to replace my precious lost diamond. I requested forgiveness in addition to the inevitable medical care I would require.

His text indicated my mother had already inquired, as she was encouraging my hospital visit. As she'd started it, she would pay the price for my indulgences.

With that out of the way, I headed into my office, turned on my new digital murder board, and went to work trying to make sense of the dead weight case. Opening several new files, I began to create a timeline. The sales of the poisoned alcohol went in first, and I registered every known instance, listing the bars that had bought the tainted booze, the date the purchase had been made, and who had sold the bottles. Every witness statement we had went into the appropriate section, although I had doubts regarding the viability of such statements.

The sellers, all of whom were large-scale wholesalers, would need to be questioned again, as I wasn't buying the hogwash they attempted to sell me. And if they tried to claim they hadn't done any vetting on the bottles for safety, I would be digging through every single one of the law books until I had a case file so thick the judge would need six months to read through it.

While Cauldron City had a healthy bar scene, the wholesalers of alcohol were required to track where they got their booze, who had sold it to them, where it had been manufactured, and when it had been manufactured. Recalls on alcohol didn't happen often, but they did happen.

When something went wrong, the wholesalers providing alcohol to the city bars were supposed to be able to give law enforcement the required information—including a certificate verifying the alcohol was safe for consumption.

We did not have any of the information we needed to identify where the alcohol had come from and if it was safe for consumption.

I wanted to know how the culprit had pulled that off. The why made sense. While most criminals were dumber than a sack of rocks, the culprit I hunted had bothered to take steps to cover his trail. That the person—or persons—managed to circumvent long-standing laws bothered me.

That the wholesalers had played the game or had been tricked into doing it bothered me more. Had one of the wholesalers sabotaged the record systems? Had they accepted a bribe to hide the poisoned alcohol? Making the wholesalers take the fall made sense.

If the wholesalers took the blame, the investigation might stop with them, thus preventing the culprit from facing justice.

But why target the city's bars?

I opened a new file, and as part of investigations involved attempting to discover the motive along with the method, I began making lists of theories on why someone might go through all the trouble of setting alcohol wholesalers up for a fall.

Playing off the high frequency of sexual offenders on

the victim list, I pursued reasons someone might want to poison the local watering holes. Going through the victim's files on my computer told a sad tale of substance abuse, ranging from alcohol to a staggering assortment of narcotics.

Most of the drug offenses hadn't made it to the paper copies of the rap sheets, however. Frowning, I grabbed my phone, stabbed the captain's extension, and pinned the damned thing between my shoulder and ear while reviewing the physical documentation I'd been given.

"What do you need, Smithson?" my captain answered. "I could have sworn I'd just seen you an hour ago."

I snorted at the opal's tone, which blended exasperation with irritation. "The rap sheets I have on the victims in the dead weight case are missing records, mostly regarding alcohol and narcotics abuse. I used our digital database to confirm the paper records are incomplete. Can you yell at someone about that, please? I can't follow all leads if I don't have all the relevant information. With the toxin on and in those bodies, their narcotics histories are relevant."

My captain issued a tiny growl, the kind warning me of mayhem in the station as soon as he figured out who had left out pertinent information from my records. "I'll take care of it. Any thoughts on that case?"

"I'm checking out a potential motive for the bar poisonings, which might be able to forge a link between the cases, but I need a complete copy of the rap sheets. I have some thoughts, and generally, I don't like those thoughts in the slightest. Any news on the wire?"

"We've got another one over in Precinct 158 in the Industrial Quarter. Their cops are handling the information gathering, and someone will be by today with pictures and evidence for you. I thought about sending you out, but as it was a more traditional case, I opted against it."

There were multiple ways I could interpret his statement, so I asked, "You mean the bodies were counterweights for each other rather than a living victim?"

"Precisely. The methodology seems to match the other cases, but we won't know until the forensics team evaluates the scene. On the surface, it looks like the first case, with the notable lack of a unicorn hanging around." My captain sighed. "There are also reports of failed kidnapping attempts of other unicorns, adult ones, which is playing well with our thought about a shaggy pony being clipped to resemble an adult. I'm going to have you go out with Hardy and Dowdren tomorrow, where you will openly have lunch containing chicken and cheese."

"I'm going to need therapy after this," I warned him.

"I'm sure an arrangement can be made. Today, I want you to keep your head down and stay at the station until we get more information on the unicorns being targeted. I don't know if we have a copycat or this is connected to our primary case, and I'd rather not find out what a copycat might do to one of my cops."

I expected if I were to get snatched, the opal dragon would have the entirety of the city buzzing worse than a hive of provoked yellow jackets. And like yellow jackets, angry dragons, griffons, unicorns, and others tended to erase mercy from their dictionaries. Granted, I'd never seen a yellow jacket have mercy on anyone before, which implied mercy had never been in their dictionary to begin with. "Understood, sir."

"I'll have complete paper records delivered to your office within the next two hours. Do your best with what you have, and I'll look into why you weren't given the full rap sheets." My captain hung up, and after returning the phone to its cradle, I eyed my murder board.

What were the requirements for an organ donor?

I suspected I'd locate some important keys to my case with a better understanding of the science. As such, I decided to impose on Dr. Erik. Grabbing the phone again, I dialed his number, considering the record for James McDonald, the most likely candidate for being the donor of a successful heart or kidney transplant.

"What is it, Jace?" the black unicorn answered.

"I have a work-related medical question for you. What are the requirements for somebody to be a viable organ donor? Age, sex, blood type, the works. What makes someone a good donor candidate?"

"It's complicated," Dr. Erik warned me. "There are a lot of criteria for someone to be a match for organ donation, living or deceased. While matching race and species is not necessarily a requirement, the reality is, different races and sub-species have variations in their immune system. Matching someone from a very different genetic background increases the risk of an alloimmunity issue—or the rejection of tissue or cells from someone of the same species. In this case, the alloimmunity issues involve where the tissue grafts occur."

I feared I would need a medical degree to understand the black unicorn, but determined to make sense of the situation, I asked, "Do you mean where the donated tissue is connected to the recipient?"

"Correct. Alloimmunity is complicated and not fully understood, especially by the general public. You are aware of how blood types work, correct?"

"Yes."

"One of the most common forms of an alloimmunity disorder is when the mother of a baby has a conflicting blood factor. Humans have two Rh factors, positive and negative, within their genetics. In order to get an Rh-negative blood factor, you need both parents to have at least one copy of the Rh-negative factor. When this happens, and the mother has the Rh-positive factor, the mother and baby conflict. Depending on the specific situation, the mother may kill the baby or the baby may try to kill the mother. Their immune systems are treating each other as something to be eradicated. We have special antibodies that the mother is given during pregnancy to control the conflicting blood factors. This is classified as an alloimmunity disorder, as mother and baby are the same species but are rejecting each other due to their conflicting blood factors."

I took a few minutes to chew on that, and when I decided I had a basic understanding of the concept, I asked, "So, in the case of organ transplants, the donor's organ may be rejected by the patient due to some unknown factor?"

"Correct. We have medications that are designed to suppress the patient's immune system and make it more likely that the donor's organ will be accepted. The closer the biological match for the organ, the less likely that rejection of the grafted tissue may occur. As all your victims are Caucasian males in their thirties with an O-positive blood type, I would look for patients with O-positive blood types, male, in their thirties, in need of either a kidney or a heart."

"Kidney or heart?" I asked.

"Most of the bodies showed damage to the heart and kidneys, with one victim having those organs removed appropriately for an organ transplant. It could just be that the operating surgeon wanted some extra money on the black market, but going through all the trouble to get convicts with matching ages and blood type leads me to believe there's something there. I'm not a detective, however. But if I were to be investigating this matter, I would be looking for the organ recipient. That's going to be difficult, as you'd have to have a reason to access medical records—or there is public information available. There likely isn't. Patient privacy is protected."

I could read between the lines readily enough. "And someone who is trying to get a black market organ is not going to advertise that they're after a black market organ."

"Correct."

"Any other gems of wisdom, doc?"

"I wish. Be careful, Jace. Whomever is behind this is good at what they do, and they mean business."

"I'll be careful," I promised. "I'll call you back if I have any other questions."

Once I exchanged a few pleasantries with him and promised to take it easy on my foot for the rest of the day, I put the information he'd given me into a note file to pursue later. As the autopsy reports would play a key role in the investigation, I went to my computer, checked the digital records to see if the autopsy reports had been loaded into the system, and upon locating the digital records, I copied them onto the murder board. I created a profile for each victim, snagged the latest mug shot for them to use as their visual identifier, and began the tedious process of gathering up all the data and making it accessible.

To help me make sense of the case, I began with a list of the first victims found along with a notation of how their bodies had been mutilated following death. Well, I hoped the organ removal had begun after death. I made a note to ask Dr. Erik if any of the victims might have been alive when their organs had been stolen. With the exception of the brain, if it was an organ, the organ thief had shown some interest in it in one way or another.

The longer I stared at the list of the basics, the more it disturbed me.

BENJAMIN PATEL: Aged 32. Caucasian, male. Species: human, non-shapeshifting. Muscle and fat removed, heart damaged.

LUKE JORDAN: Aged 36. Caucasian, male. Species: human, non-shapeshifting. Four ribs, fat, and all major organs partially removed.

ROBERT RICHARDS: Aged 34. Caucasian, male. Species: human, non-shapeshifting. Bone and bone marrow damaged or removed, fat, and all major organs partially removed.

ADAM GILL: Aged 32. Caucasian, male. Species: human, non-shapeshifting. Muscle and fat removed.

NICKOLAS OSBORN: Aged 38. Caucasian, male. Species: human, non-shapeshifting. Muscles removed, all major organs partially removed.

LEO FERGUSON: Aged 31. Caucasian, male. Species: human, non-shapeshifting. Heart partially removed.

Lane Coffey: Aged 35. Caucasian, male. Species: human, non-shapeshifting. Fat and all major organs partially removed.

Julian Cane: Aged 36. Caucasian, male. Species: human, non-shapeshifting. All major organs fully removed.

James McDonald: Aged 32. Caucasian, male. Species: human, non-shapeshifting. Heart and kidneys fully removed.

Manuel Wilkins: Aged 33. Caucasian, male. Species: human, non-shapeshifting. Muscle, fat, and lungs partially removed.

With James McDonald the only victim who hadn't been poisoned, I suspected his heart and kidneys had been transplanted into someone else. But who? There were too many possibilities. The hire, the one truly behind the killings, could be harvesting organs for the underground market, a market I knew existed. That was as far as my knowledge went, however.

On the other hand, the killer could be the one working with the surgeon. Over the years, I'd seen how far people would go due to passion. Someone capable of slaughtering so many people wouldn't have any problems with committing the crime if it meant a loved one might continue to live.

Who played who? Did the hire want the killer's ship sunk? Were they the same person? I doubted that; with the rise of kidnappings involving children linked with more deaths, *someone* wanted the chain to break. I held the belief the hire betrayed the killer, but I lacked evidence to prove it, although I also liked the idea of an ethical killer attempting to sink their unethical hire.

On the evidence front, I had a whole lot of nothing.

As misery loved company, I wheeled my chair to my door, opened it, and leaned out to check the status of Hardy's office.

His door was open.

Excellent.

As my co-workers often bothered me when I wanted to concentrate, I decided to get some payback. I inhaled, allowing myself to break every rule regarding indoor voice volume, and complained, "Why don't I have any actual evidence, Hardy?"

In the nearby cubicle farm, someone snorted, which triggered a cascade of titters.

"Welcome to being a detective," Hardy hollered back. "We never have enough actual evidence."

"This isn't a matter of having enough. This is a matter of not having any at all. This is unacceptable. Get me some actual evidence, Hardy."

The black dragon laughed, and he rolled his chair into the hallway. "What do you need, Jace?"

"Evidence. I just said that."

"Let me rephrase that. What sort of evidence are you looking for? Is there a picture you're trying to paint with the case?"

"The only evidence I have, if you can call it that, are autopsy reports showing nine of the ten victims had metabolized the toxin in addition to it being on them. One victim had not been poisoned. He had the substance on him, yes, but not in him. All victims showed evidence of having body parts, muscle, or fat removed. My guess is organ donation in a violent fashion targeting the unwanted of society, but that does not count as admissible evidence, Hardy. I want some admissible evidence." To make it clear I meant business, I pointed in the direction of the elevator. "Go get me some evidence. Precinct 158 might have some for me."

"Another one?" Hardy sighed. "Is some asshole waiting for you to come into work to add to your case? Maybe we should profile you to find out why you're so popular this week."

As Hardy liked jumping in line to imply how handsome he was, I figured I could join the party, albeit a little late. "It's obviously because I was well-raised, far more handsome than you'll ever be, and a true unicorn among men."

"You're a bastard," Hardy informed me in a solemn tone. "Are you sure I can't take you home with me?"

"I have a new rule in my life. I will only have one live-in dragon at a time, and Alicia is smarter than you, as she claimed the spot first through the attempted murder of her grandfather. It takes a great deal of skill and trickery to bring that dragon down."

"As far as murder attempts go, I'm pretty sure that mean old bastard hasn't had a health scare like that in a long damned time. Brought low by eggs."

"And bacon. I'm still ashamed my pesto was somehow involved with that travesty."

"He *ate* it," my co-worker mock whispered. "He not only ate it, he acted like he enjoyed it."

The area fell quiet as we all took a moment to marvel at the sheer courage and strength the Black Dragon of New York possessed. Unable to find a flaw in the dragon's behavior, I was forced to confess, "He is a better man than I."

"He's not a man at all, Jace. He's a dragon. He's male,

but it's important to remember dragons are *not* human. We just look human."

"I call you a man, and you don't complain," I pointed out.

"Well, yes. I am single, I am beautiful, and I don't want to be single forever. Dragons can be men when it comes to the proper wooing of women. And any female, regardless of species, counts as a woman for this. Well, assuming we're shifting to human form to have ourselves a good time."

I regretted having opened my mouth. "And here I thought you were a virgin."

Judging from the choked sounds nearby that sputtered away to nothing, my comment killed one of my co-workers in the cubicle farm.

"Damn, Jace, that's *mean*." Hardy scowled. "Are you sure I can't take you home with me?"

"Sorry, Hardy. Alicia is spending my money buying me paradise. Paradise has an entire floor dedicated to books with a bathroom to make sure I don't have to venture far should nature call." I rubbed my hands together at the thought of filling the shelves with my books. "And before I can truly enjoy the paradise I tricked a dragon into buying on my behalf, I need to solve this case before even more people die. I need evidence, Hardy, and I need you to go fetch it. While you're out, bring me some chicken from the Portuguese place. I'm going to need fuel if I'm going to have any chance of figuring this case out."

TUESDAY, APRIL 17, 2057

The Industrial Ward, Precinct 158
Cauldron City, Nebraska.

WHILE HARDY BROUGHT me my chicken, news from Precinct 158 sent us out to the scene of the crime to investigate the gruesome deaths of ten more men. The morning's first batch had only been four, and they'd all matched the basic criteria of the first group of victims. All were Caucasian males, all were missing various organs, they seemed to be in their thirties, and the forensics team managed to confirm they all had O-positive blood.

Until we could get them identified, we could only guess at the circumstances leading up to their deaths.

Their estimated time of death ranged from hours to a few days prior to them being dumped in the warehouse, and everybody treated them like they were poisoned, plagued, or both.

The last thing anyone needed was a plague tearing through Cauldron City to go with the mass poisoning.

"Hey, Dowdren?" I asked, aware I probably wouldn't get an answer out of the man. Once I had his attention, I said, "Can you shoot me an email later to remind me to look more into the mass poisoning case? I need to figure out the base number of people poisoned, how many might have been poisoned had we not started looking into the supply chain, and what types of bars the suppliers work with."

He nodded, and his attention returned to the tangle of corpses hanging from the warehouse rafters. Unlike the cases in our precinct, no pulley systems had been used. How the bodies had gotten up there remained a mystery. I could only hope someone in the forensics department had a good idea, as I could only assume magic had been involved.

Magic hadn't been involved in the prior cases, and its introduction to an already complicated case would ruin my day. Standard crimes had a way of becoming complicated, with insufficient evidence and leads resulting in the criminal successfully dodging justice. While magic left residue and traces we could use as evidence, it could also erase evidence.

I was living, breathing proof of that.

One of the local cops, a younger woman, eyed us with open suspicion. "You the boys from Precinct 153?"

Dowdren grunted, Hardy sighed, and I replied, "We are. I'll just apologize now for our messes coming to pay you a visit. I'm guessing the warehouse in Precinct 153 is currently inaccessible due to the investigation, and this outfit is just smart enough to understand we might notice something if somebody starts hauling mutilated corpses into the building next door."

She bobbed her head and eyed the bodies. "They started dripping twenty minutes after we got here at an abnormally consistent rate. Some of the dripping matches the briefing we were given from your case."

Great. More replicating poison. Beneath the bodies, someone had put down several buckets to catch the various fluids. "Has it replicated?"

"One of the substances has replicated, but we have discovered that hydrogen peroxide will halt the process. One of the forensics members decided to test, as it was getting uncomfortably close to the rim."

So much for keeping the evidence pure. Still, I'd rather have ruined evidence than poison spreading throughout Cauldron City unchecked. "Hardy, call in the hydrogen peroxide tip to the lab and have them run some tests on our samples."

"On it." The black dragon stepped away, digging out his phone to make the call.

With one problem sorted for the moment, I eyed the corpses dangling above. "Any word on how they're secured up there?"

"They fused a steel cable to the ceiling. We'll need some serious tools to get them down or figure out how they were attached to the cable. We think the bodies have been embedded with rope or a cable of some sort to secure them."

Well, that would make the forensics team work for evidence. "Think my captain would approve a demotion? I'm not sure I'm paid enough for this," I admitted.

She laughed. "None of us are, and we had the same discussion earlier. I'm Susie, and my partner over there is Emilio. Emilio won't be coming any closer, as we don't need to clean vomit out of our crime scene."

I waved to her partner, pondering how we might be able to get the victims down. "Well, dragons are sometimes useful. I'm sure we can find one capable of breaking or melting off that cable *without* bringing the warehouse down around our ears." I eyed Dowdren. "Think Hardy can handle it?"

The immediate shake of my co-worker's head worried me. "I'm going to need one of those mean red bastards for this, aren't I?"

He nodded.

"What bribe do you need to be the poor bastard to make the call?"

"Portuguese tomorrow," he replied.

"Deal. Extra spicy with two orders of fries?" I asked,

aware he viewed fries as the gift of some god determined to make us happy.

He nodded, and he headed off to join Hardy outside of the warehouse to pretend he would enjoy some privacy.

"Thanks. I'll start getting the rest of the info we need so we can let these nice folks get back to work without us underfoot." I turned to Susie and asked, "What do we need from you so we can get out from underfoot?"

"I like you," she informed me. "There are several problems with the vics, excluding the jurisdiction issues. First, we already know the identification of one, and he's on the FBI's wanted list."

I raised a brow. "Most of them in this case have been on a wanted list or another, including the FBI's. They can get in line with the other corpses. That's just a little extra paperwork at this stage."

She raised a brow. "You have more like this?"

"They're all violent crimes offenders on various levels, and most of them are on sexual offender lists," I replied, circling beneath the corpses. Sure enough, one of them had his head sticking out, and he was fresh enough for his features to not have been distorted from putrefaction. Pointing at him, I asked, "Is that our wanted vic?"

"Sure is. His name is Ryan Martin, and he busted out of a Federal prison in Maine three weeks ago. Whomever killed him walked away from a half a million dollar reward. My partner recognized him, as he likes keeping an eye on the wanted list for new additions. Martin hit the list the day after he busted out."

I retrieved my phone and shot myself an email to look into Ryan Martin, dig out the FBI wanted poster for him, and get his complete rap sheet. "Violent crimes and sexual assault?"

"He was convicted for the murder of his six-year-old daughter and her mother, but he has a history of violence crimes in addition to that. He'd gotten a life sentence without parole. I don't have details on how he escaped jail, however." Susie glared at the corpse. "Are you going to take over the interviews?"

"Yes." I assumed Susie numbered among those who felt the vics had gotten precisely what they deserved. While I agreed with her in some ways, I also understood vigilante justice wouldn't erase the crimes of the guilty or ultimately serve the community. If everyone opted to take justice into their own hands, bodies would be plentiful, mercy would never be shown, and the innocent would pay as often as the guilty. "Just send me copies of everything, and I'll make sure it's handled."

We spent a few minutes exchanging information, and I gave her several alternative contacts she could reach out to if I wasn't available. Once that was handled, I returned to the problem of getting the bodies down without mutilating them any further.

Hardy returned with Dowdren in tow, and he said, "I've got one of the mean old reds incoming, and she's bringing a forensics team over. We're also getting some help from Precinct 1. They're pissed about the colt, and they want to be involved, just in case there is a connection."

I winced, as the last thing we needed was additional complexity. "Is this our cue to leave, Hardy? Susie is going to make sure we get all the intel we need to get a move on."

"As I don't want to smell charred metal and corpses, yes. Sorry, Susie," the black dragon said, saluting the woman.

"Bring your partner over to Precinct 153 for lunch next week so we can make this shitshow up to you?"

"Only if I can try some of that Portuguese food that got your partner moving like he meant it," she replied.

"You're on. I'll get a whole batch ordered for the team dealing with this. Send Jace the numbers and when everyone will be on shift together, and I'll make it happen. Keep us looped in if any of your cases have any similarities to this one."

"Actually, we do have a few from this week that seemed weird and might match if you squint. I'll talk with the others and send over anything that might be relevant."

"We're looking for probable organ theft."

"How about corpses with their blood removed?" she asked.

My eyes widened. "Yes," I replied. Blood would definitely be a requirement if someone was trying to perform organ donations. "O-positive, by any chance?"

"A disturbing number of the vics were O-positive, yes, but there's a mix of other blood types."

That worried me. "How many corpses did you find that were missing most of their blood?"

"More than I care to think about," she admitted. "I'll send the info your way by the end of the day. Thanks for coming—and thanks for calling in the dragon, because we were all out of ideas of how to get them down."

We exchanged pleasantries before we left, and as usual, I had more questions than answers.

TWENTY-FOUR

"Why am I going to be killing and eating you today, Officer Smithson?"

TUESDAY, APRIL 17, 2057
LOWER NORTH LAKES, PRECINCT 153
CAULDRON CITY, NEBRASKA.

BRACING to face the wrath of an opal dragon, I knocked on my captain's door. He ordered me to enter, and drawing a deep breath, I stepped inside.

"You look like you're about to be executed. Why am I going to be killing and eating you today, Officer Smithson?"

Damn. One day, I would somehow figure out how to get my face to shut up when I was apprehensive over something. "Precinct 158 has had a surge of murder cases where the bodies have been robbed of their blood. According to Susie, one of their detectives, a high number of the corpses had O-positive blood."

"Just like our organ theft cases." While Captain Farthan wrinkled his nose and huffed, he did not slay me and proceed to have a unicorn snack. "I'm not sure why this makes you think you're facing your execution."

"I told Susie to send the files for those cases over to us due to probable connection."

Rather than face death, I received a slow clap. "Do I need to send you back to preschool for a few weeks to get you over this surge of uncharacteristic anxiety? That's what you're supposed to be doing. You're supposed to be claiming jurisdiction as things come up, handling interviews, and funneling all the paperwork to one place, which is your office."

I blinked. "I'm supposed to be stealing jurisdiction of other cases?"

"When it's pretty clear they're related to and connected to the case we have primary city-wide jurisdiction for, yes. You're not doing anything wrong. If you weren't acting like I caught your hand in the cookie jar, I'd be giving you a card to escape your next visit to preschool."

I allowed myself a chuckle at that. "Can I have the escape card anyway, sir?"

"I'm thinking you'll want an invitation to preschool after this week is over and all those cases hit your desk. How about I give you a card that lets you decide if you want to flee to preschool for a week or two or get out of going to preschool when you've finally screwed something up?"

As I had a brain and sometimes decided to use it, I nodded to accept his offer. "Susie asked if I would be handling the interviews. I told her yes."

"Good call, but I don't envy your day, which can start as soon as you flee my office, taking your many regrets with you." Captain Farthan reached over, plucked a pile of papers off his desk, and held them out. "We have one fresh lead for you, and the woman arrived at the airport this morning with her young child. As a fair warning, they're upset. They were on good terms with a vic. The FBI escorted her to our fair city, but as this is our case, you get to handle our chunk of the questioning. She is waiting at the FBI building in Precinct 1. I told them you'd be around a little later. She understands she's being questioned twice, consented to it, and is a willing participant, so she should be a good warmup for you. The FBI will give us the recording for evidence and training purposes. I wanted to send Hardy and Dowdren with you, but I need them elsewhere, so you're on your own. Well, mostly. Your dragoness is in the building, and I got approval for her to watch your back from the FBI. She'll be working in a conference room while you handle the questioning session. I think she's trying to finalize paperwork on your new home. Think she'll handle my real estate woes next time I have to move? She's vicious."

"She has a realtor, I think." I frowned, wondering what she was up to. "The house in question is already available, and it's on hold for me to buy, so I'm guessing there's a lot less paperwork than normal. And it's a cash sale, so it should close quickly."

"Quickly should not be over a weekend, Smithson. I'm pretty sure she has a date to get the keys tonight."

I narrowed my eyes, sat down in one of the free chairs in front of his desk, and retrieved my phone. "Do detectives use their personal cells at work?"

"You can with dual sim chips, but only if you bar people from accessing the phone. You'll have your new cell for work by the end of the day. It's fine to use your personal phone for the moment, just keep all confidential stuff off it, just like before your promotion."

Nice. “I emailed Susie’s contact information via my phone because I realized I didn’t have another way to do it. The laptop was still in the cruiser.”

“Ah, speaking of which. Your cruiser will be ready on Wednesday. It needs a paint job, but we were able to get the right make and model, and they were able to start the modification work right after your promotional flight. Technically, you’re going to have two cruisers, but you’ll be expected to share with your partner once you pick one. The other cruiser is a K9 vehicle, as you worked with Mamma Mia beautifully. Martino wants you able to work with a dog as of next week, and he’s authorized you to take Mamma Mia as needed. She’s starting to slow down.”

I winced, as Martino adored his wolf-dog, but she had been working the streets for far longer than I’d been a cop. “He needs a more active dog?”

“He needs a more active dog. Mamma Mia likes you, and she would appreciate a detective’s speed, and that’ll let us keep her around longer. She’ll still go home with Martino unless he’s not working, and if he’s not, you can drop her off at his home or keep her for the night. If you two work well together, I expect Mamma Mia will transition to being your wolf-dog with Martino holding visitation rights. We’re hoping we can transition her so you become her handler and long-term owner. You can give her the care she needs.”

Right. I was a unicorn, and I could find a vet to help keep the animal comfortable as she aged. “How old is she now?”

“She’s fifteen.”

“How long do wolf-dogs like her live for?”

“Sixteen, usually.”

I raised a brow, as I hadn't realized she had two paws in the grave. "I made an old, tired dog run around?"

"The old, tired dog hates not having a job to do, and we were told by our vet she will work until the day she dies. We don't have the heart to retire her, so there you have it. She's given her whole life to the service, and she does *not* want to retire. We're respecting that. Martino is ready to hand over her leash as soon as you're ready to take it. She's also good with kids and trauma victims."

"She looks like she could eat the kids," I confessed.

"Her method of convincing children that she is safe is to roll onto her back and absolutely writhe while lashing her tail. It's ridiculous. It's also effective. She's a smart animal, and while she never developed sentience like a few of our bloodhounds, she understands how people tick. We think she's questionably borderline."

"Any health problems?"

"Surprisingly few, but her joints are achy. Can you unicorns address arthritis?"

I nodded. "I'm not sure I know anyone who has done it for *dogs*, but we'll do it for people when the pain is unmanageable in other ways. It's time consuming."

"The precinct will pay the bill, as she's a full-time staff member and her arthritis is ultimately work-related. Just try to spare us a fortune."

I snorted. "If I'm getting her leash, it counts as 'pet of a unicorn in distress' and we don't handle that well, even if she is technically a work dog. If Mamma Mia is good with kids, and I have a distressed woman and kid at the FBI building, then it makes sense to give her some work she'll like."

The captain grabbed his phone, punched a button,

waited a moment, and said, "Martino, bring Mamma Mia to my office with Smithson's bone and her kit. She's got a job working a pair of distressed witnesses. Smithson is willing to take her off your hands, and she'll have a date with some unicorns for treatment sooner than later. Bring up two puppies when you come, the washout to go with Mamma Mia and your favorite of the lot to be trained to take Mamma Mia's place."

Without waiting for an answer, he hung up.

"Puppies?" I asked.

"The washout is another wolf-dog like Mamma Mia. She might work out, but she's too friendly at this point in time. Mamma Mia likes having other dogs around, so with a little luck, Mamma Mia can teach the puppy her manners and how to be a proper police dog. Worst case scenario, you'll be the leader of the station's dog and pony show, and we train the dog for therapy. Admit it, Smithson. You love the idea of being able to help traumatized victims with a canine sidekick. And with some work, we can train her for sniffing and other tasks. She won't be good at the offensive, however. You'll have Mamma Mia for that for a while—and if it turns out you need an attack dog, we'll figure something out. But the puppy might work out. Or she might love the perps to a near-death state, and as long as she's loving them to said near-death while on top, it works."

Rather than reply, I leaned back in my chair, crossed my arms, and engaged the opal dragon in a staring contest.

Captain Farthan laughed at me. "Every time we try to get this puppy to do anything offensive, she thinks it means she's supposed to lick us in the face. She has the same general offensive ability as down feathers—and they aren't in pillow format."

"So, she's soft, fluffy, and prone to making you sneeze?"

"Only if allergic, Smithson. Are you allergic to dogs?"

Before I had a chance to answer, Martino knocked, let himself in, and brought Mamma Mia and two pint-sized puppies wearing oversized harnesses proclaiming their status as police dogs. At roughly the five-pound range, I struggled to imagine either one coming anywhere near Mamma Mia in size when grown.

Martino tossed me Mamma Mia's leash, and I greeted the wolf dog, petting her before ordering her to sit beside my chair. "When Captain Farthan said puppy, I was thinking something closer to the six-month range," I confessed.

"These babies were weaned last week, and they're five weeks old. These two are ahead of the curve. When we aren't training them, they go back to their momma, although Misfit can head off tonight if you end up taking her home. Misfit lives for raw food at this stage, turns her little nose up at her momma's milk, and minds her manners. She's a lot like Mamma Mia, ready and wanting to please. Unlike Mamma Mia, she has zero backbone, no spite to speak of, and would rather love everyone to death. The other one is my pick of the litter, and she's basically a young version of Mamma Mia in tendencies, so if I get lucky, I'll get another great wolf-dog."

"What's the percentage of wolf?"

"Higher than you care to know," Martino informed me.

"There's no dog in this wolf-dog, is there?"

"There's just enough dog in this lot we can attach the dog and escape the rules involving wolves on the force. We got permission to try out another batch after Mamma Mia's record was evaluated. We've been planning this litter of puppies for a few years now. The wolves we're using have been questionably domesticated, so we're not just taking wild wolves and breeding them to dogs; they've been in captivity for over ten generations, they're smart, they're trainable, and the dog breeds we used have been good for mellowing out certain instincts. We have also been using some magic to make sure some behaviors are contained. Hole digging is one of those behaviors we've been working to contain."

"How about the destruction of books and furniture?"

"I will make sure that is addressed before you take them home with you tonight. I'll get a bunch of toys she can chew on. For the most part, she'll accompany you out on witness interviews, where you will work with her patience and sitting for longer periods of time. We'll try for once a week on that. Rest of the time, she'll be in puppy boot camp to learn the tricks of her trade." Martino pointed at the smaller of the puppies. "This one is Misfit. She is the runt of the litter, and I fear she'll be just as big if not bigger than Mamma Mia when she grows out. There was a lot of competition for milk, and she's just too nice to push other puppies out of the way. Since we've moved her to raw with supplemental milk in her meat bowl, she's been growing worse than a weed."

"She's that little *after* growing worse than a weed?"

"She was half the size last week."

Damn. "Well, in good news, I'm upgrading my living space soon, so this won't be a problem. Can I impose if I have to go out of town and can't take the wolves?"

Martino nodded. "I'll give you a card for our on-call caretaker. We've got a few vets and handlers across the city who can help when the cops need somebody to watch their dogs. Or wolves, as the case is. This isn't going to be a problem?"

I scratched Mamma Mia behind her ears. "She's a great animal, and if she can't work the beat anymore, she can come with me and ride around in my cruiser."

Martino nodded. "I appreciate it. When you're out and can't take her, I'll get her working with the horses so she knows her manners. It's good for the puppy to learn early."

"I'm going to need a rundown of what I can't let these pups do. I don't want to teach them any bad habits."

"Come with me, and I'll give you the basic rundown of what to avoid along with Mamma Mia's bone so she doesn't feel like she's being punished."

Tuesday, April 17, 2057
Administrative Quarter, Precinct 1
Cauldron City, Nebraska.

I ADMIRED Alicia's ability to concentrate no matter what went on around her. While I wrangled Misfit and Mamma Mia, I guided her on which direction she should walk so she wouldn't collide into someone or something. After checking in, we were escorted to the fifth floor by an agent who eyed Mamma Mia with interest.

"I wasn't aware your precinct partnered K9s with detectives."

"I'm a trial," I replied, keeping an eye on Misfit and reinforcing her command to heel, which she obeyed.

Someone had worked some foul magic on my puppy,

and I would make them pay for it somehow. How could a puppy so young actually know how to obey without extra prompting?

Foul magic, surely.

"What breed is your K9?"

"Mamma Mia is one part demon, one part devil, and a quarter saint. The rest of her seems to be wolf blended with a minor amount of domestic canine of indeterminate nature."

The agent snickered, and when the elevator door opened, he gestured for us to exit. Both animals heeled as though glued to my feet. To my relief, Alicia noticed we moved and kept up. "Thank you for your help, and I'm sorry that we're having to share turf."

The agent waved his hand. "Not a problem at all, detective. We like making a fuss with you boys in blue, but in reality, we're batting for the same team, especially when working a case like this. Up top wants this handled, and they're willing to work with your precinct to make it happen. Would you like me to accompany you for the interview? Word on the wire is you're new."

I shook my head. "If I screw it up, you good folks can correct me, as you're also questioning her. I want to see how I do first."

"I'll intercom if there's something catastrophic you're about to mess up, but otherwise, I'll make sure everyone knows you want to sink or swim on this one. A good case to sink or swim on, though. We don't usually get witnesses this open and honest."

"You have someone who can tell the truth on the team?"

"We do, and we're recording all levels of falsehood. We'll share that data with you after your interview. We caught her lying to us a few times, and I think it is because she's not comfortable with us FBI types."

That I could understand, especially if she was associated with one of our victims. "Considering the list of vics, I'm not surprised. It's not a problem for Alicia to use your conference room?"

"Not at all. We have a room already set up for her, and there's an agent who will be around if she needs anything. We'd rather the Black Dragon of New York not have a reason to come pay us a visit."

I could see the FBI sacrificing an agent to make certain nothing happened to Alicia, especially after the poisoning. "As he has been visiting me daily, I can understand your determination to prevent any unnecessary contact with him."

Alicia snorted, and she cracked a grin. "I'd say he's not that bad, but in reality, he's even worse than you're thinking. I'll just apologize now for boring an agent. Jace, what are the odds I can get a set of gemstones from you for the show?"

"Higher than I appreciate," I admitted. "If you make each gem's sale value go to a charity of my choosing, you can probably talk me into one for each event on top of the other prizes those idiot dragons will be battling over. I'll even toss in a stone or two the public can buy under the same terms."

"We'll be swamped if we do that. Great. Raffle at ten dollars a pop for a stone for charity?"

Ten dollars a pop made it accessible for most everyone. "Do a larger stone for a hundred dollars an entry as well, also for charity. Hell, do three stones. A dollar per entry, ten dollars per entry, and a hundred dollars per entry. You can have the raffle start long before the airing of the show and announce the winners of the raffle when the show airs." I narrowed my eyes. "I have plenty of smaller stones, and there's no reason we can't do a raffle for every segment or competition. As it's all for charity, it'll do great."

"Shouldn't you get paid for those stones?"

"I guess you can put in a stone at the end that I get paid for to see which dragon likes me more." I shrugged. "Just disclose which stones I get paid for. Can you work with that?"

"Yep. That'll eat most of the day. Thank you."

"Glad to help."

Five minutes later, with Alicia safely nestled in the conference room and the agent on guard understanding the woman would starve and dehydrate herself if allowed, I herded Mamma Mia and Misfit to the interrogation room where the woman and child waited.

It bothered me the FBI used an interrogation room for the pair, as they had come willing to talk, making the effort to fly in to talk with us. Lifting my chin and straightening my back, I knocked on the door before letting myself in.

From my understanding of the situation, none of us would be leaving the room until the FBI agents outside opened the door. I didn't mind general containment, but I worried for the woman and her child.

Interrogation rooms were designed to be uncomfortable to encourage those being questioned to talk.

A dark-haired woman with pale skin and brown eyes looked up from her phone, and when she spotted me, she offered a tired smile and flipped the device over so its screen faced the metal top. "Clarice, darling, a police officer has come to see us."

The child in question, a human girl somewhere between the age of three to five, stopped what she was doing on the floor.

It took a single glance to recognize the resemblance between James McDonald and the little girl.

Rather than make the woman get up, I took the seat across from her and ordered the dogs to sit. "I'm Detective Smithson. Thank you for coming out. I haven't been told anything about you," I admitted, and I forced myself to relax in my seat, hoping I communicated something she would find calming. "I hope bringing the dogs in with me isn't a problem."

"Clarice loves dogs. Clarice, look. The nice police officer brought dogs. One's a puppy."

I leaned over for a better view of the little girl, and something about her behavior warned me of trouble brewing on the horizon. She took little interest in the dogs, as though she struggled to process what her mother told her.

After a few moments, the girl's gaze landed on Mamma Mia. Without a word and with the fingers of one hand crammed into her mouth, she got to her feet, waddled over, and wrapped her arm around the wolf's neck.

Mamma Mia's tail waggled, and she stood still for the child.

The woman sighed. "I'm sorry. She's a good girl, but she has problems. I'm Brenda." She reached across the table for her wallet, which she tossed my way. "My legal documentation doesn't tell the truth. I married James McDonald a year before Clarice was born, and we hid it. We had the marriage officiated—mostly. We never filed the papers with the court properly because of his legal woes. But we wanted to be married. And so it goes. I saw on the news he had died." Brenda glanced at her daughter, and her shoulders slumped. "Clarice doesn't understand what's going on. Things like this just don't make sense to her. Little does. She knows she loves dogs, but it takes her a while to remember, you know? James was trying to find work so we could pay for medical treatments for her, but we couldn't afford much. Then he went off to do a job." Lowering her head, she sighed. "He didn't come home. I thought he'd gotten on the wrong side of the law again, but then I saw the news."

Well, so much for the hire only targeting people with nobody to miss them. "I'm sorry, ma'am. Before we begin, at any time, you may ask for an attorney to advise you. I fully know and understand you are here of your own accord, but you still have legal rights, and should you wish to exercise them at any time, simply tell me. Do you consent to having this conversation recorded?"

"Thank you for asking. I do. James trusted me with this if anything happened to him. It's too little and too late, but it's something."

Some burdens I didn't wish on anyone, and I feared what secrets her heart held—and how many of them would come to light after being locked away in the darkness. "Thank you, Brenda. You don't mind me looking through your wallet?"

"Please. It tells the story better than I can."

Pictures often did. I picked up the wallet, an old, worn leather one men typically favored. After a few moments, I realized I held James McDonald's old wallet. His driver's license, long expired from before his time in prison, remained in the clear pane. Her license hid beneath it, claiming her last name to be Patlin. Tiny pictures filled the pocket where the cash should have gone, and I took them out and spread them out in front of me.

On his rap sheet, he had ruined the lives of at least ten women, ended even more lives, and had created a trail of terror. Between plea bargains and helping to sink other criminals, James McDonald had been released for good behavior before causing trouble in Cauldron City. The photographs led me through the life of a family man who loved his daughter and wife.

Had I not known the bitter truth, I would have been convinced someone like McDonald couldn't be capable of the sorts of crimes he'd committed in his life.

"How did you meet James?" I asked, picking up the photograph of the man cradling his newborn daughter while his wife recovered. He held a bottle for the infant, and his facial expression suggested he cooed to keep his baby calm and happy.

"It was right after he left prison. He'd been on the streets, foraging for food from a dumpster. I was riding my bike, told him to hop on, and took him to the nearest fast-food joint. We got to talking, and he told me about all the shit he'd done, the time he'd spent in prison, and how he refused to go back just because he was hungry. I took him home with me, and I hid him in my basement. He had a temper, but never with me. Never with our baby, either. I know he's done things. He's done more things than you cops know. I understand that. But he had us, and he was doing his best to be a better person. He should have had a chance to try."

While Brenda didn't cry, she stared at the metal table, her expression wavering as she fought her emotions.

I wondered if she told the truth or if she lied. In the

end, I decided I would believe her even if I was wrong to. With someone listening in on the conversation, I decided I'd keep her talking and sort the mess out later.

Aware my captain would be sending me back to preschool for at least a month without any hope of parole for not following protocol, I braced for the worst and asked, "Can you walk me through your time with James from the very beginning? What made you decide to help him?"

"I'm not all that innocent either, Detective Smithson. I've done things I should probably face time for, but I've got a little girl now. And she'll have a little brother or sister within the next five months or so. I can't live with knowing what I know, but my babies need me around. And I know what I tell you might land me in prison, but it's more important that what James did isn't dead and gone like him." She wrung her hands together and continued to stare at the table. "Those FBI types look into your soul, and they judge. They hate people like me, the wives of a criminal they wanted to catch but couldn't. James was good in prison. He didn't hurt anybody, he didn't get into any fights. That was where he began when he talked with me the first time. He told me he wanted to be different, and that he tried when he was in prison. He told me the public record of what he'd done. He told me while we sat on my bike, eating shit burgers from a joint I hated because it was the closest thing to get him something warm to eat. Nobody should starve, not even crooks like him."

I checked on Mamma Mia and her charge to discover the little girl had decided it was time for a nap. The wolf served as a pillow, and I took the moment to praise her and scratch behind her ears. As I wanted the animals to stay quiet, I encouraged Misfit to lie down beside the larger wolf, which she did. Satisfied the child had canine custodians, I gave the woman across from me my undivided attention. “I’m not here to judge, ma’am.”

Lifting her head, she offered me a smile. “I know. Maybe I’m just a human, but I can hear the truth, and you’re the first person who hasn’t lied to me yet. Not even your eyes have lied. You saw my child, you recognized her father through her, and you saw me, not as just some criminal, but as a human. And because of that, I will tell you everything I know.”

TWENTY-FIVE

I couldn't imagine the woman's anguish.

Tuesday, April 17, 2057
Administrative Quarter, Precinct 1
Cauldron City, Nebraska.

IN TRUTH, I didn't interview Brenda McDonald. She talked. I listened. Every now and then, I requested a clarification. Within three hours, she'd given me the keys to James McDonald's criminal career, the location of some of the bodies he'd never meant to have found, and a long list of crimes he hadn't faced justice for.

She thought James McDonald had been off to do a contract job, likely under the table, the night he'd disappeared, five weeks prior to his death. The day before his disappearance, he'd brought home six thousand dollars doing manual labor. Brenda confessed she didn't believe the manual labor had been legal, but she'd opted to ignore the lies in favor of the truth.

He had promised nobody had been hurt during his work.

Brenda confessed the six thousand hadn't gone far. She'd spent a few hundred on a doctor for Clarice with no progress. The rest had gone to paying off bills and putting food on the table.

While I wondered what would happen to her and her children, I made a decision I'd face consequences for.

Bracing for the mother's wrath and a possible rebuke for over-involvement in personal matters, I asked, "What is wrong with Clarice? A lot of James's final year involved gathering money for doctors and bills, but mostly doctors."

"She has subacute sclerosing panencephalitis." Brenda judged me, her eyes narrowing a little.

I grimaced, as I'd endured enough medical education to understand what she faced. What she didn't know was the unicorns of Cauldron City could cure the degenerative disorder. I wasn't one of them, but help was a phone call away. "How long has she had symptoms of Dawson Disease?"

Her eyes widened, and I wondered what truth she heard in my question. "She started having problems when she was a newborn. We both got ill from measles. I gave birth to her at home. She… doesn't have a birth certificate. We couldn't afford the hospital bill. When she turned six months old, things started going really wrong."

If I recalled correctly, those with Dawson Disease typically endured a multi-year asymptomatic period, with seven to ten years being the average. It could happen much earlier, like with Clarice. Once the symptoms showed, the victim's health declined quickly. Without treatment, the little girl would die. In most cases, the victim died within three years of the symptoms appearing. The birth certificate problem could be resolved with the right magical abilities, confirming the truth of her birth, and some paperwork. Resting my elbow on the table, I rubbed my forehead and debated my options. The truth would hurt—but lying would do far more harm. "Dawson Disease is lethal without intervention, and she's already survived longer than most showing symptoms of the disease. Who gave you the diagnosis?"

"I took her to one of those family clinics for those in need, and they gave me a referral to a specialist. Once I received the diagnosis, I was told they couldn't help. I didn't ask why. They just gave me a list of things to do, and I've been doing them. They told the truth." Brenda resumed her habit of wringing her hands. "I've always done what's best for her."

While I understood I stated the obvious, I made the comment so the FBI agents observing the interview received the message regarding the child's condition. "She needs medical treatment."

"I know, but I don't know where to get it or how. Or how to afford it. That's part of why I contacted the FBI. Maybe with the reward money for those cases..."

When she didn't continue to speak, I asked, "Would James have wanted that?"

"He told me to go for the rewards if something happened to him. He told me to lead the police and FBI to the bodies. He even told me how to drop tips so I could get paid without revealing how I knew. But that all seemed *wrong*."

Once again, she fell silent. I could make a few guesses, but I tried to put myself into the shoes of someone who could hear the truth. "You can't tolerate injustice."

She nodded. “The truth comes with a price, always.”

“Would you mind if one of the FBI agents came in to discuss this more with you?” My next question would test my luck. “I can watch Clarice while you’re discussing those things, especially if the disease has to be discussed in earnest.”

“She can’t understand what we’re talking about anymore. Not really. I love her dearly, but I lose her a little each day. The happy little girl she was for the first few months of her life is gone. I… that she actually recognized your dog as something she likes is better than normal. No seizures today yet, either. They’ll come. They always do. One day, she’ll go to sleep, and she won’t wake up. It’s been a peaceful day. That worries me. The peaceful days are always followed by bad ones. I thought I’d lose her last time. I probably will this time.”

I couldn’t imagine the woman’s anguish. I’d have to ask my parents what they’d do if they had to walk in Brenda’s shoes. “If you could have her treated, would you?”

“At any cost. No cost is too great to save my baby, detective.”

Her statement brought me back to the cruel reality of the case I fought to crack. Someone felt the same.

To the killer or the hire, perhaps both, no cost was too great. We just didn’t know who needed to be saved or why. We raced against death, but unlike those behind the murder, we didn’t know when the clock might stop. Without that critical piece of information, we would always be a few steps behind, unable to guess what their next move was, jumping from corpse to corpse like some deranged spider.

Someone knocked, and a moment later, the agent who’d

escorted me upstairs stepped into the room. To my astonishment, Dr. Erik accompanied him.

Dr. Erik chuckled at my expression. "I was called in about an hour ago, and we were waiting for the conclusion of your interview. Hello, Brenda. My name is Dr. Erik, and if you give me leave, I'll go take Clarice to one of the nearby rooms for an examination with Detective Smithson. That will let you discuss matters with Special Agent Hammot. He has questions about your testimony."

"I've been told there's nothing that can really be done, doctor."

"If it's subacute sclerosing panencephalitis, as I've been told, you would normally be correct. Outside of Cauldron City, there are no successful treatments for the disorder. Many doctors outside of Cauldron City forget we have advances in medical sciences most lack."

"Can you save her?"

"I'm most certainly going to try."

She bobbed her head, and I realized she fought the urge to cry, the second time since my interview started that she'd shown such an emotion. To keep from rocking the boat, I got up, cooed to wake Mamma Mia, and gave the wolf a moment to identify me before picking up the child. Clarice's limp state worried me, but a quick check with my magic confirmed the child still lived.

For the moment.

"If you can take the leashes, Dr. Erik?" I asked, not wanting to risk a transfer and potentially waking the child.

With a little verbal coaxing from me, the black unicorn managed to get both wolves out of the interrogation room. I followed, promised I'd do my best to return her child in a timely fashion, and closed the door behind me. Once in the hall, I heaved a sigh. "They really called you in?"

"They called me around the time the child failed to recognize Mamma Mia was a dog. Her behavior was clearly abnormal, and her mother's statement initially was worrying, so they asked me to come. I wasn't invited to listen in on your questioning session, but I was texted as needed. Their attempt to spell her illness was laughable, but it was enough to get the point across. They don't like the girl's father, but none of them want to be responsible for a child's death."

"The crimes of the father are not the crimes of the child."

"Precisely so. Good memory on the disease. It's fairly rare. Did she mention how long she's had it?"

"She contracted measles as a newborn, and she started showing symptoms at six months old. I think she's been symptomatic for about two years now."

Dr. Erik huffed, shook his head, and gestured to a nearby room with an open door. "That's now my new medical office. I'm going to require a fluffy pony for this, and you're going to have to strip, else you're headed home to get new clothes."

Damn it. As there was no way I'd leave a child to fend off a lethal disease when I could help, I waited for Dr. Erik to get the wolves contained in a corner and shut the door before handing the little girl over, stripping, and shapeshifting. To my dismay, I'd conjured a saddle and bridle.

I bowed my head, and the bridle jangled. The lack of a bit appeased irritation over my inadvertent display of magic.

I hadn't meant to conjure new tack.

"I recognize that guilty pony look. You didn't mean to

create a saddle or bridle." Dr. Erik eyed my hooves. "The booties are cute, and with that frog injury, I approve."

Booties? I abandoned wallowing over my lack of finesse to lift a hoof for a better look. Silvery booties covered my hoof and ankle, and the top strap was trimmed with silver bells. I tested my new gear to determine they offered nice cushioning and general protection. "I need to do these on purpose every time. These are great." I took a few steps to find my stride a little springier than normal. The material also spared the floor. "Did I make these or steal them?"

"You're probably bleeding off excess magic, so you would have made them. The entire set matches and fits perfectly, so I'm going to guess you properly conjured them. You've had a good diet, you've been working a lot of magic lately, and you're rested. It wasn't much work to fix your frog, and you've had a few quiet days on the magic front. I'm not concerned. Now, come sniff this little girl. I want you to treat her like you had when investigating that toxin. The viral infection she's suffering from isn't the same as a toxin, but there are similarities in how we treat it."

Careful not to bump into anything and jingling all the way, I approached Dr. Erik and brushed my nose against the little girl's hair. Sure enough, something slimy and hot engulfed her entire head. "I sense it. It's hot and slimy."

"I'm going to monitor you for this, but I want you to try to cool her head down. I will be preserving her life; you will be killing the virus through lowering the virus's temperature beyond what it can survive. Once the virus is killed, we can begin the basic treatments to restore her brain's base functionality. That part will not be simple, but we can at least restore some of what she's lost. Not everything, but some. Perhaps with some time, we can undo most of the damage."

Dr. Erik sighed. "If you get the hang of identifying virus versus brain cells, we could be done within twenty minutes. You're a weird one, so we'll see."

"Because I work differently from you?"

"Right. In this case, we don't want to accidentally boil the blood in her brain. Did you know it's possible to recover full functionality of a brain that's been chilled a little more than we prefer? And before you panic, this is a *lot* easier than what you did in the ER. Truth be told? Measles and its related viruses are an easy treat for us if we catch it early enough. I charge ten dollars and a thirty-minute lecture for failure to vaccinate. In this case, you're doing the work, you're not a charging physician, and I won't lecture a woman who has clearly suffered enough."

"Clarice doesn't have a birth certificate."

"That's easily resolved. Let's get her through the day alive, and then that will be a problem I'm sure her mother will be happy to have. When you start, start slow, because I need to keep track if you're cooling her brain rather than the infection. Once the infection is killed, we will make certain that there are no breeding grounds in the rest of her body. It'll be twenty minutes tops. I'd wish you good luck, but you won't need it. I expect you'll take to this like a duck to water."

Tuesday, April 17, 2057
Administrative Quarter, Precinct 1
Cauldron City, Nebraska.

TWELVE MINUTES AFTER STARTING, Dr. Erik informed me I'd purged the virus killing the girl. He then took over, as the last thing he wanted to deal with was a shaggy pony having an anxiety attack over rearranging a child's brain matter to be better suited for life.

To comfort myself, I went over to Mamma Mia and the puppy to introduce myself. Misfit licked my nose and yipped her excitement. Mamma Mia observed with an ear cocked back, but after a few minutes, she reached out to touch her nose to mine. I blew air into her face to introduce myself, and she huffed back before bathing my muzzle with her tongue.

Dr. Erik laughed at me, and he said, "And the first treatment is done. Her body needs a chance to recover, but when she wakes up, she'll be an entirely different little girl. Let's keep some of that unicorn magic alive." Without warning, he placed the girl onto my saddle.

I braced my legs and kept still, as I would never buck a child off. I did turn my ears back, snapping my teeth at the black unicorn. Somehow, the bastard of a doctor would pay.

"Good evening, Clarice," Dr. Erik cooed, and he gave the little girl's shoulder a gentle nudge. I suspected he worked magic, as she woke up, yawned, and rubbed at her eyes. "It's time for a pony ride."

The little girl blinked, and unlike in the interrogation room, her eyes focused on me and my horn. "Unicorn!"

"Yes, he's a unicorn. My name is Dr. Erik, and this little pony is Jace. Tell Jace hello."

"Hewwo, Jace," the little girl replied, and she bounced on my back, waving her little hands. "Unicorn! Unicorn!"

The doctor had worked some sorcery on the child, and I regarded him with suspicion.

"I didn't do anything nefarious, Jace. Her mother puts on a lot of children's shows for her, and when I was working on her brain, I focused on the portions dedicated to communication and her memories. The virus hadn't killed off her brain cells. It had changed how her brain worked and reduced her ability to access memories. I simply gave her the keys to all those locked doors in her head."

"It can't be that easy," I whispered.

"Oh, Jace. It's not. I've dedicated my entire life to this art. It took over a hundred years for me to learn how to breathe life back into a damaged brain. It took decades to understand how to murder measles. I still can't conquer the common cold, because that one is… persistent. I can teach you as I do because of that experience. It only looks easy because I did the equivalent of hold your hand while you provided the magic. You'll never be able to do this level of work on your own—nor would you be happy doing this on your own. But you also wouldn't be able to forgive yourself if you hadn't done *something.* I know your type. It's a lot like mine, but we work in different ways to change lives. Now, let's take this little girl back to her momma. It's time we had a little hope rather than tragedy."

Dr. Erik opened the door and made certain to keep the little girl on my back. I took care with every step, and when we reached the interrogation room door, I snorted and bobbed my head.

Clarice giggled. "Unicorn!"

Dr. Erik praised the little girl. An FBI agent came over, knocked on the door, and let us into the room.

Brenda McDonald spoke with Agent Hammot, pointing at a map. She lifted her head, caught sight of her daughter on my back, and gasped.

"Please don't worry, Mrs. McDonald," Dr. Erik said, and he eased Clarice off my back and brought her to the woman. Brenda cuddled her child and clung to her.

Clarice hugged her mother, and she giggled before shoving her little hand into her mouth and sucking on her fingers.

"The first treatment is completed, but she will need to stay in Cauldron City for at least two months to undo the damage. We typically charge ten dollars for the base treatment, but I'm waiving the fee. We usually inflict a lecture on those who don't vaccinate against the parent virus group responsible for the disease, but I suspect you did not have the opportunity to properly vaccinate your daughter."

"She's had some through a family clinic, but not all of them."

"We will handle her vaccinations after she's been fully treated for her disease. In the meantime, we will monitor her for infection and treat her as needed. You'll want to be vaccinated as well, I'm sure."

"I can't. I'm pregnant."

Dr. Erik considered the woman through narrowed eyes before settling his glare onto Agent Hammot.

The FBI agent wisely raised his hands in surrender. "We can continue our questioning tomorrow and get additional information. We have enough to work with so far. Thank you, Mrs. McDonald."

The woman's eyes widened. "You mean it."

"I do. Because of you, we will have closure on numerous cases. Ignoring your minor infractions is a simple enough thing. We would do more harm to you and your children than any justice gained. Your husband was correct regarding how you could be paid for the tips, and I will suggest to the uppers that we pay out on these tips. It is money well spent. I'm going to have to insist we put you into a safe house while you're in Cauldron City. Dr. Erik?"

"I'll handle her family's medical care."

"But what happened to Detective Smithson?" Brenda asked. "I need to thank him."

Dr. Erik gestured to me. "The unicorn is Detective Smithson, ma'am."

"Thank you. You didn't have to."

Dr. Erik chuckled. "There is no way this shaggy little colt would ever abandon a child in need. He could help, so he did. Now, if you'll excuse us, we have other work to do. I will see you and your daughter in the morning for your next checkup. I will make sure you have prenatal vitamins, which you will take as directed."

"Thank you, doctor."

Dr. Erik cleared his throat at me, and I backed out of the interrogation room.

For the first time since starting the case, I felt like there were answers right within my reach if I could figure out how to connect the pieces. All I needed to do was figure out the motive of the person driving the effort.

Dr. Erik closed the door, and he made sure to keep Mamma Mia and Misfit contained, ordering them to heel at his side. "If you pin those ears back any more, I'll be worried you're about to ram that horn somewhere we'll all regret. What's bothering you?"

"Would a doctor resort to murder to create an underground clinic?" I tossed my head in the direction of the interrogation room. "That mother would kill if it meant her child might survive. Are there doctors who would kill to help people like that mother?"

"Yes, there are," Dr. Erik replied in a subdued tone. "Not all doctors believe in the oath we take—and not all doctors feel our system is fair. With the improvement of trauma care, organ donations are at an all-time low. Unless the person was killed immediately in an accident, we have become better and better at preventing death. That means organs are rare—far rarer than those who need an organ. We can't cure all diseases and illnesses. Little Clarice's age matters. Her brain is still developing. With help from me and some other unicorns, we will be able to work with her body's natural development to undo much of the damage done from the infection. We can't do that with many diseases."

"Heart disease?"

"That is an excellent example of something we can't readily fix. Why? I don't know. If we knew, we'd have a significantly shorter list of people needing a new heart. We can do a lot, but there are limits."

"Then how did we save those poison victims?"

"That is an excellent example of how we can bypass the limits sometimes. The memory of how the organ should be was still present, so we hitched a lift off the organ's memory. When you were working, you were matching the body's memory to the moment before it was poisoned. That's a fundamental. How you work is different from us blacks, but you've always been a little different. Your gemstone production is different. Your interests are different. You're just different. And that's not a bad thing. The basics of organ recovery are simple. If the organ was recently sickened or damaged, we can undo the damage. Children are easier. Their bodies are developing, and the memory of the organ is regenerating during that development. We can hitch a lift off that development. But we can't fix things like birth defects. That's how they naturally are. There's nothing for us to fix. We are imperfect beings, and we can't completely circumvent nature. But we try."

Yes, we did. "Do you really charge ten dollars for the treatment, Dr. Erik?"

The black unicorn smiled. "Mrs. McDonald knows the truth of that, and I'd normally say that's the only truth you need. But yes, we only charge ten dollars for the treatment. It saves us a great deal of time, effort, and money if it's treated right away. And most patients are just like Mrs. McDonald and her child. They are poor or in a corner. They aren't vaccinated for a myriad of reasons. But they suffer, and killing the virus is trivial for us. The body wants it gone, and it remembers how things were before it invaded. That memory is long. And yes, you hitched a ride on her body's memory without realizing it. Her will to live was strong. Your determination to make sure she survived was stronger. I'll do the rest of the work from here. You focus on the gift that little girl's mother gave you. But I'll give you a bit of truth of my own. She came here praying for salvation for her child. You have given her that. That is not a debt easily repaid, and she will dig up every grave her husband ever made to even the scales. You mark my words, Jace. That woman is made of secrets, and she hides her secrets behind a shield of truth."

"How do you know?"

"Call it a father's intuition if you must. I've just seen women with eyes like hers before. She has seen dark and terrible things, and she will exhume every body she knows of if you ask it of her. But will you ask the right questions?"

TWENTY-SIX

At first glance, nobody would miss James McDonald.

Tuesday, April 17, 2057
Lower North Lakes, Precinct 153
Cauldron City, Nebraska.

INSTEAD OF GOING HOME, I waged a silent war with my digital murder board, taking the transcription of the interview with Brenda McDonald and turning it into something useful. Mamma Mia and Misfit shared a dog bed crammed into a nearby corner, creating an obstacle whenever I needed to access one side of the board. As the wolves had opted for nap time, I took care with where I walked and focused on my work.

According to the FBI, the woman had been fully honest with me unlike with them, and they'd been kind enough to offer up the intel on what she had lied about in case it proved to be useful.

I began with her husband's disappearance compared to his estimated time of death.

On March 27 in North Carolina, James McDonald had disappeared, leaving his wife and child bereft.

On April 4, his life had come to an end, likely in Nebraska.

On April 5, his mutilated body had been involved with the kidnapping of my mother.

How had he gotten from North Carolina to Nebraska? The why of his selection as a victim still made sense. According to his wife's statements, they had worked hard to hide their marriage. They shared a home, but they had gone out of their way to avoid being seen together in public.

The fateful day she had taken him in had been the first and the last time they'd gone out together in public.

At first glance, nobody would miss James McDonald.

In truth, a woman grieved the loss of a man she'd loved despite his sins. That man had shown her all the love he could muster. I doubted James McDonald could have changed his tendency to be a villain and undo the harm he had done, but there was a twist to his story I hadn't anticipated.

Good men were expected to give up the love of their life for the sake of the world.

Men like James McDonald would burn the world for their love's sake. He'd found that love in Brenda and his daughter. I lacked understanding of what had brought upon the man's change of heart. But he had been willing to dirty his hands to put food on the table for his wife and child, playing the game by the rules she had set.

She tolerated his lies with the understanding he had changed his core ways.

He hadn't hurt anyone since finding her.

Even in Cauldron City, where he'd danced with the law

numerous times, he hadn't done anyone any true harm. It would send me checking through our records about the carjacking case.

I suspected we'd missed something. I worried the knowledge we needed had gone to the man's grave.

What had happened to James McDonald? What answers could I find if I went back in time, investigating the place he'd been last seen? How far back would I need to go?

Where—and when—was the true beginning of the story of James McDonald's death? I dug out the man's complete criminal record, which took over three full filing boxes and promised months of work to fully evaluate. Some cases had at least an inch of paperwork, but the case's summary sheet might give me enough basic information to work with.

I began populating the murder board by case number. Upon entering the FBI's case record, the digital murder board asked me if I wanted to populate data from the entire case. I hit yes, and it automatically imported the records I could access.

"Is this thing magical?" I blurted.

In the cubicle area, my co-workers laughed at me, and an amused Paul came in to pay me a visit. I bumped elbows with him before pointing at the registered case. "It links into the FBI's case records."

"As I'm one of the poor bastards who helped pick this beauty out for you, it will check every system it has access to for case records. When we had the vic records pulled, we got authorization to access all the associated cases, so your board is just pulling out everything it has permission to access. You also have access to all case records in Cauldron City. If there's something sealed, the board will tell you it's sealed and ask if you would like to request permission to access the file. There's one sealed record in your McDonald files." The elephant tapped the screen, pulled up a new case record, and referenced his phone before typing in a record identifier. A prompt came up. "Tap yes, and then it'll ask for your badge number."

I did as told, checked my detective badge, and input my new identifier. "I was prepared to manually input all of this, Paul."

"We were waiting for the moment you figured out this was not the case. You just won me ten bucks from everyone, as I was the only one who bet you'd register the record numbers in the board first rather than other identifiers."

"My plan had been to get all the case records plugged in, then organize them by type and input into the board as I addressed them," I admitted.

"Smart plan. Now, once you have all of them input, you will want to confirm the paper records against what was put in. People screw things up—and things will be excluded. When it gets here, use your new work phone to photograph the pages you want, use the character recognition tools to get as much of it digitalized as possible, and then work on a mix of the photographs and the digital versions. Usually, we're given some time to get a chance to play with our new toys before having to work a big case, but the captain wanted fresh eyes."

Right. My lack of preconceived notions might allow me to spot an important clue in the case, and I could be taught the rest as I went. "Dare I ask if we have anything new?"

"Your dragoness is sulking with the women of dispatch. She wanted to ride the unicorn in the pretty parade gear."

"That's not my fault. Dr. Erik barred any riders because of my hoof, and he used the fact I conjured booties against me. He took one off, and it's a solid medical boot for beautiful young stallions about to shed out of the shaggy pony stage."

Paul snorted. "You're bad enough as it is. You do not need beautiful attached to your descriptor. Having witnessed you in your shaggy pony glory, you're fine just as you are."

"Ah, but I will shame the police horses once I shed out."

"I'm sure you will." Paul stared me into submission. "Do you know what I do when the captain suggests I should run around as an elephant during one of the parades?"

"You say no."

"Loudly and with great emphasis. Refusal is allowed."

"But I'm beautiful, Paul."

Hysterical laughter in the cubicle area lured me out of my office, and I went to go make my stand where all my coworkers could witness it. Paul closed my office door after me to contain the beasts.

"The dragons started it," I announced, aware my words would get the dragons of the precinct riled up along with everyone else.

Paul followed me, and to my irritation, Captain Farthan stepped into the area. "What did we start now, Smithson?"

His presence would ruin my fun, but rather than push my luck beyond what I could handle, I replied, "You dragons claim that I'm beautiful, sir."

"Well, it's true. And you're so damned smug about it. The station rules apply. No dragons may take home their co-workers on grounds of being smart or beautiful. Good work today, Smithson. You didn't precisely have to ask many questions, but you got the canary singing. In cases like this, I don't care how you get the canary singing. If sugar works, pile it on. However, we're going to have to work on forming bonds with the witnesses. You want a rapport. You do not want worshippers at the altar of all things unicorns."

"Like hell I don't, sir!" I braced my fists on my hips. "And anyway, I wasn't going to just let the kid die for no good reason, and well, we're unicorns. I really have no idea how much Dr. Erik charges for the complete treatment he did, but the preliminary part took twenty minutes. If the FBI hadn't called him, I would have myself—and I would've paid the damned fee out of pocket."

"Yes, yes, I am aware. The FBI called me to warn of a potentially emotional unicorn headed my way. Are you emotional?"

I raised a brow. "No, sir? Why would they think I'd be emotional?"

"After you left, Dr. Erik transformed, rolled around on the lobby floor, kicked his heels, and had a tantrum. There's a video, and I would be pleased to share it with you. He has reached his general tolerance for this week. As Dr. Erik has had it, the FBI is concerned you're at the end of your rope. It seems your dragoness really wanted to ride the unicorn wearing parade gear, and he wouldn't let her."

"Has everyone heard about that?"

"Your parade gear is nice, and Deputy Inspector Hagfield swung by, claimed all your tack, and promised to return it in the next few days. He's getting you actual parade gear made and will use magic to get your current measurements. He loves your booties."

My job would drive me crazy sooner than later, and the management would be the reason I finally went insane. "He's going to be heartbroken when he discovers those are conjured."

"Well, he wants them for his horses, so don't be

surprised if he starts chasing you to get a set of booties you're willing to give up. How is your hoof?"

"It's mostly fine, although it seems Dr. Erik wants me to limit to carrying no more than a very small child. I would not take kindly to anyone climbing on my back right now."

"Outside of small, sick children."

I nodded.

"There is a reason I decided to join this party."

I sighed, as did most of the other detectives. Rather than ask, we waited for the opal dragon to decide when he wanted to drop the next bombshell on us.

"I need one pair willing to handle a bar case. It's more of the toxin, and six patrons were poisoned. There were three deaths before paramedics arrived. Any takers?"

Paul huffed, but he raised his hand.

"Try not to trumpet your dismay over the state of the bodies, Masoner. And tell Lovell I want him to take the good camera. Forensics is leaving the bodies where they're at until you arrive. Get the address from dispatch."

Paul left, calling for Lovell and beelining for their shared office.

"Next up, I need a pair to head to Precinct 102. We have a pair of mutilated bodies we need confirmed belong to our case. Once it's confirmed, notify Smithson, give him the case numbers, and claim jurisdiction. I'm sure they'll be willing to throw it at you right now."

One of the oldest detectives in our precinct, Victor Jasons, waved, got up from his desk, and said, "I've got your back, Smithson. I'll make sure the whippersnapper I've got tagging along doesn't lick your evidence."

"You partnered them with Yvon, Captain Farthan?" I

asked, wondering what Jasons and his partner, Zeller, had done to deserve such a thing.

"They can handle it. Yvon's back from preschool on parole, and assuming he can stop licking the evidence, he'll be moving up this week." The captain eyed the collection of detectives working in the cubicle farm and pointed at one of the senior detectives. "Thames, I want you to go to that other station and secure one of the beautiful maidens to serve as a sounding board for Smithson. Bring that captain back with you when you come."

The detective in question, one of our griffon shapeshifters, raised a brow. "Am I flying or taking a cruiser?"

"Fly, that way you show off those feathers you claim can charm women into doing what you want."

Everyone laughed, and the cops tasked with the captain's dirty work headed off, leaving me to endure his scrutiny.

"I'm not sure what I did, but I'm sorry, sir."

He chuckled. "As you aren't having a meltdown over the kid, you haven't done anything wrong. After hearing Dr. Erik was rolling around on his back in the FBI's lobby, I wanted to make sure you didn't need some space, something to take your temper out on, or dinner."

If I had to eat another bite of chicken or cheese, I'd put some serious thought into joining Dr. Erik in having a tantrum. Aware I'd be eating nothing but chicken or cheese for at least another week to make the binge worth my while, I checked my phone for the restaurants my mother suggested, and I eyed the listing that might result in another dance with salmonella. I texted him with the restaurant and my mother's favorite dish, along with a warning it might result in illness and that weaker species should not indulge or join me in my suffering.

The captain's pocket pinged, he dug out his phone, and he laughed. "You're out of here an hour after your dinner arrives, and I don't want to see you back here until two, in the afternoon, tomorrow. Spend the morning with your dragoness hunting houses. As they're stationary, I'm sure you can almost manage to equal a dragon this once."

"How did she become my dragoness, anyway?"

Captain Farthan snorted. "You established terms where she can't leave without passing your basic cooking criteria. Her family has agreed to this. Having seen photographs of what the Black Dragon of New York endured, it's probably a permanent arrangement. It'd be easier to ask for a miracle, Jace. It's that bad."

I checked over my shoulder to make certain the woman couldn't hear me before whispering, "He ate it."

"Trust me, Jace. That old dragon earned a great deal of respect that morning. I'm just glad he survived. Don't tell him I said this, but I'd miss him if he died from a batch of bad eggs."

Tuesday, April 17, 2057
River Lakes Park, Precinct 153
Cauldron City, Nebraska.

AS MAMMA MIA and Misfit wouldn't fit in the Black Wing due to its two-seater nature, I borrowed one of the K9 cruisers for the night. Alicia made friends with both animals in the back, cooing at them as though they were pets. With my understanding of the situation being the puppy would wash out and the old dog would live out her best wolf-dog life with us, I neglected to correct the woman regarding the proper handling of working animals.

"Where am I going, Alicia?" I drummed my fingers on the wheel while waiting for the light to change. The first step of her instructions had taken us around the North Lakes Memorial Park and Gardens, which had the usual evening traffic of those seeking to enjoy the green space and pay respects to the dead.

"You know those mansions that skirt that park with the ponds?"

"You mean River Lakes Park?"

"If that's what it's called, yes. It's the corner lot facing the park on the western side of the street."

Ah. Right. I was buying a mansion, and we were to pick up the keys from the owners, as Alicia had managed to clear the payment and only a few paperwork hurdles remained. As the owners couldn't care less about the specifics, we were getting the keys a few days early. "I feel like I'm quite the idiot right now. Logically, I understand it's a mansion. It'd have to be with the size of that library. But aren't those places ridiculous?"

"There's a gate to get into the property, a nice security system, and your driveway is half a mile long just to get to the garage."

"My driveway is how long?"

"It's half a mile long."

"Just how big is this place?"

"The lot is a mile on all sides, minus enough space for a sidewalk, five feet, and the exterior fence. It's a stone fence that's three feet tall so most people can see into the gardens. The home itself is large, mind you, but it's one of the smallest buildings in the neighborhood. The owners preferred having outdoor space. It's also one of the only lots without a pool. You have a small pond and a reading area instead. There's a fountain and an outdoor chessboard. Standard size, not one of those oversized ones. There's also a nice barbecuing and entertaining area."

"I would probably know this if I hadn't stopped looking after I spotted the library," I admitted.

She laughed at me. "You would be correct."

Nobody could blame me for falling for the library's charms. "Do I have any money left?"

"You have plenty of money left. I even managed to get the money transferred to your bank account, although there was some paperwork I had to address, which wasn't a problem."

What had I done? Had I been sensible and gone to look the place over, I wouldn't have gotten sideswiped. Accepting I'd made more than a few mistakes, I drove in the right direction, went around the park, and took the large street cutting between the rows of mansions. Most of the mansions were positioned so people could view the homes from the street, with my new property being the sole exception. The gate was open when I pulled the cruiser up. Rather than turn around and flee, I followed the driveway, which curved through an orchard of fruit trees. "I missed the orchard, too, didn't I?"

"The orchard has pear, plums, apples, and apricots. There's an area for a variety of berries, and there's even a couple of mulberry trees and elderberry kicking around. I believe there are also a few cherry trees. They'll have a book with all the various edible plants growing in the garden. The landscaping bill is a little terrifying, but there's no reason you can't sell the fruit you don't want. That's what the previous owners did."

"I bet all the deer come to my yard, too."

"The property is warded against most animals taking too much of an interest. Birds are given free range except for the fruit still on the trees, so you'll see them foraging from the ground rather than eating your crop. There's a grove dedicated to all things birds, and the landscapers take care of cleaning the hummingbird feeders. We were advised that many of the city's sentient songbirds live on the property. As you're a cop, I'm sure you won't have any problems getting along with your new neighbors. We'll have to work with Mamma Mia and Misfit to make sure they know the birds aren't lunch, though."

"I'll make sure the trainers work with Misfit. Mamma Mia should be okay with the birds. I've seen her out with the little ones often enough." I parked the SUV in front of the large steps leading up to the home's front door.

The place reminded me of a plantation in its general styling, although on a larger, grandeur scale. It consisted of the main building and two wings, and I suspected I'd missed more than a few pictures of what might be on the second floor.

I had no idea what was on the third floor, and I pointed at the covered porch surrounding the top level. "What's on the third floor?"

"Nothing, which is why there weren't any pictures. I thought you'd like to turn it into your private office and another library."

What was money? Who needed it? Not me, not when I

had an entire third floor I could turn into another library. "Perhaps a few offices with a shared library. My live-in dragoness should have an office."

She laughed. "I can work at a kitchen table with a laptop, Jace. I can survive without an office."

"Perhaps you can survive without an office, but should you? No. You need an office. We can argue over the floor plans for that third level another day." As we hadn't argued over anything except her inability to ride me until Dr. Erik cleared my hoof, I figured we could get into a good spat over it and find out how we handled each other when irritated.

"I can fit in a good fight tomorrow. It's been a while since I've been in a good fight."

"That has to be the dragon in you," I muttered, getting out of the car and retrieving the beasts from the back so Alicia could escape. At my command, both wolves heeled, and the pair whipped their tails. I praised them for good behavior, encouraged them to stay at my side, and headed up the steps.

The door opened before I could reach it, and a young couple stepped out. Before I had a chance to fend them off or protest, I received kisses on the cheek from both before they crowed their delight, dropped to their knees, and introduced themselves to Mamma Mia and Misfit.

I twisted around to regard the black dragoness with wide eyes. "You didn't sell *me*, did you?"

She laughed, as did the pair greeting my wolves. "I didn't sell you, but you're well-liked, your enjoyment of affection was betrayed by numerous parties, and your parents are here exploring your kitchen."

Ah. That explained a few things. I regarded the pair of

dragons making friends with the wolves. "Did my parents sell me?"

The man shook his head, got to his feet, and held his hand out. Once I shook with him, he said, "You haven't been sold. Your parents may have offered a child for cheap, but we took your side on this one. If we were to accept a cheap child, we'd have to give all that money back, as it'd be rude to charge our new child the price of his home."

Well, that had backfired spectacularly. "Now I'm not sure if I want to be sold or not. Oh, well. The larger one is Mamma Mia, and she's a work dog. Misfit is a puppy in training, but I've been told that her chances of successfully being trained are low. She's a little too nice and attempts to lick all opponents into submission. They're apparently my wolves now, and I'm going to need training on how to train them."

"Well, you definitely have enough space for a pair of rather large dogs, if this puppy will be anywhere near Mamma Mia's size when grown."

"I have reason to believe that is the case." I took the time to pet both wolves to reassure them they were off duty and could be treated like beloved pets rather than enforcers of the law. "Mamma Mia is an old lady, so she's going to be coming to work with me and helping me to solve mysteries rather than chase after mean criminals. Misfit is too nice, so I guess I'm going to have a freeloader taking up space in the work SUV once I get mine." I gestured to the vehicle I'd borrowed. "That's not mine, but I couldn't fit them in the Black Wing."

"And the Black Wing is mine," Alicia stated, coming up the steps to join us. She shook hands with the couple. "Jace, Lance and Rubella are the nice dragons who contacted me about the house when they found out you were in the market. Unfortunately, Lance is related to my father, and he played the distant relative card to get first crack at me. My daddy would have become sad."

I suspected a wily black dragon hid under all that innocence, and he ruled the roost by making certain nobody was willing to cross any of his lines.

"I am a blue dragon, and this may as well be a crime," Lance informed me in a solemn tone, which he softened with a wink. "Normally, I would take the little black dragoness for all she was worth, but as you're the owner and she's…" Lance's brow furrowed. "Could you please explain the relationship to me? I don't want to offend unintentionally."

With a snicker, Alicia announced, "It's okay as long as we offend intentionally in the family, even among the sad blue dragons."

"She tried to murder her grandfather with eggs. While he survived, no kitchen is safe from her. I informed the black dragons they were not getting her back until she could handle the basics," I replied, keeping my tone as solemn as his. "I'm not sure why they caved at the first sign of pressure, but now I have a live-in dragoness, and I have to keep her until I can somehow teach her how to survive in a kitchen." As Alicia was a good sport about the jokes, I did my best to mimic my sad pony eyes, directing the full force of my stare on her.

Alicia burst into giggles. "Those sad pony eyes aren't going to work on me, sir!"

"I don't see why not," I replied. "How do I get to the kitchen? I need to make certain my parents aren't doing something I might regret."

Lance laughed and went into the house, gesturing for me to follow. "They wanted to make sure you wouldn't starve, so they brought some of your things over from your apartment. According to your mother, you will go where your kitchen is, so she started ferrying things out of your apartment. Then she remembered you cannot live without your books. Between the two of them, your parents managed to move most of your books into the living room, although you'll have to take them up to the library."

The entry, which devoured a ridiculous amount of space and featured a marble floor and a crystal chandelier, led to the living room. Furnished in a Victorian sitting room theme, it appealed enough I might ask to keep the furniture. It blended a warm motif with comfort. Once my hoard of books was removed, it would be a spacious, welcoming space.

It even had a pair of bookcases and a fireplace boasting sufficient room on the floor to curl up with my favorite blanket.

While tempted to explore, I followed Lance down a hallway, and opened doors revealed a mix of rooms, from a music room, several bathrooms, a few offices, and a craft room. The kitchen waited at the end, and a chef's paradise promised many well-spent hours cooking.

My parents waged war against a cake, which they attempted to decorate. Sugar crystals could work with a cake, but not with a rather runny frosting, which did a good job of melting their creation and creating a mess. Unable to help myself, I laughed. "Full points for effort, but next time, leave the celebratory cakes to me while you make me soup."

My mother pouted while my father grinned at me. He came over, claimed a hug, and pointed at the double-decker ovens. "Your mother saw those and had to bake a cake. As we had a few hours, she baked a cake. Things got out of hand."

I suspected she hadn't let the cake cool before attempting to add the frosting, thus melting her crystals and ruining her efforts. "I'm sure it'll taste fine. Just for the record, I would not have thought to buy myself a mansion."

"With that library in here? I doubt you even saw any other pictures of the place before you decided you wanted it," my father accused.

Shrugging, I went to the refrigerator, a stainless steel monstrosity with two doors. A quick check revealed the contents of my apartment had wandered to my new home. "Did I buy the refrigerator, Lance?"

"You bought all the appliances in the base price of the house, and Alicia thought you'd like the furniture, so we cut a deal for everything. I'm sure we can afford to buy some new furniture, and it's been a while."

Rubella hopped and sat on the kitchen's central island. "We're going pawn shop and discount store hunting for a lot of it. We love turning someone else's trash into our treasures. That's how we got a lot of the stuff for this place, too. We like comfort—and comfort need not cost a fortune. Of course, I'm a green dragon, so restoration is up my alley. I restored everything to its new state for you, as I thought you'd appreciate having a chance to enjoy everything for a few years before it wears out."

"Thank you, Rubella. I really appreciate that."

She waved me off and replied, "With your job? You don't have time dealing with predatory salesmen out for all your gemstones. You'll have plenty of furniture shopping to do for the top floor and basement, anyway. Would you like the tour or a chance to eat the cake?"

Who needed pride when I could have cake? "Can I have cake while taking the tour?"

Lance snickered, went to the cupboards, and pulled down a set of plates. "We can even drink milk out of wine glasses and pretend we're civilized."

"That sounds like a plan."

TWENTY-SEVEN

"You and me both, baby girl."

WEDNESDAY, APRIL 18, 2057
RIVER LAKES PARK, PRECINCT 153
CAULDRON CITY, NEBRASKA.

MAMMA MIA DID NOT WANT to go to work.

Once given free rein to pick her favorite place in the house, she had selected the sitting room. I had placed her massive dog bed in front of the fireplace, which she had taken over with a happy huff. Once in possession of her new bone, the wolf had settled in for the night.

Misfit's had gone nearby, a safe distance from Mamma Mia, and I had put down puppy pads as directed in case she struggled to make it through the night.

The puppy hadn't needed the pads, did her business outside with admirable speed, and heeled, harnessed, and leashed like a dream.

I reclaimed the old wolf's bone, which had been gnawed to a near-death state, and announced, "You can chew on this in the SUV while Misfit worships you, but we're going to work."

Much like a husky, the wolf raised her head and warbled complaints.

I laughed at her antics, got the wolf's work harness, and shook it at her. "We are going to work, Miss Mamma Mia. I have murderers to research, track down, and arrest. You have a long and difficult day of chewing bones ahead of you while you teach Misfit her manners."

In reality, I expected Martino would come claim the puppy, working on giving Misfit exercises and maintaining her training while attempting to turn her into something other than a lovable pet.

She vocalized a long string of complaints, but she got up, came over, and stood while I put her harness on and clipped the leash to it. Once I praised her and gave her the attention she was owed, I gathered my work supplies and herded everyone out to the SUV, which was still parked at the base of the steps.

Following the cake bender and tour of the home and settling the animals, I'd relocated myself to a couch. While I had a faint recollection of Alicia attempting to coerce me into sleeping somewhere more comfortable, I'd pulled a Mamma Mia, refusing to move.

It took walking down the steps for the second time that morning for my back to announce numerous regrets over my stubbornness.

I assumed Alicia had demonstrated more common sense than I possessed, either returning to my apartment or taking advantage of one of the many bedrooms within the mansion. With the entirety of her family in town, I expected she'd been taken off again, probably by her grandfather, to do whatever it was black dragons did when the rest of the world worked.

I got into the SUV, made certain I had the fob that opened the gate along with the override code in case it didn't work, and headed for work. The gate opened automatically on my way out, which would make deliveries simplistic enough, assuming the mail chute couldn't accommodate the box in question.

The mail chute sent any packages on a trip along a slide to the basement, where I could summon the packages at the press of a button. I refused to question the magic or technology that shunted the deliveries into the elevator dedicated to them. When I'd asked about clever raccoons or humans that might take advantage of the chute, we'd made the hike over, where I discovered a painful jolt awaited any who tried to infiltrate the property in such a fashion.

Those who persisted would become trapped in the elevator, the security system would trigger, and the police would be notified.

Per an agreement between the dragons and the cops, the cops would take their time retrieving the would-be thief, although the security company would monitor the situation for any health emergencies.

Amused over having a home with aspirations to become the next Fort Knox, I headed to the station. Mamma Mia regaled me with a warbled song of her people, protesting the necessity of leaving her comfortable bed and fireplace.

"You and me both, baby girl," I told her, and I somehow kept from laughing at her antics. "You'll get days off, I promise."

While Mamma Mia didn't meet the minimum requirements for sentience, she settled down with Misfit, who did her best to comfort the older animal.

By the time I got to work, I'd come to an important decision: anyone who did anything to my wolves would be dealing with an enraged unicorn.

Pleased with myself, I herded the wolves to my office, where Martino waited.

He came armed with a new bone for Mamma Mia. "How did she handle coming in to work today?"

"There was some vocalization about how I'm the cruelest of wolf handlers, although she did let me harness her and get her into the SUV. I can't blame her. She was cuddled up in her bed in front of the fireplace. She's going to love it in winter, although I'm not going to love the bill keeping wood stocked for her."

He grinned, waited for Mamma Mia to head to her bed in my office, and gave her the bone. "Good girl. How did Misfit do?"

"There were no messes, she's heeling like a champ, and while she's friendly, she seems smart." I handed over Misfit's leash. "Please bring my puppy back one step closer to being a detective appropriate K9."

"That is probably something I can manage. I've discussed the situation with the detectives, and they don't think you'll often need a dog capable of aggressive offense. They call in K9s when it's needed, and I think you'll end up doing the same. As such, I'm going to see how she handles sniffing out bombs, drugs, and a variety of other tasks that will be useful for your investigative work. I'm also going to see about training both of them to pull wagons and litters."

I could see having a K9 trained to handle a sled being useful. "Regular mushing sleds, too?"

"Yep. While Cauldron City law enforcement doesn't get called to the outskirts much, if there's an incident deep in a park, it could be useful. And if you are called out somewhere it snows, she'll have the right idea about how to handle the sled."

"What will be Mamma Mia's weight restriction?"

"One body should be within her tolerances, and that's assuming you're walking with her. We'll test it and see if her old bones can handle it. She'll be game. She always is. The real question will be her comfort levels."

"I'll handle getting some unicorns in to check her over the weekend," I promised.

Martino saluted me, ordered Misfit to heel, and stole my puppy, leaving me with Mamma Mia.

The wolf huffed, and I smiled at the disgruntled sound. "Don't worry. Your puppy will be back later. She has to go to puppy school while you get to laze about and listen to me bitch about this case."

As the dead weight case wouldn't solve itself, I went to work inputting case numbers into the system, populating data for every victim. Fortunately for my sanity, the records resulting in an addition to one of the many watch lists were flagged as such, allowing me to easily create groups of victims based on the types of crimes they'd committed.

The ones that became public record in searchable databases would be my initial focus. It took several hours, but I managed to get all identified victims into the system and linked with their criminal records.

The one common link between them wasn't the sexual offenders registry as I expected, but a public watchdog group for homeowners that scraped public court records to vet incoming residents. A group within Block Island in

Rhode Island maintained the registry, and when I did a search for their work, I found the website within five minutes. My brows shot up at the filters I could use to locate criminals.

They even allowed me to search by age.

Damn.

I checked the boxes for both violent crimes and sex offenders, included everyone male within their thirties, and selected non-shifting humans as the species.

On the first page, I found all ten of my first victims. Every bit of public information was available at the click of my mouse, and in the summaries for each criminal, I found information on their blood types, known medical issues, and everything someone searching for an organ might want.

It even included last known locations.

Picking up my phone, I dialed my captain's extension.

"What do you have for me, Smithson?"

"Could you come to my office? I have something to show you."

"On my way."

He hung up, and I set up the digital murder board to show the added-on dates of the suspect database as a new entry. The captain let himself into my office, and Mamma Mia issued a single, soft growl to notify the dragon he entered her territory.

"I see you have that wolf wrapped around your finger already," he commented before observing me work. "Why do you have an entry listed as 'probable murderer candy land', Smithson?"

I gestured in the direction of my computer with my elbow while referencing the site on my phone. "I left a present open for you."

Captain Farthan sat at my computer, and after a few moments, he began to curse. "And all of our identified victims can be found in this database?"

"So far, yes. I'm still working on inputting data, but that's how I found the database. I used the board to find overlaps, and that was the only internet-searchable database that had everyone in it."

"The *only* one?"

I understood his skepticism; while I hadn't been a detective for long, investigations rarely went smoothly—or had such an obvious link tying all the victims together. "That's correct, sir. While there's no way of knowing who found the database and is using it, if we can get the server logs for who did searches for our victims, we might have a launching point for the investigation."

The captain got up, stepped outside of my office, and roared his frustration.

Mamma Mia huffed her displeasure before chewing on her bone. Shaking my head over his reaction to my request, I went back to work. A break of any sort in the case would do wonders, although I questioned who had made the database, why the database had been made, and if the creator of said database would end up holding legal responsibility for tracking those who *weren't* in the sex offenders registry.

Criminals still had some right to privacy, and while certain offenders were tracked, the level of tracking done by the Block Island vigilante crew went beyond what most viewed to be permissible.

If the database proved to be a critical link resulting in the murders of so many, the creators behind it might end up in a legal battle they would regret. Worse, knowing what I did about the law, the case held the potential to explode in a variety of unpleasant ways.

Many shadows darkened the case in general, and breaches of privacy were only the beginning. The fact that the database included private matters of the victims' lives would be taken into consideration. Nobody needed to know someone's blood type when monitoring newcomers to their community. From there, the case would have a place to take root.

And once it was established that the victims were chosen specifically for their blood type, the operators would have a far harder time proving, without a shadow of a doubt, they were providing necessary information.

As their information had led to the deaths of over ten people, chosen because of what should have been private medical data, the case would take on a whole new life. Curious over the differences between the private database and the government-operated ones, I went to my computer and got to work, compiling a list of differences between the primary lists and the one run by the Block Island community.

None of the government databases included private information, such as children, partners, and other family members. Medical records were also not included in the government databases. Upon closer scrutiny, I discovered that the Block Island's group also included allergies, all known preferences, and a long history of residences going back as far as the researchers could find.

Some included childhood residences.

The whole thing left a bitter taste in my mouth, as the files reminded me of a sick research diary meant to fully expose the lives of the victims.

Time and time again, I'd heard about how every murder told a story. Sometimes, the story was one of greed or passion gone wrong. Sometimes, it was a sad tale of vengeance. There were more reasons than stars in the sky for someone to kill somebody. Humanity liked simplifying things, boiling the complexities of human nature down to broad concepts. People understood passion and love. They struggled with apathy. Psychopaths and serial killers fascinated humanity due to that lack of understanding.

On the surface, someone might believe that the database operated by someone in the Block Island community was meant for the greater good.

The bodies in our morgue told a different tale.

The database might be what determined if we battled a serial killer or mass murderer, too. Unlike the mass murderer, who didn't care who was killed as long as bodies hit the floor, the serial killer had method and motive among other things. There was supposed to be a cool down period between the killings, but every other piece was present.

Until I had all the autopsy reports, I couldn't tell if there was a cool down period or not, although the corpses we had indicated that not all of the victims had been killed at the same time.

The perp had a goal, and until their goal was accomplished, more would die. Even if the database linked to all the deaths was taken offline, I feared it was too little too late. The damage had already been done.

Out of curiosity, I ran a search for men in the same general parameters, coming up with a list of twenty-seven other potential victims. I sent the list to my captain via email and suggested that some of our unidentified bodies be checked against the Block Island database.

Then I took it a step further, checking the list for rare blood types and sending that over as well, to see if that might help with the other unidentified victims who hadn't fit the initial mold. If the hire was a surgeon of some sort, working in the underground market for medical services, the organs were only the beginning. Blood would be needed along with other tissue types.

With narrowed eyes, I dug deeper at the Block Island database, searching for the organizers within the community. As though understanding they skirted on the wrong side of the law, I found no open information on who operated the list outside of referencing Block Island.

I picked up my phone and dialed Dr. Erik's number from memory, pinning the device between my ear and shoulder while I continued to work.

"Is everything okay?" Dr. Erik asked.

I eyed my work phone, wondering what caller ID registered on his end. "Why wouldn't I be okay?"

"I have received reports you opted to sleep on a couch rather than a bed last night."

Damn. The black dragoness meant business. "I seem to operate on batteries, chicken, and cheese, and the batteries ran out. Beyond a little stiffness in my back, I survived sleeping on a couch. I do need you to treat my new partner. She's getting older, probably has arthritis, and doesn't handle being a couch potato well. As such, I'm now the caretaker and servant of two wolf-dogs. Mamma Mia is the one who needs medical care, though. She would very much like to work, and her old bones need some help on that front. The puppy could use a checkup, but she's at puppy school right now."

"They really gave you Mamma Mia?" Dr. Erik sighed.

"I'll call around and figure out who is the best to help treat her. I'm going to charge you a decent diamond for the work, though."

"I better have an old wolf for at least ten more years," I muttered. "You just want my diamonds."

"I just want fair payment for dealing with your chicken and cheese bender."

"You should scold my mother, by the way. She basically told me to go contract salmonella."

"That woman!" According to Dr. Erik's tone, my mother's days were numbered. "I'll have someone come tend to your wolf. Was that all you needed?"

"Not precisely," I admitted. "I wanted to ask you if you have a way of checking to see if there are any surgeons or doctors capable of the murders living on Block Island."

"Where's that?"

"Rhode Island."

"Give me a minute. There are public records for operating surgeons I can reference. What's the population of the area?"

"A little over a thousand."

"Got a town name?"

I checked Block Island, and after a moment, I replied, "New Shoreham."

While he did his search, I resumed checking through the database, compiling other potential demographics useful for the search. Then, as I worried the surgeon might grow desperate enough to target women, I ran the search using the same criteria as the other victims except changing their gender. To my relief, there were only three records in the database, but I sent those over to the captain as something to look into.

"There is one surgeon who has a residence on the island. He is licensed to operate a private clinic for those on the island, although he only uses the license for emergencies. According to this, he is also licensed in New York, Connecticut, and New Jersey for transplant operations and trauma work. His public medical record indicates he has not been working full-time in those regions for at least six months, and his medical license is up for renewal at the end of the year."

Interesting. "When was the last time he worked in that area at all?"

"There is a note he performed an operation in New Jersey in the middle of January, filling in for a doctor who needed to take the day off unexpectedly."

"And that's public record?"

"Yes. Roughly half of the states require specific work dates and shift times to be public record. It's part of the enhancing health care acts they've been trying to implement. The theory is, if shifts are made public record, civilians can monitor if they're receiving appropriate care from rested physicians and health staff."

"The reality?" I could see that type of law going sideways in a hurry.

"Very few people actually use the records, but it has seen a decrease in general errors, as hospitals realistically can't overwork staff. Nebraska isn't one of the states with the law, but the hospital system I work for records the shifts and the data is readily available to the public on request. Our network has found the additional accountability is wise, but most of the doctors don't want the shift data to be public information." Dr. Erik paused. "Why are you asking me about surgeons in Block Island?"

"I'm testing a theory. I'll give you a second diamond if you can get me everything you can on this Block Island surgeon… and information on anyone who is closely associated with him."

"My daughter could use a new necklace. Give me something with interesting flaws or good color."

"Five carat range, uncut?" I offered.

"That'll work nicely. If you have something better suited for a teardrop cut, that would be ideal."

I had a few stones that had come out in strange shapes in the carat range he wanted. "Deal. I'll toss in accent stones for work with Mamma Mia so she's comfortable while she works."

"I would like to remind you that we can't completely erase all signs of old age."

"But you can replace degraded cartilage so she's comfortable."

Dr. Erik sighed. "You want me to also make sure her organs are in good shape and essentially turn back time for her for a few years."

"Now that you mention it, that would be very nice."

"Two teardrops, similar size, that can be fashioned into earrings," he ordered.

I chuckled. "I'll even draw a basic design for you and provide the material for the accent stones. How long to get the data on this surgeon?"

"I'll have it for you within two hours. I'm going to place a few phone calls to make sure my intel is good."

He hung up, and I went to the digital board to begin putting in notes on the first potential suspect in a case destined to push me to my limits.

TWENTY-EIGHT

"Is that mean old unicorn not paying enough attention to you?"

WEDNESDAY, APRIL 18, 2057
LOWER NORTH LAKES, PRECINCT 153
CAULDRON CITY, NEBRASKA.

A RATHER MIFFED Alicia pressed her face to the window of my office and attempted to glare me into submission. While tempted to have her stew in the hall for a while, I opened my door on route to the murder board, armed with more research on the probable unwilling organ donor, James McDonald. Outside of the Block Island database, nowhere made mention of his blood type and other medical vitals. In the process of researching him, I ferreted out some crimes from his youth in old newspapers that hadn't made it to his adult record.

I doubted his criminal record from his youth played any part in his death, but I made a notation of what I'd discovered and flagged it as a possibility.

Mamma Mia abandoned her bone to greet the dragoness, and she warbled.

"Is that mean old unicorn not paying enough attention to you?" Alicia cooed, crouching to give the wolf attention. The animal quieted her protest and basked in the glow of another servant dedicated to her general happiness.

I chuckled, made certain to save my latest update to McDonald's file, and said, "I think that was more of a mournful howl over missing the prettiest of the black dragons infesting the precinct at current."

"We really are an infestation right now. Grandpappy is downstairs trying to convince Captain Farthan he should be allowed up on your floor. He has brought Brazilian for you. It's all chicken, but at least it's a change of pace. He also brought some questionable chicken product from a restaurant your mother swears by."

My mother was trying to murder me with bad chicken—or make me even richer than I already was. "I no longer want to participate in this chicken and cheese project," I informed her.

Laughing and shaking her head, she gave Mamma Mia another round of petting before rising. "And miss a chance to welcome your newborn rock into the world?"

"That newborn rock is going to be the size of my fist at the rate I'm consuming chicken and cheese." I flopped onto my chair and leaned my head back. "And if I want this to work, after my next chicken and cheese bender, I need to transform into a unicorn nightly while regretting my choices."

"You have this nice yard you can wander around in without anyone bothering you now. That's something, right?"

"Except I'm supposed to be setting myself up for a ponynapping so the culprits behind this might be caught."

My captain poked his head into my office. "Your ponynapping has been canceled; you need to go on a trip to Rhode Island. The local police went to investigate the homes of three people associated with the Block Island website due to violated privacy laws. Apparently, their little state takes that sort of thing seriously, and the servers were run in the residence of one of the three in question. While two have been apprehended, one did not answer the door. The police acquired a warrant and let themselves in."

My eyes widened. "But it's only been a few hours!"

"The Feds politely gave the Rhode Island police a call and suggested they hurry things up before they became more involved than they'd appreciate. Rather than get steamrolled, the Rhode Island cops decided to cooperate so they have some jurisdiction instead of no jurisdiction. There are corpses, which have been mutilated in fashions similar to ours. The one who did not answer and had corpses in his basement? He's the doctor you asked Dr. Erik to investigate. Dr. Erik notified me of his findings, and he'll have more information for you later. I need you to take your dragoness to Rhode Island and talk with the police there, have a look at the bodies, and start trying to find who needs organs, who might be learning from this shady surgeon, and put an end to the murders."

Well, that would make a mess of their day—and mine. "I bet they regret sharing jurisdiction right now."

My captain chuckled. "That's one way to put it."

"You think some of them are practice runs for a second surgeon?" I asked.

A second surgeon would add complexity. Who would

murder people to learn how to be a surgeon when hospitals were scrambling for new doctors? There was always a need for more medical staff—and the various shortages had resulted in better pay, shorter shifts, and everything else needed for someone to have a successful, profitable career.

I'd been the true unicorn in my family, as a unicorn could earn a fortune without producing a single diamond in the medical field. Rather than go for the easy wealth, I'd chosen a different path.

Most hospitals in Cauldron City sponsored young doctors through school in exchange for five years of service—paid service with full benefits.

It made no sense for someone to go underground if their goal was to work in medicine.

The mystery of why would bother me for a long time to come.

As though somehow sensing I'd gone wool gathering, my captain cleared his throat before saying, "We have more autopsy reports, and yes, that's the general consensus. I'll have some of the other detectives put together something from the autopsy findings so you aren't trying to translate those and learn all the other ropes at the same time. Alicia, you're clear to fly if you'd like. The trip would be good exercise for you, and you'll have a few of your family members along in case you get tired and need a breather. Hardy will be accompanying you as well, and he'll be saddled to get used to flying long distances wearing gear."

Alicia's eyes widened. "As a dragon?"

"As a dragon. There's a saddle here that'll fit you if you want to haul my cop to Rhode Island."

I considered my old wolf, who would not appreciate a flight anywhere. "What about Mamma Mia?"

"We have a travel crate for her, it's cozy, and she's trained to handle being carted around by a dragon. The puppy can ride with her, and they'll be fine. The cage is shielded against the wind, so they'll just experience a light breeze of an enjoyable temperature. We'll give them new bones, and they'll be happy for the duration of the flight. Alicia's father volunteered to carry the wolves, and he's among the most sensible of those making the journey, I thought it wise to approve the request." My captain grinned at me. "You even get to take your firearm, as I've already gotten your carry approval for Rhode Island and every state along the flight path."

"How did you manage that in such a short period of time?"

"I made a few phone calls, assigned some of the work to a few slackers in the farm, and growled menacingly at those who disagreed with my proposals."

Well, if the opal dragon growled at me, I would have thought twice before denying his request. Any sensible being would. Once irritated, dragons created a great deal of property damage, and dragons often viewed people as property.

They did try to prevent damage to the property they *liked*, but where dragons went, trouble followed.

I wondered if unicorns could work miracles and tame the wild ways of the dragons ruling over Cauldron City. On second thought, I decided against vocalizing my thoughts. The dragons might start dividing the city's unicorns among themselves and competing to see who tamed the most, how many unicorns went mad from dealing with dragons, and who could accumulate the greatest amount of wealth through the acquisition of their very own living, breathing unicorn.

Alicia snickered. "You look worried, Jace. What's wrong?"

Well, there was a lot wrong, but I focused on the riskiest of the issues: protecting Rhode Island from the influx of irritated black dragons. "I don't know if I can protect the state of Rhode Island from your family, Alicia. You? You I can trust not to flatten the whole place. Your father? Should he run into those responsible for your poisoning? There will be no stopping him."

Both dragons blinked, and then their eyes widened.

I waited for them to work through the possibilities, and Alicia covered her mouth with her hands. "Oh."

My captain let out a breath in a gusty huff. "That is not a problem I had anticipated."

"Maybe if we repeat that they cannot devour anyone we're interviewing, it might work. Rhode Island does need to be left intact." As I worried about the mayhem the Grimstone dragons might cause, I said, "I'll put a stone up on offer in Alicia's game show, but only dragons who follow all the laws in Cauldron City, Rhode Island, and everywhere between are eligible to compete for it."

That might keep them behaved.

"Accept that offer," Alicia stated, and she attempted to stare the opal dragon into submission. "That offer will bring peace and prosperity to Cauldron City until the show's recording date. Crime rates will plummet to practically zero." With a shrug, she added, "Sure, you might be out of a job, but you wouldn't have to worry about any misbehaving dragons for a while."

"It better be a good stone, Smithson."

"I'll make it worth the show's while," I promised.

Thursday, April 19, 2057
Edgewater
Cleveland, Ohio.

ALICIA COULD TEACH the other dragons a thing or two about smooth flying. While she came in dead last for speed, she outclassed everybody else in grace and beauty. She preferred smooth elevations followed with gentle swoops, gaining speed so she could glide long distances. The other dragons made more use of their wings, ultimately circling us while she took her time.

Sometime deep in the night, we arrived in Cleveland, and the dragons landed at a park not far from the river's edge. Several women, all beauties with the look I learned belonged to the children and grandchildren of the Black Dragon of New York, waited for us with several vehicles. One by one, the dragons transformed, changing into the clothes that Alicia's father had hauled along with my wolves.

The wolves bounced around in their shared crate, ready and eager to be set free for a while. As I was no fool, I made sure to leash both animals first, and I secured a hold on Alicia's saddle so they wouldn't drag me off.

The dragoness needed to step on the leash to contain the beasts.

"You're Jace?" one of the women asked, looking me over from head to toe. "They grow them nice in Cauldron City, Alicia."

"This one is mine," Alicia rumbled, and she tilted her head to eye her relative, displaying her teeth.

The woman smirked. "Good. This is the hunk trying to teach you to cook, then?"

"He is."

"And where's that idiot son of mine?"

Ah. I realized I'd made a mistake. I beheld Hardy's mother, and my fellow cop shuffled up, pulling on a lightweight jacket. "I'm here, Mom. Please don't antagonize Alicia. She's still not feeling well."

"I swear, you're just as bad as your father, sauntering around like you own the place. Saunter less, boy. There ain't no eligible women around, so you don't have to try to exude casual sexuality."

Hardy postured. I regarded my fellow cop with a raised brow.

"Don't look at me, Smithson. You're more of an offender than I am. You don't even know you're doing it."

"I do not saunter." What the hell was even a saunter? I could understand a strut; I had sometimes strutted my stuff for Marci, but I'd always done it on purpose. What was sauntering, and how did one do it in a sexually enticing fashion?

"You saunter," Alicia informed me. "I've come to the determination you can't help it due to your species. I've determined that your gait is changing as you're growing out of your pony coat, and so rather than flounce, you saunter. Your father saunters, too."

"Flounce?" I blinked, as I'd heard the term enough times to have a basic understanding of what it meant. "But I'm not angry."

"It's more of a fake angry, exaggerating how much your co-workers are making you suffer. So much flouncing," she replied.

Thanks to the late hour, it took me longer than I appreciated to realize she teased me. Rather than fall further to her wicked ways, I crouched to check on Mamma Mia and Misfit. Both wolves showered me with affection, and I concluded they'd enjoyed their flight. "Are we taking a quick breather or waiting for morning?"

"Morning," Hardy said. "Are we staying at your place, Mom?"

"We are, and there's a warm meal waiting for you. One of your brothers is keeping an eye on everything. You're expected to go in, stuff yourselves, and sleep before heading out no later than ten. Try to pick the pace up a little, Alicia. I know you like being a gentle giant, but you're slow. Be less gentle and fly like you mean it."

"I'll try," Alicia mumbled.

Hardy sighed. "She's still not feeling great, Mom."

"She's still a Grimstone, and I don't see a single white hair on this man's head yet. He's not a dragon. He should have gray hairs by now."

"He's a unicorn, Mom. And he's a crabby one who will kick us into next week with zero sign of fear. He attacked our boss."

Hardy's mother regarded me with interest, and then she smiled. "Then you might be good enough for my little niece. Excellent. And what will you do if someone tries to hurt my little boy?"

"If your little boy doesn't eat the perp first, I'd probably be forced to stomp, stab, or sit upon them depending on the circumstances, although I do tend to prefer avoiding injury when possible. But I would stop long enough to determine if Hardy deserves being trounced."

"You can keep him, Alicia," the dragoness announced.

"I'll make sure those parents of yours are aware you have my blessing."

"I'm standing right here," Alicia's father stated.

"I don't believe that your dictator of a wife would let you out from under her for long enough for you to fly anywhere alone. You're clearly an imposter."

Alicia sighed. "She's in Cauldron City making sure my grandpappy doesn't take it over."

"Well, that's dumb of her." Hardy's mother swooped in and claimed a hug from my live-in dragoness. "Did that mean old imposter do anything shady?"

"He got his first gemstone, and he didn't do anything shady. Mom bought it for him."

Somehow, Alicia contained her aunt, who went for her father and jumped on him, wrapping her legs around his waist and hugging him. "Our precious little flower has finally grown up!"

Goodness. I stared at Hardy, who shrugged.

"There's a reason I live in Cauldron City, Jace."

Right. "Please just get us to Rhode Island intact."

"Why do you always have to ask for damned miracles?"

He asked a good question, one I didn't have an answer to.

TWENTY-NINE

"That bad?"

THURSDAY, APRIL 19, 2057
NEW SHOREHAM FIREHOUSE
BLOCK ISLAND, RHODE ISLAND.

A LITTLE AFTER two in the afternoon, Alicia landed in front of the firehouse in New Shoreham, as Block Island lacked an actual police station. When viewed through the lens of no local law enforcement, I could understand why someone might build a database of potential troublemakers. However, knowledge changed everything.

Crime could happen anywhere, even in small towns. I estimated it would take the local police at least an hour to make it to the island unless they happened to have a winged officer able to carry a passenger.

Before leaving Cleveland, Captain Farthan had called me with a few key updates, indicating that the database had likely been created as a front to gather information on potential victims. The culprit behind the database, one Dr.

Timothy Lerrans, had a motive I hadn't been given time to ferret out.

A serial killer had murdered his little sister.

Captain Farthan's warning about the man's history chilled me. The doctor's sister had been one of the lucky ones. She'd disappeared, leaving her family to wonder what had happened to her for years before finding her body and uncovering the truth. Other victims hadn't been so lucky.

The little girl had been the first of the man's kills, before he'd taken to torturing his victims. While she hadn't escaped his clutches alive, she'd died from a single gunshot wound to the head with no evidence of other trauma.

Her body had been found within a few miles of her home, and the evidence indicated she had been killed immediately after being kidnapped.

With a potential motive to go with our possible mastermind, we could begin putting together the pieces of the puzzle to build a complete picture of the tragedies that had befallen Cauldron City. Too many questions lingered, however—questions that would change the story over and over until we uncovered the complete truth. Why poison people? Why mutilate the bodies? Why disguise it as an organ transplant? Were any of the organs being transplanted at all, or was it a front to disguise something else? Were multiple groups coordinating the kills? If so, why? I doubted I'd find the answers on the picturesque island, but we might find where to search next.

I slid off Alicia's back, winced at the aches in my muscles and joints, and made a reminder to demand a good leather coat the next time I accepted a ride from a dragon. I rolled my shoulders and went to work stripping Alicia of her tack, grunting and hauling it to the nearby rail so nothing would get damaged. She lowered her head so I could access the collar surrounding her throat where her neck met her skull. Once I had her free from the straps, I retrieved her robe from the saddle pack and held it open for her so she could shift and put it on without giving everyone a show.

I enjoyed the flash of skin she graced me with, and for the life of me, I couldn't tell if she'd done it on purpose. Aware I would be sharing my new house with her didn't help matters. No matter how well my mother and father had raised me, I was still a man—a man with a healthy interest in smart, pretty women.

Alicia counted as both smart and pretty, which would cause a great deal of trouble for me in the future, and that was before considering her family.

As a cold shower wasn't part of my upcoming activities, I forced my thoughts to focus on the ever-growing list of crimes Dr. Timothy Lerrans had likely committed. I would pursue the truth, even if it meant he'd only provided the tools for another killer to do the dirty work.

Whether he'd provided the tool, had hired someone to do his dirty work, or was the killer, I would find out one way or another. I expected the investigation would take me all over the country, and I worried what it meant for me that I'd somehow been given enough jurisdiction to travel to a different state.

I freed Mamma Mia and Misfit from their cage and handed their leashes off to Hardy with instructions to foist the animals off on whichever relative needed to be kept busy while we worked.

A cop wearing a Rhode Island badge emerged from the firehouse, came down the steps, and held out his hand to me. "You must be Detective Smithson."

I shook with him. "I am."

"I'm Detective Olairs, but please call me Porter."

First names worked for me. "Jace. What do you have for us?"

"More bodies than I care to think about. We thought about removing them from the cellar, but we closed it up for you to have a look at first. Everything is being preserved; it looks like the culprit used some hefty magicker workings to keep the corpses from decaying. If any in your group have a weak stomach, I recommend that they stay outside."

I winced. "That bad?"

"It's not as bad as the hanging corpses you had to deal with over in Cauldron City, but it's pretty bad. We got to see some photos of that when we were beginning the investigation. We have some FBI types crawling around, and I'd rather work with an upstart of a fledgling detective than one of that lot any day of the week. The ones we've got are a nasty bunch."

"Oh?"

"Their medical examiner is a nasty black of a unicorn, they're mostly comprised of dragons, and they think us cops are cute."

I raised a brow, and I turned my attention to Alicia, who worked to situate her bathrobe so nothing would slip out of place. "What do you think?"

"I think we'll be romping around after work to work out a serious case of nerves. I bet you can have that black unicorn calmed down in five minutes flat, and you'll be ruling over the dragons within ten."

Interesting. I wondered if I could charm them all into working with me during the investigation with a budget of only ten minutes. "What do I get if I pull it off?"

"I promise I won't cook you breakfast."

I laughed at the threat, which would motivate me to win the cooperation of the FBI agents and their medical examiner. "And what happens if I don't?"

"I'll ride home on a shaggy unicorn."

Damn. I *could* conjure a saddle, and if I pushed it, I could cover a lot of ground in a hurry. "Only if my boss clears the time needed to do it."

"If he doesn't, I get five days of your time to carry me wherever I wish to go."

"You're on." I grinned at my fellow cop. "Where are these dragons and unicorn I need to tame? I need to secure her promise she won't be making me breakfast any time soon."

"They're inside the firehouse. Dare I ask why you don't want her to make you breakfast?"

"She almost took out the Black Dragon of New York with eggs."

Porter's eyes widened. "She's a Grimstone?"

"I'm the only one in our group who isn't a Grimstone. If I can't calm the situation down, they can, I'm sure. Just be glad that the Black Dragon of New York is still in Cauldron city." I checked on Alicia's family, determining all of them had shifted back to human. I gestured in the direction of Alicia's father. "That is Alicia's father." After a moment, I pointed at Hardy, who also wore a bathrobe and hauled his duffle towards us, my wolves in tow. "That's Hardy, and he's also a detective. The wolves are my K9s. Misfit is the one in training, and Mamma Mia is dodging retirement through working with me. Hey, Hardy? We've got a crabby black unicorn and some irritable dragons. Ask Alicia's father to trot his new prize out so he can show it off to the FBI agents. They're also dragons, and I'd rather we all get along. I dodge a round with the eggs if I get them on my side within ten minutes."

"You'll have them wrapped around your finger within two," Hardy commented. "Who is our new friend?"

"This is Porter. He's a detective, and he prefers it casual."

"I can do casual. Alicia? Charm your daddy. I don't want to attend Jace's funeral because of those eggs."

She laughed, but she hurried off to do his bidding.

Once she was out of hearing range, I muttered, "If it weren't for those eggs, I'd think about losing for the fun of it. She wants five days for a road trip on a shaggy pony of a unicorn."

"She might have to settle for a sleek stallion at the way things are going lately, but if you tie the wager, we usually go with everyone wins in our family. It keeps us from killing each other."

That I could believe, as the black dragons lived to compete with each other. I could work with a tie, assuming I could get the unicorn and dragons associated with the FBI to cooperate with me. "If I have to eat her eggs, I might not make it, Hardy."

"I really hope you tie or win," he muttered. "Finding someone else tolerable at work would be a nightmare."

"I'm so glad to know you care."

Thursday, April 19, 2057
New Shoreham Firehouse

Block Island, Rhode Island.

WE DELAYED meeting with the FBI long enough for the black dragons to get changed into appropriate apparel. I spent the time conferring with Porter, who warned me that most of the bodies had been in the process of being dissected, frozen partway through the procedure. The Rhode Island police had taken to making sure nobody who had recently eaten viewed the deceased, as nobody wanted the hassle of cleaning the crime scene and preserving the evidence.

As requested, Alicia's father came armed with his new diamond. I took over handling the wolves, got them seated together, and praised both for their excellent behavior. Once we were all presentable, the Rhode Island dragons swooped in, and I identified the black unicorn through his expression, his badge declaring him to be an FBI medical examiner, and the way he looked us over for various health problems.

Conquering the unicorn would be the easiest, so I ordered the wolves to stay, dropped their leashes, and intercepted, holding out my hand. "Doctor, thank you for seeing us. Dr. Erik already filled me in a little on the surgeon who might be behind this." In a lower voice, hopefully soft enough Alicia wouldn't hear me, I said, "If you agree to cooperate after five minutes of talking with me, I won't have to eat the eggs that almost felled the Black Dragon of New York. If Dr. Erik has to nurse me back to good health, he's going to ram his hooves up my shaggy pony ass so I earn the medical treatments I'll be receiving."

After shaking with me, the medical examiner checked his watch and replied, "I've got your back, but we're going to have to discuss why Erik might be wanting to kick you. That's a whole lot of work. I'm Illiard."

"Nice to meet you, Illiard. I'll just warn you now, I'm more stubborn than Dr. Erik is," I confessed, making sure to keep my voice low.

"That would do it. All right. You've got a few problems on your hands, so let's get that out of the way before you go try to convince the dragons to cooperate with you. They know about the eggs, so if you play that route, you might get your tie."

"How about an invitation to participate in an episode of Alicia's game show?"

"That would get you what you want."

I nodded. "With that out of the way, give me the bad news first."

"One of the victims might still be alive."

The thought of someone being trapped, frozen while undergoing dissection justified why the FBI and police warned people against eating before going to the site. "All right. Can the victim be saved?"

"I talked with Erik, and he thinks if you're helping, he's got a seventy-five percent chance. That leads to the next problem."

"Hit me with it."

"It might be a mercy to let him die. He has serious health problems, and while we can fix a bunch of it while on the table, he's a wanted criminal, and he would not have a good time through prison."

I understood the unicorn's worry. Justice and mercy rarely overlapped. "That entirely depends on if he deserves the mercy and what he did to his victims," I reminded him, careful to keep my tone gentle. "Is mercy on him worth the price the families of the victims would pay for the removal of justice?"

"That's the argument we're having," he informed me with a grimace. "He has a criminal record long enough to give us all pause, although he's gentler than most serial killers of his ilk. Don't get me wrong; he had a history of sexual violence, just nothing on the scale of what we usually work with."

"How many victims?"

"Well, over thirty we know about."

"If he's alive, you have a better chance of finding out if there are other bodies," I pointed out. "If he can be saved without the rest of his life being blatant torture, we should save him."

"He might be short a hand when we're finished, but we might be able to preserve it. I won't know until we get to work. Go talk to the dragons, and I'll get to work getting the support staff we need, the blood bags, and the rest of the field kit. We'll have to do the work where he's at. There's no way he'd survive a trip to the hospital, not from here."

"That was likely the point." Disgusted over the state of affairs, I went to my next target, the group of dragons wearing FBI gear. Aware of the ongoing feud between the FBI and local law enforcement, I said, "If you pretend I'm a strangely dressed FBI agent for the duration of this investigation, you will spare me from the eggs that almost felled the Black Dragon of New York, but you have to give me a hard time for precisely five minutes first."

The agents grinned at me, and an older man with the first hints of gray in his black hair held out his hand. "We've heard about the eggs incident, and there were even pictures. We couldn't do such a thing to a pony, so you're on. We're going to give that Grimstone a hard time, though. I'm Special Agent Tibbers."

I shook with him. "Call me Jace. Which Grimstone? There's so many of them here."

"All of them except the shy son-in-law. We can't break the will of the shy one; that mean old bastard in New York would have our hides if we hurt his feelings. That's the stone you sold?"

I regarded Alicia's father with a raised brow, as the man had swooped in for the kill, giving Illiard a good look at the uncut rock. "He must have been waiting to start showing it off, but yes. That's the diamond. I'm offering a chance to get onto Alicia's show to make this as smooth as possible, especially on the jurisdiction front. We have way too many bodies in Cauldron City, a potential illegal organ transplant case, and probably more bodies in the works to bicker over territory."

"And they sent over a unicorn colt, and we all know if we make a colt unhappy, nobody is happy as a result, though we don't usually see the unicorns in the force. Unicorns are usually medical staff."

"I'm weird. I've always been weird. I'm a white, and everyone else in my family works in the medical field in some capacity. Hell, I'm the only unicorn who *isn't* working in the medical field in Cauldron City. But, apparently, I'm good in a pinch in the ER. I heard we might have a live one?"

"We do. And we have to decide how much work we're going to put in trying to get him to testify."

"If we can save him without torturing him for the remainder of his life, we save him. Illiard mentioned you folks weren't sure if you had a complete count of his victims."

As one, the gathered FBI agents sighed.

"That's right," Tibbers agreed. "So, the good news is, our vic has had his chest cracked, but none of the organs seem to be damaged or removed. If we can get him thawed and revived, it's a matter of sealing his chest, making sure he doesn't bleed out, and transferring him to a hospital until he can be sent to prison. He's been a fugitive for a decade. He escaped prison during a botched transfer, and he's been on the run ever since. I can have a copy of his record sent to your station so you can go over it later, and I'll get you an invite to observe the interrogation—and a chance to lob a few questions of your own at him, if we can keep you safe. He's violent, and he's unpredictable."

"You'll interrogate him while dragons?" I guessed.

"That's our current plan, assuming he survives."

Special Agent Tibbers introduced me to the six other dragons. Special Agent Calvin Lawrence handled evidence gathering and registration, specializing in violent crimes. Special Agent Luis Miles specialized in shutting down drug cartels and had come to offer his expertise regarding illegal substances. Special Agent Jonathan Tran was their former attorney who decided, a year after working in the court system, that he wanted to change fields and would be able to explain any questionable legalities.

I considered Jonathan, and then I realized I recognized him. At the same time, we pointed at each other. "You almost beat me!"

His disgusted proclamation I'd bested him almost made me laugh. Throughout the entirety of university, we'd competed for the best grades, and we'd studied together.

Tibbers blinked. "You know him, Jon?"

"We went to school together. This bastard is that jackass who beat me for the top marks for our graduating year by a fraction of a point. We had a lot of overlapping classes. Watch your mouth with this one. He's smarter than I am, and he's not the kind to rub it in your face. He'll just shoot you looks of utter disappointment, which is somehow worse. I had not known you were a literal unicorn, Jace."

"And I had not known you were a literal dragon. What color?"

"Ruby, because that's far more sophisticated than red, and I am still as vain as always."

I laughed. "Does this mean we can dodge most of the bullshit? Because if we have a live body, I'd like to dodge most of the bullshit."

"Oh, we're going to give you shit for coming onto our turf and making a mess of our investigation, but unlike with the rest of the uppity local cops, we won't mean it," my former classmate informed me. "And, unlike the other uppity local cops, at least I know you have some clue what you're doing. You took your Yale degree and became a cop?"

"As was the plan from the very beginning," I replied, unable to keep the pride out of my voice. "But now you know how I paid for it, and it wasn't because I'm handsome enough to prostitute my way through school."

"It certainly explains your rather unique diet during school, that's for sure. So, what has ants in your pants over this case? I got a good look at your face when you were waiting, and I've learned when you're genuinely pissed over something. I just hadn't realized who you were. Your resting bitch face is severe enough you're going to scare the locals."

Damn. I'd forgotten I could get a stony visage once worked up over something; it'd been a long time since something had worked me over *that* much. "My face has been tattling on me again?"

"That's putting it mildly," Jon informed me. "Spill the beans, assuming it's relevant to the case."

I considered the various things that might trip my trigger, determined the entire case applied, but one thing stuck out over the rest: the little girl who'd never get to see her daddy again. "One of our vics reformed, and he had a little girl with his wife. They'd gone into hiding, and now the little girl no longer has her daddy, and her mom is missing the love of her life. Worse, the wife is pregnant with their second child. I get it. Not all of them reform—hell, most of them don't, but one of the vics did, and he got short shafted. He's also our probable unwilling organ donor. The kidnappings of the little ones has me riled up pretty badly along with the poisonings, but that one's going to lose me sleep."

The FBI agents winced, and I gave them a minute to process my statement.

"I want to say it doesn't get much worse, but in this case, it really does. I'm hoping we can get close enough on the trail of the bastards behind this to stop the poisonings and murders—at least long enough for us to catch up. If we can."

Over the years, I'd learned the bitter truth about law enforcement. For every criminal we brought to justice, two or three got away with their crimes. Magic had made it harder for us to do our jobs in some ways. Magic also made it easier.

"All right. We did get a child abduction crew to come along for the ride. They operate in groups of three to five.

This set is a quartet, and three are keeping an eye on the site while we're here. Special Agent Galretti is the one you'll want to talk to about the kidnappings." Jon eyed one of the older FBI agents, who nodded to acknowledge me. "Our forensics expert is Special Agent Hobbson, and he'll be the one who'll walk you through the condition of the bodies before we unravel the magic keeping our live body in stasis. But there's a piece of good news in this nightmare."

"There is?"

"We don't think he was conscious when they started dissecting him."

Well, that would haunt me for a while. "Do we have any other good news?"

"I wish, Jace. I really wish. This one is going to be a mess, and I've got the feeling we're just getting started."

THIRTY

When she wasn't threatening me with eggs, I enjoyed her company.

THURSDAY, APRIL 19, 2057
NEW SHOREHAM
BLOCK ISLAND, RHODE ISLAND.

ON THE OUTSIDE, the cottage seemed like the sort of place where a doctor might retire to enjoy some peace and quiet. With a view of the ocean and no neighbors in sight, it made the ideal place for a serial killer to do his dirty work. The neighbors were far enough away I doubted they'd hear the bastard's victims scream. In the time since Dr. Timothy Lerrans had gone elsewhere, leaving his basement filled with his victims, his garden had overgrown, weeds encroaching on the pathway leading to the door.

Someone had taken hedge trimmers to the path to make enough space for the gurneys we'd need to take the bodies away.

I regretted my trip to Rhode Island, and when Alicia came calling for her half of our deal, I would be guilty of a count of kidnapping, as I'd refuse to return home until forced. With the number of dragons in my life, I'd be herded back within a week, but until then, I would run fast and far, and I'd take the dragoness with me.

When she wasn't threatening me with eggs, I enjoyed her company.

"And that's your expression of impending doom with no hope on the horizon," my former classmate stated, and he laughed at me. "The last time I saw you making that expression, it was before our final batch of tests. You'd given me hope of catching you."

"Well, I can certainly understand why none of the locals would accuse him of being a murderer. On the outside, he was the perfect neighbor until he wandered off and let his yard grow wild." Wrinkling my nose, I shook my head. "Does the inside look this nice?"

"The entry does, but once you leave the entry, it gets pretty nasty. He had the place set up so nobody could see his misdeeds from the doorway or windows, and he has some potent practitioner tricks that lessen sounds and smells. His living areas are for studying and research, so it looks like you would expect from a doctor's library, although he has more than a few jarred samples kicking around. Any room he wasn't living in is an issue. There are bodies in storage everywhere. They've been dissected already, but he closed them up and neatly labeled where he was storing which organs. The cellar is the real problem. It's an unfinished basement, and he used magic to reinforce the walls rather than studs, concrete, and the things normal people use. He has some form of cleaning zone on the steps, which we'll have to remove when we transfer evidence out of here."

Every time I thought it couldn't get worse, it did. "I just

got a raise, and I think I need to ask for another raise." I sighed and eyed the cottage, debating if I could get away with fleeing and becoming a hermit. "All right. Let's get this over with. What sort of gear do we need for going into this place?"

"We're using scrubs, gloves, booties, and surgical masks. I recommend you avoid breathing out of your nose and switching to mouth breathing. If you think it smells bad, the taste after doing that is worse. Either breathe out of your mouth the entire time or use your nose exclusively. It's awful no matter which you do, but I already made that mistake. Don't walk in my shoes."

"Thanks for the warning."

After ten minutes and a run down on what the dragons could and couldn't do, we entered the home. As warned, Dr. Timothy Lerrans put up a good front, making use of a cozy entry with a pair of armchairs and a small fireplace to keep anyone from wanting to venture deeper into his domain. The presence of a bookcase supported the illusion, with a mix of fiction and non-fiction to entertain any guests.

"I am disgusted over how pleasant this looks," I informed Jon.

"We're all disgusted over it. Do you want to start with the worst of it or explore the living area first?"

"Let's get the hard work over with. If we have a live body down there, I'd like to get him treated and to the hospital. He's our chance for some closure—and he might have information on this Lerrans fellow."

To my amusement, the FBI agents put Alicia's father to work recording the titles of every book on the shelves on one of their laptops with an instruction to open each one, flip through the pages for anything hidden inside, and record any evidence with the help of one of the weak-stomached cops. Then, in what I viewed as a move of brilliance, Hardy conned Alicia into making sure her fragile flower of a father stayed put—or went outside if he somehow managed to finish logging and checking the books before we finished downstairs.

With the warning of how bad the basement would be, I eased down the steps. I cursed Jon for making me go first, but I understood why. He hovered at my back, ready to save my ass from a concussion if I proved to be like some of the other folks witnessing the carnage for the first time.

The descriptions had prepared me for a nightmare, but the reality of the situation horrified me. I identified the victim still alive; he was the only body in the room still attached to various machines, including an IV drip. According to the display, the poor bastard had been frozen in time for over six months.

On the heels of the dismay came the rage over the complete disregard and lack of respect for life.

"You all right, Jace?" Jon asked.

"It's a good thing I am not a dragon and can't breathe fire," I replied, careful to keep my tone neutral. Shaking myself out of my stunned state, I entered the room, counting partially dissected bodies and twitching when I reached ten with more to go. I went to the man who might survive, regarding the state of his body.

The demented surgeon had barely begun the work.

I concentrated, and the slimy feeling of the toxin invaded my senses. Luckily for the victim, the poison hadn't metabolized yet. Without the experience from the ER, I doubted I could do much for him, as it would metabolize sooner than later, but he'd been put into stasis before the point of no return.

He could be saved. The work would drain me dry and test Illiard's skill, but the first incision had been done to monitor his exposed stomach.

None of the other organs were damaged.

I thought it looked a lot worse than it was.

"Has Illiard looked at the body yet?"

"I haven't closely," the black unicorn admitted, coming into the room. "Only long enough to verify he might be saved."

"Am I hallucinating this, or does it look like it's all superficial and muscular?"

The medical examiner joined me, checking the victim. "You're not hallucinating. With your skills, we should be done with this within an hour unless there are underlying issues."

"Not quite. He's poisoned." I considered how long it had taken me to eradicate the pre-metabolized toxin. "Call it an hour to get the poison out, and we're going to need a bucket. I think the perp wanted to observe the toxin when it metabolized."

"It's not metabolized?" Illiard narrowed his eyes and touched the victim's throat. "Ah, I sense it. That's vile."

"That's one way to put it. I have no real medical training, but I can handle this shit. I can mitigate scars, and I can treat this crap."

"Let me call Dr. Erik, because he'll skin me alive if I let a little colt get into trouble with a patient."

I nodded. "This is going to wipe me out, and I'm going to need a bath afterwards. It gets messy. There's no evidence that the toxin absorbs through the skin, however. Or through thick pony fur."

"Yes, it seems to be dangerous once ingested, but I'd rather not take any risks. I'll have the team set up a wash stall outside so we can get you hosed off and squeegeed."

"Squeegeed?" Jon asked.

"Pony fur is thick, and if we don't get all the water out, he'll get mold in his fur and become ill," Illiard explained. "Shift and get yourself ready."

I sighed, took off my vest and the rest of my gear, handed my wallet and badge to Jon, and stepped off to the side to transform. While I'd meant to shift without summoning gear, my magic had other plans, including a new set of protective booties. I turned my head to regard the saddle, and to my disgust, I'd have to figure out how to haul it home, as the black and silver went well with my coat.

Illiard sighed. "You're bleeding magic."

Damn it. When in good health, eating well, and on a cheese and chicken bender, white unicorns sometimes overproduced magic, resulting in it bleeding out. Bleeding out usually meant a wide assortment of new tack and accessories—and the kind of gemstones people would kill for.

I lowered my head and did the unicorn equivalent of a whine.

"Have you been working on gemstones?"

I refused to look him in the eyes, which was all the answer the black unicorn needed. "Let me guess. You've been eating chicken and cheese for at least four days."

"I was supposed to serve as bait, but the plan changed. I figured I was already this far into the run I may as well get paid for it."

"You're going to get your payout by the end of the day

from the looks of it. I'll keep an eye on you, and I'll kidnap you from these mean old dragons while you suffer."

"Suffer?" Jon asked.

"The whites get a pretty raw deal when making their gemstones, and when a colt bleeds out like Jace is doing, he's in for a rough go. I'll talk to Dr. Erik and get his recommendations, but unless he's lucky, bleeding out during a gemstone run equals excessively large stones. If he's lucky, he'll have a thin casing."

"With luck, I won't give a schist," I stated in my most neutral tone.

Illiard pressed his lips together in a thin line, bowed his head, and lasted all of ten seconds before laughter exploded out of him.

Despite the severity of the situation, I tossed my head and whinnied my laughter at having broken the black unicorn's general professionalism.

"I'm going to make you pay for that," Jon informed me, and he waved his fist. "I know just enough about unicorns to understand that was worse than awful. But for your sake, I will hope you escape your schisty situation without it being a huge pain in your ass."

I trotted over to Illiard and turned my head so he could remove the bridle. "Please put it somewhere safe. I'd rather not get blood all over my new tack."

The black unicorn chuckled and stripped all my new gear off, handing it over to the FBI agents, who hauled it upstairs to give to the dragons waiting for me to finish my work. "You'll be fine, little colt. You've had a rough week, and right now, that vic will appreciate that you're bleeding out. You won't like it later, but you'll survive."

Friday, April 20, 2057
New Shoreham
Block Island, Rhode Island.

INSTEAD OF THE expected two hours, it took us twelve to save our patient's life. While I managed to purge the toxin in a record fifteen minutes, the magic that had held him in stasis had done a number on his body. Illiard credited my latest health complication for the man's survival.

Without the surge of magic, I wouldn't have had the energy needed to hold him together while Illiard and the team of black unicorns he'd called in pieced our patient back together, restored organ function, and reversed the trauma of his captivity. The surface had told us many lies, including masking the reality of the vic's imprisonment.

Dr. Timothy Lerrans had meant for the vic to suffer before dying.

Once I finished removing the scars, I ambled up the steps. In a way, I regretted that the FBI had undone the purification zone, as we would have a few hours of work ahead of us purifying my coat from the toxin and other fluids caked into my fur.

To my dismay, I discovered my parents had come to the crime scene, and they were armed with their grooming kit. I'd appreciate the combs and brushes after being soaped and rinsed, but I would resemble an oversized Shetland pony who'd run afoul of an electric outlet by the time they finished with me.

My mother led the charge, snapping her fingers and

pointing at the hose attached to a fire truck.

I reared at the idea of them using a firehose on me, and I snorted my refusal.

"Okay, okay, I'm kidding. We're not going to directly hose you off. They're going to use the hose to fill a tub so we can use the pressure washer."

"I'd rather battle the firehose," I admitted.

"We can do some target practice," one of the firemen announced, and he pointed at a section of overgrown grass a decent distance from the truck. "We can control the pressure, so while strong, you won't be hurt. The plan is to hose you down, soap you up, and then rinse and hope the pressure from the hose is enough to get most of it out of your fur—at least enough for you to get to an appropriate facility. We'll be doing the same with the other unicorns as well."

At least I wouldn't suffer alone. Heaving a sigh, I stood where told.

The impact of the water startled me into snorting and snapping my teeth at the stream. It quickly devolved into a game where I tried to dodge the hose and the firemen did their best to knock me off my hooves. I squealed every time they scored a hit, which did a good job of eradicating the filth from my fur.

After twenty minutes, they claimed their victory, as I slipped and went down with a splash onto the sopping grass. Once down, my parents converged with their collection of pony products meant to prevent a disaster with my fur and hair. As only a foolish colt disobeyed his parents, I got up and stood still while they worked.

Rather than another round with the hose, I got the squeegee and numerous buckets.

Unlike me, the black unicorns stood still for their round

with the hose, probably trying to set a good example for me.

Rather than fully dry me off, my parents escorted me to the horse trailer. Illiard joined me, although his fellow blacks shifted back to human.

"Sacrificial unicorn?" I asked.

"We couldn't get it all out of my coat on the first run," he admitted, and he snorted his disgust. "But your father asked me to escort you, as you're a grouchy colt getting ready to become a stallion. The grouchy colts always need a sensible stallion around, otherwise they kick and bite and get into trouble."

"If the chief hadn't stabbed a hole in my frog, I wouldn't have gone after him."

Illiard whinnied a laugh. "That's what I told your father. Nobody blames you for your reaction, although I've been asked to check on your frog, especially as you manifested yourself a nice set of medical boots."

"They're *comfortable*."

"Better than no shoes, huh?"

I regarded my front hooves with a sigh, and I lifted one to check for stones. Fortunately, my parents had gone over my hooves, and I'd dodged any pointed hitchhikers. "I'm notorious for picking up stones."

"Well, those boots are definitely going to protect you from stones. Smart colt—and smart magic. You don't seem to be bleeding out anymore, although I'm not sure how long you're going to last before you're down and out for the count."

Swishing my tail, I considered the black stallion. "If I can last until a proper hotel, that'd be ideal. The dragons get touchy."

"So, I've been told. Your co-worker was about five

minutes from sprouting scales and making a fuss, but I pulled him aside and explained that bleeding out magic is not the same as bleeding out blood. Once he figured out you've recovered a little *too* well and needed to expend some energy, he relaxed and went off to calm the other dragons. Your parents flew in to keep the dragons calmed down while you worked and to bring us your pony care kit so we'd avoid a temper tantrum. That was Dr. Erik's idea, as you seem to have a history of bleeding out magic?"

"Is twice a history?" I asked, eyeing the black unicorn with interest. "I think I did it as a little kid, and again when I was twelve?"

"Dr. Erik checked, and you bleed out every time you're getting ready to change your coat, so you'll be prancing around as a stallion by the end of next year. You've done it more than twice. You did it as a foal, then again as a yearling, then again when you entered your pony stage. You had some minor bleed outs here and there, but your parents noted you manifested tack or toys. You didn't need any treatments for it. You might shed out with the fall shed, but he thinks you'll hold on until the spring shed. You tend to shed out in the spring. You might bleed out again before you shed, as you've been working a lot more magic than normal. He's not sure."

Every unicorn varied, but I typically began transitioning after my fall shed and completed my transformation by the end of the spring shed. Most unicorns shared the trait, although both of my parents transitioned starting in the spring and completed when they grew in their winter coats. "I manifested toys?"

"You know your foal ball?"

I turned my ears back at the mention of my ball, which

had been bigger than me, indestructible, and offered me hours of amusement flinging myself around bouncing off it. The ball remained at my parents' place, but it would be coming home with me, and I intended on playing with it when nobody was looking. "What's wrong with my ball?"

It even had a convenient handle I could grab, and I'd spent many a happy afternoon tossing it around so I could chase and bounce off it.

"There's nothing's wrong with your ball. It's just something you manifested during your first foal bleed out. Once you grew into your pony coat, you began manifesting tack over toys, although your parents have a few more balls than they otherwise might."

I turned my ears back at the mention of my other balls, which were backups if my favorite one ever broke. "I might have a few spares."

"My fillies have six or seven balls each, and they will burn the planet down if we take away any of their balls. Don't worry about it, Jace. Fillies and colts like playing with their balls, and I've never met a youngling who didn't have a favorite ball. For the record, my favorite ball is blue, and it has been patched several times."

I whinnied a laugh at the black stallion's admission he still had a ball he played with. "Popped it bouncing off?"

"I did. I manifested my first ball growing into my pony coat, and I only ever manifested the one. I went to tack right away."

"That's tragic." I regarded him with my saddest pony eyes. "I can spare a blue one if you need it."

"I'm accepting that as payment for dealing with your schist."

"You have a deal."

THIRTY-ONE

"Your wolf is feeling great."

Friday, April 20, 2057
South County Hospital
Wakefield, Rhode Island.

THANKS TO BLEEDING out an excessive amount of magic, I reaped the rewards of my chicken and cheese bender without incident. As Illiard expected an incident, he'd locked me into one of the hospital's cleaning stalls with a proper bathroom in it in case of complications, swearing he would hold me hostage until certain I made it through without issue.

Between an ultra-thin clay casing and less than a percent of schist, I emerged unscathed. I disposed of all the unwanted material in a trash can in record time, leaving a mountain of uncut gemstones to play with, including two monster stones I might name.

The one was black, as dark as its smaller sibling, and took top spot as my largest stone. The second monster, not much smaller than the black beauty, would become the envy of every dragon on the planet if I let them learn I had it.

To keep Alicia occupied during the initial treatment of the patient in the basement, she'd gone clothing shopping for me, resulting in my change of clothes being a suit. I refused to question how she figured out what size suit I wore, but I suspected my parents had something to do with it.

Two hours after locking me in, he came in to check on me, spotted me seated on the shower floor with my pristine collection of gemstones, and laughed. "How much glitter?"

I pointed at the trash can I had nominated to hold the clay and schist.

He checked it, shook his head, and tied off the bag to take away. "I'm having you blood tested for salmonella. Your mother confessed she'd been trying to get you sick the whole time you've been eating chicken and cheese."

"I feel fine," I informed him.

"I'm having you tested anyway. I'm also going to have you tested for every other blood-based problem I can think of. A nurse is going to come in to steal some vials. After he's finished, your patient is awake. He requested the police."

My brows shot up at that. "He requested the police?"

"Yep. I've got that black dragon in with him handling the preliminaries, and there are a bunch of hovering FBI agents, but they'd like you present for the portion regarding his detainment and torture. His request, for the record. In good news, he's grateful for the rescue. I'll bring boxes for your haul, as it seems you went the gemstones route without much in the way of glitter. Do you want your glitter?"

"No, and don't let those damned dragons have it.

They'll put it up for grabs on the game show if they get their hands on it."

He laughed at me, promised he'd dispose of the evidence of my gemstone haul, and left. Within five minutes, one of his colts came in armed with everything needed to steal my blood along with several small plastic containers to stash my new stones.

"Nice haul," Illiard's son commented, handing over the tubs. With his help, I had everything put away in a few minutes. "I'm Francois. Dad is being a worrywart. All the dragons are riled up at this point, and they haven't clued in that you whites do this all the time. Any stones large enough to name?"

I snorted. "I had two monsters and a few other large ones, and had it been normal circumstances, I'd be constipated for three weeks. I am currently grateful I bled out some magic. That resulted in very little clay or schist. I would have rather done that in the privacy of some forest, thank you."

"You would have caused a mass panic attack had you wandered off and come back with a fortune of gemstones, Jace. That black dragoness would have been leading the pack. She's got enough anxiety for everybody right now. She didn't handle the terminology well. Her father helped calm her down, though, as he had a lot of questions about how unicorns bleed magic, if it was possible to gather the magic, and how it would influence your digestion."

I broke down laughing at the thought of the entire Grimstone clan having a conniption because I'd recovered a little too well. "And my wolves?"

"They are with one of the FBI handlers, who is trying to convince the puppy to do what she wants while defending life and limb from the older female. Dad sent over a few colts and fillies who like animals and can help with her arthritis and other issues."

"Ah, she got her treatments?"

"Yep. Your wolf is feeling great, which is why she's giving the handler some trouble."

Where I went, chaos followed in my wake. "I'd apologize, but I'm glad this handler is dealing with Mamma Mia right now instead of me. Hopefully, she'll have played herself out by the time I get her back."

Francois snickered before going to work stealing six vials of my blood. Once done, he applied a band aid. "Now that I have engaged in an act of vampirism, please convince the dragons you're all right before going to join the party questioning the patient. Just be aware that room is surreal. The last I heard, the patient was describing the details of his every last sin to the FBI, including locations of the bodies nobody has found yet."

"Well, that'll make some of the investigation easy." I carried my boxes of gems out of the room to discover a convention of Grimstone dragons in their human form loitering in the hallway. Hardy's parents had come out along with some of his brothers and sisters. I raised a brow at the lot of them. "Seriously? You've been getting in the way the whole time?"

Alicia's father shrugged. "We had nothing else to do."

Rolling my eyes and shaking my head, I set the tubs on the nearest chair, popped the top off one, and picked a diamond weighing in at a few carats, a nice brown one he could have cut and set into a ring. "Here. I even cleaned them all. They sparkle better when freshly cleaned. This is payment for driving off these other dragons and getting everyone to a hotel while I do some actual work. You can show off your new diamond. You can leave Alicia and Hardy here, but the rest need to go to wherever you're staying for the night. No bar hopping."

He laughed, accepted the diamond, and held it up to get a better view of it. "I can handle that. Alicia, I'll text you."

"Okay." She eyed the containers on the chair. "Are you all right, Jace?"

"I'm fine. I would have been out hours ago, but I got distracted sorting my new stones."

"We could have left him in there all night," Francois said, and he winked at the woman. "I'm going to get his blood samples off to the lab. Feed him anything other than chicken and cheese for the sake of his sanity. Protein is good for him at this stage, and if you can convince him to eat a salad or two, that'll work. Let him get some work in, and then drag him out of here by his ear if you must. Dad can swing by the hotel tomorrow morning to check on him, but he's fine. Take his parents with you but leave his grooming kit."

Alicia's father nodded to the nurse and began the process of herding everyone out, much to my relief. Once he was gone, I sighed.

"Tired?"

"I'm going to be after this questioning session. I'm hoping the FBI will hand me a file and send me on my merry way, but I doubt it." I rolled my shoulders, wincing at the cracks and pops. "I don't even remember when the last time I slept was."

"It's been at least two days, but that black unicorn said it was normal for a unicorn bleeding out magic. He described it like the magical equivalent of shooting back energy drinks. He did warn me that when it's finally bedtime, you're going to sleep it off rather enthusiastically. I'm not sure how someone asleep can do so enthusiastically."

I laughed. "I'll beeline for the nearest soft surface, and I wish you the best of luck getting me up until I've had a solid ten hours of sleep. But if you're going to kidnap me, that's when you'd do it, because nothing is going to wake me up for those ten hours. Don't worry about it. Do you know where the vic is?"

"Follow me." She guided me through the hospital and took me to the top floor. To my amusement, the FBI had a security check near the vic's room, which we breezed through.

They'd been waiting for my arrival.

When we reached the room, Alicia headed off to the nearby waiting area, wished me good luck, and left me to do my work.

I tapped on the door, waited a few moments, and let myself in, discovering barely enough room for me to fit in the mass of bodies. Hardy glanced my way, nodded, and gave his attention to the man in the hospital bed. "This is Detective Smithson, one of the unicorns who worked on you."

"You're the white one," the man stated in a rasp. "That madman rambled about unicorns. Wants to preserve your lot. He's out for your kind next. To test. To prove you're worth what he thinks."

"I'm the white one," I confirmed, wondering what I'd missed and regretting my inability to pull any one of the people in the room aside for a briefing of the situation. "Can you elaborate how he wants to test on us?"

"His drug."

The poison. "We're familiar with it." I allowed myself to scowl. "Did he tell you anything about it?"

"Only that my death would make me useful rather than being a complete waste of life. You've given me a chance to get revenge."

As the dead couldn't seek revenge, I could understand why the man might think that. "What's your name?"

"Roger."

In my time as part of the police force, I'd run into more than a few who refused to say anything other than what was necessary. Some wanted to protect themselves.

Some wanted to protect those around them. Discomfort, embarrassment, and a slew of other emotions could trigger the reaction, but I could make a few guesses as to why Roger refused to elaborate.

White unicorns had a reputation, as did he.

"Jace." I considered him, and I navigated through the maze of people, bumping Hardy with my elbow when I joined him. The black dragon bumped me back, something he wouldn't have done if he thought the situation would sour. "What sort of revenge are you after?"

Judging from the incredulous stares of the FBI agents, they hadn't expected me to go the route of the bad cop, although Jon raised a brow and flashed a grin before controlling his expression. Expectations often ruled people, myself included.

Sometimes, securing justice meant helping a serial killer with a reputation of brutality get vengeance for his suffering. If asked, I would do my best to explain my feelings on the matter, but I hoped no one approached me about the subject.

There would be no riding off into the sunset for Roger, nor would there be any hope for absolution.

But vengeance he might acquire, for himself and the other victims who'd suffered at the hands of Dr. Timothy Lerrans.

"The kind where that madman rots in all ways. He has goals. How can I help you destroy them? I'd like to see him rot in a shallow grave so that the world sees nobody cared about his disappearance enough to dig him a proper hole. I can tell you all about proper holes. That's why it took so long to tell your buddies where all my bodies went. My victims deserved that much. They deserved to be the subject of a mystery capable of captivating the hearts and souls of an entire generation. I've done that. Their bodies would not have been found without me."

The pride in his voice disgusted me, but when I stopped to think about his point of view, I could understand it.

However brutal and disgusting, Roger had wanted to leave a legacy.

Had he not confessed, his victims might have, over time, gained immortality as cop after cop attempted to crack his cold cases. Some serial killers wanted the prestige. Some desired the eternal life through becoming a legend.

"Did you tell them about all the bodies or did you save one for that legacy?" I asked, considering the man with interest.

Roger smiled. "You're the first one to ask me that. There is a crime I have committed that I have not yet confessed to, but it is not a murder. You understand I want a legacy."

We all wanted a legacy in some form or another, and denying the truth would transform me into a liar. "I do. My job is to prevent this bastard from adding more victims to his collection. If you can help me accomplish that, as far as I'm concerned, you're one of my best friends today."

Hardy was about to learn white unicorns could have dark sides, and that I could be every shade of gray in the world if it meant I could put an end to the murders and suffering in the city I called home.

"I've never had a best friend before. How do best friends work?"

While serial killers varied, they often shared traits, including a lack of empathy for other people. Roger's curiosity made me wonder.

Those who lacked empathy often failed to develop bonds with others. The lack of such bonds could readily turn into a complete disregard for life. When most said they couldn't care less, in reality, they did.

That compassion for other lives kept most from walking the path of a killer.

They did care, if only a little.

Serial killers truly couldn't care less, and so they murdered for their depraved satisfaction or for some other goal.

"Best friends help each other when they have a need. They usually spend a great deal of time together, even when things get rather uncomfortable."

Hardy snorted. "I'm a dragon, Roger. Jace is the sort of best friend who will climb onto a young dragon's back, aware he might get eaten or flung off, because said young dragon needs to learn how to have a rider without hurting someone."

"You're an idiot for even thinking about riding a young dragon, Jace," the serial killer informed me.

I laughed, as in hindsight, I agreed with him. "How does

riding a crabby opal dragon who didn't want me on his back stack up to you?"

"As suicidal, really. Do you ride dragons for fun?"

"I wouldn't call it fun, although there's something enjoyable about putting mean old dragons in their place and forcing them to recognize that they can't get me off their back unless they cheat," I replied, allowing myself a smile. "Best friends will do a lot for each other, even when they don't want to. They do this for a lot of reasons. Love is one of those reasons."

"I do not understand love," Roger admitted. "People talk about it all the time, but I've never understood it, well, mostly. My mother loved to beat me, and my father didn't give a damn."

No matter how often I checked into the reasons why someone became a serial killer, one thing stood out to me: abuse. Usually early in the serial killer's life, they'd been abused in some fashion or another, often by the people who were supposed to love them the most. The child would then continue the cycle, often targeting defenseless animals or other children, seeking power and to be the one with control. Some sought revenge on anyone like those who abused them.

Love rarely existed in the world of a serial killer, though it happened from time to time. Some only loved one person or animal above all else.

When I said nothing, Roger added, "I understand revenge. Can a best friend help me with that?"

"In this case, yes—because what you want is how the other victims will get justice. There's a fine line between vengeance and justice. I seek justice. I'm fine with you seeking revenge or vengeance, however you wish to phrase it. Working together, we might get what we both want. Our goal is the same, although we have different reasons to be pursuing it."

"This bastard poisoned my family," Hardy informed Roger in a cold tone. "If not for Jace, my cousin might have died. He targets innocents, and we don't even know why."

"He doesn't believe in humanity. He values everyone who isn't human. Unicorns. Dragons. Natural-born shapeshifters—not those fake ones who weren't born with the gift."

I twitched, as once someone discovered, found, or unlocked their shapeshifting, they irrevocably became that species. My parents had become white unicorns with the help of their parents at infancy.

I'd been born one, needing no significant guidance from another unicorn to shapeshift for the first time.

"And how does he plan to identify the natural-born shapeshifters?" I asked, allowing myself to scowl. "It's not like there are many differences between them."

"That has delayed his plans, as he expected there to be many differences between natural-born shapeshifters and their mundane counterparts. That much I learned from him. He is after natural-born shapeshifters to test his drug. He needs them to live, always. Before he did his best to kill me, he told me that much. He needed to take his hunt to where he might find many shapeshifters."

Cauldron City.

"Not New York?" I asked, raising a brow.

"He did not want to cross the Black Dragon of New York."

"Yet he managed to poison him *and* his family in Cauldron City."

Roger stared at me, and his eyes widened. "That is not going to end well for that madman."

No, it wasn't. I would help see to that. I gestured to Hardy. "This is one of that mean old black's grandsons."

Serial killers were often smart, and it didn't take long for Roger to figure out how the Black Dragon of New York might aid his cause. "That means one of his grandchildren almost died."

I nodded. "You'd be correct."

"And all I have to do is tell you everything I know about this monster?"

I would spend many an hour in the future pondering the nature of monsters.

I couldn't disagree with him, although his words would leave me wondering at the nature of people.

Anyone who would cut open a living patient to dissect him for the pursuit of how best to murder someone else counted as a monster to me—even when the victim also deserved the label. "That would help us a lot. I hunt justice, you hunt revenge. Working together, we both get what we want."

Roger took his time thinking about it, and after a while, he nodded. "Twenty years ago, I came here and murdered a few people. One of them was that madman's friend. Maybe girlfriend. Who knows? I didn't care at the time, and I still don't. She was one of them, so I eliminated her."

"Them?" I asked, although I feared the answer.

Serial killers often had a strange view of people, especially those of the opposite gender. Some delved into rape and other horrific crimes in addition to murdering their victims.

What he had done might haunt me, but if his crimes

might lead me to the bastard behind so much suffering, I would leave no stone unturned.

"She was cheating on him along with a bunch of other men in the area. I didn't rape her, in case you're wondering. She was quite willing right up until I killed her. She wanted me to take it as far as I could. She liked it right until the end." Roger paused. "Of all the people I've killed, she's the only one who went out happy about it. She didn't suffer. Well, any more than she wanted to suffer. But that's why he did what he did. I understand that. I even respect the effort he has put in seeking out his revenge. He wanted to know more about how his woman died. He didn't appreciate when I told him I had her screaming my name by the end of it."

That explained a few things, especially about why the doctor might want to dissect the man alive. Rather than point out the cause and consequence of the situation, I asked, "Did he tell you anything about the database he had made?"

"Oh, that thing? Yeah, he told me all about it while sharpening his knives. He wanted to find me, which is why he started it. It took him a while, though. He had to get access to other databases, and some can only be done with the right paperwork. He falsified being an FBI agent for some of it. He found a dirty agent, got the credentials for the database, and drew out the information that way. I'll give him some credit. He's clever. I would have been angry if some dim-witted idiot had brought me down. But no, I can't fault him on that score. He knew precisely what he was doing."

"Any chance he told you which agent?" I asked.

"Not specifically, but he kept all his information on the

guy on a laptop he kept stored in the basement. He hid it in the wall. He used magicker tricks to hide it. He's not all that bright on other fronts, though. His password is my name, and he only exchanged the space for an underscore. He didn't even bother to swap out any letters for numbers. He wanted to preserve everything I was so that he could better destroy me. He thought he had me dead, so he didn't care what I saw."

To my amusement, several of the agents left. "That's good information. And I think he'll find the tables turned soon enough."

"Are you a dirty cop?"

"I'm as far from dirty as it gets," I admitted. "Will I toe lines? Absolutely. But you'll find I stay precisely on the correct side of the line, much to the irritation of my captain and co-workers, as they're always trying to catch me doing something so they can give me a hard time."

"Understatement of the year, Jace," Hardy muttered under his breath, just loud enough for me to hear. I jabbed him with my elbow, and he grinned at me before resuming his professionally neutral stance.

"You'll take it as far as you can?"

"Ethically, yes." I considered him, angling my head to the side. "We're different breeds. I get that. But we're aimed at the same goal, and you deserve justice for what he did to you. But the families of your victims also deserve justice."

"Men like you are rare," Roger informed me.

Did someone like me even count as a man to the bastard behind the killings? When I framed the situation like that, I could understand better how so many bodies had piled up.

The mad doctor likely viewed his victims as nothing more than animals deserving to be put down.

How disgusting.

Rather than ask him why he thought I was rare, I accepted his comment with a nod before asking, "Is there anything else that you can think of that might help us bring this bastard down?"

"As a matter of fact, yes. There is." Roger paused, glanced at the gathered FBI agents, and said, "I don't think that doctor knows it, but there's a little girl. His, by that girlfriend of his. She had her early, didn't show much at all during the pregnancy, and she didn't tell him about her. She had a bad feeling and didn't want him around the kid. Before she died, she told me all about that little girl and how she wanted to keep her safe. I've been keeping an eye on her. I ain't a shining example of morality, but the best revenge I can get is to make sure that she doesn't find out what sort of monster her father is. You'd find her once you looked hard enough at her mother. That's my price. Don't let that monster get a hold of that little girl. I've killed, and if not for him and you, I'd kill again. But I wouldn't have killed her."

I doubted I would ever understand serial killers. "May I ask why not?"

"She's suffered enough."

THIRTY-TWO

"He's even crabbier than my grandpappy once he gets into a mood."

Saturday, April 21, 2057
New Shoreham
Block Island, Rhode Island.

THE IDEA that a serial killer with a reputation for brutality thought a child had suffered enough whipped the FBI into a frenzy. While they investigated the girl, where she might be, and her circumstances, I got to hunt through the doctor's little house of horrors for evidence of what he might be up to. The why remained complicated, with revenge as the obvious motivation.

Everything I learned colored my perceptions, but the evidence we found in books, on his computer, and hidden away within his walls led us to the disturbing truth of the situation. Our guesses hadn't been too far off, although we still missed a critical piece.

Why was he dissecting the bodies? Why was he adhering to transplant methodology?

Most importantly, who benefited from the doctor's work?

I wanted to head back to Cauldron City, hunt for the bastard, and bash his head into a wall. As I couldn't guarantee his survival if I were to do such a thing, I settled with thinking about it. Rather than give him the beating he deserved, I'd be happy with a clean arrest, gathering every scrap of evidence I could to make certain he never left prison alive, and winning justice for his victims.

The man's ego helped my cause, as I uncovered journal after journal regarding his gruesome workings. He detailed who he targeted, why, and everything about their health before killing them and dissecting them for the sake of science.

The situation pissed me off so much that I transformed, blinked outside through an open window, and indulged in a temper tantrum, bucking and squealing over the whole damned thing until the black dragons showed up, likely at Hardy's request.

My fellow cop waited until I'd calmed enough to no longer take flight every other second to secure a hold on my latest new bridle. "Feel better?"

I snorted in his face as he held the bridle in a firm enough grip I'd have to fight him to bob my head. "I thought about throwing the evidence," I confessed.

"I've been thinking about it, too." He escorted me to Alicia, instructing her to contain me through holding onto my bridle while he informed the others that spunky little colts tended to attack dragons when provoked. When he returned, he asked, "Did you at least take your kit off before having your fit?"

Losing my gun would cause me a great deal of trouble, especially if I couldn't figure out where it'd gone. I would need to have a talk with my magic and teach it to set my gun in the safe—and remove the ammunition and put it in its separate box. "No."

"I'll go make some calls to see if we can track down your firearm, then."

I snorted again. The recent move meant the gun and the rest of my clothes might appear at my old apartment. New homes became unique perils for those who teleported their clothing and gear across long distances.

With luck, it would be in my gun safe, which had been moved to my new home. I would accept anywhere in my new home, but I'd endure the scolding with grace—and work at teleporting what I needed back.

As bucking might injure the black dragoness, I stood still, although I issued a few more snorts to make it clear what I thought of the situation.

"He's even crabbier than my grandpappy once he gets into a mood," Alicia observed.

Hardy snickered and nodded. "Try to charm him into a better mood. If you manage that, cart him off somewhere, get him changed back to human, and attempt to tame him with anything other than chicken or cheese. For some reason, I suspect he won't want to be looking at either for a long while."

As biting my co-worker would land me in hot water, I snapped my teeth at him while Alicia laughed and did her best to contain me. She succeeded, but only because she opted to scratch behind my ears.

"Good luck, Alicia. You're going to need it."

Sunday, April 22, 2057
New Shoreham
Block Island, Rhode Island.

THERE WERE benefits to investigating while a unicorn, and my ability to dig tester holes with my hooves topped the list. Alicia helped my efforts through playing fetch, taking pictures at my request, and dealing with my temper tantrums with grace. I limited most of my tantrums to snorts, the rare buck, and pawing at the ground.

Once, I'd taken offense to one of the trees, slicing off a branch and stabbing the leaves.

She laughed at my antics.

Checking every patch of disturbed soil paid off. Dr. Laurrens hadn't bothered to bury his corpses deep. Most had been preserved with chemicals, resulting in uncovering body bags with somewhat intact corpses within. After the first body, I learned to dig until uncovering the body bag before sending Alicia off to fetch the forensics team to finish the nasty work.

After the tenth body, they'd opted to bring in a larger earth mover and investigate the entire lawn rather than potentially miss a corpse.

With my job taken over by men and women armed with heavy machinery, I relented, requested some clothing, and found a private spot to change back into a human and get dressed. Transforming helped ease my anger somewhat, although I wanted to curse up a storm over the evidence of even more lives lost at the hand of a brutal madman.

Alicia approached, and she grinned at me. "Feeling better?"

"I resent that I can't break the evidence right now," I

admitted, rolling my shoulders and forcing myself to relax. "Beyond that, I'm doing all right. You?"

"I'm feeling pretty good. Do you want the good news or the bad news first?"

"Let's go with the bad so it's out of the way," I replied, wondering what counted as bad news to the dragoness.

"Your gun is in Cauldron City. Your parents flew back home and got into your safe at our place to confirm its presence. You're being signed up for lessons on how to summon your firearm when you need it, and your father wants to start working with you on that as soon as possible. He's promised you won't like the lessons."

Yep, that counted as bad news. I thought about transforming and bolting for Canada, but the thought of having my parents and the black dragons chasing me did a good job of convincing me to go home and be scolded and educated by my father. The reward, which involved dodging being scolded by my cranky opal dragon of a boss, would make the sacrifice worth my while. "And the good news?"

"We get to return to Cauldron City by airplane. Hardy isn't clear to fly the whole way back."

I turned, eyed the gathering group of law enforcement, and spotted Hardy talking to one of the FBI agents. "Hey, Grimstone!"

Hardy said something to the FBI agent before hurrying my way. "What's wrong?"

"I was about to ask you that. Why aren't you cleared to fly the whole way back?"

"My grandpappy is a delicate little flower and is concerned I'll sprain a wing. I have exceeded his comfort levels for flying long distances this month. The captain isn't brave enough to tell my grandpappy to mind his business, so we get to take a plane. I complained until my grandpappy got us seats in business class, as there was no way in hell I'm dealing with economy. You, me, and my uncle have to head to New York first, though. He wants to show you his car collection. We'll be there for a day before heading home. He wants Alicia to have a chance to pick up some of her favorite things before returning her to your lair."

I laughed. "It really is a lair, isn't it?"

"It's even a lair built by proper dragons. You are not doing the family any shame, although we're concerned there might be a territory dispute between us black dragons and you white unicorns. Which one of you will keep your family name?"

Had Hardy hit his head? Lost his common sense upon exposure to excessive amounts of morbidity and tragedy? "What's my last name, Hardy?"

"Smithson."

"And what's your last name?"

"Grimstone."

"Which last name is the clear victor?"

"Out of familial pride, I'm forced to say Grimstone, but now that you mention it, Smithson does seem very…" Hardy held his hands up in surrender before issuing a single shrug of his shoulders.

"Dull? Boring? As common as dirt? And not the kind of dirt that might render gemstones if one is persistent enough. It's not even worthy of being called soil, as soil might contain archaeological treasures *and* gemstones, depending on where you look. I would be the first unicorn in existence with an interesting last name. Unicorns, as a general rule, use the most common last names to have ever been used specifically to hide our nature. Smithson is one of the more unusual names. Smith is more common. If it is a common last name, there are unicorns saddled with it. If there are interesting last names? There are no unicorns with them. That would draw too much attention to us."

Hardy pointed and laughed at me.

Alicia joined him, snickering at the ways of unicorns. "You have to admit, Hardy. It is wily of them to hide by pretending to be as normal as possible. And you have to admit it, he fooled you."

"He did, and I plan to make him pay. Catch the unicorn, Alicia. Once you have him secured in our family, I can begin seeking out my revenge for his trickery."

"I'm not marrying anyone solely for you to get revenge on him, you idiot," Alicia informed her cousin. "However, his ability to produce diamonds, withstand the general ways of dragons, and overall tolerance might result in him being claimed by some dragoness, preferably a black one. As he has to teach me how to cook without killing someone, I am currently the only contender for him. My sisters have already been educated."

I eyed the dragoness with interest, aware that her entire family counted as beautiful. "Can you reeducate them while I watch?"

"Absolutely. They'll forget I've staked initial claims within a week, and I'll make sure to position the brawl where you can watch and none of our trees are damaged. They'll surely come calling at the house. They want to see it."

I considered the next problem: making it back to Cauldron City without my passport or identification. I patted my empty pockets and stared at Hardy. When my fellow cop grinned at me, I repeated the motion, patting a little harder. "How am I going to fly without identification?"

"We aren't taking a public fight to get to New York City," he admitted. "My grandpappy has determined that you are too handsome and might be grabbed at the airport if we take our eyes off you, so he's arranged for a private flight to start the show. We'll be detouring to Syracuse first. Alicia's father has one of his vacation homes there, and he wants to pick something up. My uncle loves to fly, so he will do almost anything to extend his trips. One of my older brothers is winging his way to Cauldron City to retrieve your things. We'll probably take commercial from New York to Cauldron City. Your wolves will fly with my relatives, as the plane we're taking is too small for them."

"Why would anyone grab *me* at the airport?" I blurted. I also questioned the detour to Syracuse, as it was in the wrong direction, but who was I to argue with the dragons? If they wanted to extend how long it took to get to where we were going, I wouldn't complain.

Flying in planes remained a novelty. Flying on the backs of dragons fell into the life-threatening yet addicting category, depending on which dragon I hitched a ride with.

"You'll be carrying a fortune in diamonds," Hardy reminded me.

Right. The chicken and cheese bender plus bleeding magic had paid off. I had enough small gems to be willing to sell them off for some decent change. The larger stones broke records for me, and I could go my entire lifetime without eating another bite of cheese if I wanted. I even had a modest collection of fancy colored diamonds to add to my hoard. As some of the local unicorns had asked if they could practice appraising on the stones, I'd even gotten a general value on the smaller pieces, totaling in at over three hundred thousand for everything below three carats.

The small ones were fierce, with exceptional clarity to go with their color—or in my case, lack of color.

The smallest of my fancy diamonds rang in at ten carats.

I would need every last shard to pay for my upcoming expenses. Caring for a dragoness would cost more money than I wanted to think about, but I could afford her with my latest haul.

As Hardy would worry himself into a tantrum the match of mine, I said, "There aren't that many people who know I'm carting around diamonds, Hardy. Stop worrying for the sake of worrying. Unicorns don't go after other unicorns, and we're pretty good at dodging attention. And anyway, those who know about unicorns look for doctors, nurses, and medical professionals. Nobody is going to think a cop is packing a fortune in diamonds."

"We can never be too careful," Hardy replied in a solemn tone.

I wondered if he knew something I didn't, and if so, what. Rather than worry about it, I decided to focus on the remaining work I needed to finish before heading home.

THIRTY-THREE

"Well, that was interesting."

Monday, April 23, 2057
Balsam Lake Mountain Wild Forest
Hardenburgh, New York.

WHILE CONSIDERED to be one of the safest modes of transportation, planes could crash. Ours had some help, as young black dragons convinced the aircraft would smash into the ground transformed. When two black dragons transformed in a plane built for six people, it came to a rather immediate and dramatic demise.

Being shunted outside of the cabin while still strapped in my seat counted as insanity. After a ride on a demented opal dragon pretending to be a slinky, free falling barely fazed me.

It was smacking into the ground that would cause me a brief but permanent problem.

Luckily for me, I'd developed a habit of wrapping my bag strap around my ankle if in a position I worried about my personal belongings, which prevented me from having to find them later—assuming I survived.

After falling over ten thousand feet without the benefit of a parachute, living to tell the tale ranked in as sketchy at best.

I unbuckled, snagged my bag, and debated on how best to handle the situation.

Diamonds somewhere at home beat diamonds scattered all over the landscape, so I'd have to transform. Unlike my mother, I'd practiced until I could shift without my hoof touching something. Shifting wouldn't do me much good, as all unicorns needed to have a hoof touching *something* to blink, but I did it anyway. As the only sentient present without wings, I assumed the dragons could handle rescuing themselves. A quick check indicated everyone on board had followed Hardy and Alicia's example.

The tricky part would be coming into contact with something long enough to teleport. I would have to push the limits of my luck to disperse momentum and land without joining the debris scheduled to crash into the ground in a disturbingly short period of time.

Thanks to the thick forests of rural New York, my ploy stood a good chance of working, although I'd never used a tree as a launching point for blinking before.

I'd tested logs, discovering I could blink from any surface. I hadn't tried a trunk or branch still attached to a tree before, however.

If it didn't work, it wouldn't hurt for long. That thought somewhat comforted me. I'd either pull off the stunt with flying colors or splat into the ground. Either way, my predicament came to an end sooner than later.

So focused on figuring out how best to blink to avoid

being smashed to bits, I failed to notice the black dragon swooping in my direction. Fortunately for me, the dragon in question had already mastered retracting his claws before snatching me out of the air.

Unfortunately for me, the dragon lacked practice in plucking colts from the sky, resulting in a tangle of legs and wings in the boughs of the trees. The branches broke, and after some bouncing and plummeting, we hit the ground.

I did what any sane unicorn would do when in the clutches of a dragon and on the ground. I blinked, situated my hooves under me, blinked a few more times, and blew air, torn between bolting for the general safety of Canada, checking on the dragon, and digging a hole to hide in.

Alicia's father got up, stretched, and shook off, and he huffed in my direction.

Unable to decide what to do, I opted for a little of everything, bucking and charging before pawing at the ground and digging a hole to express my frustration with the situation. Once I calmed enough I wouldn't stab anyone, I peered upwards, counting two black dragons and a blue one. The blacks breathed fire and roared their fury. Alicia and Hardy squabbled with each other, and I suspected the dragoness blamed my fellow detective for the destruction of the plane despite her role in our situation.

Ruined fragments of metal rained down, and Alicia's father spread his wing over me, inhaled, and breathed flame at the incoming debris. Heat washed over me, and I crowded closer to the dragon, as his thick scales could handle a pummeling far better than my fluffy coat. A few larger chunks of the plane thumped down around us, but I dodged being crushed—and if anything had struck Alicia's father, he showed no sign of it bothering him.

"Well, that was interesting," the black dragon rumbled, and he settled his wings along his back before bumping me with his nose and checking me over. "It seems unicorns transform when startled as well."

Technically, I'd transformed to save my precious gemstones, but I wouldn't confess that to him. A quick check indicated I'd manifested a new pair of medical booties but no other tack, a warning I'd blown out all my magic and would need to rest for a while. "Someone needs to teach Hardy to avoid transforming while in a plane."

Only an idiot assigned any blame to a black dragon's daughter, but I figured Hardy counted as fair game.

"Considering we lost an engine and he'd noticed we'd lost an engine, he was going to transform. He knows enough about aviation to have understood the severity of the situation." He glanced up at the sky and heaved a sigh. "That girl is going to chase him to the city, and their grandfather is going to have to calm them down. Spooked dragons are not beings of wisdom. With luck, they'll battle over his skyscraper, which'll make it easy to retrieve them. We dragons tend to squabble over familial territory."

Dragons were beings of wisdom? I stomped a hoof, shook myself off, and took stock of the situation. My bag of diamonds had vanished off somewhere, hopefully to my new home where they'd be safe and sound. "Did the propeller stop?"

"Oh, no. It fell right off," Alicia's father stated. "It happens sometimes. Commercial planes are often designed to fly on only one engine. That one? Not so much. It can be emergency landed with no engines, although that's an art as much as it is a skill—and it's not one my uncle practices often. It seems there were some structural issues with the propeller mount. You weren't hit with any debris when the plane broke apart, were you?"

After taking a moment to look myself over and test my legs, I determined I'd escaped with some bumps, bruises, and a few cuts. "It could be worse. I didn't break a leg."

"Good. My uncle will handle making sure Alicia and Hardy get herded the right way, so don't you worry about that. He might be a blue, but he's a stubborn blue and has a size advantage over them. We'll worry about returning to Rhode Island to find out who sabotaged the plane and why. Also, until further notice, your name is Andy, you're from Tennessee, and you're my personal servant. Your job is to look like you're going to stab anyone who bothers me."

I stared at Alicia's father, certain the whites of my eyes showed. I expected such a plan from the Black Dragon of New York, not the supposedly quiet son of a blue and a red. "We're going to do what?"

"We're going investigating, and we're going to fight over the body of the bastard who broke my uncle's plane. That was his *baby*. But first, we're going to go to the airfield and question the local birds. That should give us some leads, and once we have a better idea of who was behind breaking the plane, we'll handle the situation quietly."

"But why? The instant the Black Dragon of New York finds out you and two of his grandchildren were targeted, he's going to handle the problem through any means necessary. And he'll put up a token fit over your uncle because he's your uncle. But I can offer you a clue about the culprit."

I could also make a guess at the why, and it involved me and Hardy investigating the mass murders of hardened criminals. Two wrongs never made a right, and I had no doubt the mastermind behind the killings wouldn't mind adding us to his tally.

We'd isolated three people in the New Stockham area, but I suspected there were more—and one of them had decided to help our plane break to disrupt the evidence.

How better to delay investigations than by taking out some of the investigators?

I just hoped that Alicia's father handled the news better than his family would.

The black dragon regarded me through narrowed eyes. "What clue?"

According to his tone, I invited a great deal of trouble into my life. "They know nothing of dragons, which leads me to believe it might be our dear friend Dr. Lerrans or one of his associates. The fact he lacks a solid understanding of the minimal differences between the two classes of shifters helps us. Who else would want us to disappear? It is better for us if we can gain the evidence properly, as we might get straight to the bottom of this."

"You really don't want to go to Rhode Island to investigate?" Alicia's father heaved a sigh. "Why must you be so practical? We could talk to the birds. The birds see everything."

The stress of the crash must have short circuited something in the dragon's brain. Why else would he want to sacrifice his quiet ways to partake of general insanity? "It's not that I don't want to investigate. It's more a matter of logistics. The birds have a five-minute attention span, and unless they go through practical training, they will give you useless descriptions. You *might* find out if someone tampered with the plane and how many, but unless the person did something to upset the birds, they aren't all that good at distinguishing us. Now, that said, if the person upset the birds, they might lead us right to the culprit. But it's unlikely. You'd be better off making sure your father-in-law doesn't actually destroy the entirety of Rhode Island when he finds out about the plane."

While he huffed and he puffed, Alicia's father bobbed his head. "I suppose he might react poorly if we don't show up."

Might? *Poorly?* "That's quite the understatement, Mr. Grimstone."

"I suppose we best save the entirety of Rhode Island from destruction. In good news, there are benefits to being a black dragon. When I ask someone to make a phone call for me, they usually do. And if they don't the first time I ask, I find blowing some smoke does the trick. I've only eaten two cell phones belonging to rude sentients who couldn't bother to be polite for five whole minutes."

I worried I had underestimated Alicia's father, and that despite his mixed heritage, he was truly a black dragon to the core.

I also worried about what Alicia's mother would do once she found out about the crash.

How could I, a single unicorn, hope to contain so much destruction and chaos?

Like it or not, I would be finding out.

Tuesday, April 24, 2057
Arena District Firehouse
Arena, New York.

IT TOOK us until after dark to find a town, which lacked a police station but did have a firehouse. Fortunately for my sanity, those manning the firehouse were willing to place a few calls on behalf of Alicia's father. Once armed with a change of clothes, I shifted back to human and received a bill issued in fatigue. I made it to the break room couch, where I passed out and stayed that way until a rather familiar clearing of a throat woke me.

On my mother's scale of throat clearing, I had one hoof in the grave, two broken legs, and one chance to redeem myself. In her shoes, I would have used the next stage throat clear, which indicated I was already dead and hadn't realized it yet. Rolling over on a couch resulted in a collision with the floor, and I sighed and worked on restoring coherency. I began with the first trick in my arsenal, which might buy me a few minutes of life. "I love you, Mom."

She laughed. "You're not in trouble, colt. You just refused to get up, so I had to pull out the big guns. How are you feeling?"

"Horrible." I stretched, determined the crash hadn't done me any favors, and that moving would not be my favorite activity for the next few days. "I probably don't need a trip to the body shop, but I'm not sure I want to fly in a plane again anytime soon."

My mother snorted before replying, "You'll be fine. You can take a plane, and you can do so without fussing. We made the trip just fine, and it was a commercial flight. The Black Dragon of New York is on a rampage, and now that he is convinced all his precious children and grandchildren are still alive, he is winging his way to Rhode Island. I suggested he avoid leveling the place, but I'm not sure he's in the mood to listen. Your dragoness is downstairs being shown the fire engines. Her father is strutting around, as he is quite proud of catching you out of the air without breaking one of your spindly little legs. Your friend is pacing, as he wants to talk to you, but you weren't ready to get up. The blue dragon is crying over his plane, and that has riled everyone up."

I groaned, sat up, and began the tedious process of putting myself back together so I could start my day. "Any news about the sabotage?"

My mother wrinkled her nose, a sure sign of trouble lurking on the horizon. "Alicia's father begged for somebody to question the local songbirds, but they didn't find anything useful. It wasn't that the birds weren't willing to help, but that there were a lot of new humans at the airfield, and they don't remember which ones had gone near the plane. The birds were able to identify who *wasn't* near the plane among the regular staff, which is helpful." She sighed, crouched next to me, and pulled out a comb from her pocket and went to work attempting to tame my unruly pony hair. "Your father is going to crack skydiving jokes to punish you. The black dragons are beside themselves, as it was entirely possible that poor blue dragon could have safely landed the plane with one engine. Both suffered some minor injuries from breaking the plane apart."

I sat still for my mother, wondering what counted as minor for her. As a unicorn with medical training, minor could involve broken bones. As long as she felt nobody might die, the injury counted as minor. "How minor?"

"Bumps, bruises, and your detective friend broke a toe. His toe has been set and partially healed, as there is little as annoying as a whining baby dragon with a broken toe. Your dragoness is sore, but she'll be fine. She had a rough landing once she realized Hardy had broken his toe. Landing with a broken toe is rough on the dragons, so she served as a landing pad for him to make sure he didn't hurt himself further. At that point, he was wiped out and ended up taking a nap on her while a dragon. She let him, waiting until his parents arrived to handle that situation. Then the unicorns took care of the break, he shifted back to his human form, and he slept it off. He's been up for a few hours now, thus him getting antsy."

It amazed me that Hardy counted as a baby among the dragons—a situation not much different from mine. Then again, knowing my parents, I could shed out into my draft form and still count as a little pony. I'd have to ask Alicia what counted as a baby among black dragons. How much work I put into stomping anyone who threatened Hardy depended on how the other dragons would react to him being injured while on duty.

The Black Dragon of New York in Rhode Island, unattended, worried me more than it had before my mother had clarified some of the situation.

"According to your expression, you just realized there is a cranky black dragon out for blood in Rhode Island."

Damn. My face had been telling on me again. I needed to work on my general inability to mask strong emotions, especially while working. "Will Rhode Island survive?"

"It will, but only because whomever sabotaged the plane is long gone. Once you're coherent and on the move, we'll be headed to New York before returning to Cauldron City. Yes, by commercial plane. It's a lot harder for someone to sabotage a guarded jet than it is to infiltrate a private airfield." My mother stopped trying to tame my hair and dropped a kiss on my brow. "You're presentable, so go reassure your friends, then we'll get on the road so you can get dressed down by your boss for scaring the liver out of him. Expect to be hobbled until he's satisfied you'll stay out of trouble."

As I couldn't tell if she was being literal or not, I worried. "Please don't have me hobbled."

Being hobbled sucked. Hobbling, especially when Dr. Erik's bracelet was involved, meant being legitimately stuck and unable to do jack shit until set free. I'd been hobbled numerous times as a child for doing stupid shit like bouncing out in front of cars while a foal. It'd only taken twice for me to learn not to earn being hobbled, and being fair to me, the first time I'd been hobbled, I'd been legitimately too young to learn from my mistakes.

The second time, I'd learned from my mistakes. For three hours, I endured being put in a corner, and my mother had taken away all my bouncy balls until I learned to look both ways before crossing the street.

"I wish you the best of luck convincing your boss of that, but you might dodge being hobbled if you recruit the assistance of both young black dragons. I wouldn't count on it, but you can try."

THIRTY-FOUR

As unicorns often lacked sense, I fell for the bait.

WEDNESDAY, APRIL 25, 2057
THE GRIMSTONE RESIDENCE
MANHATTAN, NEW YORK.

THE BLACK DRAGON of New York owned a skyscraper, and I loved everything about the place. Instead of ridiculous opulence, he'd gone for a forest paradise motif. An entire wooded wonderland occupied the lobby of his home with a reception and security desk near the door. I understood why Alicia's father wanted to talk to the birds in Rhode Island.

The lobby served as a preserve for at least seven hummingbird species, more songbirds than I could readily count, quails, peasants, and even a few turkeys. I'd drawn the attention of one turkey, a male as far as I could tell. Rather than spurring, biting, or otherwise attempting to remove me from the planet, he rubbed his head against me, gobbled, and showed me his tail feathers.

As unicorns often lacked sense, I fell for the bait and petted the turkey.

I kept all my fingers, my blood stayed in my body where it belonged, and the turkey rewarded me with his affection. My attempt to leave the turkey and accompany the dragons upstairs encountered a snag within a few steps.

The turkey followed me to the elevator, and he made it clear I would not be leaving without a fight. He attempted to stare the Black Dragon of New York into submission, spreading his wings and issuing an odd purring sound. While I had no idea what the bird was up to, I guessed he liked me and didn't want me to go upstairs, which was outside of his domain.

"For fuck's sake," the Black Dragon of New York muttered, and he crouched in front of the turkey, shaking his head. With zero evidence of fear, as black dragons also lacked sense, he stroked the bird's head. "All right, all right, you can keep your pet unicorn. Alicia, please get a collar and leash from the receptionist."

Alicia giggled and bounced off to do her grandfather's bidding.

None of the dragons in attendance seemed bothered by or surprised by the request, leaving me to wonder what was going on, why I counted as a pet, and what kind of turkeys the Black Dragon of New York kept in his lobby. "You collar and leash your *birds*?"

The Black Dragon of New York laughed at me. "We use some pretty hefty magicker tricks to keep our lobby inhabitants safe, happy, and contained. Sometimes this backfires, as most of our birds are either sentient or borderline sentient. This fellow is borderline sentient. His children may learn to speak, although he won't. He likes you, and he's trying to tell me he wants to go home with you. As such, he's going home with you, and I'll send you off with a flock of five or six borderline hens. I can handle teaching them their range is in your yard when we're in Cauldron City, and turkeys can be quite useful once they start talking, so you can train them for law enforcement purposes. Caretakers of sentient species get a nice commission when one of their birds is hired."

Huh. I'd assumed only the songbirds and hummingbirds obtained sentience. "Turkeys can talk?"

"They're one of the first larger birds to develop sentience, but yes. From what we can tell, it's a matter of brain size. Birds with tiny brains obtained sentience first, and now the birds with larger brains are starting to pick it up. There are only a handful of sentient turkeys right now, but I suspect you'll have a flock of talkers after the next breeding season. In good news, the borderline birds are smart enough they won't interbreed—as long as you make sure to teach them who their family is. I'll help you with that." After rewarding the bird with another round of petting, the Black Dragon of New York rose, waited for Alicia's return, and took the slender collar and leather leash from her. The turkey stood still while the black dragon secured the collar around his neck and adjusted it.

"Does he have a name?"

"Sir Blackie," he replied with pride in his voice.

I eyed the turkey, which was brown without a scrap of actual black on him. As questioning the Black Dragon of New York might result in an answer, I decided I'd accept the weird name without comment. Once I held the leash and the turkey had taken his place at my side, I waited for the elevator door to open before escorting the bird inside, careful to make sure he didn't trip into the gap or get any of his feathers caught. "Can you teach my wolves that the animals, birds, and whatever else might be living in my orchard aren't prey?"

"Easily done," the Black Dragon of New York promised. "You'll want to make an indoor habitat for the turkeys. While they will appreciate roaming in your orchard, they're spoiled indoor birds now."

Would I have any time to read any of my books with the number of animals I would have to care for? In good news, I could coerce young unicorns into helping with the chores, as little would appeal to the younger colts and fillies than a day in my yard with their bouncy balls at the price of some chores. "Dare I ask how many floors have pets living in them?"

"The first five levels are a menagerie," he admitted. "I'm currently working on renovating three more floors for animals and their habitats. My family occupies the top ten stories, and the floors below are a mix of offices, guest quarters, and so on. As my favorite of my grandchildren, Alicia has a suite on the top floor."

The dragoness snorted. "I only have it because I won a bet, Jace. Don't listen to him. We bet over the suite every few years, and as I happen to like that suite and have occupied it since the day I turned eighteen, I am ruthless about keeping the suite. I use it when I need to be at work often and don't want to fly from my regular home."

"Her regular home is the equivalent of a shack," the Black Dragon of New York muttered.

"It's a small townhouse in an older part of town," Hardy informed me. "As such, our grandpappy hates it. As he hates it, he growls rather menacingly at any challengers for

Alicia's suite. We have come to the conclusion that the suite is Alicia's for life."

I read between the lines: under no circumstances could I let anything else happen to Alicia. "But is the suite better than the mansion, Alicia?"

"Not a chance in hell," the dragoness replied.

I engaged the Black Dragon of New York in a staring contest, and as I refused to be the shame of all unicorns, I smirked.

The black dragon waved his fist at me. "Just for that, I will force you to drive three of my cars before sending you home."

If he wanted to pretend he was punishing me through exposure to his vehicles, I would accept my punishment with a smile. "I'll probably survive."

"Probably," Alicia muttered.

Wednesday, April 25, 2057
Times Square
Manhattan, New York.

IN ADDITION to an entire collection of Black Wings, the Black Dragon of New York owned more classic cars than anyone needed in even ten lifespans, and I got to take his 1964 Ferrari 250 LM for a spin. As I could pick one and only one passenger, I invited Alicia to join me while her grandfather played chaperone from the air.

To add insult to injury, the bastard had two of them, one in red, and the other in black. I laid claim over the red one.

Grateful my police training had handled manual transmissions of all types to account for every situation, I handled the task with as much grace as an excited colt behind the wheel of a beautiful car could manage.

I limited myself to the rare giggle and drummed my fingers against the wheel.

"I see your love of cars is not limited to my grandpappy's Black Wings," the dragoness teased while I navigated through the chaotic streets of New York. Thanks to the chaperone hovering above, people kept their distances.

Not even the cabbies dared to enter my space, as they were wise enough to value their lives.

"Dare I ask how much he spent on this one?"

"Very little. He's the original owner," she admitted, and she opened the glove box, pulled out a packet of papers, and held something up. At the next red light, I discovered a photocopy of the original bill of sale, which was in the Black Dragon of New York's name. "This is this first baby car, and while he wasn't a precisely young dragon then, his hoard had been mostly gemstones and other natural objects. A lot of the cars he has in his garage he bought when they were new. The black one was an old racer he adopted and had repainted, as it had been red, too. That's one of the few that he didn't buy new. He got it to reward his children and teach them how to drive properly. It mostly goes to the racetrack as a reward."

Well, that explained why he was flying overhead and keeping the streets of New York safer than normal. "And he let me drive it?"

"Let? Oh, Jace. He loves letting people behind the wheel of this beauty. She's far too lovely to just sit gathering dust. He won't leave his precious little daughter unattended, though. This is not an uncommon sighting in the area. And because she is driven so much, she's had a lot of magic done on her to keep her original parts in good working order. Some parts were replaced, but he still has them. Well, except for things like hosing. He doesn't care about that. Her original transmission is on display in his garage, as it went out before he mastered the art of restoring car parts with magic. Her current transmission is a work of art, though. He learned how to machine engine parts just so he could do the transmission rebuild himself. Now that he's learned how to restore car parts with magic, he could put the original transmission back in, but he's proud of his contribution."

"Your grandpappy is weird even for a dragon, Alicia."

She laughed. "He really is. What do you think about New York?"

"It feels old," I replied, taking the time to gawk up at the buildings every time we got stuck behind a red light. "It has a great deal of personality."

Like Cauldron City, it was home to the strange and stranger, offering a sense of familiarity.

"That it does. Before my grandpappy took it over, New York had one of the highest crime rates in the United States. When he moved the clan in, he reformed the law enforcement system and worked on cleaning up the streets. Now New York City is one of the safest cities in the world."

That I could believe. Only a fool tested a Grimstone, especially when it came to the safety and security of their family. "How does it compare to Cauldron City?"

The dragoness huffed. "Grandpappy is concerned we'll get a copycat—or worse, this Dr. Lerrans might become bold enough to target New York. If he's bold enough to damage a plane we're on, then he's bold enough to come directly to our turf to start problems."

I considered her statement, realizing that she made a good point. More importantly, her point illustrated an inconsistency I would need to pursue the instant I made it back to my office.

Until our trip to Rhode Island, the black dragons hadn't been targeted directly.

That pointed at someone else being involved. More possibilities existed than I cared to think about, but one stood out to me. How better to get everyone riled up than to target the grandchildren of the Black Dragon of New York on purpose? Had Dr. Lerrans done something to irritate a conspirator?

The little girl back in Cauldron City and her grieving mother also opened another possibility for me.

Were others in the same shoes? But, unlike the daughter and her mother, were they willing to get their hands dirty? I could believe it.

Motivation mattered. But who was trying to motivate the Black Dragon of New York to become involved? Why?

"That's quite the expression, Jace. What did you think of?"

Well, if anyone might understand the nature of black dragons, it would be Alicia. "Let's play a game. You're a mastermind murderess out for the blood of a serial killer. Let's say you wouldn't want to kill those you're targeting, but you wanted to frame someone else and have the dirty work done for you. What percentage risk of death would you assign to a plane loaded with dragons if you were to take out an engine or two?"

"Zero. We're dragons, Jace. We have wings, we can fly,

and we transform within seconds. As long as the plane doesn't explode with us in it, we can tear through the cabin like it's cotton candy."

"And let's say there is a handsome unicorn stallion on board. What percentage chance would you give the dragons of saving the unicorn?"

She giggled. "Pretty high, honestly. Judging from your question, you were unaware we actually train to catch people and things out of the air. I'm too young to be trained, as is Hardy, but it was the first thing my momma taught my pappa the instant she decided to keep him. You're the first equine we've caught out of the air, though. We usually train to catch people. My parents can catch five each if they're positioned well—six if we can get underneath them properly and they're not panicking."

Huh. When I stopped to think about it, I realized Alicia's father was large enough to catch someone in each foot and still have a hope of staying in the air. "So, that indicates the culprit behind the plane crash knows a lot about dragons, where Dr. Lerrans does not."

Alicia sucked in a breath. "You make an excellent point. It's probably not the same person, is it?"

"Considering Dr. Lerrans isn't quite clear on the difference between the various shifter types, yeah." I tapped out a beat on the steering wheel. "Want to go through the tunnel just to fuck with your grandfather?"

"Absolutely."

I had her bring up the best route on her phone before suggesting that she text her mother with our plan to tweak the old bastard's nose. Then I put aside thoughts of work long enough to enjoy the ride.

THIRTY-FIVE

"Who started fussing?"

Friday, April 27, 2057
Lower North Lakes, Precinct 153
Cauldron City, Nebraska.

A FULL NIGHT of sleep in my new home did me a world of good. I made breakfast, woke the dragoness long enough to feed her, and braced for an entertaining morning trying to wrangle a pair of wolves who'd gotten used to having time off.

Mamma Mia bounced through our morning preparations to go to work. Misfit howled at the idea of leaving her new best friend, Sir Blackie. As I couldn't afford to be late, I collared and leashed Sir Blackie, grabbed enough food to keep him satisfied, and loaded him into the SUV in his carry cage. As I couldn't afford to have a turkey run loose, his indoor play pen came with me along with the magicked pad charmed to contain his messes.

Borderline sentience did not equate to overnight litter box training.

With two wolves and a turkey heeling, I headed up to my office, drawing the attention of all my co-workers. Hardy met me at the elevator, grinning at my menagerie. "Who started fussing?"

"Misfit," I informed him, and I stared at the puppy, who insisted on snuggling with her new best feathered friend. "They slept together, Hardy. I have to pen my *wolf* with my *turkey* in my house, else the whining and the gobbling and purring and whatever the hell other noises he makes is intolerable. Mamma Mia just settled in to babysit. I'm going to have to make a playroom in the house so the wolves and turkey can sleep together *without* driving me insane. The only good news I have is that none of the animals seem interested in sharing the bed with me."

Unbeknownst to Hardy, I included the dragoness in the statement, as she'd entered the demonically tired stage before we'd gotten home and stayed there until passing out in the bedroom she'd claimed as hers. I suspected she'd wanted to join me in bed, understood she was crabby enough to flay the flesh off any mortal, and behaved to maintain the peace.

If I had to deal with two wolves and a turkey in bed with me along with a cranky dragoness, I'd lose my mind.

I would issue a platonic invitation to share a bed sometime after the dragoness's temper cooled. Survival mattered, especially mine.

As my day could get more interesting, Dowdren, Paul, and Lovell joined us. I shuffled the leashes so I could bump elbows with the elephant, who said, "Welcome home, Jace."

"Thanks. Yes, the turkey lives to be petted, and you can

come to my office later to make friends with the local wildlife. Did everyone behave while I was gone, Dowdren?"

The telepath heaved a sigh and shook his head.

That left me with Lovell, and I settled with raising a brow and waiting.

"We had a station-wide conniption over the plane crash. The ladies are ten seconds from stealing you and Hardy for the afternoon to make sure you're properly fed and cared for," he reported. "I recommend against resisting. They've already picked out the restaurant, and Patricia already took care of reminding them your dragoness will become sad if she isn't invited."

Alicia would become *sad*? No, she would shift, breathe fire, and take names while possibly making bodies. I snorted at that. "Sad is not the word I would use. When I left this morning, she was fuming over the fact I needed to go to work this morning, but some breakfast and tea tamed the beast. She went back to bed. I'm not sure she's used to getting up at dawn."

Technically, the sun hadn't even risen when I'd gotten out of bed, but I had waited until after dawn to feed the dragoness. According to her phone, which she'd left unlocked, she had several alarms set for closer to noon, with one set for one indicating she had a meeting with a television studio about something.

I would call before I left for lunch to make certain she was ready for her meeting, although I feared it involved a gameshow episode I would be forced to participate in. Rather than complain over my lot in life, I tapped the elevator button in hopes of salvation.

Salvation eventually arrived, although with two wolves and a turkey keeping us company, we barely fit.

When we reached our floor, Hardy said, "She really isn't a morning person."

"That's an understatement, Grimstone." Caring for a cranky live-in dragoness would test me, but I could handle a little excitement in the mornings. I would factor risk to life and limb into how much I took her grandfather for the next time he came calling, though.

Another date with his classic cars would go a long way towards making certain I accepted my cranky live-in dragoness with a smile plastered onto my face. As my face had taken to betraying me, everyone would know I had a price. Could anyone blame me for wanting time to play with the Black Dragon of New York's car collection?

"The captain wants to see you," Paul announced. "Both of you."

Hardy's shoulders slumped, and he bowed his head. "Ready to be sacrificed to an opal, Jace?"

"I'm not the one who thought transforming in a plane was a good idea. *I* will be fine. But I'll try to rescue you from the opal dragon. I'll bring the menagerie. Maybe that will confuse him long enough for you to talk your way out of this one." I grinned at my co-worker, and rather than go to my office, I herded the black dragon across the floor.

As expected, my turkey drew a lot of attention, and we lost twenty minutes introducing Sir Blackie to everyone.

It took less than five minutes to determine everything was perfect in Sir Blackie's world, and he showed off his tail for everybody, posed, and cuddled anyone foolish enough to come into his range.

As expected, the touchy-feely elephant fell for the turkey's charms. Paul regarded me with wide eyes and said, "I thought turkeys were supposed to be *mean*."

"Sir Blackie has borderline sentience, and the children of Sir Blackie will likely be sentient. Once we have babies, you can come to my place and see if any take to you. Hardy's grandpappy seems to think they might be suitable for law enforcement."

Much like our coworkers, the station's flock of birds ultimately fell prey to the turkey's charms with the hummingbirds taking point. While most converged on Sir Blackie, Mikhal came over and landed on my shoulder.

I smiled at the young bird and gave his breast a pet. "And how are you doing, Mikhal?"

"I am good. The captain wants me to accompany you for the next few weeks, and when I'm not with you, I'll be with Mr. Paul and Mr. Lovell." The hummingbird rubbed his head against my hand. *"I get to go home with you tonight?"*

Ah. The captain had decided to go the route of spying, using a young, impressionable hummingbird to accomplish his dirty deeds. Laughing, I reassured the little one. "You'll like my place. There's an orchard and many flowering plants you'll like. You can even bring your ladies over, where they can be kept safe if they're in one of the parks."

"They are."

In the wild, hummingbirds rarely lived more than a few years, but the birds with sentience tended to live much longer. As Mikhal would have a mix of sentient and non-sentient ladies, I expected to deal with a relentless cycle of love and loss, although the birds recovered better than most humans in the face of tragedy.

Well, mostly.

Mikhal, while young, possessed more compassion than he knew how to cope with.

His ladies would find their lives extended with the help

of some unicorns, a safe haven in the form of my yard, and comfortable accommodations immune to the harsh weather that tended to visit Cauldron City. Worrying about how to keep all the beings living at my home alive and happy would eat up a lot of time, but they were worth the effort.

"We can make an arrangement for them and their nests to come to my place with you," I promised. "Can you please tell the captain we'll be there in a few moments?"

"He expected you would be waylaid. I will tell him." The hummingbird took flight and zipped off, and I chuckled at the new word in his vocabulary.

"He's pretty advanced," Hardy commented, observing the hummingbird zip off. "But we best get a move on, as we'll be in for it if we delay much longer."

While it took some work, I convinced the wolves and the turkey we needed to leave their adoring worshippers. "I'd delay until rescue in the form of the ladies from the other station arrives," I confessed.

"Me, too."

"On a scale of one to dead, how dead do you think we are?"

"Definitely dead. I'm more dead than you are," Hardy replied, and he heaved a sigh. "Remember me fondly."

"I'm going to be dead, too. You're going to have to ask someone else to remember us. Your grandfather might, but it's looking sketchy."

Hardy heaved his most dramatic sigh and headed for our captain's office, holding open the door so I could get the menagerie inside without incident. As expected, Captain Farthan locked onto Sir Blackie, and he eyed the turkey with interest.

Rather than ask, he leaned back in his chair, redirected his gaze to us, and waited.

Hardy closed the door and joined me, and we waited for our scolding.

"Well? Where should we begin?" the captain asked.

"The turkey," I suggested, aware I might be able to buy us a few minutes of life ruthlessly using my new feathered companion.

"Why did you bring a turkey into my station?"

The truth amused the hell out of me, although I doubted my captain would appreciate it. "Well, after the plane crashed, we were sacrificed to keep the Black Dragon of New York from demolishing the entire state of Rhode Island. I was minding my own business, walking through the lobby of his residence, when I was waylaid by this turkey. His name is Sir Blackie, and he is a borderline sentient. His children should be sentient, and I have six hens living at my house, all of whom are borderline sentient and should produce sentient offspring." I crouched and rewarded the turkey with some affection before giving the wolves their fair share. "Misfit really likes Sir Blackie, and rather than deal with the apocalypse in my house this morning, I brought him to work. She'll need to be trained to understand she can't bring Sir Blackie to work every day."

According to the exaggerated way the captain rolled his eyes at me, he believed me. Then again, in Cauldron City, magic and mayhem were a way of life.

"You can bring him in on office days," Captain Farthan replied.

Well, that would make my life easier. "Thank you, sir."

Mikhal landed on my shoulder, and he did his best to hide in my hair, which hadn't been tamed to my satisfaction due to a crabby dragoness, a needy wolf puppy, and a stubborn turkey. *"His babies will talk?"*

"Yes, Mikhal. You can help teach them how to use their words if you'd like."

"I would, I would!"

With that settled, I decided I'd spare our captain from death at the claws of a clan of angry black dragons, saying, "In Hardy's defense, I probably would have shifted, too, had I just watched the engine of the plane fall off."

The opal dragon sighed, bowed his head, and after a moment, he snorted. I realized the bastard laughed at us, and I did my best to maintain as neutral an expression as possible. As saying anything else would get us into even more shit, I closed my mouth and kept it closed.

"Grimstone, nobody is actually mad you helped tear the plane up. We do discourage transformations within planes for a good reason, but when a prop plane's engine drops off, it's rather difficult to land it safely. The plane becomes unbalanced. It can be done, but it's not easy. Nobody is in trouble for transforming that poor blue dragon's plane into debris. Now, that said, you should, perhaps, warn your fellow passengers it is time to transform before doing so. We'll be working on that, as it seems we haven't gotten you quite to the point you can avoid shifting while startled or stressed. We're also going to start training you to catch fluffy colts out of the air, as it seems this may become an issue."

Nothing I could do could top my captain's plan for revenge, which involved me jumping off a dragon's back to be caught by a young, skittish dragon. As I hadn't known dragons practiced such things, I regretted my involvement in the whole situation. "When will you expect me to learn how to skydive, sir?"

"We'll give it a few weeks, as Grimstone will need his family to teach him the basics with his relatives. You'll be spotted by an entire flock of worrywart dragons for Hardy's first catch of someone who isn't a dragon and can't save himself from a rather brutal collision with the ground."

I wondered if surrendering would do me any good, and after spending a moment to consider my options, I opted to keep quiet.

"I'm sorry, Jace," Hardy muttered.

I would make the black dragon pay one way or another. Helping to care for my menagerie topped the list, along with making him ferry me lunch would be a good start. "I'm sorry, because I'm pretty sure you're in this situation because I went to Rhode Island, where one of our perps took offense to me sniffing at his trail."

"That is a good way to phrase it. Now that I've made you both nervous, sit. You're not here for your execution. I wouldn't want to have to clean your blood out of my office. You're here so I can catch you up on what's gone on, since you were gallivanting in Rhode Island."

We'd been gallivanting? "Doesn't gallivanting involve going to do something for *fun*, sir?"

The opal dragon made himself comfortable behind his desk and barked, "Sit, Smithson!"

To my amusement, the turkey and the wolves sat, and I followed their lead so I wouldn't earn even more of my captain's ire. Hardy took his time, laughed, kicked his shoes off, and rested his feet on the captain's desk.

Rather than get upset, the captain followed the black dragon's lead. "In good news, there have been no more dead weight cases since you left for Rhode Island. In bad news, there have been more poisonings, but the frequency is dropping as bars and other locations serving alcohols are testing their bottles. Alcohol seems to be the primary poisoning source in Cauldron City. The real issue is that our culprits have gone underground. In a way, we've won—for the moment. The frequency of attacks has dropped, which is giving us time to work on our investigation. Our investigation isn't going as well as we would like, as we have been given little in the ways of clues and hard evidence."

"Our perp is smart, he's driven, and he's taking steps to avoid being caught," I said, wondering what it meant for me as I delved into the depths of being a detective.

The opal dragon nodded. "Until we find something conclusive, we're stuck. As long as he goes underground, I fear we won't be able to pick up his trail. We're going to be going over all the old sites looking for new clues, but I doubt we'll find anything. I suspect a magicker is working for our mastermind—or the mastermind is a magicker."

"Dr. Lerrans is a magicker, isn't he?" Hardy asked, and he narrowed his eyes.

"He is, and he's our best lead so far. While you two were crashing planes and giving that mean old black in New York gray hair, I had a few pairs put together information and load it into your digital board, Smithson. I asked them to mimic how you were organizing things to minimize the whining."

"I wouldn't whine, sir."

"No, but you'd look at us with those sad pony eyes, which are going to be even more effective now that we know you're a unicorn," my captain replied. "No whining and no sad pony eyes unless you're being tossed in general holding again."

I'd been working for the opal long enough to understand

my fate. I would be tossed in a cell again for the amusement of my co-workers, likely as punishment for worrying everyone and not calling in the instant I'd touched hoof to ground. "Am I going to be tossed in general holding again, sir?"

"Actually, yes. I have you booked to be booked tomorrow for a full shift while your wolves go through some training. I need to boost morale, as everyone has been more stressed than I like. You and Grimstone are scheduled to be pampered by the ladies at noon, so you're off the hook until then. I expect you both to be ready to work on Tuesday, which is when we're going to go over shift assignments. You're both useless to us exhausted, so tomorrow, you'll have a light day in the station doing nothing. Grimstone, you'll be keeping the unicorn company, and you can lead him around on a line rather than store him in general holding. But you'll both be in general holding for the first hour of your day while everyone else gets their critical work done."

"It could be worse," Hardy replied, and he snapped a salute to our captain. "Rest and recovery until Tuesday?"

"Wednesday. I'll have you two working in the station on Tuesday while we bicker and brawl over shift assignments. Smithson, I want you Monday through Friday, as most of our victims have been cropping up on weekdays. You'll be staying in the station on Tuesday to do paperwork. Our killer keeps his schedule light over the weekends, and you need one day to handle the reports, else the papers will breed. Grimstone, you'll be working Sunday, Monday, Wednesday, Thursday, and Friday. You and Dowdren will be keeping an eye on Smithson while I try to figure out who might best partner with him." The captain leaned forward for a look at my menagerie, who settled in for the wait.

"That happens to be human, questionably human, or a supreme being."

Dragons. Give an inch, and without fail, they would take miles due to their confidence in their superiority. Worse, as they knew they'd take a mile, they expected everyone else to do the same. Rather than argue with him over it, I said, "We should investigate why Dr. Lerrans hadn't directly targeted dragons until the plane—and that's assuming he's responsible for the plane. I don't think he is."

"That's easy. It involves clan behavior," Captain Farthan replied, and he leaned back in his chair. "Most dragons don't go out alone. The Grimstone case is due to bad luck. They weren't explicitly targeted. Only an idiot would directly target dragons, especially the younger generations, like Hardy and his cousins. To dragons, they're only a step up from being babies, and the older dragons take offense when someone goes after the babies. Rather like unicorns from the looks of it. Where there is one, there are usually many. And if you go after one, you're going after the many. Dr. Lerrans—or someone he knows—is likely aware of clan culture and doesn't want his operation to become targeted. That his ploy hit the black dragons first means he's in for a world of trouble. Opals? He might get away with targeting opals. Of the local dragon clans, we're fairly independent. While I'm usually found with dragons of other colors, I'm not always with another opal. We're all like that. So, in theory, I could be hit without any of the others in my clan being around. But black dragons? If they aren't with other black dragons, the rest of the clan is keeping an eye on their wayward hatchling. I mean you, Grimstone."

My fellow cop shrugged, and then he laughed. "It's true, though. There aren't a lot of Grimstones here, but the other blacks definitely check in with me often. And after what happened to my family? I expect to be shadowed everywhere for a while."

"By a while, he means until this Dr. Lerrans is brought in for questioning," our captain announced.

While I believed them regarding how dragons behaved, some discrepancies stood out to me. "Dr. Lerrans, according to our sole surviving witness, seemed uneducated regarding the nature of shapeshifters."

Captain Farthan nodded. "Yes, he does seem to be ignorant in some ways. We've done some digging. There are a few hate groups out there who dislike regular humans. By that, I mean people without much in the way of magic. They take up space, and in their view, they do not contribute to society. This group seems to think that shapeshifters who were taught how to shift are stealing magic. Once hate is brought into the picture, logic tends to leave the building. So, that works in our favor. Their willful ignorance means we might be able to catch him in the act—assuming we can figure out what his end game is. His connections with a hate group help clarify some matters for us, though."

Right. Any time a large number of people got together, hate groups inevitably formed. Within the population of those without magic were those who hated those with magic. The reverse applied. Some hated others over uncontrollable factors, like the color of one's skin. Every year, our station went through training to help control and eliminate such prejudices.

In Cauldron City, nobody could afford members of law enforcement indulging in hateful tendencies. We served—and that meant we served *everybody*.

It sometimes meant we served men like Dr. Lerrans when someone did them wrong, although those cases came few and far between.

"Where does this put us with the investigation?"

"Rock bottom," the captain admitted, and he sighed. "Tuesdays, I want you beating your head against the wall on this case, trying to think of new angles, gathering data, and finding witnesses to question. The intel we're getting from the FBI is good, but it is going to be weeks before we have complete autopsy reports and anything coherent out of them. That's just how these cases go. In the meantime, I'm going to have you working on learning the ropes and helping out with another case. Masoner and Lovell are working on one they could use some help with, so I'm going to have you two, Dowdren, and them working together on it. We also have an odd community service case I'm giving to Lovell."

If I asked, the captain would answer, and I feared what sort of community service case might come our way. Unfortunately, Hardy fell for the bait, asking, "What do you mean by odd community service case?"

"Remember the string of home robberies from early last year our detectives couldn't crack?" he asked.

I'd heard of it, but as I hadn't been on any of the calls, I'd only heard a little. Hardy heaved a sigh. "That case again? It's awful, Captain. They left us with nothing except missing items."

"The community service case involves a shapeshifter who would be more than happy to show us how it was done in exchange for dodging prison time. While she isn't our culprit, she's learned the method. She would like to reform."

Uh oh. Reforming criminals sometimes wanted to

become cops, and depending on the nature of the crimes they'd committed and their skills, the courts sometimes approved a trial run. "She wants to become a cop?"

"She is interested in seeing if she can convert her tendency to steal things she shouldn't into a life of stopping people from stealing things they shouldn't. I want Dowdren eavesdropping on her—and I want Lovell and Masoner to see if they mesh with her."

Lovell would find the situation hilarious, and if the woman panned out, Paul would get more of the support he needed. "Are you going to set them up permanently as a trio?" I asked.

"That really depends on them, but I think it has potential. Smithson, I want you to mingle with the other pairs early and often. If your regular group isn't doing anything interesting, I want you to hop into the patrol car of someone who is—or follow them in yours. Oh, and one more thing."

"Sir?"

"Feel free to bring your dragoness to work. I've already opened an office for her in the support wing so she can work, and that'll let us keep an eye on her. Until we know more about this Dr. Lerrans, I want to make sure somebody is keeping an eye on her at all times. At the very least, we'll make sure she stays fed so that ulcer problem doesn't show back up. This arrangement will also let her work on that game show idea and have us accessible. She'll need to schedule all participants, and it seems like my station is being targeted." The opal scowled. "I wonder how *that* happened.

I feigned ignorance, widening my eyes. "I'm really not sure, sir."

"You will pay for what you've done, Smithson. Mark my words. You will pay."

That I believed, but I'd enjoy the ride, as I lacked any real sense of self-preservation and enjoyed yanking on the chains and tails of dragons. "What can you tell us about this community service case?"

"Well, I can tell you that the ladies wanted nothing to do with her, and the reason disgusts me," the opal dragon announced.

Puzzled, I exchanged glances with Hardy, who shrugged. I interpreted his raised brow to mean I would be the poor sucker to request clarification. Bracing for the worst, I asked, "Why don't they want anything to do with her?"

"She's pretty, she's smart, she's skilled, and she's humble about it," Captain Farthan announced.

Well, there went any hope of sense, common or otherwise, from anyone in the station for a few weeks. "Please tell me the ladies aren't jealous."

"They're not, but the last thing anyone needs is an entire station of heartbroken women because of a reforming criminal sweeping in and reminding everyone that good people can be put in bad situations. Our new recruit is a lot of things, but she grew up poor, she never had any opportunities, and she didn't grow up in Cauldron City. Had she, she would have had an education. Oh, Grimstone?"

"Sir?"

"Speak to your grandfather and ask who among your family might be best equipped to teach a young woman who dropped out before starting high school. If she wants to be a cop, she needs to have the appropriate education. Smithson, as the best educated officer we have, I want you to challenge her the best you can. She's ignorant, but she's intelligent. The court feels she needs direction. And by that, I got told by a judge that we would make certain she becomes a productive member of society."

Well, life would be interesting for the next while, of that I was certain. "Understood, sir."

"Get out of my office, and when the ladies come to claim you both for the rest of the day, get them talking about what a woman needs to thrive as a cop in Cauldron City. For some reason, we seem to lack a general understanding of what women need and want in life."

No kidding. I got up, shot him a salute, and said, "Yes, sir."

"Oh, and Smithson?"

"Sir?"

"I recommend you get tracking on all your diamonds. Reforming does not mean reformed, and she's smart enough to know about white unicorns."

I read between the lines: the woman had spent all her life poor, and her entire life would change with one diamond. However, I had a solution to that problem, although I would hope Alicia would forgive me for suggesting it without asking her about it first. "Why not reward her with a diamond if she can pull off a caper on national television? Maybe she'll be the equivalent of a cadet, but if she's pretty and she's smart, then she's perfect for Alicia's gameshow. If she pulls off the caper, she gets to keep a diamond. Her motivation for petty theft is removed, and it'll be that much easier for her to reform. I can provide a diamond—and arrange for a buyer for it so she won't have to battle her circumstances."

Both dragons stared at me with wide eyes.

As I understood they would ask why, I added, "One of those diamonds is easy come, easy go for me. I have enough of the damned things squirreled away to last numerous lifetimes. If one diamond can help Alicia with her show *and* help this woman reform, then it is a diamond well spent. It doesn't even need to be a big diamond—it just needs to have a buyer who'll pay decent money for it. And for people in her shoes, even fifty thousand dollars can make a huge difference. I'd offer a better stone than that, though. I'd make it just big enough so she's comfortable, not worried about rent, and can afford higher education if she wants it."

"Make arrangements with Alicia," Captain Farthan ordered. "If we're going to have to do this game show, at least we'll make it be worth our while in the process—and have it do some good. Grimstone? You better warn your grandfather that Smithson is going big because he refuses to go home. Also, suggest to your cousin that it's a multi-episode affair. There's no way she'll be able to fit in everything in one run."

"You got it, sir."

"No trouble until Tuesday," he ordered before shooing us out of his office. "I want you both ready to work like you mean it."

"Yes, sir," we chorused.

About G.P. Robbins

G.P. Robbins lives in California, serving two feline overladies and sharing a domicile with another human.

G.P. Robbins is a pen name of R.J. Blain. RJ also writes as Susan Copperfield, Bernadette Franklin, Audrey Greene, G.P. Robbins, and Lilith Daniels. Visit RJ and her pets (the Management) at thesneakykittycritic.com.

Bonus Short Story

Author's Note

I thought about writing an experimental pilot for this novel's bonus story, but I kept thinking about how a bunch of cops in Cauldron City might want to have some fun at the expense of the Black Dragon of New York.

This would take place between the end of Dead Weight and the next novel, Partner in Crime. There are a few days in which Jace and co can make the Black Dragon of New York pay for his crimes… and I mean, existing is a pretty big crime, right? Totally.

So, as a nice little warm up for the next book, I present to you this short story, from the perspective of the poor bastard saddled with being the lead in Partner in Crime. Sometimes, Detective Lovell has some serious regrets about joining the force.

Today is definitely one of those days…

Oh, an important sidenote. This is an *exploratory piece.*

I'm trying to get a feel for Lovell. What would *normally* happen is that I would write this to get a feel for him, and then I would shelve it somewhere without actually *sharing* it, because the character *will* change by the time I actually write his book.

I'm also trying to work on making a character different from Jace—exploratory pieces like this help to work out one character and start giving a new one a different vibe. As Jace and Lovell are both troublemakers with offbeat senses of humor, this is going to be quite difficult.

So, this story really is me just extending feelers to see how I feel about this character written this way. I'll evaluate how I handle him later, make adjustments to make sure he's got his own voice compared to Jace, and so on.

One last thing… this series will have five different leading men for the most part; after the first six books, the characters introduced as leads will be reused as needed, with me picking the cop that is best able to tell the story.

In some novels, Jace will be out and about, taking a holiday or otherwise not being in the area. In other novels, Jace will be the lead because he's the one neck deep in trouble. Having a lead cast of five or so cops gives me a good variety of characters to work with as the lead while letting the others do their things as needed in the background—without having to jury rig one character into doing everything.

Don't be surprised if the bonus material for these novels is always some form of short story getting a feel for a character. Well, at least for the first while. After everyone has been established, then I'll expand my efforts.

I hope you enjoy this little romp. No, it doesn't have much of a plot… but that's not why this story exists.

It exists so I can have a better understanding of how to write Lovell and Masoner (Paul). Welcome to this glimpse into the background world of how I write books!

Short Story: The Black Dragon of New York Must Pay.

One day, Captain Farthan would learn. On the surface, tossing a unicorn and a black dragon in general holding seemed like a good idea, but I knew better. The unicorn would cause trouble because he could, and the black dragon would help for the fun of it. Add in a set of six troublesome teens waiting for their parents to pick them up, and disaster would surely come knocking.

How had I become the most normal cop in Precinct 153? Until Jace had showed his true colors, he'd enjoyed the distinction, and I'd enjoyed hiding behind him, just another cop in a station full of them.

While I had more than a few magicker tricks up my sleeve, why did Captain Farthan think I could contain one unicorn, one black dragon, and six teens?

Could anyone contain such a combination?

The unicorn conspired with the dragon in a corner, and the pair had gotten the teens sitting around them, pretty as a picture and as quiet as mice dodging the attention of a cat.

Every now and then, one of the teens chirped up with a thought.

Jace, being Jace, rewarded the bolder teens with attention. The behavior of the kids, who basked in the unicorn's affection, implied some problems were easier to solve than others.

Attention-starved kids caused trouble. In the eyes of so many youth, any attention beat solitude. While their attempt at petty theft wouldn't give them more than a slap on the wrist, I'd talk to the captain about the situation and see if we could get the entire lot of them into a program to redirect their mischief into something useful—and something capable of filling a probable void in their lives.

Still, I couldn't tell if the pair was being punished or rewarded, as neither unicorn nor dragon seemed at all distressed they'd been tossed into holding.

My partner joined me, and he chuckled at the state of the general holding cell. "I thought you would appreciate the warning that the Black Dragon of New York just arrived, and he has plans to bust the cops out of holding." As the precinct's sole elephant shapeshifter, Paul drove everyone else crazy with his need for attention. As one of ten siblings, I tolerated the insanity well, and I bumped elbows with him.

"Demand hugs in exchange for you considering his plan," I suggested.

One day, Paul would clue in that most of the station had touchy-feeling tendencies, and I expected Jace would be the one to expose the problem and ultimately resolve it. Until that day came, I would work at making sure my partner remained stable and did as little property damage as possible.

Once distressed, elephants lacked sense, common or otherwise.

As our captain had a brain and even bothered using it from time to time, I received a small bonus every month we dodged property damage issues from the elephant's relentless need for affection.

With our job for the day making sure nothing happened to the unicorn or the dragon until we released them from general holding, I settled in to observe the chaos, questioning why I'd made the decision to become a cop in the first place. I certainly hadn't joined for the pay, although I paid the rent, kept food on the table, and even managed to go out and do things from time to time without making my bank account cry.

The next time I had dinner with my family, I would have to ask. Perhaps one of my parents or siblings might have the answer.

While it took two hours, the Black Dragon of New York showed up to lay claim over the detectives in general holding, and he came armed with a new bridle for Jace and a collar and leash for his grandson. The teens recognized the mean old black the instant he came into view. Their eyes widened, and it took me a few moments to diagnose them all with hero worship.

I could either go with the flow or get steamrolled, so I grabbed the keys for the general holding cell, opened the door, and eyed the teens. "You may go say hello to him and shake his hand, but you may not run down the hall. We'd have to stop you, and that would put an end to you meeting him."

To make certain none of the teens bolted for freedom, I inhaled, pressed my palms together, and tapped my fingertips together to draw in magic and weave it into a barrier designed to deter them from leaving the area. Without a proper focus, I would have to maintain my pose, although I'd refined my magic enough I could keep my fingers still and continue to control the working.

My magicker tricks worked a great deal better when I could focus them. I preferred carving stones with symbols and linking my magic with the stone. I kept a collection of perfectly ordinary river rocks in my desk drawer in case I needed them, and I usually had three or four on me at any time.

The teens did as instructed, and they swarmed the Black Dragon of New York. While the black dragon was many things, he was a grandfather above all, and he settled into introducing himself to the kids.

Hardy came over, shook his head, and said, "Given ten more minutes, Jace would have had those kids so charmed they would be trying to groom that pony fur of his with their fingers."

The unicorn plodded over, and I eyed the white boots he wore over his hooves. "Is your hoof still bothering you?"

"No. These are just comfortable. Not only are they comfortable, I run no risk of picking up a stone while wearing them." Jace lifted a hoof and regarded his new boot. "I'm going to talk to Dr. Erik tonight to check to make sure I'm not still bleeding magic, though. I do not need any more boots, bridles, saddles, martingales, bonnets, and bits.

I'll take a few more hackamores, though, as I'm stunning in them and I dislike bits."

"For the rest of the day, you are joining forces with me to make that black dragon pay," I informed my fellow detectives. "And not you, Hardy. You've suffered enough for one week."

"Oh, I deserve some suffering. I destroyed a plane with Smithson in it."

One day, I might succumb to the station's tendency to refer to everyone by their last name. Sometimes, I did it for clarity, although there was only one Jace in law enforcement in the entirety of Cauldron City.

There were several Smithsons, and none of them were related—and only one was a unicorn.

Upon learning Jace's species, I'd checked.

"Make sure your grandfather caters to those kids until their parents show up."

Hardy snorted, and then he laughed at me. "You're rewarding him, Lovell. Just toss the whole lot of them into general holding until their parents show up. He'll love it, especially if we take pictures and text them to my grandmother."

Paul needed no other encouragement, and he dug out his personal cell phone for the photographs, herded the lot into the cell, and locked them in.

That the Black Dragon of New York cooperated without a peep of complaint amused me. "Thoughts, Paul?"

"Hide Jace and Hardy somewhere and make a wager on what'll happen if Grimstone can't find them by a deadline. That'll drive him crazy, since he came out here just to see them."

"Hardy, you know what to do," I said. The instant word

spread the pair was playing an elaborate game with the Black Dragon of New York, the entire station would help keep the detectives safe and sound—and out of the dragon's grasp. "Paul, keep them busy. Impress upon those teens that platonic affection between adult men is a real thing and won't kill them. I'm sure that mean old bastard will bite on being a good example."

"For once in his life," Hardy muttered before herding Jace out of the general holding area. "If you see Alicia, tell her I'll give her unicorn back later. If the turkey starts crying, just tell him his unicorn will be back. Apparently, he somewhat understands English. And good luck with the wolves."

I could understand how the animals had fallen so hard for Jace. While Jace's species played a part, he walked into the room and brought peace along with him unless he was out to stir up some trouble. His trouble tended to amuse everyone.

Change came to our precinct, and only time would tell what would happen.

I suspected the other stations in our precinct had decided to give us a break for the day, as there were only three calls needing the attention of a detective. As Paul kept the Black Dragon of New York contained, I got to stay put and monitor everyone, who'd forgotten we'd come to work rather than to a playground for adults.

By six, the parents of the teens showed up, bringing the general holding party to a halt. Paul did what Paul did best, charming the kids and getting them all to indulge in hugs after the menace of a black dragon led by example. I handled the parents, and per the captain's orders, strongly recommended they be enrolled in one of several community programs. I took the time to make recommendations on which ones might keep their wayward teens out of harm's way and on the right side of the law.

The lack of charges got the parents to at least listen to me, but I suspected the teens would need to act for themselves after overhearing what I'd told their parents, rather than receiving any actual encouragement.

The Black Dragon of New York swooped in, took my stack of pamphlets, sorted through them, and handed a set out to each teen. While the parents bristled, it took one low growl from the dragon to convince them to quiet down their complaints.

Once the lot of them left with Paul to be escorted out of the building, I heaved a sigh. "Thank you, Mr. Grimstone."

"You're welcome. They're not bad kids. They just need a little motivation and a good reason to play the game in the way most adults and society appreciates. Where is my unicorn? I suppose I better see that grandson of mine, too."

As Jace became rather surly if he thought something might happen to the little dragoness he'd lured into living with him, I saw no need to protect him from the dragoness's grandfather. "That's a good question. I haven't seen them since they escaped general holding. They're probably around the station somewhere—maybe. They do like to slip off the instant they think they can get away with it."

"Those rascals!" The Black Dragon of New York huffed and puffed, and after a moment, he narrowed his eyes at me. "What's your name, boy?"

"If you have any mercy in your body, anywhere, you'll just call me Lovell. Detective Lovell if you feel a need to be formal."

I still questioned why my parents had named me Valor, and I couldn't even go by my middle name without enduring questions. Why had they thought Thomassin had been a good idea for a middle name? Some days, I thought about pretending my name was Thomas, but I gave that ploy a lifespan of precisely five minutes before dying a terrible death.

"I don't laugh at any child with the misfortune of having a parent who couldn't quite seem to get the whole naming thing right," he assured me. "But I'll call you Lovell if you tell me what your name is, as now I'm curious."

"Valor," I informed him, and I grimaced.

"I see. While a genuine and nice thought for you, I can understand why you wouldn't want people running around a police station calling out your name. Name changes only cost around a thousand to process, and I happen to be intimately familiar with them, as I will rename any one of my children or grandchildren who are unhappy with what they were given on virtue of being born. It's *their* name, after all, not mine. Nor is it their parents'. So, salvation is a name change form away. A piece of advice, if I may?"

"Don't drown my parents is the most common piece of advice I hear when people find out my name," I admitted, and I flashed the dragon a grin. "I appreciate your concern, but I view it as a glorious burden I tolerate because I do love my parents."

"That is excellent advice, but I was more thinking along the lines of either accepting or changing it, as your name does make up a significant portion of your identity as an individual. Alicia is one of my few grandchildren who has, from the moment she comprehended Alicia was her name, loved everything about her name and how it has shaped her. Hardy was originally named Olsen. He hated it with a passion, and he wanted to be Hardy when he turned three. The paperwork becomes much more complicated when the young dragon changing his name is three, but Hardy is what he wanted, so Hardy is what he got. His mother wanted to have a second middle name, so that's what she got. His father? He picked Justus. On purpose. I'd named that brat Justin, but apparently Justin was too common. So, your name is part of who *you* are. It is your legacy, not the legacy of your parents. If you don't like your name, change it. That unicorn is a smart one, so if you want help with it without relying on a mean old dragon, talk with him. He's a good paper pusher."

No kidding. While Jace had come across to me as smart, I hadn't realized how smart, until word spread he was a Yale graduate. "But is he good enough for Alicia?"

"My opinion on this does not matter as much as everyone thinks it does. That said, she becomes delightfully agitated if she loses track of her unicorn, and as a loving grandfather, what she wants is what she gets. In this case, she wants that unicorn. Now, where is he? I got him a new bridle, and I have a bow ready to gift wrap him for my granddaughter's leisure."

A better man would have sided with his friend and co-worker, but as I wanted to see what sort of chaos a bunch of dragons could create in the station, I pointed in the direction of the elevators. "The last I heard, they were escaping your clutches so you'd have to go home defeated."

The instant the Black Dragon of New York headed off, swearing he would not go quietly into the night, I smiled.

Then I followed after the dragon, ready to enjoy the show.

In what I viewed to be a confirmation of Hardy's insanity, my fellow detective made no effort to hide from his grandfather and basked in the old dragon's affection when captured. Jace, on the other hand, had fled. According to the rest of the loitering cops, the unicorn remained in the station.

Somewhere.

After twenty minutes, the Black Dragon of New York huffed and puffed, entertaining everyone fortunate enough to witness his defeat at Jace's hands—or hooves.

Not only were the detectives refusing to offer the old black dragon any clues, they delighted in giving him the run around. Nobody knew for sure if he was a unicorn or a man—and the last anyone saw him, he'd been fleeing from Alicia, who'd wanted to go home.

I suspected the only person to have half a clue what was going on would be the dragoness, and I hunted her down in the office someone had opened up for her so the Black Dragon of New York wouldn't have an excuse to take over Cauldron City.

"Seen Jace?" I asked, plopping down in the chair in front of her desk.

She pointed at her feet. "He passed out about an hour ago, and Dr. Erik said to let him nap for two hours before we go home. He's just had too much excitement, and young colts eventually run out of batteries. As he's hiding from my grandfather, I suggested he crawl under the desk. There are two wolves and a turkey under there with him."

"How'd they all fit?" I asked, raising a brow. Having a similar desk in my office, the panel keeping people from seeing my feet and chair created a tiny space barely sufficient to hide a person in.

The panel was bulletproof, which made the desks an ideal defensive boundary should someone with a gun get through our basic security.

It'd been a few years since anyone had tried anything seriously, and nobody had gotten hurt. We had, however, gotten bulletproof panels installed so we had a place to take shelter during an emergency.

"Jace is buried beneath two wolves and a turkey, but he's sound asleep, so he doesn't notice. Misfit is snuggled up with her favorite buddy, and Momma Mia is keeping an eye on everybody. It's a tight squeeze, but it's fine. I'm not going anywhere until Jace wakes up, though. He decided to hug my leg in his sleep."

Much like my partner, the new detective required a great deal of affection to get through the day. The why of it made a great deal of sense.

Unicorns belonged in herds, and we were his herd. "And your grandfather?"

"Let him stew. He'll figure it out eventually. And if he doesn't, well, that's not my problem, is it? Are you done for the day?"

"Actually, yes. I just wanted to keep an eye on the festivities."

"Go on home. I'll make sure Jace makes it to a proper bed tonight."

I wished her the best of luck with that, having heard about his tendency to pass out on couches. "All right. Call me if you need help getting that lot back home."

"I'll make my grandpappy handle it if I can't get him mobile. He might be old with one foot in the grave, but he still has some muscles in those emaciated arms of his."

I laughed, as the Black Dragon of New York was in the prime of his life and probably would be for a few more thousand years. Saluting the woman, I made my escape, wondering if anything could top a clan of black dragons out for our station's sole unicorn.

I had a feeling I would find out soon enough.

www.ingramcontent.com/pod-product-compliance
Lightning Source LLC
Chambersburg PA
CBHW020352310726
48979CB00015B/2569/J

* 9 7 8 1 6 4 9 6 4 1 3 7 3 *